Praise for the storytelling talents of bestselling author
JANET DAILEY

Books by Janet Dailey

Published by Pocket Books

JANET DAILEY

WESTERN MAN
AND
LEFTOVER LOVE

POCKET STAR BOOKS
NEW YORK   LONDON   TORONTO   SYDNEY

A Pocket Star Book published by
POCKET BOOKS, a division of Simon & Schuster, Inc.
1230 Avenue of the Americas, New York, NY 10020

Western Man copyright © 1983 by Janbill, Ltd.
Leftover Love copyright © 1984 by Janbill, Ltd.

ISBN 13 : 978-0-7434-6988-3
ISBN 10 : 0-7434-6988-7

First Pocket Books printing March 2004

10 9 8 7 6

POCKET STAR BOOKS and colophon are registered trademarks of Simon & Schuster, Inc.

Illustration by Mark Gerber

Manufactured in the United States of America

For information regarding special discounts for bulk purchases, please contact Simon & Schuster Special Sales at 1-800-456-6798 or business@simonandschuster.com.

These titles were previously published individually by Simon & Schuster, Inc.

Table of Contents

WESTERN MAN

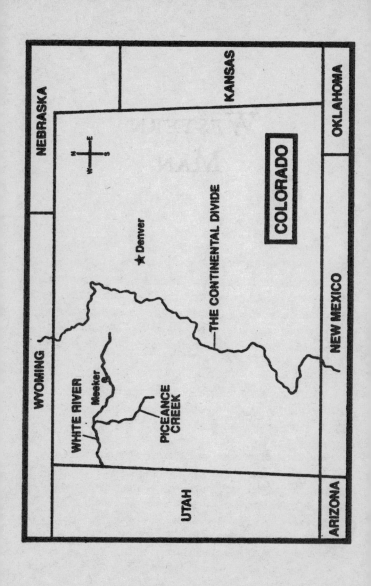

Chapter 1

The he ranch-house kitchen was filled with the warm smell of chocolate chip cookies fresh from the oven. When the last cookie on the metal sheet pan joined the others cooling on the paper spread on the counter top, Sharon Powell turned to carry the sheet pan to the table where the bowl of cookie dough sat.

Her hazel-eyed glance fell on the empty chair pushed away from the table, where a half-finished glass of milk remained along with two cookies, each with a bite taken from it. Her reaction was a combination of alarm and exasperation.

"Tony?" Sharon tossed a potholder onto the table and laid the cookie sheet, hot from the oven, on to it. There was no response to her querying call, although she strained alertly to catch any sound. Muttering to herself, Sharon started out in search of the toddler. "Now I know why they call them terrible two-year-olds. I turn my back on him for two minutes and he disappears."

This time she didn't have to search far or long to find the

boy. As soon as she entered the living room, she spied him standing at the screen door, stretching a small hand to reach the latch. A wry shake of her head sent her short, toffee-colored ponytail swaying.

"Come on, Tony. Let's go back to the kitchen." Sharon started across the room to retrieve the adventurous little boy. "Don't you want to help Sharon finish baking the cookies?"

Just before she reached him, he turned. The tow-headed boy's expression was animated with excitement, his blue eyes gleaming. "Horses, horses," he declared and swung around to press his face against the wire-mesh barrier.

With a sinking feeling, Sharon glanced through the screen toward the corral by the barn. A flaxen-maned chestnut horse had nudged the gate open and was taking its first tentative step to freedom. The five other horses in the corral, horses Sharon had contracted to train, were crowding into line behind their chestnut leader.

Her gaze never left the horse warily stepping through the opened gate as she scooped Tony off the floor and swung him onto her hip. She didn't dare leave him alone in the house while she chased the horses back into the corral. Heaven only knew what he'd get into; mischief seemed to be his middle name.

Sharon fumbled with the screen-door latch for a second, then pushed it open to race from the house. The sleek chestnut threw its head up and snorted in alarm at her approach. Her boots skimmed down the porch steps while Tony rode on her hip, laughing with delight.

"Huck! You spoiled, good-for-nothing animal! Get back in there!" she shouted at the troublesome horse, cursing its latest trick of opening the corral gate.

As the chestnut lunged to make good its escape, Sharon ran an intercepting course that would place her directly in the path of the horses and hopefully prevent them from bolting down the ranch lane to the road.

It wasn't easy doing that with Tony on her hip. She didn't dare set him on the ground. With his penchant for adventure, he'd get right into the thick of things, ignorant of any possible danger to himself. In the back of her mind, there was a silent tribute to her mother, who had probably coped with many similar situations raising her two children on this western Colorado ranch.

At her shrill whistles and waving arm, the chestnut horse broke stride. Its hesitation provided Sharon time to get in front of the horses. For a second, she thought the other horses pressing the lead chestnut from the rear might prod it into charging against her.

"Wave your arms and yell real loud, Tony," she enlisted the boy's help in raising a commotion to turn the horses. He thought it was all great fun and threw himself into this new game with such abandon that Sharon nearly dropped him.

The horses swerved, hooves clacking. She had stopped them from galloping down the lane, but herding them back into the corral was another thing. It became a frustrating game of tag. Sharon was able to contain them, but she couldn't coerce the horses to re-enter the fenced enclosure. If only she could get one inside, chances were the others would follow, but each time Sharon tried to lure the horses in, they shied away from the open gate.

Her cowboy boots were not designed for running over rough ground for long periods. Her leg muscles soon began to feel the strain, while Tony was getting heavier and heavier, his weight more awkward to balance. Her arm ached from holding him on her hip, and he didn't help the situation. Weary of the game, Tony wanted it to stop so he could pet the horses. His whining and demanding protests wore on her already frazzled nerves. She was hot and tired, choking on the dust churned up by the milling horses.

Sharon paused a second to catch her breath, wondering how on earth she was going to get the horses back in the corral on her own. Neither her parents nor her brother were due back until evening. She felt doomed.

From out of nowhere it seemed, a brown streak flashed by Sharon. It only took her half a second to recognize Sam, Ridge Halliday's cow dog. She overcame the impulse to turn around and locate its owner. The well-trained dog had already driven the loose horses into a tight circle and was pressing to herd them through the gate. All that was needed to accomplish the feat was her assistance.

With a burst of flagging energy, Sharon pushed forward. The flashy chestnut made one bold attempt to break from the pack, but the efficient cow dog smoothly turned it back. There was a rippling toss of the horse's flaxen mane, then it whirled and trotted meekly through the corral gate. The other horses followed single file.

While the dog guarded the opening, Sharon rushed to shut the gate. When she set Tony on the ground to secure the gate latch, the muscles in her arm vibrated uncontrollably from the prolonged strain of holding the child. As soon as the gate clicked shut, the panting dog ducked under the lower rail and trotted back to its master, obviously located somewhere behind her.

"Doggie, doggie." Tony lost interest in the horses to begin chasing the smaller, four-footed prey, his clutching hand outstretched in a supplicating gesture.

"Stay here, Tony," Sharon ordered sharply, fully aware the cow dog was not a pet. It required an economy of breath to speak, making her voice tautly low and impatient. "The doggie will bite you."

She spared a glance in Tony's direction long enough to ascertain that he was hesitating, unsure whether or not she was telling him the truth. There was the crunch of an unhurried stride approaching her from behind.

"Did somebody forget to shut the gate?" Ridge Halliday's low, drawling voice ran over her weary body with a soothing laziness.

"No. Wonder Horse in there," Sharon flicked an irritated look at the gleaming chestnut horse as it began walking docilely toward the gate where the humans were gathered, "opened the gate. Would you bring me a piece of that baling wire by the barn."

She pushed the waving sweep of caramel-colored hair off her perspiring forehead. She was marking time, postponing the moment when she actually had to look at Ridge, and knew it. But she needed the respite to marshal her carefully practiced, light-hearted friendliness.

If there was a course in adolescent crushes getting out of hand, Sharon could have qualified as an expert. Ridge Halliday was a fellow rancher in the basin and a contemporary of her brother—and the embodiment of every woman's fantasy. It wasn't fair to any impressionable teenager to be exposed to a man like him.

As his long shadow fell across hers, Sharon recognized the real problem—she was no longer a teenager, but that didn't stop a quiver of excitement from shooting through her. She took the proffered baling wire from his leather-gloved hand, her glance skimming him while she became irritated because of her hot and disheveled appearance.

An inch over six feet, Ridge had the loose-limbed ease of a rider about him. His long frame was hard and lean, not given to bulging muscles but a sinewed toughness. These same characteristics were stamped on his sun-browned features, except that his hard-bitten looks were made handsome by the lazy glint in his blue eyes and the grooves carved near the corners of his mouth that always seemed to suggest a lurking smile. A dusty brown cowboy hat was pulled low on his forehead, covering most of his mahogany-dark hair except at the back, where its shaggy length curled onto his shirt collar.

All in all, it was a potent combination of hard virility and a lazy sexual charm. There was a surface recklessness about him that seemed to hide the deadly serious side of him. Or so Sharon had always thought. Perhaps it was the case that he took his ranch and his work seriously—and nothing else. There was no doubt in her mind that Ridge could be an outrageous flirt at times. Heaven knew he had flirted with her enough times to lead her into believing she meant something more to him than just his buddy's kid sister, only to learn the painful lesson that with Ridge it was a case of out of sight, out of mind.

While Sharon concentrated on wrapping the baling wire around the gate post and the gate, the blaze-faced chestnut hung its head over the gate and nuzzled her shoulder in an overture of friendship. But she refused to forgive the animal so easily.

"Unless you have wire cutters for teeth, you aren't going to be able to open the gate the next time," she informed the horse as she tightly twined the ends of the wire.

"Beautiful animal," Ridge remarked and stroked the sleek, muscled neck of the horse.

"Beauty is as beauty does," Sharon retorted. "And that horse is close to being worthless. He's the yearling Sue Ann Langford's father spent a fortune a couple years ago. She's spoiled him to the point where he's nearly ruined. It was a mistake ever to agree to train him for her. Huck is headstrong and unruly, tame as a puppy but completely undisciplined. He's been here only three days and already we've had to padlock the grain bin, nail his stall door shut—and now this."

All her senses were so completely focused on Ridge that for a few moments Sharon had completely forgotten about her young charge until she heard a low growl coming from the mixed-breed dog. The warning growl alternated with an anxious whine as Sharon turned to see Tony crouched over and inching closer to the nervous dog unwilling to leave its master's side to escape the unwanted attention from the child.

In a high, little voice, Tony was trying to coax it to stay still. "Doggie. Nice doggie."

"I told you to leave the dog alone." Sharon moved, scooping Tony again into her aching arms while the dog wiggled with relief now that he was no longer being pursued by this small person. Tony struggled in her arms, wanting to be put down. "The last thing I need today is for you to get bitten," she muttered, because everything had seemed to go from bad to worse. "If it isn't one thing, it's another."

"Why don't you marry me and I'll take you away from all this?" Ridge declared lazily.

She swung around, facing him. He was leaning against the corral, an arm draped carelessly along the top rail, an easy familiarity in his blue eyes that was so unnerving. It didn't seem to matter how many times she heard that joking comment—there was always a little leap of her pulse. But she had also learned not to wear her emotions on her sleeve.

With so much practice, her laugh came naturally. "If I ever said yes to that, you'd run so fast that we'd be seeing your dust for days. You're going to say that to the wrong girl one of these days and find yourself being sued for breach of promise," Sharon warned.

Ridge chuckled, amused rather than annoyed by her response. He pushed away from the fence to move toward her. "Have you got any coffee hot?" In the past, Ridge had frequented the Powell house too often not to feel he could invite himself in for coffee.

"No coffee, but I've got a batch of homemade cookies fresh from the oven," Sharon countered, adopting the role of friend and neighbor that had served her in such good stead the last three years.

"Leave it to a woman to know the way to a man's heart." Slanting her a lazy smile, Ridge hooked a hand companionably on her shoulder. Together they started for the house.

The idle weight of his hand made itself felt, but Sharon had learned how to deal with such things. She had stopped reading anything intimate into his attitude. An arm around her shoulders meant precisely nothing. A kiss here and there meant nothing. She had stopped making mountains out of molehills. She had put aside her childish dreams that someday Ridge would look at her and discover that she was something special. It simply wasn't going to happen. Over the years, she had finally come to accept that and it hadn't been easy.

At first, she had strongly considered leaving home— leaving Colorado and seeking a job training horses somewhere. But something had warned her that Ridge's ghost would follow her and torment her with what-ifs and what-might-have-beens. So she had stayed—to face the situation and come to grips with its harsh reality.

"I want my cookie," Tony complained with a demanding frown.

"Who is the little guy?" Ridge looked around her at the boy riding on her hip again. "I know I haven't seen you the last couple of times I've been over, but not even you can keep a toddler hidden this long."

As he spoke, his gaze ran down her slender curves. He knew very well the child wasn't hers, but it amused him to tease her with the possibility. Once such a remark would have aroused a blush. Now Sharon shrugged it off without a blink of an eye.

"Tony is Rita Campbell's little boy." Rita was an old schoolmate of Sharon's. They were still friends even though marriage, a home and a family, plus a part-time job had severely cut into the free time Rita could devote to that friendship. "Her regular sitter was sick today, so I volunteered to look after Tony," Sharon explained her unusual occupation. "You need to be three people to keep up with him."

In unison, they climbed the porch steps and crossed to the screen door. His hand slipped off her shoulder as he reached in front of her to open the door.

"Stay." It was a low-voiced order issued to the dog trailing after them. With a plaintive whine of protest, the dog obediently sat on its haunches to wait for its master.

Tony twisted around as Ridge closed the door, shutting the dog outside. "Doggie come in and play," he said to Sharon.

"No, the dog has to stay outside," she insisted. "Let's go out to the kitchen and see if somebody ate your cookies while we were gone."

"Doggie wants a cookie." Tony gave her a bright-eyed look that Sharon ignored.

"I take it you're here by yourself today," Ridge inserted.

"Yes. Mom and Dad and Scott are out at the South Meadow gathering the first-calf heifers. It always happens that way, doesn't it?" She smiled in his direction. "Livestock never gets out unless you're the only person around. You could have helped," she said in a half-accusation.

"You and Sam were doing all right," he replied with a

faint grin. "I thought I should stay by the lane in case the horses got past the two of you."

"Sure," she mocked him with an exaggerated agreement. "The truth is you were standing back there so you could watch me racing around there like a mad hen with two-ton Tony on her hip." Upon entering the kitchen, she plunked Tony on his chair and pushed it up to the table. "You'd better finish your cookies and milk," she advised him, but he was still pouting because she wouldn't let the dog come in the house. He hung his head, his lower lip jutting out sullenly, and showed no interest in the cookies or milk.

Ridge wandered over to the kitchen counter where the cookies were cooling on the newspaper. "I'm going to be needing a couple of extra riders at Latigo the day after tomorrow. I stopped by to see if Scott might be able to shake free."

Latigo was the name of his ranch, which encompassed nearly a hundred square miles of Piceance Basin in western Colorado. The rough terrain of hill and gully was well suited for cattle ranching, and Latigo was one of the larger ones in the area.

"I'm sure Scott can help out," Sharon answered. Although her father and brother were ostensibly partners in their ranch, her brother often hired out for day work at neighboring ranches to lessen the drain on the ranch's finances and permit them to put more of the profits back into the ranch.

"Do you suppose I can persuade your mom to come along and cook for us—and maybe swing a rope now and then?" He arched her a querying look as he bit into a cookie.

The corners of her mouth deepened with a faint smile. Her mother was widely respected and sought after as both a cook and a cowhand, although the approval of her skill on horseback was usually grudgingly given. Of course, her father gave full credit to his wife for working at his side and building their ranch from practically nothing to the modest holding it was today. Sharon admired her because even though her mother did a man's work, she never stopped being a woman. She didn't resort to cussing or rough talk to gain male acceptance as one of them. If anything, men respected her more for that.

"You'll have to ask Mom." Sharon didn't answer for her mother.

"What I should do is arrange some sort of package deal for the whole Powell family?" A slow smile widened the line of his mouth.

"That might be arranged." She laughed briefly, pleased by the subtle recognition of her worth as a working rider. After she washed her hands in the sink, she walked to the table to begin spooning the rest of the cookie dough onto the sheet pan. It was easier to keep busy while Ridge was around. It kept her from focusing too much attention on him. "Do you want me to have Scott call you tonight?"

"Yeah, why don't you do that?" he agreed and came over to the table to watch her, a fistful of cookies in his hand. He stood idly for a minute, then pulled out a chair to sit down.

When she carried the pan to the oven, she had to step over his long legs, his boots hooked one atop the other. Ridge always seemed so relaxed, and she always felt so tense. Turning back to the table, she deliberately shifted her attention to the pouting Tony.

"Drink your milk." She pushed the glass closer to him so it was within his reach.

"No. Don't want it," he refused sulkily. "It's warm. I want another glass."

A fresh glass of cold milk from the refrigerator would probably have only one swallow taken from it, then be left to sit as this one had been. In Sharon's opinion, that was a shameful waste.

"You have to drink this milk before you can have any more," she informed him.

"No." Tony slumped in the chair and peered up at her through tearful lashes.

"Don't be so mean," Ridge eyed her with mock reproval. "I don't blame the kid for not wanting warm milk. I don't either."

With an adult supporting his demand, Tony reasserted it, banging his feet against the chair in a slight temper display. "I want milk."

"You're a lot of help," she muttered to Ridge. "I tell him no and you undermine what little authority I have."

There was an amused glint in his eyes at her flash of anger. "There is a simple solution to this that will satisfy both you and Tony," Ridge insisted.

"What's that?" Sharon asked in skeptical challenge.

"Ice." After delivering his one-word answer, he rolled to his feet in a single motion and crossed to the refrigerator, removing a tray of ice cubes from the freezer compartment. "Tony still drinks the same glass of milk, but the ice will make it cold." Taking two cubes from the tray, he walked to the table and dropped them in Tony's glass. "You see?" An eyebrow quirked in Sharon's direction.

"I hope you're right." For some reason, she was still skeptical of his solution.

"Of course I'm right," Ridge said as Tony reached eagerly for the glass.

Instead of drinking the milk, Tony tried to scoop out the ice cubes, and Sharon understood why she had instinctively doubted the wisdom of Ridge's solution.

"No, Tony, don't play with the ice cubes," she admonished and pulled his stubby fingers out of the glass to dry them with a kitchen towel. She slid a dry glance at Ridge. "Terrific idea."

"Drink your milk and see if the ice made it cold." Ridge changed chairs, sitting in the one next to Tony offering him the glass again. "Once you drink all your milk, then you can have the ice cubes." With seeming obedience, Tony took a drink of his milk and Ridge shot a complacent glance at Sharon. "You just have to know how to handle children."

"And you're an expert, of course," she mocked. "How many children did you say you had?"

"None . . . that I know about," he qualified his answer with a roguish twinkle glittering in his eyes.

It wasn't as if half the women in the county wouldn't have been willing to bear his child, Sharon thought. She turned away quickly to the oven to check on the cookies before her gaze lingered on the raw strength and maturity etched in his roughly hewn features. It was much too easy to love him—and much too hard to stop.

The cookies were close enough to being done, so she removed the pan from the oven with the aid of a protective potholder and carried it to the counter. She concentrated on lifting them one by one from the sheet pan with the metal spatula so she could block out the physical impact of his presence.

"Scott mentioned you were planning on cutting back on the number of shows you're attending this year," he remarked.

"I think so," she admitted. "It's getting too expensive to haul horses to some of the distant shows. I thought I'd concentrate on the major shows in the immediate area. I can't quit the show ring altogether or I'll lose the chance of getting new horses to train." She was well aware that competing in stock and western pleasure classes brought her to the attention of owners willing to pay to have their horses trained by a professional. Her reputation as a trainer was growing—and she had a roomful of trophies and ribbons to prove it.

As she turned to carry the empty cookie sheet to the table, she saw Tony slyly dipping his hand into the milk glass. "Tony—"

At her sharply reprimanding tone, he jerked his hand out of the glass. The suddenness of his action tipped the glass over, spilling the milk—right into Ridge's lap.

"Now look what you've done, Tony." But she couldn't keep the smile out of her voice as she deposited the cookie sheet on the table and reached for the towel. Her hazel eyes were dancing with laughter when she met Ridge's glance. "Was the milk cold?" she murmured innocently.

The anger went out of his expression as quickly as it had come in. "You know damned well it was," he muttered with a half smile and took the towel she offered to blot up the excess wetness.

"The ice cubes were your idea." Sharon took delight in reminding him of the fact.

"Maybe father doesn't always know best," Ridge conceded with a rueful look and stood up to wipe at the front of his jeans where the wet blotch spread onto his thigh. "There's one consolation. Milk is probably the cleanest thing that's touched these jeans lately."

The faded material was dusty and dirt-stained, but Sharon was more conscious of the way the work-worn fabric snugly shaped itself to his hips and thighs like a second skin. It turned her thoughts in a direction that had no place in the kitchen.

The spilled milk that hadn't initially landed on Ridge was now dripping off the edge of the table. Sharon grabbed the dishcloth from the sink and mopped up the milky film on the table. All the while Tony stayed very quiet and very small, not wanting to draw further attention to himself in an attempt to avoid possible punishment. He looked sufficiently chagrined so that Sharon didn't feel anything more needed to be said.

As she returned to the sink to rinse the dishcloth under the faucet, Ridge followed her. "I'm afraid your towel is soiled," he said, acknowledging it had picked up some of his dirt along with the milk.

"It'll wash."

Chapter 2

Taking the towel from him, Sharon draped it over the edge of the counter to dry and folded the dishcloth to lay it over the divider of the double sink. She felt him studying her with a penetrating thoughtfulness and sent him a curious sidelong glance.

"I hear you've been seeing a lot of that oil man lately," Ridge said.

"Oil man?" She frowned with an initial bewilderment, then her expression cleared. "You mean Andy Rivers," she said, realizing suddenly whom he meant. "He's a geologist who *works* for an oil company."

The Piceance Basin of Colorado contained one of the largest concentrations of oil shale. According to Andy, they estimated there were over 500 billion barrels of recoverable oil in the shale, more than the provable reserves of crude oil in the OPEC countries. It defied imagination when one considered they were standing on top of it.

"Same difference," Ridge shrugged at her answer and continued to study her with a kind of interested speculation. "Is it true it's become a regular thing?"

"More or less. Between his work schedule and my horse show dates, we don't see each other all that frequently," Sharon insisted. "But I suppose we go out on a fairly regular basis."

"Are you thinking about marrying him?" he asked.

Just for a second she searched his face, trying to find some reason for this personal interest, but there appeared to be little more than the casual interest of a family friend. She suppressed a sigh. Friends always seemed to be more inquisitive than family.

She laughed shortly and with little humor. "Why is it that if a girl sees a guy more than a half-dozen times everybody assumes she's planning on a trip to the alter? Maybe I'm just taking a page out of your book—or Scott's." She was vaguely impatient, but there was no heat of anger in her voice.

His eyes narrowed speculatively. "What do you mean by that?"

"You and Scott seem to be on the road to becoming confirmed bachelors." To her knowledge, neither Ridge nor her brother had been serious about any girl they had dated. "Maybe I'm not the marrying kind either." Her real problem was that she had to stop comparing every man she met to Ridge. Until she did that, she probably never would find a man she could care enough about to marry. "I enjoy going out with Andy. We have fun together."

Which was true. Andy made her laugh. When she was with him, she rarely thought about Ridge. Maybe that didn't seem earth shattering, but she considered it important.

"The three of us used to have some good times together. You, me and Scott," Ridge stated somewhat absently. Lifting a hand, he trailed a finger along her cheekbone and tucked a strand of hair behind her ear. "Didn't we?"

"Yes." Sharon didn't trust herself to say more.

There was a poignant drift of memories back to that time he had recalled. It had always been a threesome, although Sharon had been so wildly infatuated with Ridge at the time that she had believed her brother was tagging along with them—instead of her tagging along with them. She had built so many dreams from those innocent evenings in Ridge's company. She had wanted so much to believe he loved her that she had exaggerated every slow dance, every kiss, out of all proportion.

Long ago Sharon had stopped trying to second-guess his motives, so she didn't allow herself to wonder whether he was caught in a past memory when his calloused fingers laid themselves against the curve of her neck. He bent his head toward her, the brim of his hat partially masking the skimming inspection of his gaze.

She had learned that a kiss from Ridge was nothing more than a kiss. Avoiding it would make more out of it than what it was. The trick was to accept it *without* making more out of it than it was.

The warm pressure of his mouth covered her lips and moved familiarly to take possession. His hand tightened slightly on her neck to arch her into the kiss. An encircling arm was bringing her against his body. Sharon relaxed naturally against his hard frame, letting her hands slide around his middle.

Her lips moved under the investigative influence of his. The stirrings of hunger escaped her restraint and became a part of her response. Sharon wavered, wanting to draw back from the edge of this unexpected precipice, but Ridge pressed the issue with deepening insistence. Her indecision dissolved under the heat of raw longing.

There was a slow disentangling of their lips. Her breath was coming low and shallow, as disturbed as the uneven rhythm of her pulse. Sharon was careful not to let her expression show just how much his kiss had affected her. Her gaze she kept focused on the shoulder seam of his shirt. His face remained close to hers, his hat brim casting a shadow on her face while his moist breath warmed her hot skin.

"When did you learn to kiss like that?" His low voice held a hint of curious amusement.

The hand on the small of her back spread its fingers, testing the supple curve of her spine. It sent little waves of heat lightning flashing through her nerves, recharging their high sensitivity. His hard, sinewed length seemed indelibly imprinted on her flesh, male in its contours.

"It's been two years or more since you kissed me." If he'd asked, Sharon could have told him the place and the time. Her voice contained no trace of her tension, even though it was a little on the husky side. "I've had time to practice. Surely you didn't expect me to kiss like some innocent seventeen-year-old."

"I don't know," Ridge murmured and raised her chin, his blue eyes intent and probing in their narrowed study of her. "But I didn't expect this."

This recognition of her as a woman was the very thing she had so longed to hear. Her breath caught in her throat, as she hardly dared to believe it. Even if Ridge meant nothing beyond that, there was sweet satisfaction in being acknowledged as a desirable female. However, both her feet remained firmly planted in reality. It was the first time Sharon had met him on an equal footing—man to woman. He didn't have a starry-eyed romantic in his arms.

All this gave her a new confidence when his mouth sought to discover the mystery of her lips again. It wasn't necessary to disguise her enjoyment of this intimacy. Her lips parted under the deepening urgency of his kiss. A golden tide of warmth curled through her limbs while she spread her hands over the rippling muscles of his back.

Her senses were awash with the taste, the feel, and the smell of him. His mouth rolled off her lips as he came up for air, the heat of his breath fanning her cheek. There was a labored edge to his breathing, and her acutely sensitive hearing picked up the slightly uneven tempo of his heartbeat.

There was a bright glint in his eyes when Sharon finally lifted her gaze to meet his. Behind its surface amusement, the look was faintly accusing.

"You've come of age," Ridge murmured.

"I turned twenty-one on my last birthday," she pointed out, a fact that he had obviously overlooked, being so accustomed to regarding her as Scott's kid sister.

From the front porch there came a snarling growl that erupted into an angry bark. Sharon stiffened at the sound, then pushed out of Ridge's arms.

"Tony," she gasped the toddler's name as she raced into the living room. He had managed to push the screen door open. When he heard her coming, he hurriedly tossed the cookie at the barking dog and guiltily let the door swing shut.

"Doggie wanted a cookie." He blinked at her with wide-eyed innocence.

Fully aware that Tony was trying to make her believe he had intended throwing the treat to the dog all the time, Sharon wasn't buying any of it. The cookie had been offered in an attempt to entice the dog inside the house.

"All right, bud. It's nap time for you," Sharon informed him angrily.

The minute she picked him up Tony started wailing at the top of his lungs. "Don't want nap!" he protested. His cries immediately started the dog barking.

Between the two, Sharon was nearly deafened. She

shouted at both of them to hush up, but neither listened. When she turned, she spied Ridge leaning an arm against the doorway to the kitchen and watching the scene with detached amusement.

"Will you shut that dog up!" she demanded.

"Sam. Quiet." The two words came out hard and quick. There was instant silence from the dog, although Tony continued his whining bawl in her ear. Ridge's smile was close to a taunting grin as he moved lazily toward the door on a path that took him past Sharon. "One way or another, I think Sam and I have done enough damage for one afternoon." His glance flicked to her lips and she guessed they were still swollen from his kisses. "Don't forget to have Scott phone me tonight."

"I won't." But she'd practically forgotten the reason Ridge had stopped in the first place until he reminded her. Being in his arms had driven nearly everything from her mind.

The instant Tony realized the dog was leaving too, he sent out a fresh protest. Ridge and Sam were long gone before Sharon was finally able to quiet him down. Although he tried very hard to stay awake, Tony was exhausted from all the excitement and eventually fell asleep against his will.

When the ranch house was at last filled with silence, Sharon returned to the kitchen to put the last sheet of cookies into the oven. It was impossible not to think about Ridge. The scent of him still clung to her clothes and her skin, and the remembered sensation of his roaming hands remained with her.

She was determined not to make a mountain out of this molehill-sized kiss the way she'd done in the past. To paraphrase an old saying—one kiss did not a romance make. But it gave her a lot to think about.

Ridge—so easygoing and carefree on the surface. But there was more to the man than that, even if he never showed the serious side of himself around her. It existed—of that she had no doubt. No one could approach life with the shallow and lackadaisical indifference that Ridge showed and efficiently manage a ranch the size of Latigo. If that was the true sort of man he was, the ranch would have started going downhill five years earlier, when Ridge took over after his father's death. That hadn't happened. From the talk Sharon had heard, the Latigo was in a more solid financial position than it had enjoyed in years.

Her brother Scott probably knew Ridge better than anyone, but getting him to talk was about as difficult as extracting oil from shale economically. Scott was undoubtedly a bonanza of information, but Sharon hadn't successfully squeezed any of it from him.

When the last of the cookies were cooling on the counter, she began washing up the baking dishes. It was funny to discover that as a teenager she had been attracted to the slightly wild and fun-loving side of Ridge, always ripe for a laugh and a good time. Now that she had grown older—and hopefully wiser—she was becoming more intrigued by the more silent, and probably stronger, side of him.

It was nearly six in the evening when Rita came by the house to pick up Tony. She had to rush home to fix supper, so there wasn't time for Sharon to have more than a quick chat with her while they gathered all Tony's toys and clothing.

Supper was in the oven and Sharon had the evening chores done when the pickup truck with the horse trailer crested a hillock and approached the barns. Sharon waved to the three people crowded together in the cab of the truck and continued to the house. With their horses to be unsaddled, rubbed down, and fed for the night, it would be another quarter of an hour before they joined her, Sharon knew.

By the time Sharon's parents and brother had taken turns using the shower, three-quarters of an hour had passed before they all sat down at the table. There was a moment's pause while her father said grace. Lloyd Powell was tall and broadly muscled, with a silver mane of hair that had once been the color of his thirty-two-year-old son's dusty brown hair. Scott had his wide features, bluntly chiseled and weathered brown by the sun and wind, but he had his mother's green eyes. On the other hand, Sharon had inherited her mother's slender build and toffee-colored hair, and her father's hazel-brown eyes.

"I noticed the corral gate is wired shut," her father remarked. "Trouble again?"

"I think I'm going to change Huck's name to Trouble." Sharon identified the chestnut as the culprit and explained about the afternoon's fiasco—and Ridge's timely arrival, passing on Ridge's request for Scott to phone him that evening about working a couple of days for the Latigo.

"Day after tomorrow?" Scott repeated and glanced questioningly at his father. "I should be able to manage that with no problem."

"None that I can see," Lloyd Powell agreed with a slow nod.

"How did the baby-sitting go today?" her mother inquired.

"Don't ask," Sharon replied with a rueful grimace. "I'm convinced no woman in her right mind would take on the task of motherhood if she knew in advance what it was like. You need three sets of arms, feet, and eyes to keep up with them."

"Now you know what it was like having you two,"

her mother laughed, her sparkling green glance darting between her son and daughter.

"Is that why you waited until I was older before you had Sharon?" Scott wanted to know, drawing attention to their twelve-year age difference. "So you could have a built-in baby-sitter?"

"Your son was a bit slow figuring that one out," his mother declared as she cast a side glance at her husband.

"*My* son? When did he cease being ours and become mine?" he challenged good-naturedly.

Sharon eyed her brother with a studying look. "Isn't it time you were thinking about getting married and raising a family?" she asked. "By rights, there should already be another generation of Powells running around the house."

"Me?" He was startled and amused by her suggestion. "First, there's a little matter of a bride. If you're so eager for the folks to have grandchildren, why don't you marry your oil man?"

She lifted her head. "So you're the one who told Ridge about Andy."

Her brother appeared slightly taken aback and a little uncomfortable. "Was your boyfriend supposed to be a secret?"

"No." She smiled at the thought. "At the moment, that's all Andy happens to be—a friend. It's just that Ridge referred to him as an oil man when he asked me about him this afternoon. I wasn't aware my love life was something you two discussed."

"We don't," Scott replied evenly.

"What do you talk about?" Her curiosity was heightened by an afternoon spent wondering about such things and what they might reveal about Ridge.

"What kind of a question is that?" Scott frowned at her as if she'd asked a ridiculous question. "What does anybody talk about? Me? You? Dad?"

Put in that context, it did sound a little silly. She poked a fork at her food and shrugged. "I just wondered what men talk about."

"The weather, business, their health—and women," her father answered, "but not necessarily in that order. If they're married, you can add family to the list. Not a very mysterious list, is it?"

"No." Sharon had to laugh at her attempt to make something complicated out of a simple statement.

As soon as the meal was finished, Scott left the table to ring through to the Latigo ranch. Sharon helped her mother clear the table, stowing the leftovers in the refrigerator and stacking the dishes in the sink to wash.

"Mom!" Scott called to her from the front room. "Ridge wondered if you would be able to cook for the crew. And he wants to know if Sharon can lend a hand too."

"Tell him," her father inserted before either could answer, "that I don't know if I like the idea of him hiring away my whole crew." It was meant as a good-natured gibe between friends.

There was a moment's pause while Scott relayed the message, then came back with a reply. "Ridge says that's the risk you take when you have a good crew willing to work cheap. It isn't his fault we work for you for nothing."

Sharon heard her father's hearty chuckle and walked to the doorway. "Scott, tell Ridge I can spare two days." The new horses she was working would probably benefit from a short respite from the training routine. "But—I don't come cheap. If he wants me, he'll have to pay top dollar."

Scott repeated her answer into the telephone. A grin split his face at the response. "I don't think I'll tell her the last part."

"Tell me what?" she insisted with a wary look.

He placed a covering hand over the mouthpiece. "Ridge

said he doesn't mind paying you top dollar." He hesitated, the light in his eyes dancing brighter.

"Is that all?" Sharon knew it wasn't.

"Not quite." Scott tried to contain his smile. "He said there's always more than one way to get your money's worth out of a woman."

"Tell him not to worry. I come with a money-back guarantee if not completely satisfied." This time she was the one with the gleam in her eye and Scott was the one hesitant about passing on the message.

Her father cleared his throat and reached for his cigar. Her mother had appeared in the doorway behind Sharon and he arched her a considering look. "Might be that you should go along with this young girl of yours, Lena."

"*My* girl?" she countered. "She sounds more like you." But she glanced at her son. "Tell him I'll stop over tomorrow and check the camp kitchen and supplies to make sure nothing's been forgotten." She didn't wait to hear Scott relaying her message as she nudged Sharon's arm. "Do you want to wash or dry the dishes?"

"I'll wash." She turned and followed her mother to the kitchen sink.

When she turned on the faucets, the noise of running water drowned out the sound of her brother's telephone conversation in the front room. Mechanically Sharon began washing the glasses first, but her thoughts were turned ahead. She had never worked with Ridge before, so she couldn't help wondering about this new kind of experience with him. But she was careful not to start imagining possibilities.

"I thought you liked Andy," her mother remarked, interrupting her silent reverie.

"I do." Sharon glanced at her in surprise.

"At the table tonight, you seemed to stress the point that

he is just a friend." She took a great deal of time to wipe one glass when she usually zipped over it with a few efficient swipes of the towel.

"He is a friend," Sharon insisted. "If I was trying to make anything clear, it was simply that I'm not on the verge of marrying him—as everybody seems to think."

"You mean Scott?"

"And Ridge, too."

The mention of his name by Sharon produced a long, heavy silence. Her mother was completely aware of Sharon's previous infatuation with Ridge, and how Sharon had loved him with the blind intensity only an adolescent can attain. She didn't wish to raise the subject with Sharon because she knew what a long and painful process it had been getting over that unrequited crush.

"After he left this afternoon, Mom," Sharon spoke softly into the silence, "I had the strange feeling that I don't know him at all. I built up such a dream around him that I never saw him—just my dream."

"That's usually the way it is," her mother nodded.

"Around me, Ridge is always laughing and joking—or that's the way he's seemed." She frowned and dipped another glass into the sudsy water.

"Perhaps that's the only level of communication he's had with you," her mother suggested.

"What do you mean?" Sharon's frown deepened as she turned her curious gaze toward her mother.

" 'When I was a child, I spake as a child,' " she murmured the Biblical quote, becoming vaguely thoughtful. "You were young and carefree, always so quick to laugh and have fun. Whenever the conversation became serious at the table, you used to complain it was boring."

"Well, I'm a woman now," Sharon said with the full-blown confidence she'd found this afternoon, "and I've put away my childish things." She paused to look thoughtfully out the window. The evening darkness on the other side gave the glass a mirror-like quality, reflecting an indistinct image of herself. "It's going to be interesting to meet Ridge as an adult."

"Sharon . . . you're not—"

The hesitancy and veiled warning in her mother's voice made her smile. "No, Mom, I'm not still crazy about him. That's one of the childish things I've put behind me."

The events of that afternoon had put her on a new footing with Ridge, but Sharon didn't intend to replace puppy love with passion. Both were equally blinding emotions. And she didn't plan to walk down another dead-end street.

Spring had exploded on the rugged plateau, turning the seemingly barren terrain into a patchwork of color. Sharon walked the close-coupled bay horse, a Latigo brand burned on its hip, through a grove of aspen trees growing on the north slope below the ridgeline. She was making one last sweep through this section of range for any strays that might have escaped the first roundup before joining the crew at the holding pens.

Bushes of chokecherry and serviceberry crowded close under the shade of the aspens. The leaves overhead formed a glittering, silvery-green canopy that trembled at the slightest stirring of air. Showy blooms of blue columbine, the Colorado state flower, blanketed the ground in the aspen grove.

Emerging from the stand of aspens, Sharon kept her horse pointed down the slope toward the sage-covered valley. The muted purple-green color of the sage was interspersed with patches of wildflowers, the brilliant crimsons and scarlets of Indian paintbrush, firecracker penstemon, and scarlet gilia.

The air was sharp and clear, the morning sun pressing its warmth on her the instant she left the coolness of the north slope. Sharon reined in the bay horse and peeled off her jacket, tying it behind her saddle. Her flannel shirt of green and gold plaid was adequate covering on this exceptionally mild spring day.

A ribbon of green wound crookedly through the valley of sage, marking the course of a small creek. The scattering of cottonwood and willow trees growing along the banks offered potential concealment for an odd cow or two. Taking up the reins again, Sharon urged the bay horse into a canter and headed for the creek to investigate.

The small creek was full from the winter runoff, and the water ran swiftly over its shallow bed in a rushing murmur. There were no cattle in sight, nothing larger than a mule deer disturbed into flight by Sharon's approach. Still, she continued to walk her horse along the wide band of tall grass beside the creek. The scene was too idyllic to leave, and the general direction of the stream was one she would have taken anyway.

The strides of her horse made quick, swishing sounds in the thick rye grass that nearly reached her stirrup. Once this grass had dominated the landscape the way the sage did now, until early cattlemen had allowed their cattle to overgraze it. The Ute Indians had given this country its name, *Piceance*, which means "tall grass." Now the grass, properly called Big Basin wild rye, grew only along isolated stream beds flowing into Piceance Creek.

The bay horse whickered softly and tugged at the bit, pricking its ears toward the silver rush of water. Her own mouth felt dry after the long morning ride, so Sharon reined the horse toward a gravel bar that pushed into the stream a few yards ahead.

When they reached the narrow bar, Sharon dismounted

and let the horse bury its muzzle in the cool, clear water and suck in the liquid in noisy slurps. She removed her hat and shook her shoulder-length hair free after hours of being tucked under the crown. After the horse had satisfied its thirst, she moved a short way upstream and stretched flat on the gravel to scoop up several handfuls of water, laying her hat on the ground beside her. For safety's sake, she kept hold of the reins. The bay horse appeared to be well trained but she wasn't taking any chances.

Chapter 3

The water was crystal clear and cold, revealing the smooth and glistening stones on the creek bottom. Sharon had taken her last drink when she felt a pull on the reins. She tightened her grip on them quickly and hastily looked up. The solid-colored bay had lifted its head in sudden alertness to stare at some distant object across the creek. It snorted loudly, then its sides heaved in a questioning whicker.

As she pushed to her feet, wiping her wet hand on her jeans, she heard the drumming of a horse's hooves growing steadily louder. She shielded her eyes with her hand to look into the sun and identify the approaching rider.

The tall, lean shape could belong to no one but Ridge Halliday. A thread of uncertainty ran through her nerves at the prospect of meeting him here. Sharon was puzzled by the cause of it. She hadn't seen him since the dawn hours when he'd assigned the crew their individual tasks. There had been no resemblance to the joking, smiling Ridge Halliday she knew. Perhaps she'd been put off by the hard, authoritative figure he had presented. It had been all business and no nonsense. And Sharon hadn't been sure how to react to this change even though she had come expressly to discover it.

Her hat was on the ground near her feet. Sharon turned and bent to pick it up as Ridge slowed the liver-colored chestnut gelding into a long-striding walk. She heard his horse splashing across the creek to the gravel bar where she was standing and made a project of adjusting her hat snugly on her head before blandly turning to greet him.

The saddle leather creaked as Ridge stepped down, the gravel crunching beneath his boot. His hard features had relaxed out of the stern lines of the morning. There was a faint curve to his mouth, and the rich blue of his eyes was lit by a taunting gleam. Sharon felt a vague relief that this was the Ridge she knew.

"Looks like I caught you loafing on the job," he remarked as his horse dipped its nose into the clear-running creek.

"Just watering my horse the same as you're doing," she retorted, matching his faintly complacent smile with one of her own.

"I had the distinct impression you were lying down when I rode up," Ridge countered and let the reins fall to trail the ground.

"I was getting a drink. The water's icy cold and fresh," Sharon stated, all her senses coming alert as he leisurely approached her.

"So you were taking a break." His skimming glance was playing havoc with her pulse. That purely physical attraction was asserting its influence over her again. "That's going to cost you."

It was crazy. Sparks of sexual disturbance were shooting all over the place, charging the air with an elemental tension that Sharon wanted to avoid.

"That's where you're wrong, Ridge." She calmly applied the brakes to the situation before it could flare into something more than a stimulating exchange of banter.

"What's this?" He halted, smiling through his faintly puzzled frown. "I thought I had a money-back guarantee if I wasn't satisfied."

"Money-back guarantee," Sharon repeated the phrase to stress it. "And that's all you get."

She looped the reins over the bay's head and moved to the left side to mount. His hand closed on her arm, checking her step into the stirrup. She partially turned her head to give him a sidelong look, her glance forced to angle upwards because of his height. His piercing look was hard and probing, and the line of his mouth had a grimness to it.

"What's going on?" he demanded. "Why the cold shoulder all of a sudden?"

The warmth of his hand filtered through her shirt sleeve and spread through her arm. She supposed he was entitled to some explanation for her change in attitude, although she was reluctant to make one. The muscles in her throat were tightening.

"I'm not upset or angry," Sharon insisted. "I just didn't feel like going through with your little charade."

The pressure of his hand increased to turn her away from the saddle and toward him, subjecting her to the scrutiny of his unrelenting gaze. "Why? Because I was making an excuse to kiss you?" Ridge challenged, bringing his intention out in the open even though both of them knew it was where the conversation had been leading all along. "Or didn't you want to be kissed?"

"Not particularly." She lowered her gaze to the width of his leanly muscled shoulders, conscious of the way his chest expanded under his shirt. His nearness was creating an inner agitation she couldn't control.

"You raised no objections the other afternoon," he reminded her tersely. "In fact, you were more than willing."

"Maybe I'm just tired of playing games," she retorted with an impatient edge to her voice.

His harsh laugh had no humor in it. "What do you call this if it isn't playing hard-to-get?"

The accusation startled her into meeting his narrowed look. After those early years of chasing him, was this a sub-conscious attempt to have Ridge pursue her?

"No." It was more an answer to her own silent question than a denial of his charge.

She started to shrug out of his grip and turn back to the saddle, but Ridge tightened his hold and hooked an arm around her waist to keep her facing him. Anger flared at his forceful tactics. She brought her hands up to keep from being drawn into his arms.

A stiffness claimed him. Sharon wasn't about to antagonize him by struggling further, satisfied to show a resistance and keep the status quo. She could feel the coiled energy in his rigidly flexed muscles, the strength held severely in check. Hard blue eyes relentlessly probed her expression.

Suddenly the clenched line of his jaw relaxed. "I get it," he murmured with chilling satisfaction. "You planned all this just to pay me back."

"Wh . . . what?" Sharon faltered, completely thrown by his conclusion because she had no idea what he meant.

"You wanted me to become interested in you so you could have the chance to tell me to go to hell." His mouth crooked in a slanting line of rueful amusement. "I never would have suspected you of being vindictive, Sharon."

"I'm not," she denied his assessment.

"Am I supposed to believe that you're not trying to pay me back for the way I unwittingly hurt you a few years ago?" Ridge tipped his head to the side, hard amusement gleaming in his eyes.

"Then you know—" She stopped in midsentence, briefly horrified to discover he had known how crazy she had been about him.

"When a young girl starts mooning over you like a lovesick puppy, it's difficult to ignore." His voice was thick with silent laughter, the corners of his mouth deepening.

Sharon pulled all her feelings tightly inside herself to hide them. "It must have been very amusing for you," she replied stiffly. "No wonder you and Scott were so willing to take me with you all the time. I was always good for a laugh if things got dull."

"Sharon." He gave her a little shake as if exasperated with the deprecating way she was talking about herself. "It wasn't until the last that I guessed the way you felt about me."

"And before that?" Sharon looked at him, so cool that she felt frozen inside. "Why did you drag me along?"

There was a flash of impatience. "Why are you asking me questions when you know the answers are going to hurt?"

"I always thought it was the truth that hurt," she declared, a bitter tinge in her response. "Or maybe I'm just a glutton for punishment. But I would like to know."

Ridge studied her as if to assure himself that she meant it, then grimly set about answering her. "I guess we regarded you as a kind of mascot—a cute and cuddly little mascot."

"Cuddly." Sharon choked on the word. Suddenly she was tired of blaming herself for what had happened. "You didn't exactly treat me like a mascot, Ridge," she accused. "You did hand out some encouragement."

"Inadvertently I suppose I did," he admitted, then hit

back without pulling any punches. "But you made it plain that you wanted to be kissed. You did everything but come right out and ask. The first few times I thought you were trying some innocent experimenting on me. Later on I realized that wasn't the case." He paused, a nerve twitching along his jaw. "Hero worship can be very flattering to a man, Sharon, even when it is misplaced," Ridge added curtly.

"I'm sure it can be." It all seemed very fresh and painful. She was beginning to feel the strain of keeping all emotion inside.

"It was never my intention to hurt you—and it isn't now." He sounded slightly angry that she had resurrected the past.

"I don't know." There was something stilted in her voice and the attempted shrug of her shoulders. "I always heard catharsis is good for the soul."

"Wrong. Confession is good for the soul," Ridge corrected her wording. "My God, how did we get into this discussion?" In a burst of impatience, he released her and took a quick stride away.

"You brought it up," Sharon reminded him.

"I'm sorry—" He swung around with thinly disguised impatience. "Sorry I mentioned it—and I'm sorry if you got hurt. What else can I say?"

"Nothing," she agreed, but the apology seemed flat.

His features appeared to grow hard, the recklessly handsome lines smoothed out of them. "I suppose you're secretly wishing that I'd say something like 'I've been waiting all this time for you to grow up'—that I've always been in love with you."

Anger flashed in her hazel eyes at his mildly sarcastic taunt. "Maybe once I might have wanted to hear that, but I don't now."

"It's a damned good thing, because it isn't true," he muttered thickly. "I didn't like it on that damned pedestal. I'm a man, not some god to be adored."

"Believe me, I don't have you on a pedestal any more." Her voice trembled on an angry pitch, a direct reaction to his icy rage.

"Good. At least we're clear on that point." There was a certain rawness in the contained energy that directed his movements as Ridge gathered up the reins to his horse and swung into the saddle.

In direct contrast, Sharon mounted with a deliberate lack of haste. When both toes were securely tucked into the stirrups, she looked at him expectantly, meeting his boldly challenging gaze.

"One more thing before we ride to the holding pens," he said.

"What's that?" Coolly she continued to hold his gaze.

"The next time I decide to kiss you, I won't make any excuses or wait for any invitations. I'll simply do it—man to woman," Ridge stated flatly—and about as unromantically as one could get.

"Always supposing I let you," she countered smoothly, finding she had no qualms about slapping him down—figuratively. There was even the faintest smile on her face when she said it.

"I think I liked you better when you were all honey and sweetness," he muttered.

"And I liked you better when you were just a handsome flirt," she retaliated in kind.

Digging her heels into the bay's sides, she sent the horse across the creek at a lunging canter. Its scrambling hooves kicked back sprays of water, showering the liver-colored chestnut and its rider. She hadn't ridden twenty yards before Ridge caught up with her. Not a word was exchanged during the ride to the holding pens. A couple of times, Sharon stole a glance at his profile, its lines showing such unyielding hardness and his gaze always directed to the front.

The holding pens were a hive of activity. Dust kicked up by churning hooves hung over the scene like a dirty gray pall. The bawling of cattle, clacking hooves, and shouts from cowboys both afoot and on horseback created a ceaseless cacophony. As Sharon and Ridge approached the pens, they separated. Sharon rode over to the motorized cook wagon where her mother was in full preparation for the noon meal, and Ridge headed for the chutes to check on the morning's progress.

Feeding nearly two dozen hungry men with hearty appetites was no easy task under normal circumstances, so Sharon opted to pitch in and help her mother rather than join the crew at the chutes, vaccinating and ear-tagging calves. Conversation was held to a minimum by the amount of work to be done and the noisy competition from the pens.

When the call for noon break sounded, the activity shifted to the camp kitchen. Good-natured grumbling was customary, but this group grumbled with silent expressions. Her brother was one of the last in line. Sharon speared a charred steak and forked it onto his plate.

"What's the matter?" she murmured, her glance running curiously around the vaguely sullen group. "Nobody seems to be in a very good mood."

"It's Ridge," Scott muttered in a grudging fashion. "He's been as bad tempered as a range bull with a nose full of quills. He'd better start letting up or he's going to find himself without a crew."

Scott drew in a deep breath, briefly meeting her sobered glance, and moved on down the line for his helping of potatoes and corn. She scanned the scattered collection of cowboys sitting cross-legged on the ground or clustered around the odd barrel drum. But there was no sign of Ridge among them.

"That should be the last of them," her mother said as she wiped her brow with the back of her hand, a sight in her flop-brimmed hat, a cast-off flannel shirt of her husband's rolled up at the sleeves, and snug-fitting jeans that showed her still very trim figure.

Sharon glanced at the cowboy walking away with a plate mounded with food. "Where's Ridge?" she asked. "I don't remember seeing him come through the line."

"That's right. He didn't," her mother commented with a curious frown and looked around as Sharon had done earlier. "He can help himself when he comes. Grab yourself a plate. If Ridge is like your father, he won't show up until the food is cold. I used to wonder if your father ever ate a hot meal when he was running a crew. That's half the reason I started cooking," she admitted, smiling faintly.

When another quick search of the area couldn't find Ridge, Sharon reached for a plate. It had been a long time since breakfast. Maybe some of her rawness was caused by hunger.

The excuse her mother had offered for Ridge's absence was a reasonable one. From her own experience, Sharon knew her father always lagged behind, making sure everything was in readiness for the crew when they went back to work and no time would be lost. He was always the last one to eat and the first one to throw in his plate. There was no reason to think Ridge was any different.

Her plate was filled and balanced on her knees as she sat on the running board of the van. She was chewing her first bite of steak when Ridge approached the edge of the circle. The camp kitchen was situated upwind from the pens, so the dust and smell would blow away from the food and the noise would also be carried away from them. He was leading a roan horse, instead of the liver-colored chestnut he'd been riding in the morning.

"Hobbs, where did you pick up that unbranded yearling bull?" Ridge snapped the question at his lanky foreman. "How come you haven't separated him into a pen away from those cows?"

"Damned thing's half-wild. We spent nearly an hour this morning trying to pen it, then finally decided it was easier to separate the cows from him," the foreman Hobbs answered and immediately forked another mouthful of food.

"Is the yearling one of ours?"

Hobbs had to chew quickly to answer. "Yup. It sticks close to that half-shorthorn cow. I reckon she's his momma. I think we had her listed last year as being barren. I figure she hid that calf from us all this time."

"Did you try penning her first?" There was a faintly sarcastic edge to Ridge's voice. Sharon could almost see the foreman's hackles rise at the insulting tone.

"Nope. We didn't do that," he admitted.

There was no comment from Ridge, but his look said it all. "I'll pen her up myself." He stepped into the stirrup and swung onto the saddle all in one motion.

"If you wait a couple of minutes, I'll give you a hand," Hobbs protested.

"I don't need it." Ridge set the roan horse on its haunches and pivoted it in a half-spin, pointing it toward the corrals.

There were a few low mutters, but no one moved from their positions. Sharon was conscious that all were watching as Ridge rode his horse into the largest of the pens. After he had herded the mixed cattle to the far end, he came back and opened the gate to a small pen. He walked the roan horse back to the herd, picked out his quarry, and set about cutting it from the rest.

A sudden movement caught her attention. She turned, spying her brother as he set his half-finished meal down and walked over to the horses, climbing aboard his afternoon mount. Secretly she was relieved that someone had gone to help Ridge, although she suspected he could have managed alone.

With Scott on hand to turn back the cattle, Ridge made short work of separating the shorthorn cow and maneuvering her into the smaller pen. The yearling bull turned out to be a real test for horse and rider. Four times he escaped and rejoined the herd. The fifth time, Ridge threw a loop around his stubby horns and dragged him the length of the pen, shouting to Scott to open the gate.

The sight of the lowing cow in the pen checked the struggles of the yearling bull. Ridge shook off the loop as the yearling trotted eagerly past him through the open gate. A murmur of approval began to flow through the watching riders at the efficient job Ridge had made of it.

A moment later everything went wrong. The instant the yearling heard the squeak of the closing gate Scott had started to swing shut, it whirled and charged for that narrow gap of freedom. The cow followed her feral son.

In a lightning move, Ridge was out of the saddle and lending his strength to Scott's in an effort to latch the gate before the pair forced it open. For a second, it looked as if they were going to succeed. Sharon was on her feet, unconsciously holding her breath.

The gate popped open. Scott was thrown to the side, but Ridge stumbled into the path of the yearling bull and the cow. He tried to dodge out of the way, but the wild-eyed bull hooked at him and drove him onto the ground with a butt of his head. Then both animals were trampling over him and running to rejoin the herd.

For a paralyzed instant, Sharon stood there, staring at Ridge and waiting for him to move out of the half-crumpled ball he'd made of himself on the ground. The sounds of others running toward the scene finally galvanized her into action.

Later, she couldn't even remember climbing the fence and racing across the churned-up sod of the pen. She didn't remember seeing any of the other riders—only her brother as he knelt over Ridge's still form.

And her mother's voice, saying, "Don't move him."

Then Sharon was kneeling on the ground next to him. Her hand felt cold as ice when she pressed it to the side of Ridge's warm neck, seeking his pulse. Her own heart was pounding so loudly that she couldn't hear his, but Sharon felt the vein throbbing beneath her fingers.

Ridge stirred, moaning. There was an ashen pallor to his skin beneath its burnt-in tan. He made an attempt to uncurl from his protective ball and roll onto his back. Her eyes widened at the sight of his torn shirt, the front nearly shredded by sharp, cloven hooves. His stomach was scraped raw, but there were no other obvious wounds.

Suddenly his glazed blue eyes looked directly into Sharon's. "Help me up." His voice was a hoarse, rasping sound, completely unrecognizable as belonging to him.

Somebody ventured the opinion, "Maybe he's just got the wind knocked out of him."

"Probably broke some ribs," someone else said.

"You'd better lie still," Sharon told him and glanced at her mother.

"No." The protest was a guttural sound.

After a few seconds' hesitation, her mother suggested, "Let's see if we can't roll him onto his back."

"Help me up." This time Ridge didn't waste his throat-rough appeal on either Sharon or her mother, directing it instead at Scott who would understand the manly need to rise above injury.

Her mother placed a restraining hand on her son's arm when he would have helped Ridge. She bent closer so that Ridge could see her face. "The pain. Where is the pain, Ridge?" She spoke slowly and concisely.

The tightly clenched jaw, the betraying whiteness, and the trembling mouth that wouldn't let any sound come out were all indications that he was in a great deal of pain. Both arms were clasped around his middle, holding his stomach.

It seemed a very long time before Ridge attempted to answer the question. "My gut—" his voice was so tight and hoarse that tears pricked Sharon's eyes "—feels like it's . . . on fire."

Mrs. Powell sent a concerned glance at her son. "I think he's hurt internally. Get one of the trucks in here and find some blankets."

Somebody handed Sharon a canteen. She vaguely recalled hearing that a person bleeding internally shouldn't drink. So she took her kerchief from her pocket and wetted it down, then used it to moisten Ridge's lips and wipe some of the grime off his face. His features were twisted with pain that had him doubled up.

When the pickup roared into the pen, two cowboys hopped out of the rear bed before it came to a stop. Both carried blankets. Her mother instructed them to roll Ridge onto the blankets and use them as a stretcher to transport him to the back of the truck.

"Dammit! If somebody would just help me . . . , I can walk," he protested in a hoarse rage.

"Hell, what difference will it make now?" someone wondered, sympathizing with Ridge's pride.

"We'll make a cradle and carry him," Scott said and

waved to a stocky, muscled cowboy to give him a hand.

Together they managed to get Ridge partially sitting up, and each slipped an arm under his legs. "Let me stand," Ridge insisted. Most of his weight was already on their shoulders, so they let his feet slide slowly to the ground. Sharon gritted her teeth as he tried to take a step. His agony dominated his expression, and his face went whiter still. He sagged against the pair.

For a second, Sharon thought he'd lost consciousness again. He didn't say a word when they scooped him up and carried him carefully to the lowered tailgate of the pickup truck. More blankets were spread across some loose hay scattered over the truck bed to make a rough mattress.

"I'll ride in back with Ridge," Sharon told her mother and crawled hurriedly into the back of the truck.

His least painful position seemed to be partly hunched over, so Sharon propped herself against the back of the cab and told Scott to lay Ridge crosswise to her. She gathered him into her arms and rested his head against her shoulder.

"It's a long ride into town," Scott warned her. "Your arms are going to get tired holding him."

"We need some blankets to wrap around him," she said, ignoring his comment, perfectly aware it was true. But her body would be a better cushion to absorb the bumpy ride than the straw bed.

"Are you all settled in back there?" Her mother had the door on the driver's side opened.

"Yes." Sharon nodded and smoothed the thick mahogany-colored hair off Ridge's forehead.

"Do you want me to come with you?" Scott vaulted over the side of the truck bed to the ground.

"Sharon and I can manage," her mother replied.

Chapter 4

Only once did Ridge stir during the interminable ride to the hospital. Between the engine noise and the rushing wind, Sharon couldn't understand Ridge's unintelligible mutter, so she simply hugged him closer and tucked the blankets more tightly around him.

When the attendants at the emergency entrance whisked him away on a stretcher, it felt as if some part of her had been taken. Her aching arms were suddenly very empty, and her body missed the hard, punishing weight of his.

Both she and her mother were sidetracked from following the stretcher into the emergency room by a nurse. Between them, they were able to supply most of the information the admitting nurse needed for the multitude of hospital forms. Sharon found herself signing the list of valuables—jewelry, wallet, and the like—that had been removed from his person while Ridge was being wheeled to some other part of the hospital.

"X-ray," the nurse informed her with a benign smile. "Are you his fiancée?"

"No . . . just a friend," Sharon replied.

In the waiting room, Sharon and her mother each drank a cup of bitter black coffee from a dispensing machine and leafed endlessly through tattered magazines. Each time any uniformed person went by, Sharon tensed, expecting the doctor to arrive and advise them of Ridge's condition. It was the not knowing that was so terrible and wearing on the nerves—the uncertainty about the extent of his injuries.

"I didn't know it was like this," she murmured to her mother. "No one has ever been sick or hurt before—no one I knew well."

"He's going to be all right," her mother smiled in understanding.

"I keep telling myself that," Sharon managed a rueful copy of that smile.

"Can you imagine what we must look like?" Amusement suddenly gleamed in the green eyes.

Suddenly Sharon noticed her mother's floppy-brimmed cowboy hat, with wisps of hair sticking out from it like a witch's coiffure, the baggy shirt, and the scruffy, manure-stained cowboy boots. Sharon covered her mouth to smother the laugh that bubbled from her throat, aware she probably didn't look any better.

It was such a welcome release of tension that both of them started to titter, which succeeded in drawing curious looks at the pair of laughing loonys.

"Maybe we'd better find the ladies' room and make ourselves presentable," her mother suggested between laughing gasps for breath.

After Sharon had brushed the wisps of hay and dust from her jeans, tucked her shirt neatly inside the waistband, and removed her hat to comb her honey-brown hair, there was infinite improvement. Magically, her mother produced a tube of lipstick from her pocket to add the finishing touch to both their transformations.

They returned to the waiting room just as the doctor walked in. "Mrs. Powell?" He glanced questioningly at the older of the two jean-clad women with cowboy hats in hand.

"Yes," she nodded.

There was an efficient, scrubbed-clean look about the balding doctor with the shining face. Although he was slender and spare with silver wire-rimmed glasses, there was something about him that reminded Sharon of a roly-poly Santa Claus. Maybe it was his round cheeks and beaming smile.

"How is Ridge—Mr. Halliday?" she rushed the question, not giving the doctor a chance to impart the information.

"My daughter, Sharon," her mother explained when the doctor gave her a questioning look. "My husband and I own the ranch next to Mr. Halliday's. Ridge has practically been a second son to us."

"He's a very lucky man," the doctor declared. "There is evidence of some mild internal bleeding but it appears to be the result of some rather severe bruising of his internal organs rather than any perforations. You might refer to the loss as seepage—as when you scrape your skin and draw blood. Outside of that, he has a broken rib and two that are cracked."

A shiver of relief ran down Sharon's spine. "I was afraid—" she stopped and changed what she had been about to say "—he was in so much pain."

"I didn't mean to minimize the amount of pain he'll suffer," the doctor cautioned. "The bruising is very severe. It's a miracle nothing was ruptured. Naturally I'll want to keep him in the hospital a few days and monitor his condition."

"But—" It sounded more serious than he had first indicated.

He held up a calming hand. "There has been some bleeding. We want to make certain it doesn't recur—and we want to keep watch for any formation of blood clots. It's a precautionary measure."

"I see," she said, slightly reassured. "May we see him?"

The doctor nodded affirmatively. "For a few minutes. He's been given medication so he can rest."

When they entered Ridge's room and Sharon saw him, there was something incongruous about such a vital, healthy-looking male specimen lying in a hospital bed with tubes running into his veins. The fiery lights in his darkly brown hair appeared subdued in this setting. His blue eyes were such a focal point of his features that Sharon noticed the darkness of his thick brows and long lashes for the first time—because his eyes were closed.

She moved quietly to the side of the bed, unaware that her mother didn't step beyond the doorway. The lower part of his chest was strapped in white bandages, obviously support for his ribs. His bronze shoulders and arms were uncovered. Sharon lifted the blanket to draw it up around his chest and noticed the discoloration already showing through the raw, scraped redness of his stomach. And that was only the tip of the iceberg. She laid the blanket across his chest.

His eyelids flickered, then slowly opened. There was a faraway, dreamy quality to his look when Ridge focused on her. She guessed he was high on some pain-killer.

"Told you I could stand," he declared in a slurring whisper. Then his mouth curved in that reckless smile she knew so well.

"I guess I should have listened to you." She went along with whatever dream he was having.

"Damn right." His eyelids seemed to grow too heavy for him to hold open. A wince flashed across his face, proving the drug had only dulled the pain, not killed it. "Hurts."

"I know it does," Sharon agreed. "Try to get some sleep, Ridge."

His eyes were closed and she thought he had drifted into that other state. But when she started to straighten away from the bed, his hand closed on her wrist.

"Talk to me," he insisted.

"About what?" she asked quietly.

"Don't know." His head moved to one side of the pillow in some mute protest. "Never been . . . stomped on like this before. Not like this."

"You're going to be all right," she assured him, and realized he was fighting the drug, not wanting to let go of his wavering stream of consciousness.

" . . . gave me something," he muttered with an angry frown. " . . . told them . . . didn't want it. . . . wouldn't listen."

"Sssh." Sharon murmured things, soothing words she might have used to calm a green horse she was training. The content was unimportant; only the steady softness of her voice mattered. Her wrist was still imprisoned in his grip, but his rough fingers had loosened their circle. He was breathing deeper, slower. Lightly she took hold of his hand loosely clasping her wrist. "You can let go now, Ridge."

His fingers uncurled as Sharon lifted her wrist free. A look of disappointment flickered across his features, then they smoothed out into an expressionless mask. She retreated from the bed and tiptoed to the door to join her mother.

"He's finally sleeping," she whispered. "We might as well go."

"Yes," her mother agreed. "I spoke to the nurse a few minutes ago. She said the doctor had left instructions to keep him sedated through the night, so there's little point in coming back this evening to see him."

"He'll need his razor, a robe, and some clean clothes. We can collect them when we go back to Latigo and I'll bring them in with me when I visit him tomorrow," Sharon murmured with a last glance at the bed and the man in it. "I'm sure he can get by until then."

To make up for her less-than-feminine appearance when Ridge had been admitted to the hospital, Sharon took extra interest in her choice of dress the next afternoon. She selected one of her favorite dresses, made of yards of soft, peach-colored material gathered in at the waist by a wide belt. It had a peasant-style, elastic neckline and long, full sleeves banded tightly at the wrist. Her throat was bare of any necklace to detract from the creamy smoothness of her skin, and her tawny hair glistened in soft curls that brushed the tops of her shoulders.

As she walked down the hospital corridor carrying Ridge's small satchel of belongings, her high-heeled sandals made attention-getting clicks. Sharon was conscious of the looks that came her way. The faint smile that touched her mouth was in remembrance of the entirely different looks she and her mother had received the day before.

All the doors to the hospital rooms were open, but when she approached Ridge's room, she saw it was shut. A nurse darted out, her expression grim, and went hurrying past Sharon toward the ward station. Before the door closed behind the nurse, Sharon caught the spate of angry voices.

She quickened her stride to find out what was going on.

As she pushed the door open, she heard the tightly angry but controlled voice of a second nurse in the room. "Since you insist on being difficult, Mr. Halliday, I've sent Nurse Gaines to fetch the orderlies—"

"You can send her to hell for all I care!" Ridge snarled in response. "I told you I don't want that damned thing in my arm!"

Shutting the door quickly, Sharon moved forward a little hesitantly, trying to take lightning stock of the situation. Ridge was sitting on the edge of the hospital bed. The blanket had been pulled loose and partially wrapped around his waist, still leaving most of his legs bare. He was glaring at the flushed nurse who was glaring back.

"Do not swear at me, Mr. Halliday!" she reproved him sharply. "I am not obliged to take that kind of abuse from you or any patient!"

"Then kindly get the hell out of here," Ridge declared with a dangerously thin smile.

"Ridge!" Sharon stepped forward, drawing attention to herself. She was more than a little stunned that this man, who had the virile charm to wind this nurse around his finger, had resorted to crudeness and anger. "What is the meaning of this?" she demanded.

The look he flashed her held impatience rather than welcome. "It's about time somebody showed up," he muttered. "These damned fools took my clothes. All I've got to wear is that damned flapping gown."

The dismissive gesture of his hand turned Sharon's gaze to the crumpled hospital gown on the floor, obviously thrown there by Ridge.

"What have you got there?" His glance fell on the satchel she was carrying.

"I brought some of your things. Mom and I—"

Ridge didn't give her a chance to finish. "Did you pack me some clothes?"

"Yes—"

"Bring it here," he ordered peremptorily and extended an impatiently flicking hand to take it from her. "I'm getting out of this place," Ridge added as she brought it within his reach.

"You're in no condition—" Sharon started to pull the satchel away, but he snatched it from her before she could succeed. A rush of irritation swept through her. Like the nurse, she was fast losing her patience with him.

"All I've got is some bruises and a couple of busted ribs," he muttered. When he tried to turn slightly to open the satchel, he winced and went pale at the shafting pain that took his breath away. A moment later, he was pulling out the clean shirt and pants she'd packed for him. "Hell, I've broken my arm one day and rode the next. I'm not going to stay in here so they can keep me doped up with those damned drugs 'til I don't know up from down."

"I don't think you know up from down now," Sharon declared grimly, suspecting there was just enough of the pain-killing drug in his system for him to be numbed to the severity of his pain. "And you didn't break your arm. You are badly bruised *inside*."

But Ridge wasn't listening. The agonizing effort of getting his arms into the shirt sleeves had beaded his forehead and upper lip with perspiration. He was taking short, quick breaths to avoid aggravating the discomfort of his broken ribs. When he shook out his pants and tried to put a leg into them, the subsequent pain was so intense he groaned aloud and fell back on an elbow, swearing savagely under his breath. Involuntarily Sharon took a step toward the bed, feeling sorry for him even though she knew he was bringing it all on himself.

His half-closed eyes caught her movement. Ridge struggled to sit up again, his features whitening with the effort. "Help me get these damned pants on," he demanded through tightly clenched teeth.

"I'm not going to help you." Sharon steeled herself against the compassionate urges that tried to push her to his aid. "If you can't put your pants on, you've got no business getting out of that bed."

Her logic angered him, lighting blue flames in his eyes. "All right, dammit, I'll show you." Ridge started all over again, the strain showing in the contortions of his face as he tentatively slid a bare foot into the pants leg.

Watching him, Sharon gritted her teeth so hard they hurt. He had to keep pausing to wait for the pain to subside. By the time he managed to get both legs into the pants, sweat was trickling down his neck. He slid off the edge of the bed to pull the pants over his hips and his legs nearly buckled under him.

The nurse rushed forward to catch him, but Ridge had already braced an arm on the bed to support himself. "Mr. Halliday, please get back into bed," the nurse urged with obvious concern.

"Ridge, please," Sharon added her voice to the nurse's. It was clear to her that he was so weak and in so much pain that he could barely stand.

He shrugged off the nurse's supporting hands. "Just get away and let me get dressed." The roughness was still in his voice, but it lacked its earlier strength.

The door opened behind Sharon. She turned as the doctor came striding through, all brisk and professional. He was followed closely by the first nurse and an orderly. The cavalry was coming to the rescue, and the good doctor was leading the charge. He didn't stop until he confronted his adversary.

"What's going on here, Mr. Halliday?" he demanded sharply. "You're supposed to be in bed."

"Wrong." Ridge grabbed the bedrail for support and began inching along it.

"What do you think you're doing?" the doctor demanded with exasperation.

"I'm trying to find my damned boots so I can get out of here," Ridge muttered. "Where are they?"

"In the closet with the rest of your clothes," the doctor replied. "But you're in no condition to be released. You need at least three days of total bedrest to give your body a chance to heal itself."

"If I've got to lie in bed for three days, I'll do it back at the ranch. I'm not staying in this hospital." Clutching his stomach he staggered to the closet door. Sharon saw the doctor wave aside the orderly when he made a move to stop Ridge. Once he had his boots, Ridge more or less fell into the vinyl chair in the corner.

"It should be evident to you, Mr. Halliday, that you aren't capable of taking care of yourself." The doctor changed his confrontation tactics and attempted to reason with him. "You told me you lived alone. Who is going to fix your meals, give you your medicine, help you back and forth to the bathroom?"

The question was met initially with silence as Ridge appeared to concede that he couldn't manage alone. Then his blue gaze sought her out. "Sharon," he concluded and stuck a foot into one of the cowboy boots, seemingly oblivious to the fact he wasn't wearing socks. "She can stay at the house for a few days."

She opened her eyes a little wider at the way he took her agreement for granted, not even bothering to ask. The doctor appeared startled and glanced at Sharon as if just realizing there was a nonstaff member in the room.

After a second's hesitation, he shook his head grimly.

"I'm sorry, Mr. Halliday, but I can't agree to release you from the hospital," he stated.

"I never asked you to release me," Ridge glanced at him with laughing scorn. "I'm checking myself out of here."

"If you do, I can't be held responsible for anything that might happen," the doctor warned him.

"I never asked you to be," Ridge pulled on the other boot, then remained partially hunched over, an arm folded across his stomach.

"Are you positive you want to go through with this?" the doctor persisted in the face of the patient's obvious debilitating pain.

"Yes." He made the short, one-word reply without looking up.

Resigned to accepting the decision, the doctor sighed his disapproval and glanced at the orderly. "Bring him a wheelchair."

"I don't need it." Ridge struggled to his feet, using the chair and the wall for support, and reached inside the closet for his hat.

"It's hospital rules, Mr. Halliday," the doctor informed him. "It's required by our insurance."

There was no protest from Ridge as the orderly left the room to fetch the wheelchair. His departure was closely followed by the nurses, who obviously had other duties and patients. The doctor scribbled something on a paper attached to the clipboard chart he carried, tore it off, and walked over to give it to Sharon.

"The hospital pharmacy will fill the prescription for you," he said. "He should eat nothing but soft foods the next couple of days and there should be absolutely no strenuous activity at all. I would prefer that he doesn't get out of bed, but failing that, he should be confined to the house."

Like Ridge, the doctor was taking it for granted that she was going to look after him and wasn't wasting his time giving Ridge any advice. Sharon accepted the prescription without comment.

"I know Mr. Halliday insists he doesn't want anything for the pain," the doctor continued. "But in this instance, it will be much less wearing on his system if he does take something. Rest is the best medicine for him, but it's extremely difficult to rest when you're in pain."

"I understand," Sharon nodded, then glanced up to see Ridge staggering out of the room, minus the assistance of a wheelchair.

"The man's impossible," the doctor muttered under his breath and went after him.

Silently echoing the sentiment, Sharon hurriedly gathered his dirty clothes from the closet and stuffed them into the open satchel on the bed. As she left the room, the orderly went by with the wheelchair. Ridge was halfway down the corridor, hugging the wall as he moved with obvious care.

When she caught up with the procession of patient, doctor, and orderly, the doctor's insistence that Ridge sit in the wheelchair was falling on deaf ears. He kept putting one foot in front of the other as if he didn't dare stop.

"Look, Doc—" Ridge stopped and leaned against the corner of an intersecting corridor "—I'm going to walk out of this hospital. Let this guy follow me with the wheelchair and everybody pretend I'm sitting in it."

The doctor looked at him for a long second, then swung away in disgust. "Follow him," he told the orderly and walked off muttering to himself.

Half an hour had passed by the time Ridge signed for the hospital bill and collected his personal valuables. All the while Sharon stayed quietly in the background, slipping away once to have the prescription filled. Part of her admired the grit that was carrying him through the ordeal, while the rest of her was irritated by the sheer stupidity of his refusing all help.

When they left the office to head for the hospital exit, they found the orderly had momentarily stepped away, leaving the wheelchair unattended. Ridge was free to leave the hospital on his own. Ten feet from the door, he stopped and leaned heavily against the wall. There was a grayness to his face, weakness visibly clawing at him. His gaze flicked to Sharon.

"What are you hovering around for?" he muttered roughly.

"It's the first time I've seen a real macho cowboy up close." The corners of her mouth twitched with a smile. "You're so big and brave. I thought it would be interesting to see how long you can keep it up."

"Sharon." Ridge spoke her name in a tone that tiredly appealed to her not to hassle him. He shut his eyes and let his shoulders slump. "Get the damned wheelchair."

She went back for the wheelchair and held it steady while he gingerly lowered himself into it. There was a barely stifled moan that was bitten off, then he cradled his forehead in his hand as if he lacked the strength to hold his head up. Her fingers almost touched his shoulders in a sympathetic caress, but she curled them up tightly and pulled her hand back. Her gaze lingered on the corded muscles in his neck, testimony of his pain-wracked tension.

"Now where?" She made her voice sound falsely bright and watched him stiffen.

"Home," he answered curtly.

"How do you plan to get there?" Sharon inquired innocently and tilted her head downward in smiling inquiry.

"Sharon, for God's sake, will you take me home?" Ridge demanded impatiently.

"Oh? You want me to give you a ride home," she said as if she had just discovered his intention.

"You know damned well I do," he snapped.

At that point, Sharon had had her fill of his high-handed tactics. The full skirt of her dress swirled about her legs as she moved to the front of the wheelchair. Determination ruled her expression, making her gaze just as hard and unyielding as his.

"I'm not going to take you anywhere until we settle a few things," she informed him. "First of all, you're going to do exactly as the doctor ordered."

"I'm not staying in this hospital." An instant after the firm declaration was issued, an expression flickered across his features that invisibly reached out to her with an irresistible poignancy. "I want to go home, Sharon," he murmured, a touching ache in his voice that was nearly her undoing.

"And you'll stay in bed for three days," she added the second condition.

"Two days for sure," Ridge grudgingly conceded.

"Three days," Sharon insisted. "And I'll be there to make sure you do. Do I have your word on it?" She saw his hesitation. "I'm warning you, Ridge. I'll walk away right now and leave you sitting here in this wheelchair."

An angry frown darkened his brow. "I'll call somebody else to come pick me up."

"And I'll convince them that you should stay in the hospital for your own good," she retorted, continuing to challenge him with the steadiness of her gaze. Out of the corner of her eye, she saw the orderly approaching.

A brief spark of admiration glimmered in his eyes, although his mouth remained grimly drawn. "I'm in no shape to argue with you," Ridge replied.

"I have your word?"

"Yes," he grudgingly gave in.

Her expression softened with inner relief. "Wait here while I drive the car up to the door." She smiled at the orderly who was very careful to say nothing about finding Ridge in the wheelchair. "I'll just be a minute."

Chapter 5

The ranch appeared to be deserted when Sharon stopped the car in front of the sprawling, single-story ranch house. A golden twilight was throwing long shadows over the land and casting a yellow tinge over the buildings.

Climbing out of the car, she walked around to the passenger side to help Ridge. After he'd taken one step, she could tell he was too exhausted and weak to walk all the way to the house under his own power. She took his arm and put it around her shoulders, trying to help him without adding to his pain.

"You'd better lean on me," she advised him.

Her quick glance at his face was caught and held by his half-veiled look, so lazy and warm. There was even the suggestion of a smile around his mouth. She became conscious of the heat of his body running the length of hers, the closeness of his leanly handsome features, and the caressing warmth of his breath. A disturbance started in the pit of her stomach.

"It seems that's all I've been doing is leaning on you,"

Ridge murmured while his eyes made a slow, roaming study of her upturned face. "I leaned on you all the way to the hospital—and here I am, leaning on you again."

"I know it's hard on the male ego, but you'll survive." She was having trouble breathing evenly, so she tried to make light of his comments.

"It would be easier if you were softer." Ridge shifted his position slightly to keep her shoulder bone from poking him in the side.

It was the break Sharon needed to regain control of the situation. "Come on. Let's get you inside."

With slow, measured steps, she helped him into the house, entering into it through the living room. His bedroom was the first door off the hallway. Like the rest of the house, it was Spartanly furnished. His mother had died some years ago and the house was beginning to lose the traces of a woman's touch. Except for an odd vase or two, most of the flat surfaces were bare of adornment—an indication of a man's impatience to pick up things when he dusted. Ashtrays, lamps, radios, and clocks were practically all the movable items.

Ridge sat on the edge of his bed while Sharon plumped the pillows, one atop the other, so he could rest against them. Holding himself very carefully, he shifted to lie on top of the chenille bedspread fully clothed.

"I'll go out to the car and get your things," she said and started to leave the room.

"When you come back—" his eyes remained closed as he spoke "—would you bring me a pack of cigarettes from the kitchen? They took mine away from me at the hospital. I sure could use a smoke." The last was murmured in a tired sigh.

"Sure."

Without saying more, Sharon quietly withdrew from the

room and retraced her steps to the car. Returning to the house with the satchel, she paused in the spacious kitchen long enough to take a pack of cigarettes from the carton on top of the refrigerator.

When she returned to his bedroom, it didn't appear that Ridge had moved an inch from his previous position. The lines in his face seemed more deeply etched, giving the impression of pain being suppressed. There was a tinge of grayness around his compressed mouth and the pinched-in tightness of his nose. His eyelids were closed, long lashes casting shadows on the faint hollows under his eyes.

Sharon hesitated. There was no sign that he'd heard her come in. She didn't want to disturb him if he had managed to fall asleep or drifted into that in-between state that is neither sleep nor wakefulness. Rest was more vital to him than the cigarettes in her hand.

"If you're through staring, you can bring me my cigarettes." The roughness of impatience was in his voice.

Startled, it was a second before she noticed the narrow slits of his eyes, observing her while they appeared to be closed. Recovering, she walked calmly to the side of the bed.

"I thought you might be asleep," she said.

"If I was, I suppose you were going to wake me like those damned nurses, so you could take my pulse and check my temperature," Ridge grumbled.

"I'll bet they enjoyed sticking a thermometer in your mouth just for the pleasure of shutting you up," Sharon countered, and observed the slight widening of his eyes to more than slits.

"It's wonderful that you're so understanding," he murmured with dry sarcasm.

"I understand, all right," she assured him. "You feel rotten, so you behave rottenly to everyone around you. Misery loves company."

He shut his eyes and made no comment to her remark. "Light me a cigarette." As an obvious afterthought, he added an explanation to the demand. "Right now, the pain's bearable and I don't want to move."

Sharon shook a cigarette from the pack, then picked up the book of matches from the bedside table to light it. "Shall I smoke it for you, too?" she asked and blew out the match flame along with a stream of smoke from her mouth.

"Very funny," Ridge murmured. "Why don't you pretend it's a thermometer."

With his eyes shut, Ridge didn't see her amused smile as Sharon reached over and placed the lit cigarette between his lips. Her fingers briefly touched his mouth before she drew them away. They tingled slightly from the intimate contact with his smooth, hard lips.

As she straightened, she noticed the cautious way he lifted his hand to take the cigarette from his mouth after he'd taken a short drag. Even then, he winced as if jarred by the careful motion.

"Where would you like me to set the ashtray?" Sharon realized that it would be too painful for Ridge to twist himself around to use it if she left it on the bedside table.

"Just somewhere within reach," he said, then added hastily, "but not on my stomach. It hurts to have anything touch it—even these clothes."

"Do you want me to help you take them off?" she offered, as she placed the ashtray on the bed next to him and half-turned from the bed in the direction of the chest of drawers and the clothes closet. "Last night, Mom and I looked for a pair of pajamas and a robe to take to the hospital, but we couldn't find any. Where do you keep them?"

Ridge started to laugh, but the bruised muscles in his stomach must have screamed a protest because it ended in a groan. When he finally answered, his tight voice was heavily threaded with suppressed pain.

"I haven't owned a pair of pajamas since I was ten," he told her. "And as for a robe . . . when you live in an all-male household, you don't need one." A smile deepened the corners of his mouth at the stunned look on her face. "Do you still want to play nurse?" Ridge mocked.

She recovered instantly. "For heaven's sake, I'm not a schoolgirl anymore," she flashed in annoyance, irritated with herself—and with him for drawing attention to her brief moment of self-consciousness. "I'm not likely to be shocked by the sight of a man's body. I do have a brother."

"In that case, I would like these clothes off," he acknowledged, still watching her with a challenging gleam in his eyes.

Sharon didn't falter for a second. "Then I'll take these." She picked up the ashtray she'd just set on the bed and removed the partially smoked cigarette from his hand. "Can you sit up by yourself, or do you need some help?"

"I can manage."

His stiff and stilted movements were such a marked contrast to his usual effortless and fluid motion that Sharon couldn't help noticing it. But she stood back and let Ridge take as much time as he needed to sit up and swing his legs over the side of the bed.

"The boots first," she said and knelt down to tug them off.

Without socks to ease the friction, it wasn't easy. She closed her ears to the half-smothered, grunting sounds of pain that came from him. When both boots had been removed, she set them next to the dresser. Ridge already had his shirt half unbuttoned, so she unfastened the last few and eased one arm out of the shirt sleeve. After that, it was a simple matter of slipping it off the other.

As he edged off the bed to stand up so his pants could be taken off, Sharon avoided meeting his gaze. She was very careful when she unfastened his pants so her hands wouldn't touch the badly discolored flesh of his stomach. Her hands were steady and sure as they inched the pants over his hips and slid them quickly down his legs. The white material of his jockey shorts filled her peripheral vision, but she concentrated on her task.

Ridge lowered himself onto the edge of the bed and the pants slid onto the floor. His bare legs were in front of her. For an instant, she let her gaze linger on the silken-fine hair covering them. She had never found hairy men very attractive, but Ridge wasn't covered with a furry, dark mat.

As she straightened to hang up his clothes, she caught his eye. Amusement danced openly in the blue irises. It instantly made her conscious of the warmth in her cheeks. She had been so positive she had been a model of indifference at the sight of his lean and muscled body that she hadn't been aware of the building heat in her cheeks.

"Don't look now, nurse, but you're blushing," Ridge informed her in a deeply resonant voice as he tried very hard not to laugh because it would hurt too much.

Denying it would be foolish. She picked up the burning cigarette from the ashtray and passed it to him. "Smoke your cigarette."

" —and shut up?" An arching brow queried whether that was the rest of her suggestion.

"And shut up," Sharon agreed with a sweetly angry look and walked to the closet to put away his clothes.

"Sorry," Ridge said. "I guess it wasn't fair to tease you."

No suitable reply occurred to her, but she swallowed her anger. It served no purpose except to give him more fuel. Her expression was calm when she turned back to the bed.

"I'll be in the kitchen if you need me," she said and exited the room.

In the sunny yellow kitchen with its shiny white cabinets and windows facing to the east to catch the light from a rising sun, Sharon halted her hasty retreat from Ridge's bedroom and paused to calm her shaky nerves. There were bound to be more intimate moments like this last one during the next few days. She was going to be in constant contact with him—figuratively and literally—so she might as well come to grips with it and stop turning it into a sexual encounter every time. She was here to take care of him—as a family friend and neighbor—and that was all!

Her breathing returned to a more normal rate. A corner of her mouth lifted in a wry semblance of a smile turned inward. With considerable more aplomb, Sharon was remembering Ridge's testy behavior. It was amazing how one man could be so infuriatingly difficult—and so damned sexy at the same time!

A telephone extension was mounted on the kitchen wall. Sharon crossed the room and lifted the receiver to dial her parents' number so she could advise them of the changed situation. Her mother answered on the fourth ring.

After Sharon had informed her about Ridge's condition and explained her subsequent decision to take care of him at the ranch when he stubbornly refused to stay in the hospital, there was a few seconds of silence on the other end of the line.

"Under the circumstances, I don't see what other decision you could have made," her mother finally concluded with a trace of a sigh.

"Ridge is certainly in no condition to take care of himself," Sharon reaffirmed. Neither of them directly alluded to her past infatuation for Ridge, but it was behind every word that was spoken—a silent reminder to proceed with caution. "Would you pack me some clothes for the next few days?"

"I'll have Scott run them over to the ranch. He was planning to go to the hospital to see Ridge tonight anyway. Oh, I almost forgot," her mother declared suddenly. "Andy Rivers phoned. I told him you'd be home later tonight. He's going to call back. What do you want me to tell him?"

Sharon hesitated. It was funny, but when she tried to conjure up an image of his face, it was all fuzzy and out of focus. Ridge's overpowering personality was to blame for that. Friendship had been the mainstay of her relations with the young geologist—for both parties. But even that feeling had dimmed dangerously in the few short days dominated by Ridge or thoughts of him.

"Have Andy call me here," Sharon stated firmly, determined the Latigo Ranch wasn't going to become a desert island with only herself and Ridge as occupants. Retaining contact with the outside world was essential. "Was there anything else?"

After exchanging a few more words, Sharon rang off. She had just begun investigating the contents of the kitchen cupboards to find something soft and easily digestible for Ridge to eat when there was a knock at the back door.

An incoming ranch hand had noticed the car and came to inquire about Ridge's condition, thinking that someone from the Powell family had been to the hospital to see him. After Sharon explained that Ridge had discharged himself from the hospital, the cowboy went in to see him.

While he visited with Ridge, Sharon went back into the kitchen to prepare a meal. The cupboard had yielded a can of creamed split pea with ham soup and a jar of applesauce. Beyond that, she had to improvise. With a dish towel tied around her waist to protect her peach-colored dress, Sharon peeled potatoes to boil and mash and scrounged around to find some kind of tray to serve the meal on while the potatoes were cooking.

The ranch hand was still in the room when Sharon carried in Ridge's supper, using the top part of a TV tray she'd found tucked away in the pantry. From the little conversation she'd overheard before entering the room, she had the impression Ridge had been grilling the man on the amount of work that had been done the last two days. The cowboy seemed glad of her interruption and the excuse to leave.

"I'll tell Hobbs what you said. He'll be gettin' back with you," the cowboy said as he backed out of the room.

Sharon paused beside the bed with the tray in her hands. "How do you want to do this?" she asked. "Do you want to sit up and cushion the tray on your lap with a pillow? Or shall I feed you? I've had a lot of practice playing airplane with Tony. The spoon is the airplane and your mouth is the hangar it flies into."

"I'll feed myself," Ridge replied, unamused by her mocking suggestion.

Flattening his hands on the mattress, he levered himself into a more upright sitting position. He went white with the effort, briefly baring his teeth against the ensuing pain before clamping his mouth tightly shut. Sharon pretended not to notice, aware he didn't like the thought of anyone, especially a woman, seeing him so weak that he could barely sit up by himself. Neither would he welcome any show of sympathy, so she partially turned aside to set the tray on the bedside table and get a spare pillow from the closet to lay across his sore stomach.

When she returned to the bed with a pillow in hand, his gaze had narrowed on the tray of food. It turned sharply to her face.

"That's the same junk they tried to feed me in the hospital," he accused.

"The doctor said no solid food for a few days—and you promised to follow his orders," Sharon reminded him, letting her glance slide to meet his eyes while she gently laid the pillow on his lap and tried not to take too much notice of the sinewy, muscled width of his bare chest above his bandaged ribs. She placed the tray on the pillow, making sure it was balanced before letting go of the sides. "Now eat," she ordered and straightened to study the distaste that showed on his face as Ridge viewed the meal before him. "Maybe your disposition will improve with some food in your stomach."

The corners of his mouth were pulled in grimly with dislike. "I want something I can sink my teeth into," he muttered.

"You'll have to content yourself with snapping at me," Sharon retorted.

The upward sweep of his gaze took in the towel tied around her waist, the shallow rise and fall of her breasts beneath the peasant-style bodice of her dress, and the creamy smoothness of her throat and neck before stopping when it reached her face. A lazily seductive gleam entered his blue eyes.

"I might enjoy taking a bite out of you," Ridge murmured.

Sharon didn't immediately release the breath she drew in, her pulse accelerating under his disturbing look. It was a full second before she managed a brief laugh to break the spell over her senses.

"Don't you know you aren't supposed to bite the hand that feeds you?" she mocked him. "You might discover that I bite back."

"I hope so," he drawled in answer, a slow smile edging his mouth.

The room suddenly felt very warm. "If you'll excuse me, I think I'll go fix myself something to eat. You may not be hungry, but I am." Sharon wanted to leave before she was drawn into another word battle laced with sexual overtones. "I'll come back for the tray when you're finished."

As she turned to leave, her eye caught the change in his expression out of her side vision. The glinting, roguish light faded from his eyes and his features once again showed the gray pallor of constant pain. The suggestive looks and remarks he'd passed had provided Ridge with a mental distraction from his suffering. He wasn't really interested in her, and she'd do well to remember that.

Word that Ridge was home from the hospital had evidently spread quickly throughout the ranch. Within half an hour after the cowboy left, the foreman Hobbs knocked at the door. When Sharon showed him into the bedroom, Ridge insisted she take away the tray. It looked as if no more than a couple of bites had been taken of each item.

Sharon's mouth thinned with displeasure when she saw how little he'd eaten, but she knew she'd never accomplish anything by admonishing him in front of his foreman for not eating more. She'd grown up with the macho egos of western men and knew that such a remark, regardless of the genuine concern behind it, would be considered as undermining their authority. So she simply flashed him a disapproving look and silently left the room carrying the tray of food.

There was a steady stream of visitors throughout the evening. Her brother, Scott, was the last to come, arriving as Sharon finished washing the dishes from the two separate meals she'd cooked. He'd brought the suitcase her mother had packed for her. While Scott went in to visit Ridge, Sharon took her case into the bedroom next to Ridge's to unpack and settle in.

Like all the rest of the rooms, this one was minus any frills. Her silk nightgown and matching robe appeared out of place when she laid them on the plain blue chenille spread at the end of the bed. After she had arranged her cosmetics and toiletries in the private bathroom adjoining the bedroom, she noticed her reflection in the mirrored medicine chest and realized she was still wearing the dishtowel apron.

As she retraced her steps from the bedroom to the hallway, heading for the kitchen, she worked to loosen the knotted towel ends behind her back. Scott emerged from the open door to Ridge's room just as she went by. Her glance went to him in surprise.

"Are you leaving already?" Sharon doubted that her brother had been in the room more than twenty minutes.

"I've gotta get home." His voice was deliberately loud so that Ridge would hear his answer as he fell into step with her. Immediately it dropped to a more private level. "Didn't the doctor give him anything to take for the pain?"

"I have a prescription in my purse, but I don't know if he'll take it," she said.

"Give it to him whether he wants it or not," her brother advised. "I was in there gritting my teeth for him. He'll never get any rest at this rate unless he passes out."

"I'll see that he gets it," she nodded and slowed her steps as they neared the back door.

"Mom said to call if you need anything." Scott reached for the knob, turning it. "One of us will be over tomorrow night."

"Okay." Her smile faded as he left the house, her expression becoming serious with concern.

Before going to Ridge's room, Sharon stopped in the kitchen and absently laid the towel on the counter near her purse. Opening her purse, she took out the bottle of pills and read the written instructions on the prescription label.

"Sharon!" The interior walls partially muffled the demanding call from Ridge.

Leaving the pill bottle on the counter, she moved quickly in the direction of his room. "Coming!" she raised her voice in answer.

A thin, smoke-blue haze hung in the upper air near the ceiling when she entered. Ridge was propped in the same position as earlier in the evening, but there seemed to be a marked deterioration in his condition. His features were decidedly haggard and drawn and the glitter in his eyes seemed tortured. There was an occasional, very faint tremor in various parts of his body. Sharon had the distinct impression that he wanted to writhe with pain, but it hurt him too much to move. The last of the hospital medication had worn off, leaving him without any barrier to screen out the pain.

"Bring me another pack of cigarettes." He wadded up the empty pack and added it to the mound of cigarette butts in the ashtray. "And empty this."

"You're smoking too much," she criticized automatically, aware that he was using smoking as a distraction.

"I don't need any lectures, just a pack of cigarettes," he retorted irritably.

"What you need is rest," Sharon stated. She walked to the bed, took away the ashtray and emptied it into the wastebasket by the dresser, but didn't carry it back to the bed. "I'll bring you a couple of the pain pills the doctor prescribed. They'll help you sleep."

"I don't want any of those damned drugs," Ridge flashed angrily but in a tightly controlled voice. "That's why I checked out of the hospital."

Turning, she faced the bed, her hands moving up to rest on her hips in a challenging stance. "Still determined to tough it out, are you?" she chided him for being so foolish.

There was a moment of silence during which his hard, level gaze held her eyes. "Are you going to get my cigarettes or not?" he demanded.

"No," Sharon replied smoothly. "If you want another pack, get out of bed and get it yourself." If he tried, Sharon was positive he'd collapse before he reached the hall.

His mouth tightened into a line that matched the hardness of his flinty blue eyes, indicating he suspected the same. "You're enjoying this, aren't you?" Ridge muttered.

"Immensely," she assured him and hid the wrenching concern she actually felt. As he passed a hand over his face, she noticed the faint tremor of his fingers. She relented from her attitude of indifference and suggested, "Hot milk is supposed to relax a person and help them fall asleep. Shall I heat some for you?"

Ridge started to reject the offer, then changed his mind. "If I promise to drink it, will you bring me a pack of cigarettes?"

"That's blackmail," Sharon accused.

"Yes." He smiled briefly, the movement accentuating the tautness of his mouth.

After a second's hesitation, she smiled and uttered a surrendering sigh. "You've got a deal," she agreed.

In the kitchen, Sharon poured milk into a pan and set the pan on a stove burner. While it was heating, she shook two prescription pills out of the bottle and placed them on a square of wax paper, then used a rolling pin to grind them into a white powder. After she added it to the scalded milk, she sipped a spoonful. The bitterness pinched her lips together. To disguise it, Sharon quickly added a generous amount of chocolate syrup and then plopped a marshmallow into the cup.

With a fresh pack of cigarettes in one hand and the mug

of hot chocolate in the other, she returned to the bedroom. "I changed the hot milk to hot cocoa. I thought you'd drink it with less fuss," she announced as she entered.

"You can set it on the stand," Ridge instructed, referring to the chocolate and reaching for the cigarettes.

"No." She held the pack of cigarettes behind her back. "Drink the cocoa first, then you can have the cigarettes." She gave him the cup and watched him take the first drink, unconsciously holding her breath while she waited for his reaction.

"You got a little carried away with the chocolate, didn't you?" he remarked.

"Did I put in too much?" Sharon inquired innocently.

"It's all right." He took another drink. "It's just a little strong." He slid a sideways look at her. "I suppose I have to drink all of it before you give me the cigarettes."

"Yes—to the very last drop." She didn't want any medication settling to the bottom of the cup. As he lifted the cup to his mouth again, Sharon walked to the dresser and retrieved the ashtray. After several more swallows, Ridge tilted the cup to drain it dry.

"There, I've been a good boy. Now, how about lighting me a cigarette?" The haggardness of his features seemed more pronounced as he lowered the cup to the bed. The upward curve of his mouth was closer to a smiling wince.

Sharon lighted one and traded it for the empty mug in his hand. Ridge puffed on it, unable to inhale the smoke too deeply. The nicotine didn't appear to offer him much comfort or relief. Sharon moved toward the door.

"Where are you going?" Ridge stopped her with his question.

"The kitchen, so I can clean up the mess I left."

"Oh." His glance fell to the burning tip of his cigarette, then quickly skipped back to her, his pain-bright eyes silent in their appeal. "When you're finished, would you come back and talk to me?"

It was a request to have his mind distracted from the incessant messages of pain traveling through his nervous system being expressed, not a desire for her company. Sharon reminded herself of that as she smiled.

"Sure." For both their sakes, she hoped the medication worked quickly.

It only took her a few minutes to rinse the cup, pan, and utensils she'd used and to straighten up the kitchen. When she returned to Ridge's room, the cigarette had been crushed out in the ashtray and his head was resting against the headboard of the bed, his eyes closed. He opened them a slit to acknowledge his awareness of her presence in the room but otherwise didn't move.

"Instead of talking, I think you should see if you can't go to sleep," Sharon suggested quietly.

"Yeah." It was a tired agreement. Ridge stirred, as if intending to change his position, then subsided onto the pillows. "I can't even lie down by myself." The remark was inadvertently muttered aloud, an admission that he couldn't withstand the additional pain produced by movement. "Would you help me lie down?" Grudgingly he made the request of her.

"Of course." She suspected that his bruised stomach muscles simply couldn't withstand the strain of slowly lowering his torso into a prone position.

At the side of the bed, Sharon lifted the full skirt of her dress out of the way so that she could rest a knee on the mattress to give herself leverage. Bending over Ridge, she slipped one arm behind him while she removed the pillows propping him up with her other hand.

Chapter 6

Although Ridge tried to help when Sharon began to lower him gently onto the mattress, his strength and capacity were severely limited, and she was obliged to support the bulk of his weight. When he was finally lying flat, she found herself in a ridiculous position, with her arm pinned under him while she leaned over him, trying very hard not to touch his sore ribs or stomach accidentally. She made a wriggling attempt to free her arm, without success.

"Can you lift up just a little so I can get my arm out?" she asked, out of breath from the exertion.

His face looked ghastly white under its tan, and beads of perspiration had gathered on his upper lip. "Wait a minute." His voice was unnaturally thin and taut.

Despite the care she'd taken, the change of positions had obviously released a whole new series of stabbing pains. Sharon made no reply as she patiently waited for the fresh throbbings within him to dull. In the meantime, she had a hand braced on the pillow by his head and her arm trapped beneath his weight while her face hovered above the point of his shoulder near the slashing angle of his jaw. His eyes remained closed, black lashes lying thick and roughly spiked together.

The color returned slowly to his face as his breathing began to return to its normal steadiness. Lifting his lashes, Ridge looked at her through half-closed eyes. Their blueness held a mixture of relief at the subsiding pain and self-mocking chagrin at his weakness.

"Are you okay?" she asked, now that he seemed to have recovered.

"Yeah." His mouth twisted wryly. "I never realized how impossible it is to move without using your stomach muscles."

"That's why the only cure for you is complete rest. If you had stayed in the hospital, they have beds that crank up and down." She was becoming cramped in her position, half-leaning over and half-lying down.

"I thought nurses took care of their patients without complaint," Ridge chided.

"I'm not a nurse." Sharon wiggled her arm under his back to remind him she was still pinned by his heavy weight.

"No, that isn't a uniform, is it?" he said with a slow perusal of her dress and the soft folds of its full skirt falling over him and the bed. "What color is it?"

"Peach." In her position, the peasant-style neckline was threatening to expose a bare shoulder.

"Nice." He fingered the hem of her skirt, which was closest to his hand. "Soft," he remarked on the texture of the fabric, then his half-closed gaze slid back to her.

She felt the disturbing difference in his attention, something that had been bred by the forced intimacy of their positions and that had been growing ever since. This sudden tension seemed to snatch at her breath and heighten her senses. She was conscious of so many things all at once, the smell of him tinged with hospital antiseptic and tobacco smoke, the sight of the throbbing blue vein in his throat, and the touch of his calloused hand rasping over the smoothness of her nylon-clad thigh.

"You should wear dresses more often." His voice was pitched low and velvety husky. "I never noticed your legs until today. You have beautiful legs."

"Really." Sharon tried to sound calmly indifferent, but her voice came out all thick and disturbed, throbbing with the attraction she was feeling.

"Really," Ridge repeated her response with mocking emphasis. "Do you mind that I noticed your legs? You seemed quite interested in mine earlier."

She chose to ignore his comment. "This is very uncomfortable. Would you mind moving so I can get my arm out?"

"I think I would," he replied thoughtfully.

His hand ceased its absent stroking of her leg and came away from beneath her skirt to slide up her back and tunnel under the weight of her hair. Sharon resisted the slight pressure his fingers exerted to move her closer to his mouth.

"Ridge, let me go." There was a trace of exasperation in her voice as if her patience with him had been pushed to the limit.

"Careful," he warned when her resistance started to take on a more physical aspect. "You wouldn't hurt a guy when he was down, would you?"

"When it's you, I might," Sharon retorted, but she couldn't bring herself to inflict any additional pain on him, unintentionally or not.

"No, you wouldn't." Ridge was very confident about that as she let herself be coerced into seeking contact with his mouth.

He rubbed it over her lips, warming them with his touch and his breath. She found herself enjoying just the feel of her sensitive lips moving against his, nuzzling and exploring in a purely sensuous fashion. His hand slid down to the side of her waist, no longer possessing the strength to ensure that she maintained the intimate contact. It wasn't necessary.

Of its own accord, the mutual investigation grew into a long, breathless kiss. The thudding of her heart sounded loudly in her ears when Sharon finally drew an inch away from him. She felt the light touch of his finger under her jaw. It glided to the point of her chin, then shifted to trace the outline of her lips, still warm from his possession of them.

"You have the softest lips," he murmured.

The lift of his chin invited them back. The last kiss had been marked by gentle seduction, but this time Sharon sensed a frustrated urgency in the moving pressure of his mouth. His hand dug into her waist with unconscious force, as if he wanted to pull her into his embrace and dared not. She, too, wanted to relax against him and feel the hard contours of his muscled body against hers, but she held herself rigidly away from him. Her weight on his broken ribs and badly bruised stomach would cause more pain than pleasure. Before the ache inside became any stronger, Sharon broke off the kiss.

"It's no good, Ridge. You'd better let me up." Her voice was softly taut with things better left unsaid.

"I ought to make you stay here all night," he retorted thickly. " 'Beware of Greeks bearing gifts.' "

Sharon didn't see what one thing had to do with another. "What?"

His gaze narrowed at her briefly and then moved to the shoulder bared by the drooping neckline of her dress. He shifted it back into its proper position, then let his finger hook itself on the elastic neckline while it traveled to the middle front until it rested against the slope of her breast, creating a tingle.

"You put something in that cocoa, didn't you?" Ridge accused.

After a brief hesitation, she openly admitted her trick. "Yes. You needed something to dull the pain, so I ground up two of the pills the doctor prescribed for you and dissolved them in the milk."

"I thought I felt odd," he muttered.

For some reason, his remark struck her wrong, hardening all her sympathies into stone. Without caring any more whether it hurt him, she jerked her arm out from beneath him. Remorse flashed for an instant at his involuntary grunt of pain. Already she was pushing off the bed onto the floor.

"You didn't have to be so rough," he snapped.

"I thought you were a big, tough guy," Sharon countered, with a hint of mockery. "It only hurts for a little while."

"All that honey and sweetness has turned to vinegar, hasn't it?" His mouth thinned. "What's the matter? Are you sore at yourself for kissing me?"

"Rest is the cure for what ails you," she retorted. "Not sex."

"Is that part of the doctor's orders?" Ridge mocked.

"No. It's mine," she flared.

The sudden ringing of the phone on the bedside table startled Sharon. She whirled to face the noisy interruption, then quickly took a breath to calm her jangled nerves before reaching to pick up the receiver.

"Latigo Ranch." Her voice was unnaturally low but steady when she answered.

"Hello?" An uncertain male voice came back, vaguely familiar, but Sharon just thought it was some neighboring rancher calling to find out how Ridge was doing. "Is . . . is this Sharon?"

"Yes." Her forehead became knitted with a small frown.

"It didn't sound like you," the voice replied with relief. As if sensing from her blank silence that she still hadn't identified him, the caller eliminated the problem. "This is Andy . . . Andy Rivers. Your mother told me where you were when I called the house a few minutes ago."

"Yes, I told her to have you phone me here," Sharon remembered belatedly.

"Who is it?" Ridge demanded from the bed.

She threw a glance at him, not wanting to carry on an essentially personal conversation with Andy in his presence. "Just a minute Andy," she said into the phone, then clamped a hand over the mouthpiece while she answered Ridge's question. "It's for me."

"Andy, the oil man boyfriend." Ridge had caught the name and connected it, a trace of sarcasm in his disparaging tone.

Sharon wanted to snap back some kind of denial, both at his description and at his tone, but Andy was probably calling long distance. She didn't want to keep him waiting on the line while she argued with Ridge.

"I'm going to take the call in the kitchen," she informed him stiffly. "Would you hang up the receiver here after I've picked up the one in there?"

"Talk to him here," Ridge challenged. "Or are you too embarrassed to whisper love words in his ear while I'm listening?"

"It's a personal call, which I wish to conduct in privacy." She refused to let him goad her into taking the call in his room. She took her hand away from the mouthpiece and spoke into the phone again. "Hold on a second, Andy, while I switch to the extension in the kitchen." Not trusting Ridge, she added, "If we *accidentally* get disconnected in the process, call me back."

After she had passed the receiver to Ridge, she moved the phone within easy reaching distance so he could hang it up once she was on the extension. He eyed her coolly.

Without waiting for Ridge to continue his attempt to incite an argument, Sharon left the room and hurried to the wall phone in the kitchen. She picked up the receiver and tried to force the tension from her body.

"Hello, Andy." She waited until she heard his puzzled but affirmative response before she said to Ridge, "You can hang up the phone now." There was a long moment before she heard the click of the extension going dead. It was funny, but she didn't feel as relieved as she had expected. "Sorry to keep you waiting on the line for so long, Andy, but I . . . just gave Ridge some pills to help him sleep. I didn't want my conversation with you to disturb him."

"Your mother mentioned something about Halliday having an accident. What happened?" he inquired.

Sharon retold the story as briefly as she could and made an even sketchier explanation of how and why she had volunteered to look after Ridge in his home. But he didn't seem to think it was either unusual or improper. Sharon smiled at herself, wondering why on earth she had thought Andy would be upset or possibly jealous. A guilty conscience, she supposed.

Finally the conversation came around to the reason for his call. "I'm going to be in town over the weekend. I thought we might take in a show together Saturday night."

"It sounds great," Sharon accepted the indirect invitation. "Ridge should be up and around by then, so I'll probably be home. Why don't you call on Saturday to be sure?"

"I'll do that," Andy agreed. "If you aren't there, I'll understand the movie date is cancelled."

"No." She rushed to eliminate that conclusion, not entirely sure why she didn't want to accept an easy excuse. "Even if I'm still at Latigo, we can go to the movies. Scott can come over and visit with Ridge if he isn't in any shape to be left alone."

"As long as you're sure that isn't going to create any conflict, I'll see you Saturday night around six," he said.

"Just be sure to call first to find out where I am," Sharon reminded him.

Goodbyes were exchanged and they rang off. Sharon bit thoughtfully at the inside of her lip as she turned from the wall phone and moved slowly in the direction of Ridge's bedroom. She had the uncomfortable feeling that she was trying to use the Saturday-night date with Andy as some kind of shield—as if it could protect her from the long-held attraction she had for Ridge. If that's what she was doing, it was both childish and cowardly.

"Did you and lover boy have an argument?" His taunting voice halted her when she would have walked past his doorway.

"No. Andy was calling long distance." Or so she had presumed. Ridge's earlier comment prompted her to add, "So we kept it short and sweet."

His face bore a disgruntled look. "I guess I owe you an apology for the way I snapped at you earlier—and for some of my remarks." Apology didn't come easily to him, and it showed in the tautness of his wording. Perhaps it meant something because it was honest, rather than an insincere attempt to smooth over an argument. "It doesn't seem to take much to rub me the wrong way—not the way I'm hurting. It isn't much of an excuse but—I do appreciate you staying here to look after me. I sure as hell can't do it myself."

Not five minutes ago, Sharon had been prepared to stay angry at him for the duration. But all that resentment was fading in the wake of his apology and his grudging admission that he needed her.

"Apology accepted, Grumpy." A small smile touched her mouth.

A glint of humor entered his drug-tired eyes. "If I'm Grumpy, you must be Doc. And those pills you put in my cocoa must be Snow White. Either that or they were the poisoned apple."

"Why don't you stop fighting it and close your eyes?" suggested Sharon. "You need the sleep. I'll be in the next room. Just call out if you need anything."

"Okay," he said and let his eyelids drift shut, the potent drug taking its effect.

Unfortunately, Sharon didn't find it so easy to fall asleep. After she'd taken a bath and climbed into bed, sleep eluded her. The day had been so packed with activity that she couldn't seem to bring it to an end, despite the late evening hour.

The combination of a busy day, a strange bed, and the knowledge of Ridge sleeping in the next room denied her sleep until sometime after midnight. Even then, Sharon slept lightly, alert to any sound. Twice she went to check on Ridge in the middle of the night, positive she'd heard him. Both times he was sleeping deeply, and Sharon went back to crawl into her own bed to make another attempt to do the same.

Exhaustion had taken her into a dreamless slumber when a loud crash shattered her sleep. She sat bolt upright and listened. The yellowing streaks of dawn were spreading through the grayness of the sky outside her bedroom windows. Sharon was still trying to decide whether she'd actually heard something or merely imagined it again when a muffled curse came through the wall between the two bed-rooms.

Sharon grabbed for her jade-green robe as she scurried out of bed and went flying into the hallway. She was franti-cally trying to tie the sash as she reached the open door and stopped to stare at Ridge. Half-naked, wearing only his jockey shorts, he was holding onto the footrail of his bed.

"What are you doing out of bed? Why didn't you call me?" she demanded angrily and hurried to his side without waiting for an answer. Taking his arm, she draped it around her shoulders so she could help him back to bed.

"I made it this far. I can make it the rest of the way," Ridge grumbled and pulled his arm away. To prove his point, he began hopping along the edge of the mattress until he was at the middle of the bed.

"What's wrong with your foot?" Sharon frowned.

"I stubbed my toe on a corner of the dresser," he mut-tered. His answer explained the noise that had awakened her. As he sat on the edge of the bed, he made all sorts of faces in an effort to hold in any vocal expression of pain. Lying down was a different thing. He threw her an irritated look. "Don't just stand there. Help me."

As she helped him lie flat, she was careful not to get her arm trapped again. She lifted the weight of her sleep-tousled hair away from the side of her face. "How did you manage to get out of bed without help?"

"As the old saying goes—it was as easy as falling out of bed. Nothing to it," Ridge insisted dryly, his features smoothing out as the pain subsided. "What time is it? It looks like it must be close to five in the morning."

Sharon glanced at the alarm clock on the table. "It will be in another ten minutes."

"Good. I'm starved. How about fixing me some break-fast?" he asked.

She really wanted to crawl back into bed and get some of the sleep she'd missed, but she stifled a yawn. "I guess it's time to be getting up," she agreed wearily.

"I'll have three fried eggs over easy, hash-browns, and a couple of rashers of bacon," Ridge ordered. "Toast and jelly, too. Juice and milk and coffee."

"You can have oatmeal with either applesauce or mashed bananas, or hot milk with toast," she informed him. "The juice, milk, and coffee part of your order is okay."

He gave her a not too pleased look. "How long do I have to eat this baby food?"

"Until you stop acting like one and start doing what you're told." The faintly barbed exchange was chasing away her tiredness. Mental alertness was always essential around Ridge.

"Is that right?" Behind the mockery of his vague smile there was a glint of amusement in his expression. "Is that why you mix my medicine into my food—the same way you would with a baby?"

"If the bootie fits—" Sharon murmured.

Ridge chuckled, although not too vigorously because of the pain in his ribs and stomach. "I'll have oatmeal and applesauce. No pills, please—at least not for the time being. I don't want to become dependent on them. If I do have to end up taking them, I want them on the side with a glass of water."

She smiled her approval. "You don't like being called a baby, do you? I wouldn't worry about it. All men are big babies, no matter how tough they act."

"And where did you glean that bit of priceless information?" he said mockingly.

"From years of observing my father and my brother. The only difference between men and little boys is the size and the price of their toys," she chimed. "They like being spoiled and having their own way."

"What do women like?" Ridge gingerly crooked an arm under his head, elevating it a few inches and changing the angle of his view.

"Now that would be telling," Sharon laughed.

"From my limited observation of the opposite sex—" he began to make his own guess, watching her with lazy interest, "—I'd say they enjoy mothering—which includes everything from spoiling to giving orders."

"I don't think I would say that," she hedged against agreeing with his answer.

His mouth crooked into a half-smile. "Look at yourself. You like the feeling of power you have over me—telling me what I'm going to eat and giving me my medicine even if it involves tricking me. A part of you is glad that I'm laid up, because it makes me dependent on you. So you can be nice and loving—or stern and commanding."

The more she thought about his observation, the more accurate it sounded. Sharon wasn't sure that she liked it. Even though she had accused him of liking to be waited on, she had never thought of herself as liking to wait on him.

"Maybe it's true," she conceded. "And maybe it's simply human nature—on both parts."

"How come you don't want to admit that you like telling me what to do because you know I'm in no condition to do anything about it?" Ridge challenged with a taunting gleam in his eyes.

"It's definitely a unique feeling," she admitted, although she was uncomfortable admitting to anything beyond that.

"And you like it?" he persisted.

"I suppose I do." Her chin lifted a fraction of an inch, tilting to a challenging angle. "It's nice to have the upper hand once in awhile." Since he claimed she did in this instance, Sharon took advantage of her position. "Stay in bed and don't try to get out by yourself while I'm fixing your breakfast."

"Yes, ma'am." His submissive reply was deliberately mocking, denying the obedience and respect implied by the words.

"I think I liked you better when you were Grumpy," Sharon declared in a parting shot as she turned to leave the room.

"Just like a woman." Ridge's taunting voice trailed after. "You like to have the last word."

A vague sense of irritation threaded through her nerves as Sharon swept into the hallway. There was always an element of truth in generalizations. So to that degree, the things Ridge had said were true. It simply wasn't the whole truth.

She had the feeling that she hadn't handled the conversation very well. She had started out in control, but somewhere it had shifted into his hands. Shaking her head, Sharon realized it was silly to make a contest out of every conversation she had with Ridge. There was no need to feel she had to compete with him at every turn. There might be times when she needed to defend herself against one of his advances—and that was only because her heart was vulnerable where he was concerned, not because she was physically afraid of him.

After fixing his breakfast, Sharon added a second cup of freshly brewed coffee for herself to the tray and carried it to the bedroom. A few minutes were spent helping Ridge maneuver into a sitting position before she could arrange the tray on his lap. He noticed the second cup of coffee as she took it from the tray.

An eyebrow lifted in querying arch. "Aren't you eating breakfast?"

"Not now. I'll fix myself something after I've washed and dressed." She sipped at the coffee, cupping the mug in both hands.

There was a slight narrowing of his eyes, although they continued to shine with a blue gleam. His glance flicked from the bowl of oatmeal on the tray to her face.

"I suppose I'm expected to eat this and, later, endure the aroma of bacon sizzling in the skillet." There was a hint of amusement behind the accusing statement.

"That would be cruel, wouldn't it?" Sharon agreed with an impish look in her hazel eyes. Actually her menu plans for breakfast had consisted of dry cereal and toast, but she didn't enlighten him at this stage.

"You know it would," Ridge countered and picked up the spoon on his tray. It hovered just above the bowl of oatmeal while he cast another glance at her. "There are no knock out drops in here, are there?"

"None," she promised and lightly crossed her heart, making a playful gesture of taking an oath. She turned from the bed and started for the door with her coffee cup.

"Where are you going?" His question came quickly, light with surprise at her intention to leave.

Sharon half-turned to glance at him. "I'm going to my room to get dressed."

"You can do that later. Stay here and keep me company while I eat." The request was accompanied by a crooked, coaxing smile that was almost impossible to resist.

When he chose to exercise it, Ridge was a master at the fine art of persuasion, relying on his potent charm rather than male dominance to get his way. Sharon was by no means immune to that brand of appeal. She was conscious of wavering, an invisible force in those glittering blue eyes pulling her back to the bed.

The first step was taken before she even realized it. The

discovery seemed to jolt her. Sharon quickly altered her course, angling away from the bed toward the dresser where a radio sat.

"It's just about time for the market reports," she said. "You can listen to the radio while you eat your breakfast." After she turned the radio on, she made sure it was tuned to the local Colorado station carrying the grain and livestock reports. The announcer's voice spilled from the speaker, and Sharon turned to glance over her shoulder at Ridge. "Is that loud enough?"

"Yeah, but it isn't much company." There was a degree of wryness in the slanting line of his mouth. "A radio just talks; it doesn't talk back."

"That should make you happy," Sharon replied dryly and headed again toward the hallway. "I'll be back to pick up the tray a little later."

Chapter 7

Numerous washings and wearings had faded the jeans Sharon wore until they were a color between pale blue and blue-white. Her blouse was a blue and gray madras plaid, its bleeding pattern seeming to match the jeans. A pair of tortoise-shell barrettes pinned the sides of her toffee-brown hair away from her face, and a pair of dun-colored cowboy boots with run-down heels clad her feet. It was the usual garb she wore around the family home, and Sharon didn't dress differently in Ridge's house.

On her way to the kitchen to fix a light breakfast for herself, she swung by his room to pick up the tray. The radio was twanging out a country song when she entered. Ridge was reclining on the pillows supporting his back, a bare, muscled arm curled behind his head. A half-smoked cigarette dangled from his mouth. Although the curling smoke screened his gaze, she felt his slowly scanning study.

"All finished?" Her airy question was an attempt to break the trace of tension she felt. Even before Sharon reached for the tray, she had already noticed Ridge had eaten nearly every bit of his breakfast.

He lifted a hand to remove the cigarette from his mouth. "You can take it away." With a turn of his head, he made sure he tapped the cigarette into the ashtray on the bedside table. His glance ran sideways to continue its slightly narrowed inspection of her. "Those jeans don't do anything for you."

Sharon faltered at the unexpected, and uncomplimentary, remark. "Thanks a lot." There was no humor in her laughing retort.

His mouth lifted at the corners but didn't finish the movement in a smile. "If I hadn't seen you in that silk robe and nightgown, I wouldn't have known you had such a nice shape. It's a pity you didn't leave it on. It clung to your figure in all the right places."

She hadn't been aware he'd noticed, but very little escaped those keen blue eyes. "I could hardly run around all day in my night clothes," she declared with a scoffing laugh that was on the weak side.

"I wouldn't have objected in the least," Ridge murmured dryly.

"Well, I would," Sharon responded with a certain stiffness, a little unsettled by the physical interest he was expressing, and walked to the door with the tray of breakfast dishes. "I'm going to the kitchen and fix myself something to eat. Was there anything you needed before I do?"

There was a hesitation, as if Ridge considered a possible answer and rejected it. "No," he said finally. "But you can bring me another cup of coffee after you've finished."

"Okay."

Taking Ridge at his word, Sharon ate her breakfast of corn flakes and toast, washed their combined dishes, then poured his second cup of coffee and took it to him. The disc jockey on the radio was giving the day's weather forecast when she entered the room.

"—highs in the upper 60s today. Looks like summer's just around the corner, folks," the drawling voice concluded.

"It's going to be a nice day," Sharon observed after darting a glance at the radio. "Here's your coffee."

"I was beginning to think you forgot." He shifted his position slightly and winced.

"I didn't." She set it on the table near the ashtray, conscious of his bare-chested form and the rusty darkness of his hair in her side vision.

When she turned to leave, Ridge inquired, "Where are you going now?" with a trace of exasperation in his voice.

She turned again to the bed, vaguely defensive. "I was going to make my bed and straighten up the house. Why?"

"When am I going to get my bath and a shave?" he asked, folding his arms across his middle, an action that exhibited both patience and challenge.

"What?" Sharon blinked at him.

"When are you going to give me my bath?" Ridge repeated the question, a dancing light appearing in his blue eyes. Dumb struck for an instant, all Sharon could do was open her mouth. He mockingly chided her for wearing such a blank look. "All babies get a bath in the morning. I remember you telling me before breakfast that I was just an overgrown baby. So how about my bath?" When she continued to stare at him in disbelief, he reasoned, "If I were still in the hospital, a nurse would be giving me a bath."

"You can't be serious," Sharon managed to breathe out shakily.

"I'd do it myself if I wasn't so sore I can hardly stand to move," he replied, again in a reasonable tone that conflicted with the taunting gleam in his eyes. He rubbed a hand across the bristly growth of a night's beard. "I'd like to get cleaned up—and you're here to look after me."

It was extremely difficult to argue either with his logic or his request. As a matter of fact, Sharon couldn't find any legitimate excuse to refuse him, although she searched wildly for a plausible reason.

Heat began to rise in her face at the thought of washing him all over. Sharon turned away from the bed so that Ridge wouldn't see her reddening cheeks. If it was his intention to embarrass her, she didn't want to give him the satisfaction of knowing he had succeeded.

"I'll be back in a minute with a washbasin and some towels." She cast the statement over her shoulder in a remarkably level voice and headed quickly toward the private bath that adjoined his room.

The task of finding a washbasin and gathering washcloth, soap, and towels gave Sharon the necessary time to pull herself together. A degree of detachment was required and she struggled to achieve the necessary poise and quiet her jittery nerves.

Armed with a pair of thick bath towels, a basin full of soapy water, and a washcloth, Sharon emerged from the bathroom, appearing outwardly calm and, she hoped, professional. She ignored the faint smile that played around the corners of his mouth as she walked directly to the bed and placed the basin on the nightstand.

In her baby-sitting days, she'd had more than ample practice bathing toddlers and young tots. The trick was to pretend Ridge was the overgrown child she had claimed him to be.

"How do you want to go about this?" Ridge asked, not cooperating at all. "Do you want to begin at the bottom and work your way up? Or at the top and work your way down?"

It was a simple question, but the way her mind was working, she read something much more suggestive into it. And she suspected that Ridge had counted on that. Distance from those taunting blue eyes seemed preferable. Also, Sharon didn't think she'd find anything very sexy about his feet, so she opted for them as a beginning.

"The bottom."

Striving to keep that air of clinical detachment, she tossed aside the bedcovers to expose the lower half of his body and draped one of the bath towels across his hips. She could sense the laughter in his glance at that action, but she steadfastly kept her attention on what she was doing. She shook out the second towel and lifted the leg farthest from her, sliding the towel under it so the bedding wouldn't get wet.

When she turned to the basin to wet the washcloth and soap it up, she was conscious of Ridge's glinting look. Silently he lay there, giving every indication that he was enjoying all this immensely—at her expense.

The knowledge fed an inner irritation. Sharon was a bit more vigorous than was entirely necessary when she began scrubbing his leg and foot. His soap-slicked skin made her more aware of the rope-hard muscles in his calf and thigh. She concentrated on his foot.

"Be sure to get between my toes," Ridge instructed and wiggled them slightly to draw her attention to them.

After an instant's hesitation, Sharon complied. Her lips were clamped shut against the building tension inside. *He's just a little boy*, she kept telling herself, adding, *with big feet*.

"When my mother gave me a bath, she always played 'This little pig went to market' with my toes." The thickness of dry amusement was in his voice.

His reference to himself as a small boy completely destroyed her pretense. By no stretch of the imagination could she kid herself into believing any longer that this wasn't a man's leg she was washing.

"This is ridiculous," Sharon muttered under her breath and wetted the cloth again so she could rinse the soap from his leg.

"Is something wrong?" Ridge asked in false innocence.

"Whatever gave you that idea?" Her answer was terse, with none of its implied amusement, as she rinsed the soap from his leg and dried it.

"I thought I heard you mutter something," he persisted dryly.

"Well, you must have been hearing things." She shifted the towel under his other leg and began washing it with an air of determined indifference to mask her heightened sensitivity.

She was conscious of his watching eyes and calmly folded arms. It increased her awareness of the amount of bare flesh exposed to her sight. Sharon wished she could pretend Ridge was a stranger. Maybe then she wouldn't be wondering what was going through his mind.

It was worse when she rubbed the washcloth over the top of his thigh and the smoothly muscled flank. Her heart racketed against her rib cage in disturbed reaction.

"I guess you don't want to play 'Piggy went to market,' " Ridge concluded when she had finished scrubbing his foot and moved back up his leg.

"No, I'm not going to play 'Piggy went to market.' " She stepped to the basin and rinsed out the washcloth. "But if a rubber ducky will keep you quiet, I'll see if I can find one."

He tipped his head back to look at her. "Am I bothering you?"

"Do birds fly?" Sharon retorted and briskly wiped the soap from his leg to dry it.

Ridge waited to reply, timing it for the moment when

she began washing his outstretched arm. "What made you think about birds?"

Her hand paused along his flexed bicep as Sharon darted a glance at the lazy and inquiring expression on his face. In her mind there was an immediate word association of "birds" with "bees." It was hardly surprising. Since she was engaged in the intimate act of washing him, how could she not be aware of his sex—and her own? She began to feel very warm, and a growing agitation within started to affect the natural rhythm of her breathing.

"I really couldn't say why I did." Sharon attempted an indifferent shrug but answered truthfully.

To wash his other arm, she had to lean partially across him. The focus of his attention was on the nearness of her face rather than on what she was doing. As he lazily inspected her, he observed every nuance of her expression, adding to the havoc he was already creating in her senses. Her pulse was behaving erratically—slowing down, skipping beats, then taking off again.

"Having someone bathe you is a very enjoyable experience," Ridge commented idly.

"I'm glad someone's enjoying this." It was a low retort, close to being muttered. Sharon rubbed the soapy washcloth over the muscled ridges of his shoulders, under his throat, and across the top of his chest, taking care not to get the elastic bandage around his ribs wet.

"Aren't you?" A smiling knowledge lurked behind the blue surface of his eyes.

"I'm having a ball," she mocked. Rinsing out the washcloth, she went over the same territory again.

"I thought so," he murmured.

Sharon nearly blushed because it was true, despite all this self-consciousness. She was enjoying this excuse to touch nearly every part of him, not once but a total of at least three times, when she counted washing, rinsing, and drying. Through with the washcloth, she dropped it into the basin and picked up the towel to pat dry his damp skin.

"When I get up and around—" Ridge had to lift his chin high to avoid the bulky towel when she dried his throat and chest "—remind me to return the favor and give you a bath."

Sharon faltered but recovered quickly and straightened, all brisk and efficient. "I think I'd rather manage by myself."

"You don't know what you're missing," he warned.

"I guess that's my loss," she countered and dipped her hand into the basin for the washcloth again. "Do you want to wash your own face, or shall I do it for you?"

During a small hesitation, Ridge seemed to measure the glint in her hazel eyes. "I think I'd better do it myself," he decided. "You look like you might want to push that washcloth down my throat."

"Me?" Sharon returned innocently. "The thought never entered my mind." But she had been thinking about the hard contours of his face beneath her fingers, so it was just as well that he did the job himself. She soaped up the washcloth and handed it to him, then put the towel within easy reach. "I'll bring your razor and comb from the bathroom while you finish up." When she reached the doorway to the bathroom, she paused and turned to look over her shoulder. "Don't forget to wash behind your ears."

There was a sound of amusement, close to a laugh that didn't get finished, checked by painful rib and stomach muscles that wouldn't permit it without severe protest. Sharon swung on into the bathroom to collect the items.

Ridge had finished when she came back and crossed to the bed. Before she handed him the electric razor, she reached behind the bedstand and plugged the cord into the outlet, then passed the razor to him.

"Do you need a mirror?" she asked. "Or can you shave just by feel?"

"I can get by without a mirror," he said, rubbing a hand over the stubble on his jaw.

The hum of the razor filled the room as Sharon gathered up the damp towels and the washbasin and carried them back to the bathroom. By the time she had hung the towels and washcloth up to dry, rinsed out the basin, put it away, and returned to the bedroom, Ridge had shaved and combed his mahogany dark hair.

"How do I look?" he queried.

As long as she ignored the bandaged ribs and bruised stomach, he looked vitally fresh, able to take on anything or anyone and win. But Sharon kept that opinion to herself.

"You look fine," she said and gathered the razor and comb from the table. "I'll just put these things away."

"You can bring me some clothes, too," Ridge instructed as she headed for the bathroom again.

"You don't need any," she retorted as she set the items on the bathroom sink counter and came back out. When she saw the argumentative look in his face, she reminded him of his promise. "You're going to stay in bed and rest, remember? Since you're spending the day in bed, there's no need to get dressed."

Grim and restless, he swung his gaze away from Sharon, flashing it around the room, then slicing it back to her as she approached the bed to reposition the sliding pillows supporting him.

"Dammit, I'll go crazy in here with nothing to do," he protested.

"You can listen to the radio and I'll bring some stock magazines for you to read." She punched the pillow into place behind him and straightened to leave.

"Where are you going?" His calloused fingers made a rough band around her wrist to detain her.

The warmth and strength of his hand seemed to flow into her veins. Sharon tried to react calmly to his hold, so that her pulse wouldn't leap against his thumb.

"I still haven't made my bed or straightened the house," she said. "And I need to find something to fix for your lunch."

"Stay here and keep me company," Ridge urged with a persuasive gleam in his lazy blue eyes.

When he was in this sexily cajoling mood, his male charm could be a potent thing. She felt its caressing tug on her emotions and shook her head in wary resistance.

"I'm here to take care of you, Ridge, not to keep you entertained," she countered smoothly, but his grip only tightened when she tried to pull her hand away.

The glint in his eye became more challenging and seductive, a kind of dare in its mocking depths. "I promised to stay in bed and rest, but only if you promised to stay with me." The pressure of his grip pulled her closer to the bed until she was awkwardly unbalanced, with her knees butting against the mattress while she leaned over it.

"You did no such thing," Sharon protested and tried to brace herself to keep from being pulled further by stretching her free hand on the mattress.

Ridge caught it, too, and held both wrists captive. It was too soon after bathing him to be this close. She'd barely had time to calm her hotly disturbed senses. Now the fresh scent of soap clinging to his bare skin was igniting them all over again.

"Sleeping alone is one thing," Ridge drawled. "But I'm not used to lying alone in a bed during the daytime. It isn't natural."

Needing leverage to combat the steady pull of his hands, Sharon put a knee on the mattress, but that left her with only one foot on the floor to act as an anchor. Before she could set herself to tug against his pulling hands, Ridge was dragging her across him.

"Be careful," she gasped, suddenly more worried about falling on his injured middle than she was about being hauled into the bed. "You're going to get hurt again."

"Not if you pay attention," he taunted and helped her climb over him to the wider side of the bed.

As soon as she was clear of him, she tumbled in an ungainly sprawl onto the mattress beside him. For several seconds, she lay there, vaguely irritated because she knew she hadn't struggled very hard to avoid this. It was no use pretending that she hadn't fought harder because she was afraid of hurting him. That was just a handy excuse.

The mattress moved under his shifting weight. Sharon turned her head to look at him warily, one wrist still shackled by his encircling grip. He had slid off the pillows and was now stretched alongside her, half turned, with his dark head supported by a bent arm. The glinting caress of his mocking blue eyes tightened her stomach.

"This is ridiculous." Her protest was hardly more than a husky murmur. "I have work to do."

"You're here at Latigo to take care of me, not to make beds or clean house." Ridge let go of her wrist, but she wasn't free of his touch as his hand moved to the side of her neck. His fingers were gentle and caressing while his thumb lightly stroked the curve of her throat. "Taking care of me is a full-time job."

A sweet tightness of tormenting misery welled in her throat at his comment, choking off her voice. It was a full-time job she wanted desperately—all over again. She hadn't learned a thing. Her adolescent crush had grown into love. It wasn't that Ridge had the power to disturb her so completely. It was the love she felt for him that gave him that power.

From experience, Sharon knew that Ridge didn't love women. He made love to them, but there was never any emotional commitment behind it. Knowing that, she had to guard against ruining her life over him a second time.

Bending his head he nuzzled her lips, reveling in their softness before settling firmly onto them. The slow and heady kiss dragged a response from inside her. She returned the slow, sensual movement of his mouth against hers. The sweet intensity of her pleasure bordered on pain, but she managed to suppress most of her longing.

Momentarily satisfied with the response to his first intimate foray, Ridge drew back to study her through half-closed eyes. Sharon tried to show no reaction as his fingertips explored her features, spending a lot of time around her mouth.

"Ridge, you're going to hurt yourself." Sharon attempted to reason with him. "You're supposed to rest and take it easy."

His mouth came back to make another claim on her lips, while her pulse skyrocketed at his seductive insinuation. Her hands moved tentatively to the top of his chest and the hard bones of his shoulder. Their contact with his flesh was limited by his injuries, as Sharon subconsciously avoided aggravating his soreness. His strongly stimulating kiss was skillfully drawing out her responsiveness, not letting her contain it.

The roaming caress of his hand had moved down to the back of her hip, gently applying pressure to urge her closer. In absent compliance, Sharon shifted nearer until she came up against the barrier of his long legs. She became conscious of a new assault as the solid outline of his mus-

cular thighs became imprinted on her legs and the heat of
his body burned through her clothes.

As his mouth followed a slow, wandering trail across her
cheek to her ear, her self-control became undermined by
the eroding force of her desire. His warm breath was a sexual stimulus to the sensitive opening of her ear, sending
excited quivers over her skin. Sharon sunk her teeth into
the soft inside of her lower lip, biting back the moan that
rose in her throat.

His fingers pushed the collar of her blouse away from
her neck as his warm lips moistly nuzzled the pulsing cord.
She struggled to surface from this whirlpool of raw sensation when his hand continued down her blouse collar until
it encountered the first button. She felt his fingers working
to loosen it and brought her hand down on his wrist.

"You are really into children's games this morning,
aren't you?" The pitch of her voice was husky and disturbed
as she challenged him.

"Why?" He was distracted from his nuzzling study of
her throat long enough to look at her, most of his interest
centering on her lips.

"Isn't this a version of 'Button, button, who's got the button'?" she accused on a breathless note, her hand tightening on his wrist even as the first button was slipped free of
its buttonhole.

His lip corners were tugged upward. "Ah, but it's the
adult version," Ridge informed her with dryly mocking
amusement, and bent his head again to her neck. His fingers were already moving on to the next button in line.

Sharon let go of his wrist and tried to get in the way of
his hand. "Will you stop unbuttoning my blouse?" There
was a tinge of desperation in the exasperated tone of her
protest.

"I'd be happy to," he murmured against the throbbing

pulse in her neck, "if you'll tell me some other way to get the thing off."

Her breathing became agitated and deep as she tried to interfere with his deftly working fingers. Suddenly, something in their actions reminded her of the handslap game she'd played as a child. The situation struck her funny and laughter bubbled in her throat, venting some of the sexual tension that had brought her nerves to a state of panic.

The laughter tumbled helplessly from her, turning her weak. Confused, Ridge lifted his head to gaze at her, the blue of his eyes reflecting some of the amusement that had her in its throes.

"What's so funny?" he asked.

"Doesn't this remind you of two kids playing that handslap game?" Suppressed and breathless laughter was in her voice as she sought to share her humor with him.

Giving in to the laughter had been a grave mistake, a fact Sharon discovered when she felt the warm sensation of his hand gliding under the material of her blouse and onto her ribcage below the underswell of her breast. While she was laughing, he had finished unbuttoning her blouse. There was nothing funny about the situation anymore. It was purely erotic, made even more so by the lusting desire in his lazy eyes.

"Damn you, Ridge Halliday." Her voice trembled in disturbed reaction. "You don't play fair."

"How the hell do you think I win all the time?" he taunted softly and leaned to bury her lips with the hard pressure of his kiss while his hand cupped itself to the taut underside of her breast.

She was lost in a mindless blur of sensation that swept her deeper and deeper into his embrace. The smell of his skin and the hot taste of his tongue were aphrodisiacs to her senses. Her restless hands were fascinated with the hard sinew and bone of his naked shoulders, his flesh warm and vital to her touch, the elasticized band around his ribs always reminding her of his injuries.

Caught between conflicting needs, Sharon felt hopelessly torn. The instinct of self-preservation insisted she must stop this before it went any further, but his warm lips were already nuzzling the valley between her breasts, then mounting a slope to encircle its pointed peak. With deliberate thoroughness, Ridge was conquering her body one area at a time. The part of her that loved him was willing to concede the battle.

Slowly he began to backtrack to her throat and neck, his body shifting slightly away from her. At first, Sharon didn't understand his intention until her stomach muscles contracted under the touch of his hand as it moved to the waistband of her jeans. There was a wild fluttering in the pit of her stomach, raw longing rushing intensely through her.

"Ridge—" The sane half of her that wanted to protect her from future hurt attempted a protest.

"You're enjoying it, aren't you?" His teeth gently tugged at the lobe of her ear.

"Yes," she admitted with groaning reluctance.

"We can fool around like this all day," he murmured with suggestive promise.

It was a poor choice of words, but she was ultimately glad he'd used them, because they swayed her out of her indecision. She rolled away from him, taking advantage of the soreness that didn't permit him to move swiftly, and swung off the bed. Sharon heard his muffled grunt of pain when he tried to follow her, but she didn't turn around as she hurriedly, though shakily, rebuttoned her blouse.

"What are you doing?" Ridge finally asked after he'd gotten his breath back from that shafting pain.

"I told you I have work to do," she stiffly reminded him.

He didn't accept that explanation. "Come back here and tell me what happened." The invitation was lazily offered.

"No." She could feel his eyes on her.

"Why?" he countered smoothly.

Swiveling at her hips, Sharon half-turned to meet his steady gaze. Hard determination burned cold in her hazel eyes, able to look at him impassively.

"Maybe I don't want to be the one who winds up being the fool when you're through fooling around," she stated in a hard, flat voice.

She saw the brief, upward flick of his eyebrow and the subsequent narrowing of his eyes as he reassessed her. At the moment she didn't care what lay behind those solid features or his silence. She left the room while she had the chance.

Chapter 8

It seemed she was going in and out of his room all day long. Everytime she turned around, Ridge was impatiently calling for her. Sometimes it was for something as trivial as emptying his ashtray, sometimes he wanted a cup of coffee or to complain that the radio was still too loud and keeping him from taking a nap. Naturally, an hour later he wanted the radio turned up.

Late in the afternoon, he relented and took a pain pill. Sharon was able to fix supper without any interruption from him. When she carried the tray into his room she caught him out of bed. Although Sharon couldn't say that she had gotten used to seeing him lying half-naked in the bed, partially covered with a sheet, it was certainly more unnerving to see his long, lean body out of the bed, clad only in a thin pair of soft cotton jockey shorts. Anger seemed the best way to cover up the effect he was having on her.

"What do you think you're doing?" she demanded as she watched him moving gingerly across the room to the bed.

"I thought I told you to stay in bed. What are you doing out of it?"

"I had to use the bathroom. Somehow, I just didn't think you'd want to lend your assistance in that department," he shot back in faintly taunting sarcasm.

Sharon flushed darkly and continued into the room, averting her gaze while he managed to climb into bed on his own. "I could have helped you to the door and back," she insisted stiffly.

He had noticed the high points of color in her cheeks and smiled in satisfaction. "Your poise is slipping, nurse," he mocked. "Remember, you have a brother, so a man's anatomy isn't likely to embarrass you."

There was no response for that, but she tried. "Maybe I was more embarrassed by my imagination than by your body?" Sharon suggested coolly and set the tray on his lap. "Eat your supper."

When she started to turn away from the bed, his hand lightly touched her arm. "Sharon, I'm sorry." It was a low, rough apology, offered reluctantly, as usual. Ridge sighed heavily. "Hell, I'm bored and miserable—and I'm just taking it out on you because you happen to be on the spot." She could understand that even if it wasn't an adequate excuse. "Will you bring your food in here and eat with me?"

His drawling appeal for her company was very tempting. Against her better judgement, Sharon found herself agreeing.

It turned out to be a very companionable meal without a lot of conversation. Ridge seemed to be on his best behavior, not needling her with any of his bold remarks. It was as if they were back on a friendly footing, although Sharon knew it would take only one misstep for everything to go haywire.

While she was washing the dishes, her parents came by to see how Ridge was doing and whether there was anything Sharon needed. She had written out a short grocery list of soft foods to fix for Ridge, which she went over with her mother.

"While you're in town, would you buy him a pair of pajamas and a robe?" Sharon added. "He doesn't own any."

"His lack of proper attire is slightly indecent—or so your father thought," her mother laughed softly. "Of course, he thought that only because you're here taking care of Ridge."

"Sharon!!" Her name was shouted from the bedroom, the voice unmistakably belonging to Ridge.

"What?!!" she hollered back, then said to her mother in an aside, "I've learned to shout first. That way I don't have to walk back to get whatever it is that he wants."

"We need some coffee!!" came the answer.

"Coming!!" She reached for the coffeepot and glanced wryly at her mother. "I haven't decided whether he simply enjoys having me at his beck and call or if he's only trying to get back at me because I made him stay in bed all day."

"It's probably a combination," her mother replied wisely.

It was late in the evening before her parents left. Her father stayed in the bedroom and talked ranching with Ridge while Sharon and her mother sat in the kitchen. Naturally, she found herself hopping up about every fifteen minutes to fetch something for Ridge.

When she said goodbye to her parents at the door and watched them walk to their pickup truck, it left her with an odd feeling. It was as if this house was her home—where she lived with Ridge on a permanent basis. She closed the door and looked slowly around at the walls and ceilings with a sense of belonging.

"Stop dreaming, girl," she mentally gave herself a hard shake. She paused at Ridge's door long enough to tell him goodnight and then went on to bed.

As she lay awake in the melancholy darkness of her room, Sharon wished Ridge had been made differently. He was one of the Western breed, not exactly a rare type of man, because she'd met a few others who shared his characteristics. Cowboying and ranching were their life, and there wasn't any room for a wife and family. They enjoyed women and a wild time, but that was about the only role a female played in their lives.

Rolling over, she shut her eyes tightly and wondered why she had to fall in love with a man with lazy blue eyes who wouldn't settle down. It wasn't fair, not when she'd come so close to getting over him.

The second day was practically a repetition of the day before, except that Sharon suggested that Ridge do his own bathing and there wasn't any tussle in bed. Other than that, she insisted that he spend most of the day in bed, and Ridge found a hundred reasons to call her into the room, fetching and doing things for him. Her mother stopped by in the afternoon with the groceries Sharon had wanted, plus the pajamas and robe. Sharon delayed giving the latter two to Ridge until the next morning.

When Sharon carried in his breakfast tray, Ridge was ready to do battle. There was a hard gleam in his eye as she approached the bed. She was reminded of a range stallion, penned for the first time in his life.

"I'm not staying in bed today," he announced. "If I don't start moving around, I'll be so stove up I won't be able to move."

"I'm sure you're right," she said, taking him by surprise when she didn't argue with him.

While he was eating breakfast, Sharon went into her room and got the package containing the new pajamas and robe. She carried it into his bedroom and laid it on the sheet beside him.

"What's that?" Ridge glanced at her suspiciously.

"It's kind of a get-well present," she shrugged.

There was a smile in her hazel eyes as she watched him open it. The pajamas were on top, a deep blue cotton trimmed in a lighter, sky-blue shade. He held them up, chuckling in his throat, and slid her a sparkling blue glance.

"No doubt I'm expected to model these," he said, lifting out the matching robe.

"Indeed you are." She smiled back. "But that can wait until after you finish your breakfast."

"Tomorrow morning it's back to bacon and eggs," Ridge decreed as he looked at the bowl of cream of wheat with distaste.

"We'll see," was the only comment Sharon made before leaving him to eat the rest of his breakfast.

Later she came back for the tray. Since he didn't ask for any help dressing, Sharon didn't offer. She was in the kitchen, washing the breakfast dishes, when she heard his hesitant footsteps approaching. She turned as he reached the doorway and leaned heavily against the doorframe for support.

"Well? How do I look?" He lifted a hand in a modeling gesture to indicate his outfit.

But her first glance went to his rugged features, taking note of the haggard lines of suppressed pain. She could well imagine how very stiff and sore he was. Then she let her glance sweep over the blue robe covering the pajamas. The color seemed to intensify the brilliance of his blue eyes and the darkness of his coloring.

"You look terrific." She tossed out the compliment lightly, but it was true.

"I feel like some damned actor," he declared in a tone of self-disgust. "But at least if someone comes, I don't have to dive under the covers." He sighed heavily and looked at her. "I'll be happier when I can put on a pair of boots and jeans again."

"I know." She turned back to the sink, aware that when that day came, there would no longer be a need for her to take care of him.

There was a long pause, then Ridge asked, "What are you going to do this morning?"

"I thought I'd do some baking. Why?" She had all the ingredients to make a butterscotch pie, which had always been a favorite of Ridge's when he'd eaten at their house.

"No reason." He hesitated, then very grudgingly asked, "Would you help me into the other room? I'm not as mobile as I thought."

She quickly dried her hands on a towel and went over to his side. Grimly he put an arm around her shoulders and used her body for extra support. Every step seemed to jar him as she helped him into the living room. Her side glance caught the twinges of pain that managed to break through his severely controlled expression.

"Do you want to lie down and rest for awhile?" Sharon could tell that even this small amount of exertion had tired him.

"No." He rejected the idea out of hand. "Take me to the desk. I seem to have only enough strength to sit, so I might as well do all that paperwork that's been piling up." There was anger and self-disgust in his voice.

"Maybe it would help if you took a pill?" she suggested as she led him to the large desk.

"No. I want to make it through the day without any . . .

if I can," he added the reluctant admission that maybe he couldn't endure as much as he thought.

Before the morning was over, Sharon discovered that just because Ridge was out of bed, it didn't lessen the number of his demands on her. His short temper quickly made it clear that he resented needing her help as much as he resented his own inability to take care of himself.

When she looked back on the morning, she could remember Ridge saying only one nice thing and that had been at lunchtime after he'd eaten his second slice of pie. "That's better than your mother's," he'd said.

After an hour of paperwork in the afternoon, Ridge finally admitted to being tired and lay down on the sofa to rest. He refused to go into the bedroom. Sharon put a casserole in the oven for supper and moved quietly into the living room to find him sleeping soundly, a frown creasing his face.

The house was quiet and very still. She could feel the tension in her shoulders and neck. Between suppressing her natural feelings for Ridge and the incessant demands he'd made on her in the last four days, it had been hectic. Not once had there been any break.

Her gaze strayed to the window, where the sunshine of a Colorado afternoon blazed in. There was no better opportunity to take a walk than now, while Ridge was sleeping. Stealthily, she slipped out the front door.

Outside, Sharon wandered away from the house and its ranch buildings. A wind swept over the rugged tableland and lifted her toffee-colored hair to rush its fingers through it. She turned a farseeing gaze to the land around. It was a wild stretch of country, caught between the rugged canyon-lands to the north where Butch Cassidy and his gang had once roamed and the raw, spectacular mountains of the Colorado Rockies to the south and east.

It was a land of cattle and sheep ranches and not much else except perhaps its untold fortune in oil shale. The Piceance Basin and the Book Cliff Mountains were her home. She pulled her gaze in, studying the Latigo range. The ranch showed the care and pride of its owner. Its fences were strong and well built; its buildings were painted and in good repair; and its livestock were sleek and well fed.

Wildflowers were sprinkled along the fenceline, as many-colored as a painter's palette. The minute she saw them, Sharon knew they were just what the house needed to give it some life. She picked a big bunch so that she could make several bouquets.

She was humming to herself when she entered the house by the back door with her armload of flowers. She nudged the door shut with her hip and started for the sink.

"Where the hell have you been?" Ridge demanded, lurching into the doorway. "I've been through this whole damn house looking for you, calling until I'm damned near hoarse!"

"You were sleeping, so I went for a short walk. I haven't been gone that long," Sharon replied with a confirming glance at the wall clock.

She wasn't about to apologize for taking a walk. She felt she had earned that much. She began opening cupboard doors until she found the shelf where she'd seen the flower vases.

"Why didn't you tell me where you were going?" Ridge demanded as he crossed to the sink.

"I would have had to wake you up to do that, and I didn't think that would make you very happy," Sharon explained with a calmly unmoved glance at him.

"You're supposed to be taking care of me—not out somewhere walking," he muttered in a disgruntled tone. "When I woke up and realized you weren't here, I didn't know what to think." He ran a hand through his hair, rumpling it more than it already was.

"Don't tell me that you actually missed me?" She ran a wondering eye over him as she filled the vases with water.

His gaze at her became steady. A hint of a smile began to break through his angry expression. "Yes, I missed you."

A little thrill of gladness went through her, despite her attempts not to let his admission mean too much. She busied her hands with the wildflowers, arranging a bunch of them in a vase.

"The next time you decide to go for a walk while I'm sleeping," Ridge said as he hooked a hand around her waist, pulling her sideways so that she stood closer to him, "I want you to either wake me up and tell me where you're going or leave a note pinned to my chest."

His gaze was lightly mocking as he made his request. Sharon pushed at his hand, trying to shove it off her hipbone. She was all too conscious of her shoulder resting against his chest and the nearness of his mouth.

"Ridge, will you behave yourself?" she demanded patiently while she tried to check the rush of her pulse.

"Not until you promise me." His finger caught the point of her chin and turned it so that she faced him.

The smoky blue of his eyes held her gaze, absorbing her completely. "I promise." She could hear the huskiness in her voice.

Bending his head, he rubbed his mouth over the outline of her lips, tantalizing her until she could barely breathe. The man smell of him filled her senses as her faint breath mingled with the warm force of his.

"Damn, but you have the softest lips," he said against them.

"Damn, but you swear a lot," she murmured, wishing he would stop talking and kiss her.

Instead, he pulled his head back at her reply. "Does it bother you?" There was a concerned look on his face.

She found his question curious and tested it. "Why? Would you stop it if I did?"

His mouth quirked wryly. "Probably not, but I'd watch my language a little more closely around you."

"Well, it doesn't bother me," Sharon assured him and turned back to her bouquet, but his willingness to make the attempt indicated a respect for her. She liked that. But she held that knowledge close inside her, not letting him see how much a little thing like that meant to her.

The back door opened and Ridge released her, shifting his position to create a space between them as Scott walked into the kitchen.

"You're finally up and about," her brother observed. "How are you feeling?"

"Better," Ridge nodded affirmatively and levered himself away from the sink counter.

Out of the corner of her eye, Sharon noticed the way he disguised the difficulty he had walking as he moved toward the table and chairs in the kitchen. He didn't want Scott to see just how much trouble it was for him.

"Sit down." He motioned her brother to a chair. "We'll have some coffee. Sharon, pour us a cup."

It was on the tip of her tongue to point out that he'd been standing beside the coffee pot and could just as easily have poured himself a cup and carried it to the table, but she held back the words. Instead, she took two cups from the shelf, filled them with coffee, and carried them to the table for Ridge and her brother. Scott glanced at her as if he expected her to join them, but Sharon went back to the sink and began arranging the wildflowers in the vases.

As she listened to the hum of their voices, the moment

seemed part of a familiar pattern. She'd lost count of the number of times she'd been a party to their conversations over the years. If there had been any change, it was simply that she had stopped blindly adoring Ridge. She loved him, but not blindly—futilely, probably, but not blindly.

Satisfied with the riot of blossom and color in the three vases, Sharon carried two of them into the living room, setting them in strategic places to liven the room. The third, a small vase, she set at the back of the kitchen table where it would be out of the way when they sat down to a meal. Then she stepped back to study the effect critically.

"How does it look?" she asked absently of the two men at the table. Her brother had an eye for such things as background color and proportionate sizes of objects in their settings.

"That's fine," replied Scott, never one to elaborate when something was right.

"Look what happens when you let a woman into your house for a few days," Ridge mocked, sliding Sharon a dryly amused glance. "All of a sudden, she starts setting flowers all over the place. I'm surprised she hasn't rearranged the furniture."

"I've been thinking about it," she retorted, vaguely irritated by his chiding comment.

"Well, don't," he smiled slowly. "I like things the way they are."

It only confirmed what she already knew. He was satisfied with his home and his life the way it was, minus a woman's touch.

"I can believe that." Her voice was flat and cool as Sharon broke the pattern and didn't stay in the kitchen to listen to them talk. She went into another part of the house and searched for something to do.

Before Scott left, he went to look for her to see if there

was anything she needed. Ridge stood in the background, watching her with a keenly assessing eye. It was slightly unnerving to have him taking her apart and examining each piece.

"Why don't you stay for supper, Scott?" Sharon invited, suddenly wanting her brother's presence to shield her from Ridge. It was one thing knowing that he didn't need her in his life, but it was another to hear him say it.

"I can't tonight," her brother refused. "I promised Soames I'd be over to his place tonight and take a look at that round baler he wants to sell."

"It's just as well." Ridge tried to hide his hobbling gait as he moved closer to include himself in the conversation. "You wouldn't like the food. You should see what your sister's been feeding me."

"Come over tomorrow night," Sharon issued a second invitation to her brother, ignoring Ridge's mocking complaint about his diet of soft foods. "Ridge should be able to handle a *real* meal by then. I'll fix some roast beef and you can help him celebrate."

"I'll come," Scott accepted.

While Ridge had a last word with her brother, Sharon excused herself and returned to the kitchen to check on the casserole in the oven. It was bubbling away, so she turned the oven temperature to its lowest setting and started fixing the side dishes she intended to serve with it.

After Scott left the house, Ridge hobbled into the kitchen, keeping a hand on the wall for support. Sharon barely glanced up when he entered, then swung away to remove the dirty cups from the table.

"You might as well sit down. Supper will be ready in a few minutes," she informed him in a brisk voice.

As she carried the cups to the sink, she heard the scrape of a chair leg on the tile floor. She picked up the damp dishcloth and walked back to the table to wipe its top. Ridge was standing behind the chair he'd pulled out, leaning both hands on it to rest before exerting his sore stomach muscles to sit down.

The small vase of wildflowers on the table seemed to taunt her with their presence—as unwanted as she was. As soon as she had finished wiping the table, Sharon picked up the vase. When she swung away from the table to carry the vase to the counter, Ridge's hand snared the crook of her arm.

"You can leave the vase on the table. It won't be in the way," he said.

She raised a cool glance to his face. "I thought you didn't like flowers sitting around," Sharon challenged.

"After being cooped up in the house all this time, it's nice to see a bit of the outdoors," Ridge replied with a vague shrug and released her arm to touch one of the red blossoms with his finger. "They won't last long. In a few days, they'll be dead."

"I know." Abruptly, Sharon set the vase on the table and turned away, smoothing her hands down the front of her jeans as she walked to the stove, fighting a sick, clammy feeling.

The flowers wouldn't be in the house for long and neither would she. When she was gone, Ridge wouldn't miss her any more than he would miss the flowers. Quickly she began dishing the food into serving bowls before realizing she hadn't set the table.

All through the meal, Sharon was conscious of the hooded study of his gaze. When they had finished eating, she poured them each a cup of freshly brewed coffee and began clearing the dirty dishes from the table while hers cooled.

"I wasn't completely honest with you the other day

when we had that heated discussion," Ridge said, breaking the silence that followed the meal.

"Which one?" Sharon asked smoothly, because there had been several discussions that might be described as heated, and continued covering the bowls of leftovers and stowing them in the refrigerator.

"That day at the creek, before I got stomped on by that bull," he replied.

For an instant, his answer made her pause in midmotion, then she went back to her task more vigorously than before. She remembered the conversation much too vividly—and the bitter hurt and wounded pride that had ensued.

"I think just about everything was said that day," she said curtly and walked to the sink, conscious of his watchful eyes.

"Not quite everything," Ridge paused. "Would you come over and sit down? It's difficult to talk to somebody when they keep darting all over the room."

"I can hear you just fine. I don't have to sit down to listen," Sharon countered and began running water in the sink so she could put the dirty dishes in to soak.

"Your coffee is getting cold."

"I'll warm it up when I'm through here," she stated.

A heavy sigh came from him. Then his chair was pushed back from the table and she tensed at his unsteady approach. She squirted detergent into the water filling the sink and began setting the supper dishes into it. She felt the touch of his hands on her shoulders, stilling her movements.

"You accused me of giving you encouragement when you had that schoolgirl crush on me, and I admitted that I did." His voice was low, the vibration of it seeming to come through his hands to go inside her. "What I didn't tell you was that I found you to be a very tempting morsel. The problem came when I realized I wanted to do a lot more than just kiss you—and I knew you were so crazy about me that you'd let me."

Her cheeks grew hot. His hands started to move down her arms, their action too close to a caress. Sharon grabbed the dishcloth and began scrubbing at the dishes in the sink, forcing his hands off her arms, but they settled on her waist.

"I'm not even sure about that," she said tensely, denying she had been so besotted with him back then that she would have gone all the way. "If that's what you believed, what stopped you?" she challenged bitterly, not wanting this conversation to continue any more than she'd wanted the last. "Don't tell me your conscience wouldn't let you?"

"It wasn't my conscience as much as it was your brother," he stated.

"My brother?" Sharon frowned in confusion, her body poised motionless at his response.

"Scott was my best friend, practically a brother. You don't mess around with a guy's kid sister and expect him to stay your friend," Ridge explained. "That's why I kept 'hands off.' "

"What's the point in telling me this now?" Her lips came together in a grim line as she began washing the same plate over. "Is it supposed to make a difference?"

"The situation has changed." His hands began to move to the front of her waist, sliding across her stomach and causing her muscles to contract automatically at his touch.

"How?" She tried to breathe normally as she sliced a look backward out of the corner of her eye, feeling his breath stirring her hair.

"Because you've grown up." His crossing hands had drawn her against the full length of his body—her shoulders touching the solidness of his chest, her hips feeling the rub of his thighs. "Big brother is no longer under any obligation to protect you. You haven't done a bad job of taking care of me, so you must be able to take care of yourself."

"So?" Sharon didn't trust herself to say more than one word, afraid the thick disturbance within her would creep into her voice.

"So—while the situation has changed, I think other things haven't. Namely—that I still think you're a tempting morsel and I still want to do more than kiss you—and you want me to do more than that, too." His head dipped to graze his mouth along the curve of her neck.

Just for a second, Sharon let her lashes drift shut at the sheer sensuality of his caressing touch. Shuddering, she recognized that what Ridge had said was true. Knowing it also drove her out of his arms and spun her around to face him in a trembling fury.

"I think I hate all you maverick cowboys." Her voice was low and taut, riddled with bitter hurt. "Give you a good roping horse, some cattle, and a good time on Saturday night and that's all you need! Well, the rest of us want more than that! Some day I want a ring, a marriage license, and some children—in that order! You don't need those things—and what's worse, you don't want them!"

The beginnings of a glowering frown appeared on his face, narrowing his eyes to blue slits of color. Her hands were doubled into rigid fists as Sharon glared at him, fighting back the tears stinging her eyes.

"You turn me on, Ridge. I won't deny that," she declared. "But you were right when you said I could take care of myself. So from now on, you can just leave me alone!"

Hot tears were on the verge of spilling from her lashes. With long, angry strides, Sharon swept out of the kitchen. She had meant everything she'd said, and she didn't want to weaken her statement by breaking into tears. She didn't stop until she had reached her bedroom and shut the door, leaning weakly against it while silent sobs shuddered through her body.

It wasn't long until she heard the sound of Ridge moving along the wall outside her room. She stepped away from the door and impatiently wiped at the tears on her cheeks, breathing deeply to stop them. He knocked at her door.

"Sharon?" When she didn't answer, he knocked again, louder. "Sharon." He became more demanding. "Sharon, answer me!" She pressed her lips more tightly together. "Dammit, Sharon," he swore a warning.

"What?" The response was whipped out of her, but it angered her that he could prod her into speaking when she had vowed not to say a word.

There was a long silence before he spoke again, his tone considerably subdued and terse. "Don't bother with the dishes. I'll do them tonight."

She looked at the ceiling, wanting to laugh, but it hurt too much. He didn't even need her to wash the dishes! After a few seconds, she heard him moving away from her door.

Chapter 9

The next morning they didn't have much to say to each other, although his lidded blue gaze strayed to her often. Sharon was in the kitchen washing up the lunch dishes when she heard the heavy tread of cowboy boots.

When she turned, Ridge appeared in the doorway, dressed in snug-fitting jeans and a chambray shirt with a brown, work-stained cowboy hat shading his face. His rugged vitality and masculine roughness seemed to grip her by the throat.

"I'm going with Hobbs this afternoon and look over the ranch," he announced. "We're taking the truck."

It was on her tongue to ask if he felt up to it, but she doubted Ridge would admit that he wasn't. The same ridiculous male pride that had insisted on discharging himself from the hospital was now driving him to climb back into the seat of authority—even if it killed him.

"All right." Sharon swung back to the sink, tight-lipped in her disapproval.

She listened to his footsteps as he moved gingerly to the

back door, knowing that as soon as he was with his fore-man, Ridge would be gritting his teeth and walking as if he didn't hurt at all. Men, she thought with angry exasperation as she heard the door shut.

The dishes were done and she was putting the roast in the oven to slow-cook it to a tender doneness when the tele-phone rang. Sharon crossed the room to pick up the wall phone.

"Hello, Sharon?"

"Andy!" She recognized his voice with surprise. "I didn't expect you to call."

"You said to call on Saturday. Did you forget we have a date tonight?" Behind the joking tone there was a sugges-tion of hurt.

"No. I didn't forget." It had just slipped her mind. "I guess I didn't realize it was Saturday already."

"You're still staying at Latigo, I take it," he said, stating the obvious. "Isn't Halliday up and around yet?"

"He's up, but I think there's a difference of opinion about how well he's getting around," she murmured dryly.

"Is our date still on for tonight?"

Sharon hesitated only for a second. "Of course." After last night, the timing of this date couldn't have been better if she had planned it. Besides, Andy had always been able to boost her spirits, and they certainly needed boosting now.

"I'll pick you up between five-thirty and six."

Since her mother had sent over only every-day-type clothes, Sharon put on the peach-colored dress she'd worn the day she'd brought Ridge home from the hospi-tal. Her light caramel hair was freshly shampooed and curled loosely on her shoulders. It was ego building to see her reflection in the oven door's glass window, even though she had a towel tied over the front of the full skirt to protect it.

The roast and its accompanying vegetables were done; there was a salad in the refrigerator, and some peas were in a pan on the stove burner ready to be warmed. The evening meal was virtually ready, except for the last-minute dishing up.

She turned around and skimmed the table with a glance, then realized there wasn't any bread out. Scott could eat half a loaf at one sitting. As she walked to the cupboard bread drawer to correct that oversight, she heard the back door open. A wave of tension tightened her nerves. When she turned back to the table with the loaf of bread in her hands, she was mentally prepared to meet Ridge.

Stiff legged and holding himself carefully, he entered the kitchen and more or less fell into a chair. He swept off his hat and dropped it on the table, then slumped against the chair back. There was an ashen quality about his face and the dullness of pain in his eyes. He was breathing in a slow, halting rhythm.

Without a word, Sharon left the bread on the table and went back to the cupboards, fetching him a glass of water and a pain pill. She set them in front of him. "Here you go, tough guy," she said unsympathetically. Ridge glanced at the pill and threw her a look, then tossed the pill into his mouth and washed it down with the water. "I probably wasted my time cooking this supper for you." Sharon declared, irritated with him for aggravating his condition. "Your stomach is liable to revolt at the first bite of roast beef."

"I'd forgotten I was going to get something to eat tonight for a change." The sharp edge in his voice was attributable to the pain he was obviously feeling. "How come Scott isn't coming to dinner?"

"As far as I know, he is." Sharon gave him a blank look.

"Then how come the table is only set for two people?" Ridge gestured to the two place settings, then his gaze swept over her, taking in the full-skirted dress. "And how come you're wearing that?"

"I'm going out tonight. I have a date with Andy Rivers," she announced into a room that suddenly seemed deadly quiet. "He should be here any time to pick me up."

"And what happens to me while you're out with your oil man?" It was a half-snarling demand. "You're supposed to be here to take care of me. That was the deal."

"I'm sure you'll manage to survive," Sharon murmured dryly. "Or you can ask Scott to stay and hold your hand if you're afraid of being alone for a few hours." Ridge lapsed into a thick silence that prickled her nerve ends. "Everything is ready for dinner. All you and Scott have to do is warm the peas and slice the meat."

There was no response. From outside came the slam of car doors. Sharon looked out the window to see her brother and Andy coming up the walk together after arriving separately. After a short glance at Ridge, she untied her apron and went to the door to greet them. He remained seated in the kitchen chair, all his attention centered on the cigarette he'd just lit.

The tension became electric after Sharon invited Andy into the house to wait while she got her jacket and purse. Ridge didn't say five words to him. She was seething at his rudeness when she walked out the back door with Andy.

"I'm sorry Ridge wasn't very polite to you, Andy." She felt she had to apologize for him. "He isn't in the best of moods right now."

"I'm used to it," he shrugged to show it hadn't bothered him. "There's a lot of ranchers that see red when they meet some guy who's interested in the oil shale that might be under their rangeland."

It seemed wisest to let Andy think along those lines. There was no reason to enlighten him about the circumstances that had preceded his arrival at the ranch. Tonight she had every intention of putting Ridge out of her mind.

Andy was fun, undemanding company. Even if she wasn't able to forget Ridge, Sharon did find herself relaxing and enjoying the outing. They made a long evening of it, driving all the way to Glenwood Springs to take in a show and eat afterwards.

It was well after midnight when he drove to the end of the long lane into the headquarters of Latigo Ranch and stopped in front of the house. All the ranch buildings were dark, but lights burned in the house windows.

"It looks like somebody's waiting up for you," Andy observed as he switched off the engine.

"Ridge probably just left the lights on for me," Sharon reasoned, certain that after the strain of the afternoon, Ridge wouldn't have the stamina to stay up this late.

Andy climbed out of the car and came around to open her door. His hands rested companionably on her shoulders as they walked to the house, both fairly well talked out after the long drive.

"I enjoyed myself tonight," Andy said, then slid her a boyish grin. "I guess I always say that when I take you home, but it's true just the same. I guess it's because I feel I never have to prove anything to you—or come on like some heavyweight lover, which I'm not. I can just be myself."

"Me too." Sharon agreed with all he said, from her point of view as well.

"Some guy's gonna marry you one of these times and

I'm gonna come back here and find out I've lost a friend," he declared with a mock shake of his head, stopping as they reached the door.

"We'll always be friends, Andy," she insisted.

"Not if you marry one of these 'cattle-or-die' ranchers." With a nod of his head, he indicated the occupant of the house where they were standing.

It wasn't necessary to reply as Andy bent his head to kiss her goodnight. The outside light suddenly flashed on, its brightness blinding both of them and startling them into moving apart. The door opened and Ridge loomed in its frame, glowering at the pair of them.

"It's you," he muttered harshly and Sharon wondered who else he expected it to be. "I thought I heard a car door."

"You did," Sharon said, resentment starting to build at the way he continued to stand there, holding the door open.

"Are you coming in or not?" Ridge snapped impatiently.

She was ready to defy him, but Andy took the opportunity away from her. "Good night, Sharon. I'll give you a call when I'm going to be in the area again." There was almost a smile on his face as he bent his head and discreetly kissed her cheek.

"Good night, Andy," she returned and tossed a glaring look at Ridge.

Stubbornly, she waited outside a few minutes and watched Andy walk back to his car while Ridge impatiently cooled his heels at the door. Then, and only then, did she enter the house, her chin held at a coolly defiant angle.

The door was barely shut when Ridge pounced on her with an angry demand, "Do you know what time it is?"

"It must be after midnight," Sharon replied noncha-

lantly and swept into the living room. "How come you're
still up? I thought you would have been in bed ages ago."

"I always stay up this late," he taunted her with the lie
the way she had taunted him with her question. "I've been
waiting up for you! What the hell do you think I'm doing
up at this hour?!"

"That's what I thought." She turned on him, no longer
trying to contain her anger.

"Just where the hell have you been?" Ridge demanded.

"That's none of your business!"

"It is my business!" he snapped. "You're staying in my
house, so that makes me responsible for what happens to
you."

"That's ridiculous," she declared scornfully. "Where I go
and what I do are none of your affair."

"In case you don't know it, your brother doesn't think
much of your oil man—and neither do I." He towered in
front of her, bristling with anger.

"I don't care what you or Scott think of him. All that
matters is what I think about Andy." She pointed at herself
for emphasis. "I date whom I please—and stay out as late as
I please. No one, not even my parents, tells me what to
do—and you're certainly not going to."

"I suppose you think your oil man is going to give you a
ring and a marriage license and those kids you said you
wanted last night," Ridge jeered.

"He could," Sharon countered, angrily baiting him.

"Well, you can just forget him because you're not going
out with him anymore," he informed her coldly, a muscle
jumping in his jaw.

"Why? Because you say so?" she mocked him sarcasti-
cally, then hurled, "You don't own me, Ridge Halliday!"

"Do you wanna bet?" The taunting words were ground
through his teeth as he roughly pulled her into his arms.

She fought him wildly, pushing and struggling against the steel band that pinned her to his chest. By twisting her head, she managed to elude the mouth moving hotly over her face, but it was only temporary. "You're going to lose," Ridge said against her throat, his breath coming roughly. "And you know it."

Her own breath was coming in taut little sighing gasps as her pulse careened wildly out of control. It wasn't his strength she was fighting. It was the sensation of his lean, muscular length, the smell of his skin, and the husky sound of his voice that she fought to resist.

"I hate you," she said through her teeth, because he knew what he did to her when he touched her and he was taking advantage of it.

His mouth reached the corner of her lips. Of their own accord, they turned to seek his bruising kiss. Her fingers slowly uncurled from the balled fists she'd made of them and spread across his shoulders to dig fiercely into his shirt and the hard flesh under it. For long, hot moments, their lips mated in an angry union until it spawned passion.

She strained against him, arching her spine to shape herself more closely to the hard angles and planes of his body. Blood rushed through her veins, fevering her skin already heated from the restless, pressing movements of his hands, alternately caressing and molding her body to his needs.

When Ridge pulled his mouth from hers and came up for air, dragging in heavy, labored breaths, Sharon pressed her hot face against his chest. She could hear his heart pounding, loud and fast, competing with her own drumming pulse. His hand moved over the silkiness of her tawny hair to the side of her face and lifted it away from his chest. She tipped her head back to gaze up at him, seeing the smouldering satisfaction in his half-closed eyes. Ridge stroked his hand over her neck and throat, caressing its curving length. There was a faint tremor in his touch, betraying how disturbed he was.

"I'll never understand—" his husky voice was lower than a murmur and deep with desire "—how one person could have such incredibly soft lips and soft curves and still be so hardheaded and hard-nosed. Tell me now," he insisted, "where were you and that oil guy all this time?"

"We went to a show in Glenwood Springs, then ate afterwards," she whispered, her body aching for the thrust of his hips.

"He didn't make love to you?" His fingers tightened ever so slightly on her neck, briefly applying pressure.

"No." Sharon turned her head in a negative movement. "Andy's a . . . friend."

"Why didn't you explain that to start with?" Ridge demanded gruffly. "Why did you put me through all this hell, wondering where you were and what you were doing with him? It kept getting later and later and I . . ." The rest was lost in a smothered groan as he punished her lips for the torment he'd been through, kissing them roughly and thoroughly, then drawing away. His hand tugged the elastic neckline of her dress off one shoulder to allow him to nibble on the sensitive bone, sending shivers of delight over her skin that raised her flesh.

"Were you jealous?" Sharon was dazed by the idea.

"Of him?" The look of amused scorn on his face when Ridge glanced at her, laughed away that fragile wisp of hope.

Crestfallen, Sharon lowered her gaze to the darkly tanned column of his throat. It had been a foolish thing to think, but just for a little while, she'd wondered. Then his warm lips were on her cheek, running over it in stimulating circles, and she closed her eyes to enjoy the heady bliss his touch created.

"Sharon," he murmured, tormenting her lips with the closeness of his mouth. "Let's stop fooling around and make love." His hands moved restlessly over her body, teasing her hips and breasts with his fleeting touch. "It's what we both want."

Although his statement wasn't a question, Sharon answered it like one. "Yes."

While her whole being seemed to clamor under the sweeping urgency of his kiss, some tiny fragment of her mind forced a recall of the words that had been said between them. It started an icy stream of thoughts that eventually chilled her ardor. As much as she loved Ridge and wanted him, she couldn't tolerate being a one-night stand in his life—and nothing he'd said had indicated he was offering her more than that.

She pushed with her hands to break free of him, inadvertently doing it against his cracked and broken ribs. His strangled cry of pain as he doubled over made Sharon realize what she'd done, but she felt little remorse. Considering how much he'd hurt her emotionally, he deserved to feel some pain of his own even if it was physical.

"What the hell are you trying to do?" he gasped and looked up at her with a frowning scowl. "They were just starting to heal and you damned near broke them all over again."

"You hypocrite!" She hurled the accusation at him.

"What are you talking about?" He straightened slowly and carefully, holding his rib cage and continuing to frown.

"You, pretending to be so righteous and upset because I was out so late with Andy Rivers!" Her scornful gaze raked him with disgust. "Trying to claim that you felt responsible for my reputation because I'm staying in your house. It was all lies! And I nearly believed your forked tongue. You come on 'holier than thou,' like Big Brother, and not ten minutes later, you're trying to proposition me into your bed!"

"It isn't like that, Sharon," he denied roughly.

"Oh, no?" she scoffed. "I told you last night and I'll tell you again. I'm not interested in what you have to offer, Ridge! I'm greedy. I want more than you can give me."

As she started to leave the room, Ridge tried to take a quick step to stop her and flinched at some inner shaft of pain. "Sharon." His hard voice called after her. "The last time you accused me of encouraging you. If I stepped out of line tonight, it was after I got encouragement from you."

"Then that makes us even, doesn't it?" She stopped long enough to throw the words at him.

For an instant, Sharon was held there by the sight of him, a lone figure in the middle of the room. His feet were planted slightly apart and his long arms were hanging loosely at his sides. His head was up and level. Nothing could be read in his features, ruggedly drawn in impassive lines. But it was the unstated things Sharon saw—the absolute self-reliance and the proud strength.

"Yes, we're even," Ridge acknowledged in a voice that rang flat and hard.

Turning, Sharon entered the hallway and walked past his room to her own. With unnatural calmness, she undressed and hung her dress up properly. It was as if she was trying to be as controlled and unaffected by events as Ridge appeared to be.

But when the lights were off and she was alone in the dark, it didn't seem so important anymore. Lying in bed, she slowly began to shake with sobs. As they grew stronger, she turned into her pillow and tried to muffle the sound in the feathery mass. It muted her crying and sopped up the tears running from her eyes.

A radio was turned on in the next room—Ridge's bedroom. The strains of a melancholy country song took up the silence. With it playing, Sharon didn't have to worry about Ridge hearing her, so she stopped holding back the violent ache that wrung her heart.

She finally cried herself into an emotionally exhausted sleep with the radio still playing its music in the background.

The next morning, Sharon drenched her puffy eyelids in cold water until her skin felt taut and frozen. She didn't take any pains with her appearance, skinning her hair away from her face and twisting a rubber band around its toasted-gold length. Her jeans were an old pair with patches on the seat, and her blouse was plain white cotton with a buttoned-down collar and long sleeves that she had rolled back at the cuff. Its whiteness, so close to her face, only emphasized her colorless, frozen complexion.

Her suitcase lay open on the bed, her underclothes lining the bottom of it. Gathering her few clothes on hangers in the closet, Sharon carried them to the bed and laid them beside the suitcase to begin folding them. As she slipped a blouse off its wire frame, she heard footsteps approach the door to her bedroom.

Since rising, she had ventured no further than the bathroom. No sound had come from the adjacent bedroom, so she had presumed that Ridge was still asleep—until she heard the footsteps. When she first awoke, the clock had shown the time as barely six in the morning. Evidently Ridge had been up before that.

The doorknob turned and the latch clicked in release.

Her hands faltered slightly, then continued folding the blouse with steady precision. She didn't look at the door when it swung open, although her raw nerves were tensely aware of Ridge standing in the opening.

"I thought I heard you moving around in here," he said.

She laid the folded garment in the suitcase and reached for the next blouse, flicking a brief glance in his direction. But that swift look took in everything about him from the jeans and work shirt he wore to the impassive mask blanking out all expression from his male features except for the lazy sharpness of his blue eyes.

"If you want breakfast, you can fix it yourself," she informed him, her voice flat and emotionless.

"You're leaving," Ridge stated.

"Brilliant deduction." But her voice was too dry to put any sting in it.

"I thought you'd stay a couple more days." He sounded calm as he moved into the room, coming toward the bed.

"I only came to look after you while you were laid up," Sharon reminded him, her voice cool as she folded the blouse, laid it beside the first, and picked up the next one. "You're on your feet. You don't need me anymore, so there isn't any reason for me to stay, is there?"

She made a project out of buttoning the blouse, waiting for his response to her faintly challenging question, even at this stage hoping against hope that he would express regret to see her go.

"No, I guess there isn't," Ridge agreed easily, and frissons of pain broke over her nerves.

"Then there's nothing left to be said, is there?" she said tightly and pushed the half-folded blouse on top of the others in a short burst of raw impatience.

When she reached for the pair of jeans, she suddenly

felt his hand under her chin, turning it so he could see her face. Except for that one brief glance when he'd entered, Sharon had kept her head averted, never looking directly at him. She quickly jerked her head away, but not before his alert gaze had swept the tautened skin around her eyes and the drained look of her complexion. She braced herself for some comment, but none came. Nor was there another attempt to inspect her face.

"As soon as I'm packed, I'll call home and have someone come pick me up," Sharon said into the silence.

"There's no need to have someone make a special trip over here to get you. I'll have one of the men drive you home," Ridge stated, showing that his arrangements were final by turning and leaving the room.

Alone again, Sharon pressed the jeans against her quivering chin. There had been no arguments, no protests, no regrets from Ridge, only a calm acceptance of the news that she was leaving. She asked herself what she had expected, but there wasn't any answer to that now.

When she finished packing, she discovered Ridge had left the house. She glanced out the kitchen window and saw him standing with Hobbs and another cowboy beside one of the ranch's pickups. With a touch of grim wryness, Sharon realized he'd wasted no time carrying out her transportation arrangements.

She left the house by the back door, carrying her suitcase, and crossed the yard to join the men standing by the truck's cab. She was painfully conscious of Ridge's gaze watching her all the way, its shuttered look never altering under the hat pulled low on his forehead.

"Have you got everything?" Ridge took the suitcase from her and passed it to the cowboy to be stowed in the bed of the truck.

"Yes." Everything that was hers to take.

His steady gaze was leveled at her, not allowing her to look away. "Thanks for coming."

A flash of bitter and taunting mockery broke across her tautly held features. "It was the neighborly thing to do." There was a twist in the smiling curve of her mouth.

Sharon swung away and climbed into the passenger side of the pickup. Ridge stepped away from it as the motor turned over and revved to life. Before the truck pulled away, he had already turned and begun talking to his foreman. Her eyes were painfully dry as Sharon stared out the front windshield.

Chapter 10

Okay, Huck, now it's your turn." Sharon looped the reins around the chestnut's neck and made sure the hackamore was properly adjusted roughly three fingers above the flaring nostrils before she swung into the saddle.

The sleek gelding stood quietly, waiting for the command to move away from the fence where the bay filly stood tied, finished with her morning training session. A faintly satisfied smile touched Sharon's mouth as she walked the chestnut into the dirt corral. With six horses contracted to break and train, she usually split them into two groups, working one in the morning and the other in the cool of late afternoon. The spoiled and unruly chestnut was an exception, the only horse she worked morning and night. Two weeks of that steady routine were showing results, even if they hadn't changed the horse's mischievous personality.

Her opinion of the animal's worth was slowly being revised—upward. She put the chestnut through his paces—walk, trot, canter, change leads, round turns—until she was satisfied the horse was working nicely and responding well to the pressure of the hackamore.

Bringing the horse down to a walk, she reached forward and patted the sleek neck under the flaxen mane. "I think you're ready to start learning a 'fancy whoa,' Huck," she said and watched the horse's ears swivel back to catch the sound of her soft voice.

The fancy whoa was the sliding stop where the horse seems to sit on its haunches and screw its tail into the ground. Sharon changed her grip on the reins, taking one in each hand in a "squaw's hold." She lifted the chestnut into a slow jog and waited until he was relaxed in the gait, then squeezed lightly with her legs to urge his hindquarters forward. At the same time, she applied slight pressure with the left rein. The instant the chestnut began to respond, she slacked off the left rein and tightened the right rein, then continued alternating the pressure. She sensed the horse's confusion as it came to a slightly jerky stop.

After reassuring the gelding with a few soft-spoken words, Sharon put him into a trot again and repeated the procedure. It didn't take too many times before the chestnut started to lower its rump the minute he felt the leg pressure. She gave him time to balance himself before she checked his head.

There was a strong sense of accomplishment in knowing the chestnut had stopped challenging her authority and struggling stubbornly to have his own way, and had begun to enjoy learning. More than the other green horses, Huck had given a purpose to these last two weeks since she'd left Latigo. Except when she worked the horses, Sharon lived in an emotionless void, one day sliding into another, the dull ache inside always with her.

As she debated whether to test the chestnut's response at a lope or to wait until the evening session for the next step,

Sharon heard the pickup truck drive into the ranch yard. Absently her glance swung around to identify the visitor. A queer sense of panic rushed through her nerves when she recognized Ridge climbing out of the cab. She jerked her gaze to the front and struggled to calm the leaping of her pulse. It was the first time she'd seen Ridge since leaving his ranch that Sunday morning.

All over again, she had to come to terms with these occasional meetings that were bound to occur as long as they lived on neighboring ranches. After overcoming her teenage infatuation with him once already, it didn't seem fair that she had to go through this anguish again. Sharon kept consoling herself with the knowledge that she had succeeded once, so she could do it again.

As the chestnut circled the corral at a jogging trot, she saw Ridge approach the fence instead of going to the house. He moved with loose-limbed ease, obviously recovered from his stiffness. She jammed her hat further down on her forehead and lifted the gelding into a canter.

Tension ripped through her nerves when Ridge climbed the fence and sat on the top rail to watch her working the horse. Sharon wanted to scream in frustration. The blaze-faced chestnut was sensitive to the change in mood and began acting up, breaking stride and dancing skittishly around a turn.

Irritated with herself, Sharon slowed the gelding to a walk, trying to settle him down. The horse did a side-stepping jig, refusing to stride out cleanly, and tossed his head. She reined him to a stop, but the chestnut wouldn't stand still, moving nervously beneath her.

It was a lost cause, she realized. The horse was picking up her tension and agitation. It was pointless to fight the chestnut and risk souring his training to this level. As she gave up and walked the horse toward the fence where the bay filly was tied, she noticed her mother was standing at the fence with Ridge. Sharon avoided his eyes.

"Are you quitting?" her mother asked. Then she commented sympathetically, "He was working so well."

"I've pushed him a lot lately," Sharon replied, as if that explained the chestnut's actions this morning.

Ridge vaulted lightly to the ground and walked to the chestnut's head, catching hold of the bridle and rubbing its nose while Sharon dismounted. Without looking at him, she hooked a stirrup on the saddlehorn and began loosening the cinch.

"He isn't even warm," Ridge observed, running a hand down the horse's chest.

"I ride him morning and night so I don't work him 'til he's hot," Sharon explained shortly. "I don't want him going stale on me when he's still learning."

She was stiff with tension, all her muscles tightly coiled and her nerves on edge. There was an electricity in the air, crackling in the stillness broken only by the idle stomping of a hoof and groaning of saddle leather.

Her mother came forward. "There's fresh coffee at the house. Would you like a cup, Ridge?"

"Not now, thanks," he refused. "I'll give Sharon a hand with the horses." Turning, he untied the filly's reins and prepared to lead her to the barn.

"I can manage without any help," she insisted, feeling brittle and breakable.

"I know it," he replied easily and calmly. "But I want to talk to you."

Sharon flashed an anguished look at her mother, but her only response was a pair of raised eyebrows and a faint smile. If Ridge was determined to talk to Sharon, nothing would stop him. Her mother knew that. Gritting her teeth, Sharon scooped up the chestnut's reins and headed for the barn.

The barn was full of hay dust and horse smells, shadowed and cool, as Sharon led the chestnut into his stall and clipped on his halter before removing the hackamore. Ridge led the filly into the adjoining stall and began unsaddling her, working in silence.

Unbuckling the double cinch, Sharon hauled the saddle off the chestnut and swung it onto her hip. She scooped the saddle blanket and pad off the horse's back and headed for the tack room with her double burden. Ridge followed her, not seeming to pay any attention when she stole a glance at him. The saddles were heaved onto their racks and the blankets and pads draped over them to air out the horse sweat.

The continued silence grated on her nerves as they returned to the respective stalls of their horses. Sharon picked up a currycomb and began brushing down the sleek chestnut while it nosed at the manger full of hay. Her jaw was clenched so tightly shut that her teeth hurt.

"You wanted to talk to me," she finally challenged Ridge, without breaking the rhythm of her brushing strokes.

"Yeah." The sweep of a second currycomb filled the pause that accompanied his bland acknowledgement. Sharon waited, the moment stretching out. Almost idly, Ridge said, "Those wildflowers you picked finally died. I threw them out yesterday."

"I'm surprised they lasted so long." She couldn't seem to keep the curtness out of her voice.

"So was I," he replied.

There was another interminably long silence. Sharon finally threw him a tight-lipped glance over the back of the chestnut. "Is that what you wanted to tell me?"

He stopped abruptly and rested his arms on the filly's dark back, the currycomb hanging loosely from his fingers.

His head was tipped to the side, his rolled hat brim at an angle that shaded his expression. He swore softly under his breath and pushed away from the horse, his hard gaze boring into hers.

"I've come to accept your terms," Ridge stated.

"My terms?" Her mouth stayed slightly open. In puzzled confusion, she watched him walk around the horse and come to the corner of the stall where she was standing.

"Yes, your terms," he repeated and reached into his bulging shirt pocket.

Instead of taking out a cigarette as Sharon expected, he removed a small square box and stepped forward to push it into her hand. She stared at the ring box, then hesitantly opened it, darting him a wary look. His features remained cut in stern lines.

A pear-shaped diamond sparkled in its mounting on a narrow, gold band. A raw joy flamed through her, but Sharon was afraid to believe in it. She lifted her gaze and searched his face.

"Why are you giving me this?" There was a trace of hoarseness in her low-worded question.

His blue glance flicked at the ring then back to her. "You said that's what you wanted," he reminded her with a certain flatness. "I can't get you the marriage license until we get blood tests. And we'll have to work on the kids you wanted." She felt the pinning thrust of his gaze. "I believe those were the three things you said you wanted—in that order."

Her fingers gripped the small jewelry box, a tremor of pain running through her. That was what she had said she wanted, but foolishly, she had left out love. She was angry and hurt, somehow feeling insulted.

"Well?" Ridge prompted roughly.

The hurt blazed in her hazel eyes. "This has to be the

most unromantic proposal I've heard in my life!" she retorted, snapping the box shut and ramming it into his hand as she pushed her way by him.

But Ridge was no longer hampered by his injuries. His hand grabbed her arm before she had taken two strides away from him and spun her back around. Impatience and irritation flared in his eyes.

"What do you expect me to do?" he demanded. "Get down on one knee and beg for your hand in marriage?"

"That would be equally laughable!" She pulled her arm free of his hand with an angry yank and turned again.

"Sharon." There was an ache in the way he said her name that made Sharon pause. His hands moved onto the back of her shoulders, trembling slightly as they touched her. All her senses strained to search out this difference. "I want you to come home with me—back to Latigo."

A warmth was spreading from his hands as Ridge moved closer. Sharon was afraid that his physical influence would somehow undermine her control. She swung around to face him and pressed her back against the rough boards of the barn wall partition, flattening her hands against it, too, while she eyed him with wary hope.

"Why?" she asked tightly.

He moved in, bracing his hands against the wall on either side of her, effectively trapping her. The intensity of his gaze unnerved her as he leaned closer, tipping his head down, which made it seem nearer to her face. She felt enveloped by his closeness, a captive of his tough and rugged male vigor.

"It never bothered me to walk into an empty house before," he said. "But I can't get used to you not being there. Every time I walk into the kitchen, I expect to see you. In the mornings when I wake up, I listen for the sounds of you stirring somewhere in the house. You didn't take everything when you left," he accused. "Your ghost is there, haunting me with the way it was."

"You'll get over it in time," she suggested huskily.

"That's what I've been telling myself for the last two weeks," Ridge agreed. "That's what I said yesterday when I threw those dead flowers out. But I could still smell them in the room—the same way I could still smell you."

His head dipped closer as if inhaling her scent. Her lashes fluttered, nearly closing at the rush of exquisite pain his reply brought. But she had gone through too much heartache to be so easily swayed by him.

"God knows I tried not to think about you," he said huskily. "You'll never know how hard I tried."

"Then why did you?" Her voice was turning into a whisper, the look in his eye beginning to melt her weakening resistance.

"I was satisfied with my life the way it was before you came. I thought I'd be content with it again after you left. But you don't really miss something until it isn't there. There's a void where you were, and I want you to come back and fill it."

"Why?" She kept asking the same question in a different phrasing, trying to get him to say the answer she wanted to hear.

"Because I miss you." His mouth was almost against her cheek, his breath spilling warmly over her skin. Their hat brims were rubbing against each other, but it was the only contact, although she could almost feel the sensation of his mouth moving to form the words he spoke. "I want you to come home with me, but I know how stubborn you can be. I knew you wouldn't agree unless it was on your terms."

"That's why you bought the ring?" Sharon breathed the question, feeling so boneless that she needed the barn wall for support. Inside she was a quivering mass of emotion, barely held in check.

"Yes." He was in front of her mouth, hovering close to her lips. "Will you come with me now?"

"It won't work, Ridge." It cost her a lot to deny herself the kiss he was offering. "Not unless it's what you want, too."

"I want you. Hell, I need you," Ridge muttered thickly. "I'll take you any way I can have you. And if that means marrying you, then we'll get married."

"Are you sure it's what you want?" she insisted because his answer had been far from reassuring on that score.

"I'm damned sure *you* are what I want." His mouth closed onto her lips, burning into them with hunger.

Her hands went to his waist as he gathered her away from the wall and pulled her into his arms. He crushed her to his length, unable to get enough of her as he strained to absorb her whole. It was a spinning world, a carousel ride, and she had the brass ring within her reach.

The crushing band of his arms had lifted her onto her toes while the driving force of his kiss arched her backwards. Her hat was swept off her head and sailed to a pile of straw in the corner. Sharon reeled under the desperate urgency of his kiss, which revealed a hint of vulnerability that gave her renewed hope.

When he dragged his mouth from hers, a hand cupped the back of her head and pressed it to his shoulder as if he didn't want her to see what was written in his face. Sharon felt the shudder that went through him. There was a soaring lift of her heart in reaction.

"Ridge, it doesn't have to be all on my terms," she said, listening to the wild run of his heartbeat. "I do want children, but—what about you?"

A short laugh became mixed up in the roughness of his

breath. His hand relaxed its pressure on her head, letting her draw away from his shoulder to look up at him. A fiery satisfaction burned blue-bright in his eyes.

"Shall I be honest?" he asked with a quirk of one brow.

"Yes." Never in her life had she wanted him to be more honest about something than now.

"I keep remembering how you looked that day with that little boy riding on your hip while you tried to chase those loose horses back into the corral—and I remembered how it was in the kitchen that day . . . you baking cookies while little Tony and I ate them." His gaze moved randomly over her upturned face, memorizing its features. "I think about that and imagine what it would be like if that was our son and all the things I could show him. I might like it better if we had a girl, though." His callus-roughened hand stroked the tawny silk of her hair while he studied its color and texture. "A little girl with toffee-colored hair who would sit on my lap and tell me about the boys who teased her in school and pulled her braids."

"You mean that, don't you?" Sharon realized with breathless wonder.

"Yes." His gaze smoldered on her face once more. He drew back, their hips keeping contact while he ran his hand down the valley between her breasts and came to a stop on her flat stomach. "I'm looking forward to this little stomach of yours growing round with our child. I want it, whatever sex it turns out to be. But—" Ridge paused "—there's two things that have to come before it."

She was so enthralled with the discovery that he wanted a family—that he wanted *their* family—she didn't follow his meaning. "What two things?"

"First is the ring, if I haven't lost it." He felt in his side pocket where he'd shoved it for safekeeping when she'd thrust it into his hand and started to leave. This time, he took the diamond ring out of the box and slipped it on her trembling finger.

It seemed to wink at her, as if it knew a wonderful secret. Happiness was tumbling from her, crystal bright and clear like the cascading waters of a Colorado stream running swift and pure.

Her heart was in her eyes when she looked at him, then she threw her arms around his neck and kissed him with all the pent-up emotion of those long years. She clung to him fiercely, openly showing him how much she cared, until the frustration of holding it back for so long was spent.

"I love you so much it hurts," she declared and hugged him tightly.

"The way I am?" There was an earnestness in his demand.

Sharon set back on her heels and gazed at him, a smile beaming. "The way you are—no pedestal and no shining armor. I love the grumbler that snaps when he's irritable. I love the tough cowboy that doesn't want anyone to see he's hurt—"

"Except you. You wouldn't let me hide the pain from you," he remembered.

"I don't want a hero, Ridge," she assured him. "I just want the man I love. I don't want you to be anything but what you are. When you're hurt, I want to know it. And when you're happy, I want to be happy with you. That's all."

"Maybe if you had seen me like this a long time ago, I would have forgotten sooner that my best friend was your brother," he mused idely. "It's funny. Now I think of him as being your brother, instead of you being his sister. Sharon, what have you done to me?"

"I haven't done anything to you."

"Haven't you?" Ridge mocked. "You've put me through

a wringer and taken the starch out of me. I think Scott is convinced that bull did more than stomp me."

"Scott? Why?" Sharon couldn't recall her brother saying a word to her about Ridge's behavior. Of course, every time Ridge's name had been mentioned in her presence lately, she'd left the room.

"Because of the way I grilled him the other night about that Rivers fella. It was all I could talk about—all I could think about," he admitted. "Scott didn't improve the situation either with his constant chuckling."

"You said you weren't jealous." She eyed him, beginning to doubt his disclaimer.

"I wasn't," he denied, then lifted a shoulder in a reluctant shrug. "Maybe I was. I know I was mad clean through."

"Why?" Sharon questioned, studying him more closely with a speculating gleam in her look.

"Because you were wearing that dress," Ridge admitted, a trace of a vaguely chagrined smile showing at the corners of his mouth. "You had it on that day you brought me home from the hospital. I guess I thought of it as 'my' dress. I can't explain it. But when I saw you wearing it to go out on a date with another guy, I felt betrayed somehow."

"It was all I had to wear except jeans."

"You didn't have to go out with him," he reminded her grimly. "You were supposed to be taking care of me, not gallivanting all over the countryside."

"You seemed well enough to manage on your own for one evening," Sharon murmured.

"I was. As a matter of fact, I think subconsciously I took my time about getting better. I liked having you around, and it was one way to keep you there longer."

"When I told you I was leaving, you didn't put up any fuss," she remembered. "I had the feeling you were glad to see me go."

"That's because when you left, I thought things would go back on an even keel. And I also knew if you stayed, I'd end up making love to you—by fair means or foul," he sighed briefly. "I knew I'd have trouble looking you—or your family—in the eye if I had taken advantage of the situation. Mainly, though, I realized I couldn't do that to you when I heard you crying in your room. I didn't want to hurt you again."

"You heard me?" Sharon frowned. "But the radio—"

"I turned it on. You have your pride, too, and I thought you'd rather I didn't know you were crying." His finger touched her cheek as if seeking traces of those tears. "I didn't know it could hurt me so much to hear someone else's sobbing."

"I only cried because I loved you so much. I knew I had to leave and I didn't want to go," she explained.

"Now you can come back to stay."

"Are you sure you won't get tired of having me around all the time?" she asked, melting against him as his arms tightened in possession.

"You never get tired of having people around that you love," Ridge chided and didn't understand her choked cry of elation, because he'd finally said the word she'd been longing to hear, but he understood the outpouring of desire in her kiss.

LEFTOVER
LOVE

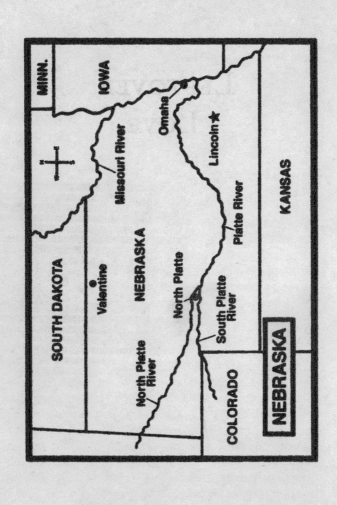

Chapter 1

"A leave of absence? Are you serious?" Clyde Walters leaned back in his squeaking office chair and stared at the woman standing in front of his desk. "Beth's on maternity leave. Ed's home, sick with the flu, and Frank is hobbling around here on a broken leg after that damned skiing trip to Vail. You can't honestly believe I'd consider such a request!"

"You know I wouldn't ask if it wasn't important," Layne MacDonald insisted firmly.

In the background there was a hum of activity—telephones ringing, voices talking, and the light tapping of fingers feeding stories into the computer terminals of the newspaper office. With the deadline approaching for the afternoon edition, there was always a wire-taut tension about the staff. But Clyde Walters had been a keen observer of people for too long. Layne MacDonald was tense—as edgy as a feline surrounded by icy water. And it had nothing to do with any newspaper deadline.

As an editor, it was part of Clyde Walters' job to know

the idiosyncrasies of his staff. A man in his position shouldn't have favorites, but Layne had occupied a special place ever since she joined the staff fresh out of college. In many ways she was a contradiction. She could be as tenacious and ruthless as a pit bull in interview situations, not caring how much her questions made someone squirm. And he'd seen her in tears over some simple human interest story. Some accused her of being heartless and cold-blooded, while others declared she was a sucker for a sob story.

Even her appearance contained contradictions. Her chestnut hair, a gleaming rust-brown color, was femininely long, but it was smoothed into a businesslike plait. Her olive-brown eyes could be piercing in their scrutiny, yet her lips were full and soft. The white blouse she was wearing had a high ruffled collar and ruffled cuffs, long sleeves puffed at the shoulders, and a wide jabot at the neck—a softly feminine creation. Yet her gray skirt was divided, full trouser pleats down the front, and the fabric was a menswear herringbone.

"What is it? A family emergency?" he challenged.

"You could call it that." She glossed over her answer and rushed to enlarge on her request. "I'll only need a few days—a week at the most."

"A week! It's out of the question." He sat forward and switched his attention to the pile of papers on his desk. "That 'crime in schools' piece still has to be finished for the Sunday edition, not to mention the interview with—"

"I have all the legwork done on the school feature," Layne cut in. "Beth can write it while she's home. And you can pull Janna Phelps off the Woman's Page to cover the rest of my assignments this week."

"You've got it all thought out, don't you?" His glance was marked with impatience. "Maybe you'd better tell me what it is that's so important," he suggested roughly and observed the barely contained stir of agitation.

Her gaze faltered briefly under his direct look, then met it. "I uncovered a lead on Martha Turner this weekend."

Clyde Walters took a deep breath at her answer and struggled to keep from sighing in irritation. In his opinion, Layne was dredging up a past that was better left undisturbed.

"What kind of a lead?" he asked.

"I found an obituary notice on August Turner, her father, dated twenty years ago. It made mention that he was survived by his daughter, Martha Turner, of Valentine, Nebraska."

"That's a real hot lead," Clyde scoffed. "Now you're following a trail that's only twenty years old. After all this time, I doubt if it would make any difference whether you waited a week or six months before following up on it. I wouldn't call it urgent."

"Maybe to you it isn't. But I finally know where she went—and that twenty years ago she was still single. She might still be living there now."

"And maybe she moved," he argued.

"I'm going to find out," Layne stated with a determined lift of her chin. "I haven't looked this long and this hard for her to wait now."

"Well, I can't spare you, so your personal business will have to wait." He was deliberately gruff with her.

"If you won't grant me a leave of absence, Clyde, I'll have to quit."

His head reared back at the blatant challenge in her voice. "I don't like being threatened, Layne."

"It isn't a threat, Clyde. I'll do it," she informed him without hesitation.

"You'd throw away your job to go off on some wild-goose

chase after a woman who's a total stranger to you?" His gaze narrowed sharply on her. "I gave you credit for having more sense than that."

Appealing to her logic was not the way to handle an issue that was purely emotional. Her actions were not dictated by reason. Finding Martha Turner was an obsession that bordered on compulsion. In her mind everything was clear-cut. If Clyde Walters didn't support her in this quest, then he opposed her. In which case, she had no qualms about defying him. It didn't have to make sense.

"I've followed so many dead ends that I'm not going to sit on the one good lead I've found," Layne declared. "If that means giving up this job, I'll do it. I'll go to work for some other newspaper. I am a damned good writer."

"But you're not indispensable." He bridled at her selfish attitude. "You could have some consideration for the mess you're leaving me in."

"You'll manage," she retorted. "As you said, I'm not indispensable." She swung sharply around and headed for the opening in the partition that gave some semblance of privacy to the office. The heels of her tall, black boots made decisive little thumps on the floor, but Layne stopped short of leaving. As she paused to look hesitantly over her shoulder at the balding man behind the desk, regret became mixed with her single-minded determination. "I'm sorry, Clyde. I don't blame you for not understanding. It's just that I've got to do this."

"What happens when you find her?" Clyde looked at her sadly. "What do you think you'll gain?"

"I don't know," Layne admitted with a small shrug. A quick smile came and went on her lips. "But it'll make a good story. You can have an exclusive on it."

"I damned well better have," he retorted. "You may be a good writer, but I'm not sure you're a good reporter. A reporter observes what happens. You're going out to make a story. I guess maybe I envy you a little." Then he sobered. " 'Course, I also think you're opening a can of worms."

"Maybe so," she conceded.

Mutual respect flowed silently between them. The harshness of their previous exchange was forgotten as Layne left his office. For all intents and purposes, she was out of a job even though she hadn't formally quit and Clyde hadn't accepted her abrupt resignation. But someone else would have to be hired temporarily in her stead. Still, Layne was confident that Clyde would make room for her on the staff when she came back.

It was almost better this way—with no time limit set, dictating when she had to return. She could pursue this lead as far as it took her, exhaust every possibility. She had some savings set aside, enough to carry her for a little while. For eight years she had been actively searching for a woman named Martha Turner—ever since she was eighteen. Perhaps it was time to make one all-out effort to locate her. It would depend on what she found in Valentine whether the road led to another dead end or put her onto a new trail.

Hardly any attention was paid to her as Layne stuffed the few personal items from her desk into her purse. In anticipation of the bitter Nebraska-cold February outside, she pulled a knitted cap over her head and buttoned her winter coat high around her neck.

"Where are you off to?" her co-worker, Sally McGraw, inquired with idle curiosity.

"I'm taking some time off to handle some personal matters," Layne explained as she pulled on a pair of heavy woolen mittens.

"Oh. Who's covering your desk for you?"

"You'll have to ask Clyde," she returned and waved as she headed for the elevators.

It was a blustery day with threatening gray skies. The wind whipped around the tall buildings of downtown Omaha, driving the wind-chill index to a subzero level. Her boots crunched on the salt-covered sidewalks as she hurried to the lot where she'd left her car parked. She kept her head down and her chin tucked into the thick wool of her collar to protect her face from the biting chill.

She made a mental note to check the weather forecast and the road conditions between Omaha and Valentine. She wasn't crazy about the idea of venturing into the Nebraska Sand Hills if a winter storm advisory had been issued.

On the way to her apartment Layne stopped to have her car serviced for the trip, and again at the branch post office to arrange to have her mail held until she returned. It was the middle of the afternoon before she finally arrived at her apartment. Packing for the trip wasn't an easy process, since she wasn't sure how long she'd be gone. It was difficult to find the happy medium between taking too much and taking too little.

There was one item Layne did not hesitate to pack, although it was the last thing to go in the large suitcase. She carefully folded the hand-made baby quilt, pink on one side and blue on the other, and laid it on top. Her fingers absently caressed its much-washed softness as she drew her hand away to close the case and lock it.

In the morning she'd put her cosmetics and toiletries in their small case, and she'd be all set. Not quite, Layne mentally qualified as she carried the suitcase into the small living room to set it by the door. There was still a phone call she wasn't looking forward to making.

The buzzer sounded in her apartment just as Layne passed the front door. She swung back to open it and admit her visitor. A twinge of guilt flashed across her expression when she saw her mother, but Layne was quick to smile.

"Hi, Mom. I was just going to call to see if you and Dad had any plans for dinner this evening." She injected a cheerful note into her voice.

"We thought you'd stop by the house yesterday evening when you came back from North Platte." The slim, blond-haired woman paused in the center of the room, her glance spying the suitcase by the door. "Haven't you unpacked yet? Honestly, Layne, I don't know how you manage on your own," she declared with a chiding laugh.

"I meant to stop but I got sidetracked," Layne fibbed and headed for the kitchen bar that jutted into the living room. "Shall I put on some coffee?"

"Not for me, dear." Her mother shrugged out of her fur-trimmed coat of emerald wool and draped it over the sofa back. "This suitcase . . . you surely didn't take it for just a weekend trip? Or are you going someplace again?"

Her mother was much too astute. Layne went through the motions of filling the coffeepot with water and ladling fresh grounds into the basket, even though she wasn't interested in drinking any coffee either. It gave her a reason to avoid direct eye contact with her mother. She didn't want to lie to her but she didn't want to hurt her either.

"As a matter of fact, I'm off to Valentine, Nebraska, in the morning. You know how Clyde is. With Valentine's Day coming up, he got this corny idea about doing a piece on the town of Valentine, then expected someone else to come up with an original slant." It was a flurry of words that came out, followed by a long silence from her mother.

"When you were a little girl," her mother said finally as she approached the counter bar where Layne stood, "I always knew when you were lying because you talked too fast. Your tongue just seemed to run away with itself. You're twenty-six years old and you still do it." There was something poignant about the look in those blue eyes when Layne briefly met them. "Am I supposed to believe that story? Or does your trip have something to do with what you found out in North Platte this weekend?"

"Don't ask, Mom." Layne's throat was tight as she fiddled with the cord to the coffeepot before finally plugging it into the wall socket. "I don't want to hurt you. I never wanted any of this to hurt you and Dad. I love you both. I'll always think of you as my parents."

"But still, you want to find her." The weariness of defeat was in her mother's reply.

"Yes." Layne's eyes were bright with unshed tears when she turned to the woman. There was no resemblance between the two, not in coloring or features. "You'll always be my mother even if some other woman gave birth to me. Finding Martha Turner won't change that. I wish you could understand why it's so important to me to find out who and what I am."

"I think *I* do." There was a faint stress on the personal pronoun.

"I know." Layne sighed dispiritedly. "It's Dad who doesn't understand."

"He's afraid of losing you. When you were a little baby, he used to have nightmares that she'd come back to take you from us even after we had legally adopted you. It's a fear that has always haunted him. He loves you."

"You don't have to explain it to me," Layne insisted with a wan smile. "Maybe it's better that you don't tell him I quit my job, though."

"You didn't," her mother protested.

"I think Clyde will take me back on when all this is through." The coffee was perking noisily beside her as Layne climbed onto a tall, wicker-backed stool at the counter. "I've decided to follow this lead wherever it takes me—concentrate all my attention on it instead of making haphazard forays to find some trace of her."

"What if you don't find her?"

There was a small shrug of one shoulder. "Then I'll know I made every attempt." She began to pull out the pins that held her chestnut hair in its smooth plait. It fell loose, cascading about her shoulders like russet-brown silk.

"Have you ever considered what you'll do *if* you find her?" Colleen MacDonald questioned with a worried look.

"A thousand times." Layne laughed without humor. "I've practiced what I'd say to her so many different times— and so many different ways—that it all sounds silly now. I just want to get to know her . . . find out what she likes and how she feels."

"Layne . . ." Her mother paused. "Have you ever considered the possibility that she might not want to see you? That you might represent a bad memory in her life that she won't want to recall?"

"Yes. It has occurred to me." Layne nodded and a sweep of hair fell across her cheek. She tucked it behind an ear and gave her mother a shrugging smile. "I'll just have to take that chance."

"But are you being fair to her?" her mother reasoned. "After all these years, for you to walk up to her and announce that you're her daughter—it's bound to be a shock, perhaps an unpleasant one."

"I've thought about that," Layne assured her.

"Have you? Have you really considered what her feelings might be? What about the home and family she probably has now? What if she hasn't told them about you? Don't you think that would make things awkward and uncomfortable?"

"Please. I've made up my mind and you aren't going to

talk me out of it." The questions seemed to hammer at her conviction until Layne felt she had to protest.

"I'm not trying to talk you out of it." There was something tenderly patient and indulgent behind that concerned smile. "I know it isn't your intention to hurt this woman. All I'm asking is that when you find her, think about it carefully before you say something that might do more harm than good. For your sake, I hope it turns out that she is as curious about you as you are about her."

With an early start the following morning, Layne made good time on the drive to Valentine. The roads and the weather cooperated. The only slick patches were the early morning frost on the bridges, and there wasn't a cloud in the diamond-blue sky. Her only complaint was the unrelenting glare of the sun off the ice-crusted snow covering the countryside, and a pair of dark glasses had alleviated that.

After the highway had left most of the towns behind to thread into the Sand Hills, she seemed lost in a glittering world of blue and white—the unrelieved blue of the sky and the white of the snow-coated hills. Except for the gray ribbon of the road to point the way, there were few signs of civilization for long stretches of miles.

Her few ventures into the Nebraska Sand Hills had not taken her into their northern end. When the first buildings of Valentine poked their roofs against the skyline, she released a breath of relief. Although it was lunchtime, she decided to check into a motel first and freshen up before looking for a place to eat. She pulled into a small, clean-looking motel.

Not bothering with a jacket, Layne stepped out into the brilliant sunlight, which offered little warmth to take the chill off the brittle cold. She hurried quickly inside the heated building, her breath making smoky little vapor clouds.

A bell rang overhead when she entered, but it was several minutes before an elderly man came shuffling out of a back room. Wispy tufts of white hair made futile attempts to refute the fact that he was nearly bald.

"What can I do for you, miss?" His glance was bright with curiosity.

"I'd like a room, please." Layne stopped rubbing her sweatered arms to pick up the pen and fill out the registration card he set on the counter.

"We don't get many guests, especially this time of year, unless the weather's bad and motorists find themselves stranded. Oh, I suppose we get our share of cattle buyers and grain dealers—and the salesmen," he observed talkatively. "Are you here on business or pleasure?"

"A bit of both." Layne hedged away from a direct answer.

"From Omaha, huh?" he said, looking at the address she'd listed on the card. "Did you just drive in?"

"Yes." She decided to be the one asking the questions. "Do you know a woman named Martha Turner? She'd be somewhere in her middle forties."

"Martha Turner," he repeated thoughtfully. "There's some Turners that live around here, but I can't say that I remember any of 'em were named Martha. You might want to check the telephone book."

"I will." Layne nodded, mentally reminding herself not to overlook the obvious.

"She a friend of yours?" He passed her a room key.

"In a way." She took the key and waved to him as she headed for the door. "Thanks."

Only half a dozen Turners were listed in the local telephone directory. Even though it was a long shot, Layne decided that lunch could wait until she'd made the calls from her room. The first five all disclaimed any knowledge of a woman named Martha. As the sixth phone was ringing, Layne was suddenly frozen by the thought—what if the sixth person said yes? What would she do? What would she say?

There was a moment of panic when a voice answered. Her heart was racing like a steam engine, almost choking off her breath. "I'm . . . I'm trying to locate a Miss Martha Turner," she finally managed to get out.

There was a small pause before the voice replied—a man's voice. "Well, you're a little late. The only Miss Martha Turner I knew died ten years ago."

"Died? But . . . that can't be." It had never occurred to Layne that her natural mother might have passed away in the intervening years. The possibility left her stunned.

"Well, you couldn't expect her to live forever," the grumpy voice retorted. "As it is, that old maid lived to be ninety-three."

"Nin—" With a faint laugh of relief, Layne realized they were talking about two different Martha Turners. "The woman I'm looking for is much younger than that."

"I'm afraid I don't know her."

"Thank you very much." There was a faint tremor in her hand when she hung up the phone.

For one sheer instant she had thought the search was over. The reality of it left her shaken. It took some mental sorting to come to grips with the problem. Over the last eight years that she had been looking for her natural mother, the expectation of finding her had not been there. Each time Layne searched, it had always been for a clue that might lead her somewhere else. Even on this trip, she had not come to Valentine to find her mother, although that had been her professed intent. She hadn't really believed she would succeed. At this rate she'd find only what she believed she would find—another dead end. This trip might only be the first leg of a longer one, but Layne was determined that it would not end as the others had.

When Layne ventured out of the motel, she was bundled in her winter parka. There was a small café across the street. She waited until the traffic had cleared, then darted across. The café was filled with a noon crowd. Layne managed to shoulder her way through the throng of cowboy hats and boots and sheepskin-lined or quilted jackets to an empty counter stool.

An aproned woman in her fifties slid a water glass in front of Layne, along with some napkin-wrapped silverware. "What'll you have?"

"Just a hamburger and some coffee." Layne took off her mittens and shoved them inside the large pockets of her coat. She unbuttoned her parka but didn't take it off, since she was sitting in a direct line with the front door. Each time it opened and closed, it sent a draft of frigid air over her.

All around her there was talk of cattle and the outlook for the spring calf crop, along with frequent mention of the weather. An empty cup was set in front of her and filled with coffee from a glass pot. A cowboy-clad man beside Layne pushed his cup forward for a refill, and the waitress obliged.

"It's busy," Layne observed.

"Always is at noon," the waitress said with a nod. "But the rush is over. The noise will start quieting down once their food's set in front of them."

Twenty minutes later the waitress's prediction proved accurate as the loud hum of voices was reduced. The clatter of silverware became dominant, punctuated by the odd, continuing conversation.

"See what I mean?" The waitress smiled faintly as she stopped to refill Layne's coffee cup.

"I do." Layne returned the smile. "Are you from here?" It was her nature to be inquisitive, so the purpose of her visit to Valentine only added importance to the answers.

"Born and raised right here in these Sand Hills," the older woman admitted with an air of pride.

"You wouldn't happen to know a woman named Martha Turner, would you? She moved here about twenty years ago, and we've lost touch with her since then." Even though it was a relatively small community, Layne knew it would be blind luck if she stumbled across someone who knew or had known her natural mother. Still, she had to ask.

"Twenty years ago?" An eyebrow was lifted in a skeptical arch. "That's a long time." But the waitress paused to think. "Martha, you say her name was." She shook her head, as if the name was meaningless. "Who was she married to?"

"She wasn't married."

"Well, if she was here very long, that all changed. A woman doesn't stay single in this town for long. I oughta know. I've been married twice." She paused again. "Now if that's the case, let's see . . . there is Martha Atherton, but she was a Pitts girl before she got married. And Martha Hoverson, but she's too young. Marge Blyson, but her given name is Margaret, not Martha. I just can't think of anybody," she said to Layne. "It could be she got married and moved away."

"Yes," Layne conceded.

"Hey, Susie! How about some more coffee and a piece of that chocolate pie?" a male customer called to the waitress from the opposite end of the counter.

"Be right there." To Layne she said, "Good luck. Hope you find out what happened to her."

"Thanks."

After she had finished her coffee, Layne collected her check and worked her way to the line of customers waiting at the cash register to pay for their meals. Although fairly tall herself at six inches over five feet, she felt engulfed in the sea of hats crowning the heads of the men standing in line. Mixed in with the smell of tobacco smoke were the spicy scents of after-shave lotions and the smell of animals clinging to the woolen coats.

As she was digging out the correct change for her meal check, she was roughly jostled. Layne staggered a couple of steps sideways before she could recover her balance and stop short of a table full of men. By some miracle, she hadn't dropped anything.

"Sorry, miss," a deep and gravelly male voice said. "I guess I didn't see you standing there."

When Layne looked at the person who had bumped into her, her glance encountered a mountain of a man. Her eyes were on a level with his wide chest, the impression of bulk intensified by a thick, fleece-lined jacket. He was a long, lean bear of a man, well over six feet tall by three or four inches.

"No harm done." As she offered the assurance, her gaze finally lifted its attention to his face.

With a build like that, she had expected to see some craggy male face that resembled the models in cigarette advertisements. A keen sense of shock registered for a split second. There was nothing remotely attractive about the blunt contours of his sun-leathered features. They were all lean and harsh, his eyes darkly hooded by brows that grew thickly together. A dark brown Stetson was pulled low on his forehead, the jutting brim shadowing most of his face. If he were a Hollywood actor, he would have been typecast as a bad guy or an outlaw, she thought.

The man seemed to sense her purely instinctive recoil from him. His lips came together in a severe line that only added to his uncomplimentary looks. Layne regretted that she hadn't hid her reaction better. Broad, callused fingers gripped the pointed brim of his hat in a courteously respectful gesture as he made a place in line for her in front of him.

"Thank you," she murmured as she stepped into the opening.

While she waited in line, she couldn't help stealing looks at him. There was something oddly fascinating about a man so completely unattractive. Layne recalled her initial impression that he was a bear of a man. On reassessment, she discovered it was an appropriate comparison, because the man did possess a kind of animal appeal. He was a lonely male brute, Layne decided, then wondered why she thought of him as being lonely.

If he noticed her covertly eyeing him from time to time, he showed no awareness of it. But he kept well clear of her, making sure there was plenty of space around her, so there was no more accidental contact. Layne was just as glad, since the last brushing had nearly sent her sprawling.

After she'd paid for her lunch, Layne left the café. The blast of cold air drove out all thoughts of the man as she hurriedly buttoned her parka and dug her mittens out of her pocket. Despite the bright sunlight, the temperature was frigid.

Chapter 2

One advantage of working as a reporter was that Layne was familiar with all the public information sources available to her. It was long, tedious work, checking through files and public lists. After a day and a half she had not come up with a single reference to a Martha Turner in any of the old records she'd checked.

It appeared more and more likely that the waitress had been right the other day when she'd suggested that Martha Turner might have gotten married and left the area. It was her only remaining alternative. On the off chance that the marriage might have taken place within Cherry County, Layne spent the morning of the third day going through the marriage license records from twenty years ago and forward.

It was always a nagging fear of hers that after going through so many documents and names, she might miss seeing the one she was looking for and skip over it without recognizing it. Yet when Layne finally did run across it, the name Martha Turner nearly leaped off the page at her.

Eighteen years ago she had married a man named John Gray, and both had listed rural Valentine, Nebraska, as their home. According to the ages given at the time, Martha was sixteen years her husband's junior.

Layne jotted the information onto a sheet of her notebook. With her purse, coat, and knitted cap bundled under her arm, she carried the record ledgers back to the registrar's counter. The male clerk didn't appear to be much more than thirty years old, yet the top of his hair was thinning to the point of premature baldness.

"Did you find what you were looking for, miss?" He smiled his curiosity as Layne dumped the record books on his counter.

"Yes, thank you." She caught the cuff of her ivory wool sweater with her fingers so the sleeve wouldn't ride up her arm when she shrugged into her jacket. "Would you happen to know a man named John Gray?"

A slight frown creased the clerk's forehead as he appeared to struggle with a recall of the name. "I think he was a rancher." He smiled again, almost apologetically. "I was born and raised in town, so I'm not too well acquainted with people in the rural areas. Everything's too spread out. But I seem to remember recording the death certificate of a man by that name when I first came to work here—that would be about four and a half years ago."

"What about his widow? Is she still around?" Layne asked.

"Sorry." He shook his head. "I wouldn't know about that."

"Thanks anyway." She headed out the door.

The next stop was the local newspaper office for a search of the obituary notices over the last five years. Layne knew she was close to the end of her search, and an underlying thread of excitement laced her nerves. The trail was no longer twenty years old; it was only five.

Not many people were interested in reading the back issues of the newspaper, so her request was regarded as unusual by the woman at the newspaper office. Layne was much too eager to get on with her search to pay much attention to the woman's obvious but silent curiosity.

The newspaper had neither the finances nor the facilities to microfilm past issues, which meant that Layne had to go through each old copy. A small area was cleared for her on one of the worktables and the first batch of previous issues, dated five years ago, was brought out. Layne went through that stack and two more before she found the notice of John Gray's death.

"'. . . survived by his widow, Mattie.' Mattie," Layne repeated. Although her legal name was Martha, it was obvious that she was commonly known as Mattie. Which might also explain why no one had recognized the name Martha Turner. They had probably known her as Mattie Gray for too many years.

Layne read on. No children of the marriage were listed in the notice. Evidently she had no half brothers or sisters. Home was listed as the Ox-Yoke Ranch, with Creed Dawson named as the surviving partner in the operation. In a happy daze, Layne noted the facts on her tablet sheet. Even if her natural mother no longer lived on this ranch, someone would know where she had moved to. It was just a matter of time before Layne finally saw her, after waiting and looking for so long.

She was sailing on a high that knew no limit as she crossed the newspaper office to the front counter. The whole wonder of it still had her dazed when Layne pushed open the half-gate that separated the reception and work areas of the office. She wanted to laugh out loud, but the smile that wreathed her full mouth spoke volumes about the inner happiness that radiated from her.

"I'm all finished," Layne said to the woman behind the counter, who had carted out the back issues of the paper.

With her head already in the clouds, that second's distraction to speak to the woman prevented Layne from seeing the man who entered the newspaper office in time to avoid him. She careened off his solid shape as though she had bounced off a wall. A huge pair of hands caught and steadied her. When she looked up, she was gazing into a dusky pair of hooded brown eyes and the outlaw-tough features of the man from the café. It was a face not easily forgotten.

"I guess it's my turn to apologize," she said with a laugh, partly from self-consciousness but mostly from the inner good spirits that just wouldn't be dampened. "I'm sorry. I wasn't looking where I was going."

"It's okay." There was a dismissive quality to the husky roughness of the man's reply as he immediately released her and stepped back.

Her flesh tingled where he had gripped her arms, the circulation returning. It was an indication of the power in those hands. She was in too good a mood to be put off by his standoffish attitude. A smile lay too easily on her lips for her to care whether his hard-favored features cracked with one.

"We seem to be making a habit of running into each other," she said. It was a lighthearted reference to the similar circumstances of their first meeting in the café, but the humor of it seemed to be lost on him.

"It isn't likely to happen again." There was a flatness to his steady gaze.

A little bit stung by such a cool rejection of her attempt at friendly banter, Layne redirected her attention to the woman behind the counter. This time she had to force her smile to broaden.

"Thanks again for your help," she said.

"Did you find what you were looking for?" Curiosity got the better of the woman as she tactfully tried to find out what it was Layne had been seeking. "You sure went through a bunch of old issues."

"I know." Since she had disrupted the woman's work, Layne felt she was entitled to some sort of explanation. She settled on a half-truth. "Sometimes you have to go through a lot of old records to fill in the missing gaps in the family tree."

"Oh, you're tracing your roots, are you?" Curiosity vanished with the dawn of understanding. "I have a friend that's into all that genealogy stuff."

"It's a challenge that only pays off if you're persistent." And she was closing in on her reward. The knowledge brought back the lightness of spirit. "Have a good day." Layne smiled at the woman as she turned to leave, and let the smile linger in place to drift over the tall hulk of a man, standing with statuelike patience to one side. There was, predictably, no response.

The whole incident was forgotten when she stepped outside and faced the distinct possibility that soon she might be seeing her natural mother—the one who had given her the red lights in her hair and the olive-green color of her eyes. Anticipation was a heady thing, building excitement to a fever-pitch intensity. Obeying a need for privacy, Layne went straight from the newspaper office to her motel room.

The minute she entered it, her glance fell on the telephone directory. Like a magnet, it drew her across the room. She flipped through the much-worn pages until she reached the 'G' section. Near the bottom of the column of names, she found "Gray, M." with a rural route address and the phone number. There weren't any other choices.

Her hand was shaking as she reached for the phone.

Now that the moment was at hand, she was scared. Layne took a deep, controlled breath and tried to calm her jittery nerves. She made two unsuccessful attempts to dial the number before she got the digits in the right order. The sound of the phone ringing on the other end of the line seemed to set off the fluttering of a thousand butterfly wings in her stomach.

There was a click in mid-ring and a woman's voice said, "Hello?"

"Hello." There was a frozen instant during which Layne clutched the phone tightly. "Who . . . who is this?" She was so nervous and scared that she was close to tears.

"Mattie Gray. Who is this?" There was an instant, responding demand.

A lightning thread of thoughts all weaved themselves together in a single second. There was no more need to look further for her natural mother. She'd found her. But she wanted no impersonal meeting with her over a telephone.

"Hello?" The woman's voice questioned the silence.

"I'm sorry," Layne blurted out. "I must have the wrong number." She quickly hung up the telephone.

For long minutes she could only stand and stare at the phone. In a way it was all so crazy. She had not anticipated that she would experience such an emotional reaction at hearing the mere voice of the woman who'd given birth to her. Maybe she hadn't outgrown all those childhood fantasies after all—the wonderings and the yearnings for this unknown person despite the constant outpouring of love from her adoptive parents. For so long she had convinced herself that this search was to satisfy her own curiosity regarding her personal family and background. It was vaguely startling to realize that her interest was not quite as detached from her feelings as she had once believed.

It took a few minutes for Layne to pull her scattered thoughts together. After that, deciding what to do next was a foregone conclusion. She left her motel room, retrieved the road map from the car, and went into the manager's office to get directions to the Ox-Yoke Ranch.

An hour later she slowed her car on the major highway and checked the map again. According to the motel manager, the turnoff to the ranch should be just ahead of her. She scanned the surrounding landscape, certain that she was in the middle of nowhere. She hadn't seen anything for miles except the snow-crusted hills, rolling and tumbling in an endless tangle of ridgelines.

Dirty gray snow flanked the sides of the cleared highway as Layne drove slower and slower so she wouldn't accidentally miss the turn. Suddenly there was a break in the fenceline; tall posts reared up to signal the location of a gate. A weathered signboard was nailed to one of the posts with the simple identification of "Ox-Yoke Ranch."

The gate was standing open, leaning crookedly away from the ranch lane. It wasn't much of a road, as Layne soon learned when she turned onto it. The snow hadn't been bladed off of it, but frequent vehicle traffic had left well-worn tracks in the dirty snow-slush. The frozen ruts put the springs of her car to the test.

The ranch lane curved into a labyrinth of ridges and valleys where windswept hills sloped into small pockets. She drove deeper and deeper into the rough country without finding a sign of habitation. She was almost convinced she had taken a wrong turn when she noticed a spider-thin curl of smoke rising into the blue horizon just ahead.

When she rounded the shoulder of a high ridge, the headquarters of the ranch was spread out before her. It was easy to pick out the main house from the collection of buildings. It sat among some winter-bare trees, its dark branches forming a cobweb. The ranch yard itself was criss-crossed with tracks and footpaths, in places exposing the frozen ground.

A long-haired dog came rushing out of one of the sheds to bark at Layne's car when she drove into the yard, but the dog seemed to be the only one around to observe her arrival, outside of the shaggy-coated horses in the corral and the herd of cattle wintering in the broad sweep of valley beyond the buildings.

Since she didn't see anyone around the barns or sheds, Layne drove straight to the house and stopped the car in front of it. Her mouth and throat felt dry, and her pulse was tripping over itself in an excited rush of apprehension. Her legs felt like rubber when she stepped from the car.

She took a moment to button her parka and muster her nerve before she approached the house. Her jeans were tucked inside the tops of her high-fashion cowboy boots, their tall heels designed more for style than serviceability. They definitely weren't made for easy walking over rough ground. Layne finally reached the shoveled sidewalk that led to the porch steps of the two-story white-frame house.

The large shepherd dog sidled around her, wagging its tail in an ecstatic fashion and grinning with almost silly delight. Layne rubbed its head and the dog panted with joy, its hot breath turning into great, vapory clouds. Its very friendliness seemed to give her courage, although it didn't follow her when she climbed the three steps onto the porch.

At the door she paused to mentally brace herself for this face-to-face meeting. She wanted her emotions securely tucked away where they couldn't be seen. Finally Layne rapped a mittened hand on the door and waited for several long seconds, but there was no sound of anyone stirring within. She knocked again, louder this time, and still there was only silence. She started to shift to one of the windows that fronted the porch to peer inside the house and see if anyone was about.

"What can I do for you?" The question came from behind her.

Layne turned with a startled little jump to face the front steps. The voice had the same no-nonsense inflection as that of the woman who had answered the phone. Layne stared at the woman before her.

An inch or so shorter than Layne, she was firmly packed into a pair of man's jeans. One of the pockets of her quilted winter jacket was torn at the side. A yellow and brown plaid wool scarf was bundled around her neck and a work-stained hat was jammed low on her head. Red wisps of henna-dyed hair poked out the under sides of the hat. The cold air had reddened her cheeks and nose, but it hadn't frozen out the collection of freckles that gave the woman a youthful look despite the crowtracks around her eyes and mouth.

"Was there something you wanted or are you lost?" A pair of faded green eyes studied Layne closely.

The question prodded Layne out of her tongue-tied silence, subtly making her conscious of her wide-eyed stare. "No . . . that is . . . you must be Mattie Gray." She finally managed to get a complete sentence out.

"I am. And you are . . . ?" Mattie waited expectantly for Layne to identify herself.

There was an earthy directness about the woman that instantly appealed to Layne. It took some of the tension out of her smile when she replied, "I'm Layne MacDonald."

Mattie's expression was mildly speculative, neither friendly nor unfriendly. The keen sweep of her glance took in Layne's fashionably heeled cowboy boots, her designer jeans, and the pale gray wool of her parka, an impractical color since it showed the smallest smudge of dirt.

"You're not from around here, so you must be from the city," she observed.

"Omaha," Layne admitted.

Inside there was a debate going on whether or not to disclose her identity. Her mother's cautionary words kept coming back to her. She didn't want this to be her one and only meeting with Mattie Gray. Yet that was the risk she was taking if she told Mattie who she was.

"A man in town gave me directions on how to get here to your ranch." She stalled, taking advantage of the precious extra minutes to observe little details about her natural mother—like the clear and direct way she looked at Layne, and the close way she listened as if weighing each word that was said.

"I see." There was a slow nod, as if she finally comprehended the reason behind Layne's visit. "You heard we were looking for a hired hand." With a wave of her hand, she staved off the protest Layne was about to make. "I know. You've always wanted to work on a ranch. And you thought, since I was a woman, you stood a chance of getting hired. What kind of experience have you had?"

This was not the turn Layne had expected the conversation to take. It caught her flatfooted and slightly baffled. "Actually, none—" she began.

"But you love animals and you can ride. Right?" Mattie Gray guessed with the confidence of someone who had heard the story many times before.

"Well, yes—"

"There's a lot more to it than that, honey. It's chapped skin, broken nails, and a cold that'll freeze your boots off. You're a lovely girl—beautiful in fact. This kind of work isn't for you."

This time it was Layne's turn to look her over, from the mud-and-manure-caked rubber of her high-buckled overshoes to her work-stained gloves. "You do it, don't you?" Layne countered in a kind of challenge.

"Sure," Mattie Gray conceded with a small shrug. "But that doesn't cut any ice. Sorry you came all this way for nothing. You might as well come in the house, have a cup of coffee, and warm yourself up before you make that long jaunt back home." She mounted the porch steps and walked past Layne to the front door.

"Thanks." Layne's mind was working, wheels turning with an idea that had so unexpectedly presented itself to her.

Rugs covered the hardwood floor just inside the front door. Mattie Gray stopped on one of them to unbuckle her muddy overshoes and leave them to sit on the newspapers. Although her own boots were clean, Layne was careful to wipe them thoroughly on one of the rugs before following Mattie, who padded silently across the floor in a pair of white woolen socks.

It was an old house, all toasty warm and comfortable. Layne took off her knitted cap and shook her chestnut hair free of her coat collar. She had time for no more than a glimpse at the traditionally styled furniture in the front room, but the predominant colors seemed to be shades of gold and tan—earth tones.

The kitchen was a cheerful yellow, with genuine solid oak cabinets and a wooden table covered with a plastic cloth in a multicolored daisy design. Mattie shrugged out of her overcoat and tossed it on the back of a chair. Underneath it, she wore a gray sweatshirt over a dark plaid shirt. Even though her figure had thickened at the waist and hips, she still had a nice, if rounded, shape to her.

"Do you take anything in your coffee?" She offered no apology for the dirty dishes in the sink as she took down two clean cups from an overhead cabinet.

"No thanks." Layne removed her parka and draped it over the back of a chair, then sat down. A pumpkin-colored cat was curled on an old, faded pillow lying on the kitchen floor by the stove. It gave Layne an unblinking, green-eyed stare, then stretched lazily and ambled over to her chair to aloofly nose her. "Hello to you too," Layne murmured, and the cat disdainfully swished its tail and walked away.

"Fred only tolerates people." Mattie set two steaming cups of black coffee on the table, then reached for a tissue from the decorative box on the counter. "Cold air always makes my nose run," she said, then proceeded to noisily blow it.

Layne marveled at the lack of pretension about this woman. She was completely natural, not trying to impress Layne one way or another. Layne either liked her the way she was or she didn't. It didn't seem to greatly concern Mattie one way or the other.

Layne preferred it this way. By blood, they were mother and daughter, but that wasn't a sufficient basis for a relationship. They could only learn to know each other as people. More than anything Layne wanted that to happen, without any awkwardness or tension between them because of the past.

"I guess you must get requests from a lot of inexperienced people like myself to come to work on your ranch. You had all the answers before I even asked the questions," Layne said, opening the conversation.

"Yes, and they're all young and eager to learn." Mattie's smile showed tolerance as she sat in one of the other chairs at the table.

"Have you lived here all your life?" Layne knew better, but it seemed a normal question.

"I'm from North Platte originally. I came here when I was only twenty-two. I answered an ad in the paper for a housekeeper and cook. At the time I couldn't tell a stallion from a mare, but I soon learned. I might have been hired as a housekeeper, but when they needed a body to hold a calf while they dehorned or vaccinated or whatever, guess who got called into duty?" There was a trace of wryness in her soft laugh. "Then, five years after coming here to keep house for him, I married John Gray. I became house-keeper, cook, wife, and cowboy. We had a good life and a good marriage—working side by side whether on the range or in the house. He taught me practically everything I know about the cattle business—unconsciously, often unwillingly." There was a small, reflective pause. "I lost him . . . five years ago in May."

"That's quite a story, starting out in the stereotypical female role of housekeeper and becoming a rancher."

"I do have a partner—a man—but Creed and I work well together." She sipped at her coffee, holding the cup in both hands. Her nails were trimmed short and her hands were work-roughened and chapped from the cold weather. "It's a case of mutual respect, I guess."

"I've met a lot of women who claim to be liberated, but you seem to be the real McCoy," Layne observed with silent admiration and interest. Usually it was just so much talk, especially among friends her own age.

"Strange you should say that." Mattie was oddly contem-plative, smiling vaguely while she swirled the hot coffee in her cup. "There was a time, especially when the feminists were creating such a furor, that I believed I always had been liberated. After all, I worked at my husband's side, doing a man's job, sharing a man's responsibilities. There were no special favors because I was a woman. But looking back, I can see that I was never treated quite the same as a man."

"What do you mean?" Layne frowned slightly, puzzled by this unexpected denial.

"As I said, I was completely green about ranch life. I wound up learning just about everything the hard way. And men are not the most patient creatures God ever created. John was forever yelling at me about something, whether I brought him a crescent wrench when he wanted a socket wrench, or I let *out* the cow he wanted *in* the pen. Most of the time I'd take just so much, then I'd go storming to the house." A quick, bright gleam entered her eyes. "There's the difference. It's very subtle, almost unnoticeable. You see, John would have expected a man to take getting chewed out, but I was a woman so it was perfectly reasonable for me to go to the house—where I belonged." She separated the last phrase from the sentence for emphasis. "I may have been out there—I may have been working with him—but a woman's place was still in the home. I've seen the same thing with ranchers' daughters. They may go with their daddy but the threat's always there, either implied or stated, that if they don't behave, they'll be sent back to the house. With a son, it's different. If he misbehaves, he'll be straightened out either with a belt or a good talking. There is a double standard out here, a subtle one, but it exists."

"I hadn't realized that," Layne mused, honestly fascinated by this revealing look at western life from a woman's point of view.

"Sorry. I didn't mean to go into a whole lecture on the subject. One thing about getting older, you can say what you think and people say you're opinionated instead of sassy." She smiled, and Layne caught the glint of humor in the washed-out green of her eyes. "Of course, the young people usually say you're boring."

"Not hardly," Layne said with a laugh. "But you have given me an idea. I never had a chance to mention that I've been writing features for the Omaha newspaper." She mentally crossed her fingers as she told a white lie. "I was interested in getting a job working for you on the ranch so I could write an article about the everyday, unglamorous side of ranching. I'd still like to do that, but I want to incorporate some of what you've just told me . . . sort of . . . the modern woman, how she fits in and where she doesn't." Layne paused, watching the flicker of interest in Mattie's expression. "I don't suppose you'd reconsider hiring me, would you?"

"Well, that's a novel reason for wanting the job," Mattie conceded.

The absence of an outright turndown gave Layne hope. "A couple or three months working here should give me enough material for a whole series of articles from winter work to spring calving. I could do one story just on you."

"That's very flattering, but . . ." Mattie was hedging away from an agreement.

"You can say what you think," Layne reminded her. "Besides, I can ride and I like animals. What better qualifications could you have for a job than that?"

"Do you know I think you're crazy?" Mattie leaned an elbow on the table and rested her chin in her hand while she studied Layne with amused interest. "If you take this job, you're going to have to work harder and longer than you've ever had to work before, in conditions that are often the worst you can imagine—and the pay is lousy."

"I'd do it for nothing." It was a heaven-sent opportunity to get to know this woman in all types of situations. She knew that Mattie was on the brink of agreeing to her wild plan and she held her breath.

"I must be crazy too." Mattie sighed and shook her head. She lifted her coffee cup in a saluting gesture. "Here's to the new hired hand." Triumphant laughter bubbled from Layne's throat as she clinked her coffee cup against Mattie's. "I just hope you don't regret it," Mattie added before sipping her coffee.

"Not a chance." Layne was beaming with confidence as she drank from her cup. "When do I start?"

"As soon as you want. The sooner the better as far as we're concerned," Mattie said. "Normally, the hired help sleep in the bunkhouse. Since the accommodations there aren't designed for coed living, you can have the spare bedroom upstairs."

"I don't know what to say." This additional windfall of luck robbed Layne of a reply.

"Don't worry. There's a method behind my madness. You can help with the cooking for the men." Mattie advised her that the arrangement was not without benefit on her side.

"All my things are at the motel in Valentine. I can drive there, pack, and be back here by early evening," Layne stated.

"I hope you have some clothes and boots with you that you won't mind getting dirty," Mattie said with a skeptical glance at the expensive pullover sweater and silk blouse Layne was presently wearing.

"What I don't have, I can buy in town." That was the least of her worries.

Chapter 3

The upstairs bedroom was small. The double bed took up half the floor space, leaving room for only a chest of drawers. A domed ceiling fixture provided the only light in the room. The clothes closet was small and narrow. By the time Layne had finished unpacking, she was glad for the drawer space. "Cozy" was the word that would have been used to describe the room in a newspaper advertisement. But Layne didn't mind the cramped quarters. It reminded her of those campus days when she'd lived in the college dorm, sharing quarters not much larger than this with another girl.

Besides, there was a homey feel to it, especially with the orange cat posed in a Sphinx-like attitude atop the quilted bed coverlet, surveying her activities with regal aloofness. The tomcat was his usual, unapproachable self, lashing his tail as if to silence her any time Layne attempted to address a comment to him.

"I'm not supposed to speak unless I'm spoken to, is that it?" Layne murmured to the proud feline.

The tail whipped the air again as the cat disinterestedly turned its head, bestowing its attention in another direction. Layne laughed softly to herself and finished arranging her underclothes in the top dresser drawer.

A new pair of very ordinary and low-heeled cowboy boots sat on the floor of the closet along with a new pair of flat snow boots, lined for extra warmth. Three new flannel shirts were hanging in the closet; two insulated sweatshirts were folded in the second drawer of the dresser. In addition, Layne had bought several pairs of heavy woolen socks and a pair of jeans to go along with the two pairs she already had.

This new venture had required almost a complete new wardrobe, but she was confident that she was prepared for anything. If she had tried to plan for all this to happen, it would never have gone this smoothly. When she thought about living in the same house with Mattie Gray, working with her and eating with her for the next couple months, it still didn't seem quite real.

Outside, the sunset, which had a habit of lingering for so long over these hills, had finally lost its yellow-rose color to the invading darkness. The single bedroom window now reflected the interior in its pane.

From downstairs, Layne heard the front door open and subsequently close. The muffled sound of a man's voice filtered through the walls and ductwork of the heat registers to drift into her room. Layne took only passing note of it as she finished her unpacking and stowed the suitcase on the upper shelf of the closet. Mattie had mentioned that her partner, Creed Dawson, would be by that evening, and Layne surmised that he had arrived.

There was a small thump as the big cat jumped off the bed and strolled to the opened door onto the second-floor hallway. With a haughty turn of its head, it paused to look back at Layne. "Miaow!" It was a wearily imperious call. Layne almost laughed at the sound of it and the marked patience in its tone.

"Am I supposed to come too?" she joked at the impression she was getting.

A small sound came from the cat's throat that seemed affirmative in nature. Then the large and sleek pumpkin-colored cat turned and walked with stately and unhurried grace into the hallway. Out of curiosity, Layne followed. The tomcat stopped once to look back, as if to make sure she was coming, then continued to the enclosed stairwell.

Totally bemused by the animal's almost human behavior, Layne was halfway down the stairs before she heard the rumble of anger in the man's voice, coming from the living room. She caught something that was oddly familiar about that voice, and it puzzled her.

"You did what?" The deep voice rolled into a clap of thunder.

Mattie responded to the demand in a calm, rational tone. "I hired a young woman this afternoon to—"

"A woman! What the hell was going through your mind, Mattie?" That husky edge to the man's voice sparked a flare of recognition. It sounded remarkably similar to the voice of that big brute of a man she'd seen in town. Layne faltered at the possibility, remembering how brusque he had been with her in those previous meetings. "You know the kind of work that has to be done around here! It's physically hard—"

"I know," Mattie cut in. "I've been doing it for twenty-some years myself. The girl is young and strong. I think she can handle it."

There was a lengthy pause. Layne had the impression that the man was attempting to control his anger. She hesitated, debating whether to descend the last two steps and let her presence be known before she was discovered eavesdropping.

"Which ranch is she from?" There was some semblance of calm in the question, however tautly held. "Is it one of Faber's girls? They're good on a horse." He seemed prepared to accept the situation, but Layne was aware that he didn't know all of it. Instinctively she shut her eyes in anticipation of an explosion when Mattie began her reply.

"No, it isn't. She's a newspaper reporter from Omaha. She wants to gather some firsthand information about working ranches so—"

"Of all the—" The rest was bitten off before it could be completed. Then he tried again to express himself in a voice that sounded like a contained growl. "It's bad enough that you saddled us with a woman, Mattie, but a green one on top of that! Whatever possessed you to do such a thing? We haven't got time to be leading her around by the hand, in the first place. And if she's used to sitting behind a desk, she won't be able to handle the kind of labor we'll need done."

"So? If the job's too tough for her, she'll quit in a couple of days. And if she can handle it, that's what we're looking for anyway. It doesn't seem to me there's any harm done on either side, except maybe a little aggravation in the beginning," Mattie reasoned.

"Hell, it's done," he muttered. "But this is one damned time I wish you would have talked to me before you hired this woman."

On that disgruntled but conciliatory note, it seemed a propitious time for Layne to enter. The high heels of her fawn-colored boots made hardly any sound on the carpet runner covering the stairs as she descended the last two steps to the ground floor.

When she rounded the opened stairwell door, her gaze

automatically sought the man in the room. It was the first time she'd seen him with that bulky winter jacket unbuttoned. His hands had pushed the front open to rest themselves on his hips. Even though he was a big, wide-shouldered man, there was a lean, flat look to his muscled chest and stomach. A pair of faded jeans hugged his narrow, male hips and lean, hard flanks. But the whipped-in toughness of his build was deceptive. He could still make two of her.

The dark brown Stetson was pulled low on his forehead, where he typically seemed to wear it so the brim constantly shadowed his blunt, flat features. At the moment his head was pulled back, his chin tipped slightly up. It gave the angle of light from the ceiling a better play over his face and highlighted his too dominant cheekbones. His attention was centered on Mattie, so far unaware of Layne's presence.

Layne took a step into the living room. "Hello."

Although he didn't turn his head, she saw the shift of his gaze to her. A visible jolt of recognition stiffened him. Then there was nothing. All expression was erased from that roughly unattractive male face.

"Come here, Layne." Mattie was oblivious to the byplay between them, treating the situation in her usual matter-of-fact way. "I want you to meet my partner, Creed Dawson." She waited until Layne had crossed the room before supplying her full name. "Layne MacDonald."

"It's you, is it?" It was a flat statement, condemning in its lack of expression.

"Yes, it is." Layne was rather glad she hadn't extended her hand. She had the feeling he would have ignored the friendly gesture. His attitude puzzled her, because she could think of nothing she'd done that could have led him to dislike her. And he was giving her every impression that he didn't care for her at all.

"You two have met?" Mattie's eyes were sharp with question.

"Not really. We just ran into each other a couple of times in town." The pun was completely unintentional. Layne had meant it only as a figure of speech, but his mouth tightened with some form of displeasure. It irritated her slightly the way he kept making her feel she was somehow in the wrong. She thrust her hand forward in a kind of challenge. "How do you do, Mr. Dawson."

There was the smallest hesitation before there was a slow swing of his hand off his hip. Large callused fingers folded briefly around her hand, exerting hardly any pressure, but the implication of powerful strength was still there.

"Miss MacDonald." The contact was broken almost as soon as it began, and she was subjected to the study of his dark gaze. "I thought you were in the area to trace your family roots. That's what you told Dorothy in the newspaper office."

It was a direct challenge of the story she had given Mattie. Somehow Layne knew she had to come up with some plausible explanation for the differing reasons for coming to the Sand Hills. Maybe Mattie would never suspect in a thousand years that Layne was her daughter, but Layne didn't want anything to turn her thoughts in that direction.

"That isn't quite true. You see, when my aunt found out I was coming here, she asked me to check the records to see if I could fill in some of the missing details about her husband's family." She was talking fast, a sure sign that she was lying. "She's having an elaborate family tree made for him as a birthday present, and there were some dates she didn't have. So I promised her I'd look to see if I could find them. It didn't take much of my time to go through the old records and files."

Her explanation seemed to satisfy Mattie, but Mattie had no reason not to believe her. Layne had the uneasy feeling that Creed Dawson was reserving judgment. Or maybe her own sense of guilt was prompting her to read things into his reaction that didn't exist. It was entirely possible that he disapproved of her being there simply because she was inexperienced at the job, and a woman. She was probably taking it all too personally.

"I see," he murmured, then seemed to rouse himself like a great bear, shrugging aside an item that had lost his interest. "Your day starts at six in the morning," he informed Layne, then briefly swung his gaze to the older woman. "See you tomorrow, Mattie."

For a man of his size, he moved with cat-footed ease to the front door and walked out into the night. There were a lot of questions Layne would have liked to ask about Creed Dawson, but it didn't seem wise to question Mattie about her partner's seemingly odd behavior.

"Are you all settled in?" Mattie inquired with mild interest.

"Yes, I am," she confirmed.

"You might want to have an early night tonight," Mattie advised. "The day starts at six, but that means breakfast at five thirty."

Which was a good deal earlier than Layne was used to getting up in the morning. "You get a head start on the sun, don't you?"

"In the summer the day begins earlier than that. There's a lot of work to be done. I have a stack of paperwork waiting for me, so I'll see you in the morning." Mattie left her to walk to the door of the side parlor, which had been turned into an office.

Deprived of the chance to become better acquainted with Mattie that evening, Layne eventually returned to her room and took Mattie's advice about getting an early night.

The alarm clock went off at four thirty the next morning. The harsh, clanging noise drove Layne out of the bed and into the darkness of the unfamiliar room. She groped for the wall switch. The overhead light nearly blinded her with its sudden glare, but she spied the clock on the dresser and finally silenced its dreadful clatter. Half asleep, she scooped up her toothbrush and cosmetic case and padded down the hallway to the bathroom. She absently noticed that there were lights on downstairs and realized she wasn't the first one up.

By the time she had dressed in her new workclothes and boots, the aroma of frying bacon was permeating the house. When she walked into the kitchen, Layne noticed that the table was set for five. Mattie was at the stove, deftly turning the strips of thick bacon sizzling on the grill. She spared one glance over her shoulder at the sound of Layne's approach.

"Good morning," Layne said, although she wasn't sure she was fully awake yet.

"Morning. Check the oven and see if those biscuits are done," Mattie instructed.

Bending, Layne opened the oven door to peer inside. A long sheetpan of biscuits sat on the middle rack of the hot oven. The dough had risen, but the tops hadn't started to brown.

"Not quite." She carefully closed the door.

"There's jam and honey in the refrigerator." With the bacon turned, Mattie started breaking eggs into a mixing bowl with pancake meal. As Layne walked past her to the refrigerator, Mattie's glance made a skimming sweep of Layne. "I'd forgotten what it's like to be young." Her mouth quirked briefly in a wry line. Layne gave her a curious look, wondering what had prompted that remark. "There you are with lipstick and mascara, and most of the time I don't do more than run a brush through my hair. Of course, it would take a ton of makeup to cover all these freckles." She sent another glance at Layne. "You're lucky you don't have any, even though you've got that hint of red in your hair."

"I like your freckles. They make you look young." With her hands full of jars of preserves and honey, Layne pushed the refrigerator door shut with her hip.

"That's nice to hear. Inside you always feel young, but it's the outside that gives you away," Mattie declared while she vigorously beat the pancake batter. "In another couple of years I'll be fifty. Life seems to be over before it's begun."

"Do you have any children?" The atmosphere in the kitchen seemed to lend itself to personal questions.

"No." Mattie set the bowl on the counter and began to scoop up the strips of crisp bacon. "John couldn't have any."

"Were you ever sorry?" Layne pretended a mild interest while she studied the woman closely. It didn't surprise her that Mattie had made no mention of the child she'd given up.

"Sorry? I don't know." She shrugged vaguely. "Does it ever do any good to be sorry about something in the past? It's over and there's nothing you can do to change it, so why make yourself miserable with regret and forget all the good things that did come your way?"

"I guess that's true." But Layne experienced a twinge of disappointment. She realized she was clinging to a girlhood wish that her natural mother regretted giving her up for adoption. It had nothing to do with what was wise or practical. It was strictly emotional.

There was the clump of boots on the steps outside the

back door just as Mattie began to ladle the pancake batter onto the greased grill. "I timed that right."

Two men filed into the kitchen ahead of Creed Dawson. The first was an older, heavyset man in his fifties with iron-gray hair. The weight of his big torso seemed to be carried on the big trophy buckle of his belt. Coats and hats were peeled off and hung on wall pegs by the door.

"Mornings" chorused around the kitchen in an exchange of greetings. The second man self-consciously combed a hand through his hair, flattened by his hat, and grinned widely at Layne. In his middle twenties, he was slim and sandy-haired. Layne smiled back as she stopped at the oven to remove the biscuits, baked to a toasty golden brown.

Creed pulled out a chair at the table. Layne had never seen him when he was not wearing his hat. The springing thickness of his hair was the rich brown color of roasted coffee. Its wayward order seemed to invite a hand to smooth it into place. Layne smiled to herself at such a fanciful idea and piled the hot biscuits onto a plate.

When she approached the table, Creed made very brief introductions. "Stoney Bates," he said, first indicating the older man to her. "Hoyt Weber, Layne MacDonald."

The older man, Stoney Bates, merely nodded to her as he scooted his chair up to the table, but the young cowboy was not the silent type. "After looking at these two characters every day," he said with a gesture at Creed and Stoney, "your face is going to be a welcome addition."

"Thanks." She laughed at the compliment.

There had been a moment when she wondered what the reaction of these two co-workers would be. They could easily have shared Creed's opposition to her sex. But it appeared that Hoyt Weber, at least, had no such hang-up about working with a woman.

Hands were already reaching for the biscuits as Layne moved away to fetch the coffeepot and fill the cups around the table. "Where's the food, Mattie?" It was the bold and talkative Hoyt who made the good-natured demand.

"Coming right up." It was a literal statement as Mattie crossed to the table carrying a platter of bacon and sunny-side-up eggs, and a plate with a tall stack of pancakes. "More pancakes are on the way." She motioned to Layne. "Sit down and eat."

The only unoccupied chair, besides the one at the head of the table, was next to Creed. Layne hesitated only a second and then sat down. Without ceremony, the food was passed around the table. Layne took considerably smaller portions than the three men, limiting her breakfast to one pancake and a rasher of bacon.

"Is that all you're going to have?" Hoyt Weber said as he critically eyed her plate.

"I'm not used to eating much in the morning." There was already more on her plate than she usually ate, but Layne also knew it was a long time until lunch. She half expected someone to remind her of that, but no one said anything or encouraged her to take more.

"Where are you from?" Hoyt asked.

"Omaha."

"Oh, yeah?" His interest heightened. "I have a sister that lives in Omaha, out by the racetrack. I usually go see her a couple of times a year." He started asking her about places he knew. Soon developed into a whole discussion of its own, a friendly getting-acquainted exchange.

Although Creed didn't take any part in their conversation, neither was he silent. Layne was conscious of the vibrations of his deep, gravelly voice beside her as he replied to comments made by Stoney that ranged from the weather to the condition of the cattle.

Whatever his personal prejudices were against females working on the ranch, it was obvious they didn't extend to the sexist belief that her presence would be disruptive to his men, since he made no attempt to discourage, either by action or word, the budding friendship between Hoyt and herself. It made Layne feel a little easier because it indicated that his objections were likely based on her ability to do the job.

It was going to be hard work, but she was confident she could do it, given a chance. And she liked the idea of walking in Mattie's shoes, so to speak, finding out about her way of life so they could meet on some common ground.

After they finished eating, a last cup of coffee was poured and cigarettes were lighted. As soon as those were gone, chairs started getting shoved away from the table. Layne stood up to help Mattie stack the breakfast dishes and carry them to the sink.

"I'll see to this," she was told by the woman. "You go to the barn with the others."

"Okay." And Layne went to fetch her coat, scarf, hat, and mittens.

When she returned, Creed was waiting for her by the door, already hatted and coated with a gloved hand resting on the doorknob. She hurriedly pulled her knitted cap down over her ears as she walked quickly to the door. There was no indication that he was either impatient or irritated with her. Indifference was closer to the mark as he followed her out of the house.

In the predawn hour the sky was a peculiar charcoal color, tinged with the merest hint of rose. It was all very still and very quiet as the tall yard light shone down on a frozen world. As awkward and cumbersome as the layers of clothes were, Layne was glad of the thick protection of flannel shirt, sweatshirt, and coat.

The crunch of Creed's footsteps on the icy ground was a companionable sound in the lonely silence. From somewhere ahead of them, she could hear Hoyt's voice murmuring something to Stoney. The still quiet of the morning seemed to encourage hushed tones.

"I don't suppose you've ever milked a cow before." The low-voiced comment from Creed came as they reached the barn and he stepped ahead to push open the large, wooden sliding door.

"No, but I have a pretty good idea of how it's done," she said to indicate that she was game to try.

His measuring glance briefly swept over her. "All right," he agreed and led the way into the barn.

Bare, dust-coated light bulbs were spaced at intervals to light the barn's interior. There was the vague smell of hay and animal odors, most of it muted by the cold temperatures. A Holstein cow was standing in one of the stanchions, observing their approach along the wide corridor. The animal was contentedly munching the grain that had been put out for it, a dusting of it covering its broad nose.

Layne had thought Creed Dawson would take a few minutes to show her how to hand-milk the cow. Instead he merely supplied her with a metal milk pail, a three-legged stool, and a wet cloth. His instructions were simple.

"Wipe down her bag before you milk her."

With that, she was left on her own. Briefly stunned, Layne watched those high, broad shoulders as Creed walked away. Finally she let out a quick breath and began to pull off her mittens to tackle the chore.

"I guess it's just you and me," she murmured to the cow.

The black-and-white-spotted animal turned its head to look at her with its big, luminous brown eyes and lowed with seeming encouragement. Layne couldn't help smiling as she crouched down to wash the cow's milk-swollen udder.

Once she had the milk pail and stool in place, she bent to the task. It was not the most comfortable position, all hunched over with her head turned at an awkward angle in an effort to see what she was doing. Her first few squeezing tugs of the cow's tits were rewarded with small squirts of milk. Soon she wasn't even getting that.

No one had mentioned the hazards involved in milking a cow. Layne quickly discovered that the swishing tail was almost a lethal weapon after she was slapped in the face by it a couple of times. Cows kicked, which was a possibility that also hadn't occurred to her. Twice the cow kicked the pail over, spilling the precious little milk she had managed to extract. All the while the beast chewed its grain with seeming contentment.

Struggling with her frustration and ineptitude, Layne carried on. But her hands were getting cold and her muscles were cramping. She didn't know how long she'd been at this, but it seemed like forever. Outside the sun was rising, and there were sounds of the ranch stirring with activity, the drum of hoofs and horses whinnying in the corral.

Hinges squeaked with the opening of a side barn door. Layne released a grimly drawn breath when she heard the shuffle of boots along the concrete corridor. But it was Hoyt Weber instead of Creed who appeared.

"How are you and Flo doin'?" he inquired with a jaunty smile.

Layne straightened, grimacing slightly at the stiffness in her back. " 'Flo' is not 'flowing,' " she admitted.

"Let me show you how it's done," Hoyt volunteered.

"Gladly." She let him switch places with her. Almost immediately, there was a steady stream of milk squirting from alternate tits into the pail. "What's the trick?"

"No trick. Just a lot of practice," he countered with a

short laugh. "There's nothing to it once you get a rhythm going."

In a matter of minutes the small pail was half full of milk. Hoyt handed it to her, then released the cow from the stanchion and slapped its bony hip as he turned it outside.

"Thanks," she said. "I would have still been here at lunchtime."

"You'll get the hang of it," Hoyt assured her.

Together they walked to the big door. The loud put-putting of a tractor shattered the peace of the morning. Layne had her first good daytime look at the layout of the ranch yard. Creed was backing a tractor up to a flatbed hayrack over by the machine shed. The long, low building, near the grove of trees where the house sat, was the bunkhouse and cook shack. In conjunction with the barn, there were pens, corrals, and loading chutes. Stoney came walking out of one of the corrals leading two haltered horses.

"Gotta go," Hoyt said. "See you later." He split away from her to join up with the older cowboy.

The noisy tractor motor idled and died. Layne's glance absently wandered in that direction as Creed swung down to the ground. "All finished?" He lifted his voice to call the question to her, puffs of steam billowing from his mouth.

"Yes!" she answered. "With some help from Hoyt."

There was a nod, no more than that, acknowledging that she hadn't accomplished the chore alone. "Take the milk up to the house, then come back here so we can take some hay out to the cattle."

There were no criticisms, no snide comments that he'd known she wouldn't be able to milk the cow by herself. As long as the job was done, it didn't appear to matter to him how she had accomplished it. Creed Dawson was definitely a strange man. She couldn't figure him out. He wasn't following any predictable pattern.

When Layne entered the kitchen, Mattie was putting away the last of the breakfast dishes. She showed Layne where the milk strainer and filters were kept while Layne related her frustrated attempts to milk the cow. After Layne had strained the milk into a pitcher, she rinsed out the pail and carried it back to the barn to meet Creed.

By the end of the day Layne was ready to swear that the hay bales weighed a hundred pounds, at least. Ice had to be broken in the stock tank. They'd ridden for miles in the cold, looking for a dozen head of cattle that had strayed. There wasn't a bone or a muscle in her body that didn't ache, and she'd wound up with blisters from the new boots.

Within an hour after the supper dishes were done, she was in bed, utterly exhausted. She slept straight through until the alarm clock went off at five the next morning. As she hauled her sore and aching body out of bed, she wondered for a moment if all this was worth it. At least she understood now why Creed had doubted that she had the strength or stamina to do the work. It was a question she asked herself when Creed mentioned at the breakfast table that the day's agenda included cleaning out the barn.

Chapter 4

At breakfast Hoyt had assured her that winter was the best time to clean out barns. "When it's hot, the smell gets so strong it'll knock you over." Maybe that was so, but he wasn't the one doing it.

Each time she tried to raise the pitchfork higher than her chest, the muscles in her arms started to quiver uncontrollably. She just couldn't find that last ounce of strength to heave the forkful of manure-packed straw into the spreader parked just outside the door.

Since she was unable to lift it over the side of the wagon, Layne tried to toss it in. But something went wrong with her coordination. She swung the pitchfork too high. When the manure came off the tines, it went straight back and landed on her face and head. She barely muffled the shriek of dismay when it hit her.

For an instant she stood motionless while the biggest clods tumbled off of her. Finally she dropped the pitchfork and gingerly began to brush the smaller particles off her face. With the thick mittens covering her hands, it was like wiping her skin with a big powder puff.

When she bent her head to see how much was still on her clothes, a clump fell off her hat. It was all suddenly so ridiculous that Layne started to laugh. She heard the heavy sound of running feet outside, but it didn't make any real impression on her as she continued to brush the wisps of straw and manure off her clothing while she silently shook with laughter.

"What happened?"

Somehow Creed Dawson had managed to squeeze his big frame between the wagon and the barn to reach the open doorway. His tall bulk loomed in front of her, blocking out the sunlight and momentarily startling her.

"Nothing. I—" Layne still wasn't sure how it happened. "I went to throw some manure into the wagon but I threw it on myself instead."

"That's why you screamed?" he asked with an accusing rasp in his low voice.

"You'd scream, too, if you had a forkful of manure land on your head," she retorted and brushed at her sleeves.

"Next time try to save the yelling for emergencies." He shifted to one side, allowing the outside light to fall on her. "Hold still. You have some in your hair."

Obediently she stood motionless while his gloved fingers brushed at her head. She was eye-level with the front of his thickly padded jacket with its fleece lining and row of leather-covered buttons. There was a vague surprise at how light and gentle his touch was.

Almost absently she lifted her gaze to his face. It was such a highly unusual face, browned by the sun and the wind and creased with strong male lines. There was something oddly compelling about features that were so unattractive. The blunt ridges of his cheekbones were too prominent and his cheeks were too lean; his nose was crooked and his brows were too thick. About the only thing she found to like was his mouth.

Layne idly wondered at his age. Thirty-six? Thirty-seven? It was difficult to tell with a face like his. She couldn't imagine a younger version of it. It would still be all hard, uncompromising lines, only now carved with experience.

A distant part of her was aware of him carefully picking out small pieces of manure that had become lodged between her scarf and the sides of her neck. A hooked finger was very deftly scooping them out.

Her attention shifted to the impenetrable dusty brown color of his eyes. They always seemed shuttered, closing in his thoughts. When their focus shifted to her eyes, Layne barely noticed. She wasn't even conscious of how rudely she was staring at him, fascinated by his irregular looks. There was a sudden smoldering of anger in his eyes, dark and thundering. Layne glimpsed it for a moment, then he was looking elsewhere and it was gone.

"I think you'll survive," he announced gruffly and reached down to pick up her pitchfork. "Here. You'd better get back to work."

"Thanks. . . ." Her voice trailed off onto a flat note as he abruptly turned away without waiting for any expression of gratitude, polite or otherwise. Layne sighed, wondering what she had done to offend him this time, then shook her head. She didn't know what sort of hang-up he had, but she wasn't going to waste precious time wondering about it.

After supper that evening Layne was quickly indoctrinated into the practice of calling the evening meal "supper." In the city it might be dinner, but out here it was supper. After supper that evening she took a long, hot bath to soak some of the soreness out of her muscles.

With the sash to her long terrycloth robe securely belted, she started downstairs. Her chestnut hair was piled atop her head in a loose knot. The bath had left her feeling almost human again. She was halfway down the steps when Mattie opened the stairwell door at the bottom.

"Feel better?" Mattie's smiling glance seemed to indicate that Layne looked it.

"A thousand percent," Layne said.

"I think I'll take a turn in there and see if a bath can't rejuvenate some life in this body," Mattie declared wryly.

As they passed on the stairs, Layne paused to ask, "Is it all right if I use your phone to make a collect call? I want to let my parents know where I am." She had planned to write them a letter but it seemed wiser to call and allay any fears they might have about the situation.

"Go ahead. There's a phone in the office."

When Layne opened the door to the parlor-study and switched on the light, the orange cat marched into the room after her, in a bit of a royal huff. It seemed to doubt that she had permission to be in there and followed when she crossed to the small walnut desk. When she picked up the telephone, the cat hopped onto the desk top and laid down, wrapping its long tail across its feet like a red-gold cloak.

Its slow-blinking eyes watched Layne as she put the call to her parents through the operator. Her mother answered the phone, and Layne waited until the reversed charges were accepted and the operator put her through.

"Hi, Mom," she said and settled into an old-fashioned wooden and leather-cushioned office chair behind the desk.

"Hello, Layne. I wondered when we were going to hear from you. How are you?"

"I'm fine. I've been meaning to write, but with one

thing and another, I've been so busy I haven't had time."

"How's it going? Were you able to find out anything new?" The questions sounded forced.

"Better than that." Layne wrapped her fingers around the coiling telephone cord, glancing briefly at the orange cat when it hopped off the desk. "I've found her."

"You have?" There was a certain vagueness in the reply. "Have you seen her? Talked to her?"

"Yes. I don't know how to describe her. She's so natural and down to earth that I . . ." Layne paused, sensing the hurt silence on the other end of the line. She immediately regretted letting so much of her enthusiasm and excitement creep through. "Mom . . . I love you and Dad. Please don't let any of this upset you."

"We won't, darling," came the quick assurance, but there was an underlying thread of nervousness and anxiety in her mother's voice. "What did she say when she found out about you? Was she happy to see you or—"

"I haven't told her," Layne admitted. "I thought it would be better to wait until later . . . after I've had a chance to see how things work out. By the way, if you need to reach me, I'm staying at the Ox-Yoke Ranch. You'd better write down the number." She read it off to her mother.

"Is this her home?" her mother asked.

"Yes. I'm working here as a hired hand. Can you imagine that?" Layne joked.

Conversation was awkward. Layne almost wished she had written instead of calling, but she knew her parents needed to hear that she still cared about them as much as before. She kept the conversation brief by promising to write a long letter, telling her mother all about everything. After she put the telephone receiver in its cradle, she stared at it for a long moment without moving.

"What didn't you tell her?" The sound of Creed's voice startled her.

Her gaze jerked to the doorway in dismay. His long shape was propped against the frame, his stance giving every indication that he'd been there for some time. The big tomcat was rubbing against his legs, a smugly smiling expression on its face when it opened its green eyes to look at Layne.

Her heart was hammering in her throat as she tried to think of some way to get out of this. She decided to bluff her innocence and uncrossed her legs to stand up.

"I'm sorry, did you want to use the phone? I had to call my parents so they wouldn't start worrying about me," she stated, sounding very nonchalant as she moved unhurriedly across the room to him, although her destination was actually the doorway he was blocking. "And I reversed the charges, so the call shouldn't appear on your billing."

With a negligent push of his shoulder, Creed straightened to his full height. "You still haven't said what it is that you haven't told Mattie." His hat was pushed to the back of his head and his dark eyes were narrowed with suspicion.

"Did I say Mattie?" Layne stalled for time as she tried to recall. She was almost sure she hadn't mentioned Mattie's name in the conversation. "You must have misunderstood something. It's easy to do when you only hear one side of a conversation. It's hard to be sure what someone's talking about."

"You said you hadn't told her yet, and wanted to wait until later." He continued to eye her skeptically, but Layne was satisfied with a little doubt.

"I was probably referring to my girlfriend," she lied. "I didn't tell her how long I planned to be gone, since I wasn't sure myself." There was an impulse to challenge him for listening in on a private conversation, but instinct told her that that was the wrong tactic. A shift in topics seemed wisest at this point, so Layne glanced down at the pumpkin-colored tomcat, curling against Creed's leg. "Fred certainly likes you."

Creed acknowledged the cat's presence with a brief glance, then moved leisurely out of the doorway. "He's a cat."

The explanation puzzled Layne. Creed was no longer blocking her path, but she didn't take advantage of his shift into the room. She half turned to study him with a curious tilt of her head.

"What does that have to do with it?" she asked.

"A cat has a different set of standards for judging a person." Which was not a much more informative response than the first. Creed paused in the middle of the room and met her look. "Your story checks out, by the way."

"My story?" Layne didn't follow his meaning.

"I called the newspaper in Omaha yesterday and they confirmed that you worked for them and that you had taken an extended leave of absence."

Bless Clyde, she thought, and said aloud, "It was sensible of you to verify it. I guess I never got around to supplying Mattie with any references. They didn't seem necessary at the time."

"Your decision to leave the paper was rather sudden, wasn't it?" It was a rhetorical question, indicating that Clyde might have let something slip. "I suppose a love affair turned sour and you wanted to get away to mend your broken heart."

The apprehension that had been building shivered away in a faint sigh of relief. "My heart is unbroken. It's been cracked a few times but it's still intact. I promise you I'm not running away from any affair." She laughed briefly. "No lover is likely to pursue me all the way here, if that's what you're thinking."

"No. I was just trying to find a reason for your sudden decision to come out here. A broken romance seemed the logical one." There was still something vaguely speculative in the way he looked at her.

"I came because it was something I had always wanted to do, and I couldn't think of one reason why I wasn't doing it," Layne stated confidently because there was a degree of truth in it. This was the culmination of eight long years of searching.

"I can see why Mattie hired you. You're a lot like her." He couldn't know the warm pleasure his comment gave her. "She can be as bold as brass sometimes—and rash in her decisions too." There was an implied criticism in the comparison that stiffened Layne just a little.

Still she managed to smile. "My daddy always told me that the people who never make mistakes are the ones who never do anything."

"Your daddy is a wise man," Creed agreed easily.

The conversation was threatening to turn into one of those battles for the last word. Layne turned again to the door. "Mattie's upstairs. Shall I tell her you're here?"

"No need. I just came by to pick up some papers she was going to leave on the desk for me."

As he walked over to the desk Layne hesitated another second, then left the room. The minute his questions were answered, Creed appeared to have lost interest in the conversation. It was becoming obvious to her that he was not one for idle talk.

That fact became more and more evident to her as the days went by. The work on the ranch didn't get any easier in that first week, but her body began to become conditioned to it, most of the soreness easing to a few minor aches.

Yet in all the working hours, some of which Layne spent in his company, Creed rarely had anything to say to her unless it was in relation to the job being done. Otherwise he seemed to treat her as some sort of nonentity. At first it bothered her because Layne was used to people liking her. Finally she chalked him off as being antisocial by nature.

When the end of the week rolled around, Layne had her first day off. But she had learned long ago that a day off meant that she had to regroup before starting again. She gathered her pile of dirty laundry and carried it downstairs to the kitchen, where Mattie was finishing up the breakfast dishes.

"Would it be all right if I used your automatic washer to do my clothes?" she asked, hoping she wouldn't have to lug them all the way to the coin-operated Laundromat in town.

"Sure. There's dirty clothes in the basket if you need some to fill out a load," Mattie said.

The enclosed back porch had been converted into a utility room, housing an automatic washer and dryer as well as a scrub sink. Mattie followed Layne onto the porch and showed her where the detergent was kept.

"It's going to be a good day to hang the clothes outside," Mattie observed with a glance out the frosted windows. "They'll freeze-dry in an hour."

"That's for sure." While Layne put the first load of light clothes into the washer, Mattie started separating her basket of dirty clothes. "Who washes Hoyt's and Stoney's clothes?" Layne asked.

"They do," Mattie replied. "That's one of the first things I tell a man when he hires on—I don't do laundry. I think Hoyt has sweet-talked some girl into doing his wash for him, but Stoney just takes a duffel bag of clothes into town and throws them all into the same machine. It isn't just his head that's gray. It's every stitch of clothing he owns."

"Gray but clean," Layne laughed and added the pile of Mattie's light-colored clothes to her small load in the washer. "What about Creed? Who does his?"

"He does. A typical bachelor, too set in his ways," Mattie declared. "Everything has to be done in a certain way or it's not right. John was that way." She paused to think about it and frowned. "No, John was worse. He wasn't set in his ways; he was hardened in cement."

"How did you manage?" Layne wondered.

"Don't forget. I came to work for him as his house-keeper, so I was paid to do it the way he wanted it done. If he wanted his shorts ironed, I ironed his shorts no matter how ridiculous I thought it was. Of course, he didn't think it was too funny when I started putting starch in them."

"What made you decide to answer that ad in the paper and come to work here?" It was a perfect opening to ask Mattie about the events immediately following her birth. "Couldn't you find any work in North Platte? You did say that's where you were from, didn't you?"

There was a slow affirmative nod from the woman. "I probably could have found work there but I wanted to get away." She shrugged idly. "It's one of the oldest stories. I'd fallen in love with a rodeo cowboy. They're the worst kind," she informed Layne with a dry look. "They live too fast, love too fast—and leave too fast. But he was the hand-somest devil you've ever seen. And intelligent. He could talk circles around anybody, so a fresh redhead from North Platte was easy pickings. He was going to call me every week, see me when he could. 'Course, it was all a line."

"He didn't come back." It didn't take much guesswork to figure out that that man was her father.

"No. Broke my heart, he did. I swore off men. I didn't want to have anything to do with them. I wanted to get far away from everybody. That's why I answered that ad in the paper," Mattie explained while she mocked those earlier, exaggerated feelings of pain and rejection. "I was a very bitter young girl when I came here, soured on life and all its supposed tomorrows. I slapped away every kindness that was shown to me. Pride is a terrible thing, Layne," she mused almost absently. "It makes you reject the very thing you want the most."

The shrug of Mattie's shoulders seemed an attempt to dismiss the somber subject as she again bent to the task of sorting clothes, briskly tossing them into the appropriate piles. Layne could only wonder whether that had been a direct reference to the illegitimate daughter she'd given up for adoption, or if Mattie had been generalizing.

"I guess John eventually changed all that," Layne said idly.

"It took a while—a long while. He had no patience with people who felt sorry for themselves. I had worked here almost four years before I realized how much that man meant to me. No one could have been more surprised than I was at the time." She straightened, her face slightly flushed from all the blood rushing to her head, and studied Layne with a speculative look. "All this must be boring to you. Or is this research for your article?"

"I was interested in your background, but we can keep the personal part of it off the record if you want." Avoiding that gaze, Layne poured detergent into a measuring cup and added it to the clothes in the washer tub.

"None of it's a secret, but it's all in the past and I'd rather keep it there," Mattie stated.

"That's okay with me," Layne assured her and set the washing machine to start its cycle.

"It looks like you're all set here, so I guess I'll go see if I can't get that plane started this morning. Enjoy your day off," Mattie offered wryly, knowing one kind of work was being exchanged for another.

"I will." A small smile touched Layne's mouth as she watched Mattie disappear through the door to the kitchen.

That copper hair might owe some of its color to a henna rinse, but Layne suspected that Mattie was still as strong-minded and adventurous as she ever was. Experience might have given her a sense of caution but it hadn't lessened any of her spunk.

Only a small percentage of the current female population were licensed pilots, but Mattie had stopped logging her hours ten years ago when she had flown more than a thousand. The boundaries of the Ox-Yoke Ranch encompassed twenty-five thousand acres, and another ten thousand acres were leased. With a plane a lot of territory could be covered in a hurry—broken fences spotted, strayed cattle located, and overall range conditions checked.

Thoughtfully Layne leaned a hip against the washing machine as it filled with water. In many respects Mattie hadn't lived up to Layne's image of what her natural mother would be like. She didn't possess the tender, motherly attributes Layne had tried to associate with her. But, woman to woman, Layne liked and respected Mattie. Maybe that was a discovery in itself.

The machine kicked into its wash cycle, and the agitator splashed water onto her. Layne jumped with a start, then shook her head when she saw that she'd forgotten to close the lid.

The following week a warm spell came and melted the snow from the hills. The complexion of the rolling landscape changed from its glistening white to a faded brown, the color of the thick grasses that blanketed the land. Billowing, white clumps of cotton clouds chased each other across the wide blue sky, changing shape and size.

The dense grass absorbed the thud of cantering hoofs as Layne rode alongside Hoyt Weber. A cow had fallen on some ice and badly scraped its front legs. Layne had ridden out on the range with Hoyt to catch the lame cow and doctor its injuries. The animal had not been the most cooperative nor grateful patient. But the task was accomplished and they were heading back to the gate where the pickup and horse trailer had been left.

All the swells and dips of this undulating land looked the same to her. Layne realized how easy it would be to become lost once a person went beyond the sight of the ranch buildings. She was completely turned around and trusted that Hoyt knew which way to go.

They crested a hill and headed down its slope. At the bottom one of the many lake ponds that dotted this region was sprawled in their path. It was ringed with trees, dark skeletons around the ice-packed surface that still held patches of snow. Instead of riding around its long, curving shoreline, Hoyt aimed his horse at a narrow finger. Layne started to pull up, checking her horse's pace. Hoyt glanced back when she started to fall behind.

"It's okay. The lake's still frozen solid. No sense riding around it when we can go across," he called to her above the groan of saddle leather and drumming hoofs.

Still a little uncertain, she followed him. When they entered the trees, Hoyt slowed his horse to a walk and approached the snow-crusted ice covering the lake. Layne waited until he had started across before urging her own mount onto the rough ice. The shaggy-coated sorrel blew out a nervous snort at the slick footing as it moved gingerly across the frozen lake, its pricked ears in a constant flux of direction at the ominous cracking sounds beneath its hooves. On the opposite shore it made a slipping lunge onto solid ground.

"See? That wasn't so bad." Hoyt grinned at her.

"Lead on," she laughed in return.

He kicked his horse into a canter to climb the slope of the next mounded ridge. At the top of the hill Layne caught a glimpse of the cartwheeled spokes of a windmill. It had to be the one located by the gate. It was a relief to finally get her bearings and know for herself which way to ride.

The windmill grew steadily bigger as they approached, looming on the horizon. When they topped the last rise, Layne noticed the mud-spattered pickup parked beside the stock tank at the base of the windmill. Her curious glance made another sweep of the wide pocket of range. That pickup was the one Creed usually drove, but she saw no sign of him in the immediate vicinity. The tailgate of the truck was lowered, and an opened toolbox was sitting on the ledge it made.

"It looks like Creed is finally getting that broken shaft fixed," Hoyt observed.

The comment pulled her gaze back to the windmill. On the platform atop the tall wooden structure, a dark shape was crouched next to the convex blades. Its bulk couldn't belong to anyone else but Creed.

"Hello!" Hoyt shouted the greeting and Creed's head came up, and a hand was briefly raised to acknowledge their approach. Hoyt reined in his horse while they were still several yards short of the windmill's base where he still had an angle of view at the man on the platform. Layne stopped beside him. "We got that cow treated, so we'll be heading back to the house."

"Before you go"—Creed moved to the edge of the platform and looked down—"one of you bring me up a crescent wrench."

Hoyt hesitated and glanced at Layne. "You do it," he urged. "I get nosebleeds every time I climb on anything taller than a horse."

The look in his eye advised Layne that he wasn't joking. His phobia about heights was very real. High places had never bothered her, so she didn't offer any objection to his request.

"Sure, I'll do it," she agreed and swung out of the saddle.

Bending, Hoyt reached for the reins of her horse. "While you do that, I'll get the horses loaded in the trailer."

"Okay." She passed him the reins.

The pickup and horse trailer were another hundred yards distant, beyond the fence gate. Layne didn't object to walking that far. After so much riding, she needed to exercise her legs a little. As Hoyt led her horse away, she walked to the toolbox on the tailgate of Creed's truck.

"The crescent wrench should be lying right on top," Creed called down to her. It wasn't but she quickly found it among the other tools.

"Got it." She started for the base of the windmill.

"Are you sure it's a crescent wrench?" he questioned with a hint of skepticism.

She didn't bother to look up as she continued confidently to the crossboards that served as a ladder. "Don't worry. I know what it is."

Chapter 5

The boards were rough-cut and quick to splinter, but Layne had borrowed a pair of Mattie's lined leather gloves to ride that morning. If she'd worn her mittens to climb the windmill, they would have been shot with slivers of wood. She paused to glance up and check how much farther it was to the platform.

When her gaze came back level again, she suddenly noticed the view of the Sand Hills from this high vantage. She could literally see for miles and miles. She stared, her imagination caught by the bigness and the emptiness of it.

"You okay?" The graveled edge of concern in Creed's question snapped Layne from her absorption. She looked up quickly to see the rough crags of his broad features as he peered over the edge of the platform.

"I'm fine," she assured him and hurriedly started climbing again.

When she was at the top, his hand closed around her arm just above the elbow and hauled her the rest of the way onto the platform with little apparent effort. Layne scooted away from the edge and passed him the wrench. She noticed the way his half-glance identified the tool, then came back to her face, something flickering briefly in his expression.

"I used to help my dad a lot when he was monkeying around in the garage," she offered in explanation. "So I was indoctrinated early in the world of wrenches and ratchets."

He held her gaze for another beat, then turned toward the stationary windmill blades and began to tighten the bolts that secured the metal shaft. With the wrench delivered, Layne was free to climb back down, but the view from atop the windmill platform was too compelling. She leaned back on her hands to gaze at the vast stretch of rolling hills.

"It's quite a sight from up here, isn't it?" Layne murmured.

"Yup." But Creed never paused in his task to take a look.

His lack of interest didn't alter hers. All the statistics Layne had heard and read over the years about the Nebraska Sand Hills came to her mind. They comprised some nineteen thousand square miles of long ridges and mounds—the most extensive dune formation in the Western Hemisphere, likened to the Great Eastern Erg of the Sahara Desert.

Only here, the desert was an oasis because the vast dunes sat atop great aquifers. The abundant supply of moisture gave the wind-sculptured sand its lush mantle of grass—a veritable sea of waving grass.

Having driven through the area, Layne knew it was large, but nothing had prepared her for the immensity to be seen from this high viewpoint. There was nothing for mile upon mile but small, angular peaks and flat, broad mounds, heaving and swelling like the ocean. Here and there the smooth ripple of grassland was dotted with trees and thickets growing up around half-hidden spring runs.

There was an odd patch of white, too, marking the location of one of the many lakes and ponds that were strewn through the area.

"Cherry County is supposed to be larger than Connecticut, isn't it?" She directed the question at Creed without turning to look at him.

"Yup."

"Is it true that there's a part of Cherry County—larger than Delaware—that doesn't have a town or a post office?" Once that had seemed a gross exaggeration. Now Layne was prepared to believe it was possible.

"That's what they say." Creed leaned his weight into the wrench to tighten the bolt that last fraction.

Slightly miffed at his indifferent response when she was seeking information, Layne sent him an irritated glance. Having a conversation with him was like pulling teeth.

It goaded her into challenging him. "Don't you ever talk?"

There was a small pause in his work as Creed cast a sidelong glance at her before his attention reverted to the long shaft. "When I've got something to say."

Layne stubbornly persisted in her subtle attack on his laconic attitude. "The Scots have a word to describe men like you. It's 'dour.'" But it didn't seem to faze him. "Do you ever smile?"

"When there's reason." He made one last adjustment.

Half turning, she rested her weight on one elbow to closely study him, her eyes gleaming with curious speculation. "What would it take to melt that iron composure of yours? What would I have to do to coax a smile out of you?"

His glance raked her briefly as he straightened away from the wind wheel. "You could try climbing down the windmill. I'm all finished up here."

With a barely concealed sigh of exasperation, Layne

maneuvered around to swing her feet onto the crossties and begin her descent. Creed followed her, keeping a cross-board empty between them so he wouldn't accidentally step on her hands.

When she neared the bottom, Layne started to push off to jump the last couple of feet. But the slick sole of her boot slipped on the rough edge of a board. Her feet became tangled and she fell, landing heavily on her back. The impact drove the air out of her lungs, momentarily seeming to paralyze them. For a dazed second she wasn't quite sure what had happened to her.

She blinked her eyes. When she opened them again, Creed was crouching over her and she was looking into his broadly lean features. She was fascinated by the concern that animated them, when they were usually so masked.

"Layne." He pulled off his glove and laid a callused hand along her cheek while a finger sought the pulsepoint in her neck. "Are you hurt?"

Unable to make her lungs work to operate her voice, she could only shake her head negatively against his rough palm.

With a frown Creed watched her labor for air. "Are you sure?"

She nodded mutely and grabbed at his arm to try to pull herself upright. Then his hands were gently and carefully lifting her so she could sit up. Conscious of his close scrutiny and the strong, supporting arms that stayed around her, Layne knew he wasn't convinced.

After the first tentative gasps of air she managed to vocally assure him. "It just . . . knocked the wind out of . . . me. That's all."

His features relaxed and the corners of his mouth lifted slightly at her answer. She noticed the small movement that altered the straight line of his mouth. Like a child captivated by the thing that had charmed her, she wanted to touch it. With hands still shaky from the fall, she tugged off a glove and reached up to let her fingertips rest lightly along an indented lip corner.

"You're actually smiling," she marveled.

When she glanced up to his eyes to seek confirmation of this amazing fact, they were very dark, yet glowing with an intensely warm light. It wasn't until then that Layne noticed how fast her heart was beating—a reaction from the fall, no doubt.

There was a suggestion of movement toward her, a barely discernible dipping of his head closer to hers. For a second she thought he intended to kiss her. Then something changed, and he was taking hold of her hand and lowering it away from his mouth. All in one motion, his hands were gripping her clothes-padded sides to help her stand.

"Come on. Let's get you on your feet," he urged with a faint gruffness.

In her mind the actions ceased to be two separate incidents. The tilting of his head had been a preliminary movement to helping her stand up. There was no reason to attach any special significance to it. She did a haphazard job of brushing herself off while Creed stood back.

"Hoyt's waiting for you. You'd better get a move on," he said and swung around to walk to the pickup and put his tools away.

Her legs felt a little rubbery the first few steps. By the time Layne crossed the long stretch of grass to the truck and horse trailer, she had walked off most of the effects of the fall, although a few spots remained tender.

"Took a flyer, did you?" Hoyt observed as she climbed into the cab of the truck.

"My foot slipped."

"You're just lucky you weren't another five feet off the ground, or you would have broken your neck," he declared and started the motor.

"Thanks for making me reel better," she countered dryly. As they drove away, her gaze was drawn to the solitary figure standing near the windmill. It tugged at her.

By the end of her third week on the ranch, Layne was beginning to feel like an old hand. Despite the three big meals she ate each day, she was slimmer and every ounce of flesh was solid. She could sling eighty-pound bales of hay like a pro and stay in the saddle when a horse did a fancy rollback in pursuit of a cow instead of getting left in midair while the horse ran out from under her. Mastering the art of milking a cow was another milestone.

The orange sun was lying flat on the flanks of the distant ridges as Layne carried the pail of milk across the yard to the house. She had managed to finish her evening chores and milk Flo and be done before the others.

When she entered the house through the back porch, the smell of fried chicken awakened her appetite. She used the bootjack to remove her muddy boots and kicked them into a paper-strewn corner of the porch.

"Smells great," Layne declared as she entered the kitchen and crossed to the sink to strain the milk into a clean pitcher. "Need help with anything?"

"I don't think so." Mattie turned the chicken and dodged the spitting grease. "Oh, damn, I didn't fix any dessert. Well, the boys will just have to be satisfied with some fruit sauce again tonight. Look in the cupboard and see if I have a jar of peaches up there, Layne."

Layne checked the cupboard and said "There is, but I think we have a little bit of peach sauce in the refrigerator, as well as some small containers of apricots and pears."

"You can set them out, but I doubt if this picky bunch will eat leftovers."

"They'll never know it," Layne assured her. "I'll chop up the fruit, add this small can of fruit cocktail that's in the cupboard, and mix it all with some coconut and whipped cream. *Voilà*, you have ambrosia."

"Sounds good."

"It's a trick I learned from my mother."

"Go ahead and fix it," Mattie urged. "I might even have some of that."

None of the men exhibited Mattie's enthusiasm for the dessert when Layne set it on the table that night. Stoney tentatively spooned some into a dish and questioned Mattie about the ingredients. He didn't appear eager to try it until he found out what was in it.

"Ambrosia, huh?" Stoney frowned at the uncommon name that didn't give him much of a clue about the taste and slapped at Hoyt's hand when he dipped his spoon into Stoney's helping of the dessert to sample it before taking any for himself.

"Hey! This is good," Hoyt said with some surprise and filled his dish to the top before passing the bowl to Creed. "Did you make this, Mattie?"

"Layne did." Mattie was quick to give her the credit.

"It's my mother's recipe," Layne explained.

"Well, if your mother knows any more dishes that taste as good as this, be sure to fix them," Hoyt insisted, hardly letting his attention stray at all from the dessert.

"I gotta admit, Mattie, this is almost better than your coconut cream pie," Stoney warned.

Creed was the only one who hadn't said anything about Layne's dessert. She watched him calmly eating it, apparently unimpressed by its taste. His silence was galling when she wanted to hear his opinion.

Grudgingly she asked, "Do you like it, Creed?"

"It's good." He nodded but the answer was so bland it was almost meaningless.

"Good?" Hoyt reacted to the passive compliment. "Is that all you can say about it?"

"He'd say the same thing whether you set a can of peaches in front of him or some French pastry," Mattie declared. "Nothing gets singled out for special praise."

"Well, just ignore Creed," Hoyt advised Layne as he reached for the bowl to have a second helping. "This is delicious. What is it? Some kind of Swedish dish?"

Layne shrugged. "I guess you could call it an 'American leftover,' like me." It was a phrase she'd used so often that she said it out of habit, the words hitting her after they were out.

A confused frown knitted Hoyt's forehead as he gave her a curious look across the table. Even Creed's spoon paused halfway between his dish and his mouth.

"What do you mean by that?" Hoyt asked. "I never heard of anybody calling themselves an 'American leftover.'"

"It's kind of a family joke." Layne had a brief debate with herself, then decided to tell the truth. "You see, I was adopted. When I was growing up, I didn't know what my family's nationality or background had been, like the other kids in my class. So my dad made up this story about children God had 'left over' and how he put them in different countries for childless couples to love. That's how I came to be an 'American leftover.'"

While she made her explanation, Layne was conscious of how silent Mattie had become at the head of the table. She listened intently to every word and studied Layne closely with those faded green eyes. Layne held her breath, almost afraid Mattie would guess, and scared that she wouldn't. It was crazy.

When she had finished recounting the story, there was a short lull. Then Mattie spoke quietly. "That's a lovely explanation, Layne. He must be a very special man."

"He is." Her voice was taut with emotion, too choked to say more.

The comments seemed to remove the reluctance on the part of the others to ask about her past. "What about your real parents?" Hoyt inquired. "Did you ever find out anything about them?"

Mattie spoke, almost defensively, before Layne could respond. "I'm sure Layne regards her mother and father as her real parents. After all, they did raise her and love her."

"I'm sorry." Hoyt looked uncomfortable. "I didn't mean—"

"It's okay," Layne inserted, including Mattie in the assurance that she wasn't sensitive on this issue. But this time she chose a half-truth. "The adoption agency told my parents that I came from an unwed mother who elected not to keep her baby."

"When you found that out . . ." Mattie began, then paused, hesitating over the question, "did it bother you?"

"For a while it did. I felt rejected, abandoned . . . even though I had two wonderful people who loved me more than anything. It hurt to think my natural mother hadn't wanted me. Then . . . I did a series of articles on teenage pregnancies and unwed mothers. After talking to those young, and sometimes frightened, girls, I discovered it was never a casual decision to give up a baby. Even the ones who were the most confident in their minds went through emotional turmoil. And gradually I learned to accept that my natural mother had made a decision that was best for both of us at the time."

But that hadn't affected this driving need to find the woman who had given birth to her, and get to know her.

Now it was happening. She was even getting a chance to tell her side of the story. Best of all, no one was getting hurt.

"How about some coffee?" Stoney leaned back in his chair, rocking it on its rear legs. "Is there any more in the pot, Mattie?"

"There should be." Mattie started to rise, but Layne motioned her to stay seated.

"I'll get it," she volunteered, feeling that it was a wise time to change the subject.

As she went to bring the coffeepot from the kitchen counter, there seemed to be a general shuffling of interest to fill the lull. Hoyt patted the empty breast pocket of his shirt, then nudged Stoney.

"Can I bum a cigarette off you?" he asked. "I'll buy you a pack when I get paid."

"It's more like three packs," Stoney grumbled, but obligingly shook an unfiltered cigarette from his pack and offered it to Hoyt. "At the rate you're smoking my cigarettes, I ain't gonna have enough to last me till the weekend." Layne filled his cup first. "Thanks," he said.

"Hey, that's right. We got a payday weekend coming up," Hoyt realized as a wide smile sprang to his face. Layne stopped by his chair, holding the coffeepot. "Yeah, I'll have some," he affirmed in answer to her inquiring look. "Have you made any plans for the weekend, Layne?"

"I haven't even thought about it," she said with a shrug.

Hoyt wrapped an arm around her hips and pulled her closer to his chair. "Let's you and me take off for North Platte. We'll do the town in style and have a ball."

"On whose money?" Layne laughed, too used to his playful exuberance to be offended by his familiarity—or to take him seriously. "Mine? Or yours?"

"We'd go dutch, of course." Hoyt grinned up at her.

"Meet Hoyt Weber," she taunted. "The last of the big spenders."

The noisy scrape of a chair leg across the floor distracted her. She looked around to see Creed looming tall above the table. His dusty brown glance briefly met her eyes.

"I'm going to skip the second cup of coffee," he said and started toward the back door. "I've got some things to get finished at my place."

"See you in the morning," Stoney called after him, but Creed was already shrugging into his coat and donning his hat as he walked out the rear door.

His departure seemed rather abrupt to Layne, but no one else appeared to take any undue notice of it.

Hoyt's arm tightened around her hipbones to pull her attention back to him. "What d'ya say? Shall we head for North Platte this weekend?"

"Sorry." Layne shook her head in a smiling refusal and picked up his hand to unwrap it from around her. "But Stoney told me that you couldn't be trusted."

"Stoney, you old hoss!" Hoyt accused in mock anger. "Why'd you go telling tales on me?"

"Somebody's gotta protect girls like Layne from the likes of you," Stoney retorted in kind.

The two went round and round in a mock argument, the old cowboy and the young playing the same game. Mattie eventually shooed them out of the kitchen after their coffee was finished so she and Layne could clean up the dishes. Layne thought the subject of her adoption might come up once they were alone but it didn't, and she didn't raise it.

On payday weekend Layne collected her wages on Saturday, like the others, and went into Valentine in the afternoon to cash her check and buy a few odds and ends. It felt strange walking around in regular clothes and the high-heeled boots after wearing jeans and flannel shirts for days. And the noise of the town seemed unusually loud after the silence of the country.

After she had browsed through the stores and finished her shopping, she called her parents from a telephone booth and talked to them at length. Then she went to the same small café for supper. It was crowded, as usual, but the waitress recognized her from the last time she had been in.

When she'd taken Layne's order, she asked, "Did you ever find that woman you were looking for? That Martha something or other?"

Layne hesitated a second, then forced a smile. "No. You were right though. She got married and moved away."

"It was a good bet that had happened." The waitress nodded in a knowing fashion, then moved away from Layne's small table to bring the supper order into the kitchen.

With the meal finished, Layne lingered over her coffee. Mattie had said she was going to a neighbor's that night, so Layne wasn't in any rush to return to an empty house. Yet the night was young and she didn't know what to do with it—alone and on her own in a strange town. She almost wished she had taken Hoyt up on his invitation for the weekend. He'd have been good fun, if a little rowdy.

As she was leaving the restaurant she noticed an advertisement for the local cinema posted on the wall. The motion picture currently being shown was one she hadn't seen. It seemed a logical if unexciting way to spend the evening. The cashier gave her directions to the movie house. Since it was close enough to walk, Layne decided to leave her car parked in the lot.

The popular film drew a sizable crowd. There weren't

many vacant seats when Layne entered the darkened theater. With some buttered popcorn and a box of chocolate mints for company, she watched the film from an aisle seat in back. The jokes didn't seem quite so funny when she had to laugh alone, and her eyes barely misted over in the sad parts.

Still, she concluded when she emerged from the theater, it had been an entertaining two hours. It was dark outside, with only the streetlights illuminating the night. She paused outside the movie house to get her bearings and button her coat while the crowd filed out behind her. The night air was brisk, a suggestion of a nip in its winter temperature that made her breath visible.

The ebb and flow of voices was all around her; the slam of car doors as people began to get into their parked vehicles. Layne adjusted her knitted cap to cover her ears, then thrust her hands into her coat pockets and started to walk in the direction of her own car.

When she crossed the street to the next block, she took only passing notice of the car stopped at the crosswalk. As she reached the other side, a long, low wolf whistle came from the vehicle. Ignoring it, Layne kept walking. The car turned the corner and drove slowly alongside her. In her side vision she could see the two young men in the car with the window rolled down, and she kept facing straight ahead.

"Hey there, good-lookin', wanna ride?" The grinning one on the passenger side had stuck his head out the window to call the invitation. Layne pretended not to hear. "Bob and me will take you wherever you're going. Won't we, Bob?"

Some laughing affirmation came from the driver, but Layne still didn't respond. In her experience, it was better to ignore such overtures. Invariably these types lost interest if they didn't get a response. It took the fun out of their game.

"Hey, come on, honey. Don't be so stuck up," the first one complained, still in a coaxing tone. "We're nice guys."

"Yeah, we wear white hats," the driver, Bob, added with a laugh.

Glancing ahead, Layne saw the café sign on the next block and calmly continued walking. When the car speeded ahead of her, a faint smile of satisfaction edged her mouth at having once again proved her theory about handling such situations.

A second later she realized she was mistaken. Instead of driving on, the car had pulled up to the curb and parked. The front doors were flung open and the two men, in their early twenties, came piling out and jogged to meet her. Layne halted only an instant, then resolutely continued on. Neither of them looked particularly threatening.

"We decided a pretty girl like you shouldn't be alone." The wide-smiling one who had made the first remarks to her quickly shifted direction to fall into step beside her.

"Yeah, and since you didn't want to ride with us, we decided we would walk with you," the driver, Bob, added.

Layne resisted the urge to walk faster. The public street was well lighted and heavily traveled, and it was just another short block to the café.

"You're new here, aren't you?" The one called Bob was walking sideways so he could watch her. A cream-colored cowboy hat was pushed to the back of his head and a thatch of dark hair fell across his forehead. "I don't remember seeing you around before. How long you been here?"

"And where've you been hiding all this time?" The first one swung ahead of her to walk backward. He was huskily built with the thick neck of a football player. "We must be slipping up, Bob, to miss noticing this gal around town."

"How come she won't talk to us?" Bob questioned his buddy in a mock demand.

"Maybe she don't talk to strangers" was the suggestion while Layne determinedly tried not to look at either of them, but this innocent harassment was beginning to strain her nerves.

"Then we'll introduce ourselves. I'm Bob and he's Mike." He quickly solved that problem. "Now, what's your name?"

On a burst of impatience, Layne broke her self-imposed vow of silence. "Look, guys, I'm not interested. Okay?"

The one identified as Mike grabbed at his chest and staggered in an exaggerated reaction. "She talks! This vision actually has a voice."

Irritated with herself for giving them anything that might be regarded as encouragement, Layne released an exasperated sigh and quickened her steps to walk faster. The café was just ahead.

"Where are you going in such a hurry?" Bob wanted to know.

"Yeah, we wanna go there too." Mike was forced to turn around and walk frontward to keep up with her.

Then Bob spotted the lights of the café. "I'll bet she's goin' in there for a cup of coffee and a piece of pie or something. After a movie you always stop and get something to eat, right?" he reasoned to his pal.

"We can't have a newcomer to town eat alone. We'll keep you company, won't we, Bob?" Mike offered generously.

It didn't seem wise to have these two jokers follow her to her car, so the café was the logical alternative. Sooner or later they'd get the message that they didn't appeal to her at all. One of them, Mike, hurried ahead to open the door for her and made a low, mocking bow.

"After you, madam," he insisted with absurd formality.

Layne was weary of their whole childish game. Inside the café she paused to patiently inform them again of her disinterest. "Look, fellas, you're wasting your time," she began. It was a sheer stroke of luck that her glance around the café tables happened to catch sight of Creed sitting alone. His presence provided her with the perfect means to send her persistent suitors on their way with the minimum of argument. "You see, I'm meeting someone," she announced, smiling coolly.

Their surprise showed, a trace of skepticism gleaming. "Oh, yeah? How come you didn't say that before?"

Not bothering to reply, Layne walked confidently through the restaurant straight to Creed's table. Without looking, she knew the two men were trailing hesitantly behind her just to see if she was telling the truth.

Chapter 6

When Layne pulled out the empty chair across from him, Creed looked up, his thick brows lifting slightly in a show of mild curiosity. She sat down, depositing her purse and mittens on the seat of the chair next to hers.

"Hi," she said brightly and reached for the menu propped beside the napkin holder. "The movie just got out. Have you been here long?"

There was a faint narrowing of his gaze; then it darted to a point beyond her. Layne continued to smile in unconcern, guessing that Creed had spied the two men following her. She heard the shuffle of their footsteps approach the table. When Creed's glance returned to her, it was cynically hard and speculating.

"About an hour." He lifted the half-filled cup of coffee in front of him and took a drink of it.

Mike and Bob paused by the table, eyeing Creed with skeptical glances. "Is this the guy you're meeting?" The doubt in Mike's voice was almost a challenge. "What is he, some relative?"

"Not hardly," she laughed and flashed a conspiratorial smile at Creed, but his hard, knowing expression never changed. "You guys can stop pestering me now. I'm not in need of your company." It was a subtle attempt to explain to Creed that this pair had been giving her a hard time and she was using him for cover.

With unhurried ease Creed pushed out of his chair and towered beside the table. Layne assumed he was using his intimidating size to reinforce her position and send the brash pair on their way. They were already sidling away from the table. Instead Creed reached into his pocket and tossed some change on the table.

"She's not with me," Creed told the pair, then slid a dry and challenging look at Layne. "Sorry, but I'm not going to be your patsy. If these boys are bothering you, you'll have to get rid of them by yourself. You're a big girl. I'm not going to fight your battles for you."

Her mouth dropped open in shock. Too stunned to speak, Layne watched in numb disbelief as Creed walked away from the table. He was actually leaving.

The clatter of chair legs being dragged across the floor sharply broke her dazed astonishment. She turned to see Mike and Bob preparing to sit down and join her at the table, laughing at the way she'd been abandoned.

"Shame on you for pretending to be meeting him," Bob mocked. "Why, anyone would think you didn't want our company."

It took a lot to make Layne lose her temper, but once lit, it had a short fuse. And the way Creed had just walked out on her had been the igniting spark. She pushed stiffly from her chair before either of the two could sit down.

"I've had it with both of you!" Her low voice trembled with the seething rage of her anger. "I've done everything, short of being downright rude, to make you understand that I want you to bug off! I'm not interested in flirting with you! I don't want your company! And I don't want you following me!"

They were stung into reacting. "You don't have to get so uptight about it," Mike protested with sullen resentment at this public rejection.

Layne was so furious she was vibrating. She was angry with these would-be Romeos for starting this whole thing and angry with herself for creating a scene in the restaurant. But most of all, she was mad at Creed for abandoning her and forcing her to be so brutal when the whole thing could have been handled with a little tact.

"Nothing else seems to get through your thick heads!" she retorted. "If you so much as look at me again, I'll call the police and have you arrested."

"We never did anything to you." The one called Bob scowled at the threat. Both of them were trying to edge away from her, embarrassed by the onlooking witnesses and trying not to show it.

"Then just stay away from me!"

Angrily, Layne grabbed up her purse and gloves and swiftly crossed the restaurant to storm out the door. She didn't bother to button her jacket. Her blood was running too hot to feel the chilling draft of winter air.

Outside, she paused only a second to scan the lot of parked vehicles. Layne had no trouble spotting the tall, dark shape moving among the shadows toward a pickup. She pushed off the steps and crossed the graveled lot at a running trot, catching up with Creed as he approached the driver's side of his truck. She stopped next to the left front fender.

"What was the idea of abandoning me like that in there?" Layne demanded. Creed halted short of the driver's door, angling his body toward her. "Why wouldn't you help me get rid of those two?"

His glance made a small sweep of the area just beyond her. "I don't see them around, so you must have managed on your own."

"No thanks to you." Her anger was taking on an impatient facet.

"What did you expect me to do? Maybe get into a fight with those two punks over you?" Creed suggested and released a short, audible breath that derided the idea. "No thanks."

When he reached for the door handle, Layne crossed the last few steps to grab at his arm and stop him from leaving. "What is it with you?" she demanded. "You haven't liked me from the start. Why? What have I ever done to you?"

"You've got all the rest tied around your finger. Why don't you be content with that?" Creed challenged in a low, harsh voice.

"What are you talking about?" She was impatient with his avoidance of a direct answer.

"You flattered Mattie into hiring you, saying you'd write a story about her. Hoyt grins like a damned puppy anytime you're around. And you've even got Stoney looking after you like a Dutch uncle. But you aren't going to be happy until you add me to the list," he muttered roughly.

"Since when is it wrong to want people to like you?" Layne snapped, her hands moving to her hips in a challenging and defiant stance. "Every time I try to be friendly to you, I end up talking to the wind."

"You want to be my friend? Then take the hint and leave me alone." The natural huskiness in his voice became more pronounced as its pitch deepened to vibrate through her.

Confused and incredulous, Layne could only protest his unreasoning attitude toward her. "What is it with you? Do I suddenly acquire two heads when you look at me? Is it the way I dress? The way I talk? What is it about me that you can't stand?"

An exasperated sigh, heavily laced with anger, came from him as Creed briefly looked away, then leveled his gaze at her once more. There was less than a foot between them in this confrontation. A streetlamp threw a harsh light across the blunt, angular features of his unhandsome face.

"Lately you've done everything but stand on your head to get me to notice you. If it makes you feel any better, I have noticed you've got hair the red-brown color of a new-born calf—and how sweet-smelling your skin is." A tautness was coming into his voice, a fiercely checked roughness that quivered along her nerve ends.

The tension between them seemed to take on a different quality that electrified her senses. The underlying heat was still there, but it was more sexual in origin. The beat of her pulse became shallow and uneven as a threat of confusion began to weave itself into her emotions.

"And I've noticed your lips," Creed was continuing, his voice dropping lower and lower. "The way they—" His mouth came shut on the incomplete sentence, the angle of his jaw hardening.

His large hands reached out and snared her arms before Layne could jump backward to elude them. She was hauled roughly against him, her arms pinioned to her sides. There wasn't time to draw more than a breath of surprise before the air was choked off by the bruising crush of his mouth.

Not an inch of maneuverability was allowed her as her head was forced backward by the brutal pressure until she thought her neck would snap. It was all pain, from the scrape of his short, whisker stubble to the grinding of her lips against her teeth.

When the initial shock passed, there was a roar of blood pounding in her ears. The heat of his breath seemed to set fire to her skin. Layne raged at her own impotency, trapped in the bear-grip of his arms with no chance to escape or struggle.

It was not the kind of kiss that had a beginning or an end. It was seizure and release, both in abrupt actions. Layne backed quickly from him, not sure if Creed intended to follow up that attack with another. The back of her hand was instinctively pressed to her sore and throbbing lips while she eyed him with wary revulsion. But he merely stood there, breathing roughly, his arms at his sides.

"Are you happy now?" he snapped at her like a wounded animal, which was crazy. She was the one who'd been so savagely attacked. "I've made a pass at you, so now you can stop wondering whether there's something wrong with you. You can go on to your next conquest now."

With that, the truck door was jerked open and Creed swung into the cab. The door banged loudly against its metal frame as it was pulled shut. An instant later the motor was gunned to life and the headlights glared across the lot. Layne moved to the side and pressed herself close to the car parked in the adjoining space as the truck pulled out. She had a short glimpse of his blunted profile, lean and ruthless in its stony contours.

Slowly Layne walked to her own car, still shaken by the incident. For a long time she simply sat behind the wheel, mindless of the cold, and tried to figure it out. Despite Creed's rough looks, what happened seemed out of character. He was an intelligent man, so he must have known how she would react to such sexual abuse. If he did, then that meant it was deliberate on his part.

It was sobering to think he disliked her so much that he was willing to make himself repulsive to her so she would stay away from him. It was obvious that Creed wanted nothing beyond a work relationship. She should have taken the hint when her friendly overtures weren't reciprocated, Layne decided. If that's the way he wanted it, then she would oblige him.

The spate of mild weather didn't last. A winter storm ushered in the month of March, complete with snow and cold north winds. Its arrival coincided with the calving of the first cows, which added a few complications to the natural procedure. A bovine nursery was set up in the kitchen for the odd weak calf that needed the warm shelter from the bad weather for a day or so until it had the strength to return to its mother.

As a child, Layne had been present when a neighbor's dog had puppies, and had seen films of larger animals giving birth to their young, but she had never attended any other birthing before. No matter how cold and tired she got, she always felt a tingling sense of awe that she had witnessed a little miracle when a spanking-new white-faced calf made its first wobbling lurch onto its feet.

With all her morning chores finished, including the milking, Layne crossed the yard to the barn area where the tractor was parked. It was already hitched to the loaded hayrack, but Creed wasn't in sight. Figuring he'd be along directly, she wandered over to the fence and huddled against a post to look out over the cattle in the winter pasture.

The hayrack with its stacks of bales acted as a windbreak to shield her from the blast of the north wind. A bleak, gray cloud cover hung over the land, pressing its gloom onto the morning and making the temperature seem colder. A wool muffler covered her mouth and nose, but her face still felt numb and stiff.

In the pasture the cows were gathering expectantly along the circuitous tracks made by the tractor and hay wagon on the previous morning's feed. The snow was trampled in that area, stray wisps of dirty hay mixing in with the snow and frozen soil.

Not far from the fence stood a cow with a calf not more than two days old. The little heifer calf eyed Layne curiously while it hugged close to its mother's side. Its white face seemed whiter even than the snow, and its deep russet-brown coat appeared burnished. But it was the calf's eyes that fascinated Layne. They were so big and luminously brown, and the lashes were incredibly long and curling.

Behind Layne heavy footsteps crunched on the frozen ground, moving her way. All tightly bundled around the neck, she had to half turn before she was able to see Creed walking toward her. She was reluctant to leave the windbreak of the hayrack, so she let him come to her rather than going to meet him.

Since the incident in the parking lot a certain terseness had existed between them. They rarely spent enough time in each other's company for it to become an uncomfortable situation. Layne knew she harbored no bitterness on her part, and it appeared that Creed didn't either. An unspoken agreement seemed to exist that they would keep their distance.

"Ready?" Creed pushed next to the fence to issue his one-word question.

"I guess so," Layne agreed reluctantly and let her gaze stray back to the young calf. "They're beautiful little creatures, aren't they?" Her half-frozen lips had trouble forming the words as she attempted to share the wonder she felt at the sweet innocence of the baby calf. "So perfect in every detail."

"Everything is beautiful when it's a baby." There was a

certain flatness in his voice, which didn't seem attributable to the cold, as he glanced at the object of Layne's interest. "But it doesn't last. That face will never be so white again. When that calf grows up, it will be just as ugly and ungainly as its mother."

His blunt and unflattering assessment of the cow seemed unfair and severe. Yet when Layne looked at the grown animal, its tongue came sliding out to lick the mucousy slime from its broad nostrils. Its shaggy coat was dirty and stained, its white face discolored to a yellow gray. Layne had to admit the cow was neither graceful nor beautiful, except maybe to a bull.

"Come on. Let's get the hay out to those cattle." Creed pushed away from the fence with a visible effort. "You drive the tractor this time. I'm liable to fall asleep if I stop moving."

Layne opened her mouth to protest that she'd never driven a tractor before, but one look at his leaden strides reminded her of the weariness that dragged at him. He'd worked around the clock during the calving, and she doubted if he'd slept more than two hours in the last forty-eight, so she kept silent about her inexperience. After all, it couldn't be much different than driving a stick shift. She trailed a few steps behind him as he trudged through the snow to the hay wagon and hauled himself bodily onto the flat rack.

Bundled in so many clothes, Layne climbed awkwardly up to the tractor seat and eyed the confusing array of foot pedals and gear handles with misgivings. It didn't look as simple as she thought it would be.

Reluctantly, she half turned in the cold seat to shout at Creed, "How do you make it go?"

His head lifted and she could see the exasperation in his expression. "Don't you even know how to drive a tractor?" he retorted impatiently.

"If I did, I wouldn't be asking," Layne flared. His tiredness was no excuse for ridiculing her lack of knowledge. Besides, it was cold up there on that tractor seat, exposed to the bleakly stinging wind.

"You can begin by starting the motor, then release the clutch to put it in gear," Creed replied with a trace of dry scorn in his raised voice.

His caustic instructions weren't much help, since she wasn't sure which pedal was the clutch, the brake, or the accelerator. And Layne was too stubborn to ask for more explicit directions, choosing instead to hazard it out on her own.

There was a reluctant grinding of the motor when she tried the ignition. With a rumble and a chug, it finally vibrated to life to puncture the stillness with its noisy roar. When she tried to coordinate releasing the clutch, shifting the gears, and giving it gas, the tractor made a halfhearted buck forward, then the motor stalled and died.

"Dammit, I said release the clutch—slowly!" Creed shouted in irritation. "If you can't drive the damned thing, just say so!"

"Maybe if you'd quit yelling at me and simply tell me how the damned thing operates, I'd be able to manage it!" Her voice rose in an angry response to his intolerance.

Layne didn't wait for him to reply as she again started the tractor. At the same moment that she let out the clutch, she tromped her other foot onto the accelerator. The tractor leaped forward, jerking the hay wagon after it. Behind her, she heard a muffled yell and turned in the seat in time to see the high-stacked bales tumbling onto Creed. In alarm, Layne slammed her foot onto the brake, stopping the tractor as abruptly as it had started.

With an alacrity that belied the many layers of warm clothing, she peeled off the tractor seat and jumped to the ground to race back and see if Creed was all right. The motor was silent, but Layne didn't know whether she had killed the engine again or unconsciously turned it off.

When she reached the hayrack, all she could see of Creed were his boots and part of his legs. The rest of him was buried under the fallen bales. As she clambered onto the rack, they started to move. She could hear him swearing under his breath. Hurriedly Layne began to lift the top bales and throw them onto the wobbly stack. As she lifted the third one Creed threw off the others with a heave of his body. When he sat up and reached for his hat, she knelt down quickly to assure herself that he was unharmed.

"Are you okay?" Her anxious glance searched his brutish features as he slapped the hay straws from his hat.

His dusty brown eyes gave her a long, dryly expressive look. He was slow in answering, waiting until his hat was pushed firmly onto his head to reply. "Yeah, I'm all right."

Relief sighed through her even though Layne could almost hear what he was thinking. "I'm glad." But if he made one comment about women drivers, she was tempted to hit him just on principle. "I—"

His glance shot past her on an upward angle. Before she could complete her sentence, she was being grabbed. The action was accompanied by a clipped "Look out" as she was twisted down.

Layne had a glimpse of a bale toppling from its precarious perch atop the unsteady stack before Creed's bulk blocked it from her sight as he protectively hunched his body over hers. The weight of the bale struck his shoulder and glanced off. The impact drove him against her and flattened them both.

For a few seconds after the danger had passed, neither of them moved in case more bales came tumbling down.

Layne was completely buried under the hard crush of his body, its muscular length and breadth encapsulating her more slender frame. His face was pressed into the edges of the wool scarf wrapped around her neck. She was conscious of the moist heat of his breath warming her skin.

There was a hesitant lift of his head, as if Creed expected another bale to come crashing down on them. As he started to turn to look, Layne also turned her head. The instant she felt the accidental brush of his mouth at the corner of her lips, she froze. Her heart seemed to make a startled lurch at the unexpected contact that held Creed motionless too.

The moment seemed to stretch itself out until Layne wasn't sure how long it had lasted—mere seconds or longer. Then, very slowly, a fraction of an inch at a time, his mouth edged onto the curve of her lips. The pressure was so faint that their lips touched and no more, their breath mingling.

Layne held herself still, wanting more than he was giving but unwilling to invite it. The memory of that other abusive kiss was too vivid in her mind. She didn't want to risk a repeat of it, yet she was a little shaken to discover that she wanted Creed to kiss her.

It didn't seem to matter that she found his looks physically unattractive to her. There was something very earthy and virile about him that touched an inner, responsive core in her own being. It was an elemental desire, female for male.

Gradually his mouth eased onto hers, mobile and exploring. The utter sensuality of the kiss quivered through Layne, supremely seductive in its slow-building heat. His long body shut out the winter cold as warmth seemed to spread all through her system.

She responded pliantly to his kiss, liking the firm texture

of his mouth and the warm taste of him, made tangy by tobacco. When Creed initiated a withdrawal, their moist lips clung together for another second, seemingly of their own volition, before the contact was broken.

His breath continued to fan her lips, its rhythm slightly irregular. As she slowly opened her eyes to look at him, Layne was vaguely dazed by the sensations the kiss had aroused. The bluntly chiseled contours of his face were so close to hers that she could see every sun-leathered groove. The light of wonder was in her green-flecked eyes.

This time she lifted her head to seek that disturbing contact with his mouth and ignite again that tingling pleasure. It was her initiative and her turn to explore the masculine curve of his lips. She felt the throb of excitement in her veins and the heady sweep of warmth through her when his mouth rocked onto her lips in response, gentle in its possession yet nearly shattering in its passion. She was filled with a wondrous ache that yearned for a more unrestrained embrace.

Yet when Creed dragged his mouth from hers a second time, she didn't protest. Like Creed, she had carefully controlled her responses, keeping them in check and releasing them a bit at a time. This eruption of passionate desire was too sudden and too new. She had been burned the last time something had exploded between them, and she didn't want that to happen again.

As she gazed into the warm and smoldering light in his dark eyes, Layne marveled at the contrast between this time and their previous encounter. A faint smile touched the corners of her mouth, still warm from his kiss.

"I knew you could be gentle," she told him in a softly husky voice.

Something leaped into his eyes that made her catch her breath, then an invisible shutter fell to hide it. His head dipped away from her. The moment of intimacy passed with an abruptness that almost negated it. Creed shifted position, lifting the crushing weight of his body from hers. She hadn't noticed he was so heavy until the pressure was removed. When Layne heard the cattle bellowing impatiently in the field, she realized she had been oblivious to many things.

"We'd better get this hay out to the stock." Creed's voice was so low and gravelly that the wind nearly whipped away the words as he rolled to his feet.

He extended a hand to help her up—an uncharacteristic gesture of assistance from him, which seemed proof that the fiercely gentle passion they had shared had touched him in some way. When he had pulled her upright, her gaze tried to penetrate the expressionless set of his features. He returned her look for an instant, a vague hesitancy showing in his dark eyes before they hardened into blankness.

"Under the circumstances, I'll drive the tractor," he stated.

"I thought you were tired," Layne protested as Creed vaulted off the flat rack to the frozen ground.

"That north wind is cold enough to keep me awake." Creed threw the answer over his shoulder as he walked to the tractor.

His remark made her conscious of the bitter blast of frigid air blowing on her face and chilling her lips, which only moments before had been heated by him. Layne hunched her shoulders against the wind and sought the protection of the hay bales, sitting down and resting against the shelter of their stacks.

While the tractor and hayrack bounced across the rutted pasture, she wrapped her arms tightly around her middle and hugged her body to keep alive the sensations so she could examine these new feelings. This sexual attraction seemed to have sprung from nowhere.

How long had she known Creed—a month? Certainly not much more than that. Never once had she regarded him as a potential lover. Creed Dawson was unquestionably a homely man, yet she had never denied that he had an animal quality about him that was both male and virile.

But if it was merely male companionship she wanted, the physical caress of a man, then Hoyt seemed the more likely candidate. Layne continued to puzzle over her reaction to this hungry bear of a man.

In the parking lot outside the café he'd been so rough with her, deliberately repelling her with his advances. Only now did she remember the compliments that had preceded the savagely cruel kiss—the remarks he'd made about the color of her hair and the smell of her skin, the tautly suppressed emotions that had vibrated in his voice. The suspicion formed that Creed had been attracted to her before that night—a grudging attraction.

But if that was so, it didn't explain why he had shown no regret over the way he'd treated her. Layne was confused, and she was usually so good at reasoning things out calmly and analytically. But none of it made sense—not her attraction for him nor his behavior toward her.

The tractor had slowed and the cattle were crowding around the hayrack before Layne noticed they had arrived at the feeding grounds. She scrambled to her feet and began to break the twine-bound bales to scatter the hay to the livestock. There wasn't much time to consciously think about anything except the cold and the work and keeping her balance while the hayrack lumbered slowly over its route.

When the last bale was broken and tossed over the side, Layne slumped tiredly against the upright post at the tail of the rack to make the long, cold ride back to the ranch yard. Once they had cleared the feeding cattle, the tractor rumbled to an unexpected stop. Layne glanced curiously at Creed, wondering what was wrong. He half turned in the seat and motioned to her.

Stiff with cold, she awkwardly swung off the rack to the ground and walked to the tractor. When she looked up, Creed was watching her. The collar of his parka was turned up against the invading wind, the bulk material adding to his massive appearance. The tractor motor continued to idle noisily.

"Do you want to learn to drive this thing?" he asked, raising his voice to make himself heard.

The question briefly took her by surprise, but she didn't hesitate in her answer. "Sure."

As she climbed onto the tractor Creed slid out of the tractor seat to stand beside it, hanging on to the back of it for balance. This time his instructions to her were clear and precise. Once she understood, she had no trouble mastering the tractor.

When the hayrack had cleared the pasture gate, she stopped the tractor and switched off its motor. There was a faintly triumphant gleam in her eye when she looked at Creed.

"Don't you have any more comments you'd like to make about women drivers?" She dryly teased him about his reaction to her previous attempt at operating the tractor that had felled him with the toppling hay bales.

"They do all right when they have a man to teach them." His low voice mocked her with a deliberately chauvinistic statement.

Laughter came from her throat, warm and easy. She liked the quickness of his mind and that ability to match her dry humor.

As Creed stepped to the ground Layne swung out of the tractor seat to follow him. His gloved hands were there to lift her, and his strength made her feel almost weightless when he swung her down. They were standing toe to toe, and her hands remained on his arms. Her gaze searched his features, trying to decide what it was about his outlaw-rough exterior that she found so strangely handsome.

"Do you know you actually had me convinced that you didn't like me?" Layne tipped her head to the side as she made the subtly challenging remark.

"Did I?" It was neither a question nor an answer.

"Why?" she persisted. "You're an intelligent man. I don't understand why you would want me to think that."

"It shouldn't be so hard to figure out. No man with any pride wants to look the fool. A beautiful woman like you can do that to a man without half trying." There was a faint narrowing of his gaze.

"I doubt that." She lightly scoffed at the implication that she was some sort of femme fatale.

"Do you? Look at me and tell me what you see," Creed challenged with seeming idleness. Words momentarily failed her as Layne searched for a response that was both tactful and complimentary. His mouth tightened at her small hesitation. "That's what I thought." He appeared to smile, but there was no warmth or amusement in the fleeting expression. "Your parents taught you well. If you can't think of anything good to say about a person, don't talk at all."

"Creed, that's not fair." Her hands dropped into fists at her side as he stepped away from her. She was impatient with him for reading something into her silence that didn't exist.

"Why? I wasn't looking for a compliment—only the truth. It shouldn't be a difficult thing to have between friends." There was a faint stress on the last word that seemed to draw a line on the limits of their relationship. "Go shut the gate before the cattle get out." He hauled himself into the tractor seat once more, effectively bringing an end to the conversation by starting the motor.

Irritated with herself for not speaking plainly, Layne stalked to the open gate. She had been trying to protect his feelings and instead wound up spoiling things. The truth was that she still wasn't comfortable with this attraction for such a rugged, homely man.

Chapter 7

All day and throughout supper Layne was preoccupied with her troubled thoughts. She didn't understand the cause of Creed's ambivalence toward her. The most logical course of action would be to confront him with it. In the process she might settle some of her own uncertainties.

With a decision at last made, she wasted no time in following through with it. There was nothing to be gained by putting it off to another day, so Layne tugged on her light gray jacket and wrapped a blue and gray plaid scarf around her bare head. Her boots clumped loudly on the steps as she hurried down the stairs to the front door.

Mattie was watching television in the front room. She glanced curiously at Layne when she emerged from the stairwell, then darted a look at the mantel clock. Its hands were poised near the nine o'clock hour.

"Are you going out?" she questioned Layne, more out of surprise than a desire for an accounting of her movements.

"Just for a short walk." Layne didn't bother to explain that the short walk would take her to Creed's house. She didn't want to make up an excuse about why she wanted to see him.

"Watch yourself. It's bound to be icy out there," Mattie advised and absently watched Layne until she went out the door before letting her attention return to the television screen.

There was a crystalline quality to the air as Layne stepped into the night. A full moon glittered like a big silver dollar, lighting the sky and flooding the ranch yard with its pale beams. Layne picked her way along the ice-slick foot trail through the trees to the second, smaller house. Woodsmoke was coming from its chimney and curling straight up in the windless night.

In the distance a coyote wailed its mournful cry to the moon, the only sound that accompanied the crunch of her footsteps. She was conscious of the frigid nip in the air, but her attention was too concentrated on the light shining from the window of the small house to pay much attention to the cold that turned her breath into a smoky vapor.

When she reached the front door, she paused only an instant, then opened the storm door and knocked on the inner door. The glass panes were steamed over. Even if she had tried, Layne couldn't see inside. But there was only a short wait until the inside door was pulled open and she faced Creed. His gaze narrowed on her as she stood poised on the threshold.

"May I come in?" she requested when he failed to immediately invite her inside.

He inclined his head in an agreeing manner and stepped to the side to permit her entry. Layne walked past him into the main room, where logs glowed a cherry-red in the fireplace, blue-white flames licking over them. The room was small, and the oversized furniture in it was out of proportion to its dimensions but in keeping with the size of the man who occupied the house. The tan leather sofa was long to accommodate Creed's tall frame, and the recliner, too, was large to fit him comfortably. There was a gun rack on the wall where the desk stood. An oil painting of a wildlife scene occupied the only other vacant wall space.

Halfway into the room Layne turned to wait for him. Her scarf slipped off her chestnut hair and fell loosely about her neck. She unbuttoned her coat but made no attempt to take it off. Without looking at her, Creed walked to the fireplace and added a split log from the woodbox to the hot fire. Backlighted by the fire, his silhouette appeared so deceptively lean.

The flames crackled noisily over the new fuel to fill the silence. It became obvious to Layne that Creed was waiting for her to speak. She stifled a rush of irritation at his laconic obstinacy. As a teenager, she had often thought she wanted to fall in love with a man who was the strong and silent type. But after meeting one in the flesh, namely Creed Dawson, it seemed to be his silence she couldn't stand.

"I came here tonight because I wanted to talk to you alone," she stated.

"About what?" He sounded disinterested.

Remaining by the fireplace, Creed angled his body toward her and rested a foot on the raised hearth. The pale blue of his chambray shirt appeared almost white in the firelight as it stretched across his wide shoulders and tapered to his narrow hips. Most of the light in the room came from the fireplace. It softened the harsh contours of his face. A kind of tension knotted her stomach.

"I'd like to know just exactly what our relationship is supposed to be," Layne said, coming straight to the point of her visit. "I don't know whether we're friend, foe, or what."

"That's simple," he replied smoothly. "I'm the boss, and you're the hired hand."

"And you have a policy of not fraternizing with the hired help, is that it?" she guessed stiffly.

"No, it isn't." Creed appeared to be untouched by the tension that gripped her. "But to this point, that is the extent of our relationship. If you've read more into it than that, then it's your problem."

Struggling to keep her calm, Layne smiled coolly. "It's funny that neither Stoney nor Hoyt mentioned to me that you are in the habit of kissing your help."

Something close to a smile quirked his mouth, then he turned to prod at the fire with a brass-handled poker. "When a man finds a beautiful and willing female in his arms, it's second nature to kiss her. But one kiss hardly changes anything. If you cross-examine every man who kisses you to see how it's affected his attitude toward you, I pity them."

He was making her sound like some romantic, idealistic fool. A hotly angry retort trembled on the edge of her tongue, but Layne swallowed it. This was not the first time she had questioned someone adept at avoiding the issue. She noticed a coffee cup sitting on the desk in the corner.

"I suppose you're right." She appeared to concede the point. "Acorns turn into oak trees, but it doesn't necessarily follow that mountains grow out of molehills." She rubbed her hands together as if to warm them. "Do you have any coffee? It's awfully cold outside tonight."

The upward slant of a thick brow seemed to silently speculate on the motive behind her request, but Creed didn't comment on her forwardness, not only inviting herself into his house but also asking for refreshments.

"Sure." He pushed away from the hearthstone and headed for the small kitchen Layne had noticed just to the right of the front door.

After unwinding the scarf from around her neck, she removed her coat and pulled the scarf through one of the sleeves. She draped her coat over the armrest of the sofa and wandered to the fireplace. From the kitchen she heard the clatter of a cup. She was forced to admit she had doubts in her mind, a question whether her imagination might have been overactive or that the attraction was all one-sided. Layne held out her hands to the heat radiating from the glowing logs.

When Creed returned to the room with a coffee cup in his hand, she glanced briefly in his direction. She absently noted again how lightly he moved for a man of his size. He crossed to the fireplace and handed her the cup of steaming black brew. As he resumed his casual stance by the fireplace, his presence seemed to fill the room.

"This is a very compact house," Layne remarked idly. "How big is it?"

"Just three rooms—this one, a kitchen, and a bedroom. Four rooms, counting the bath." He eyed her with a side-long glance, a waiting look in his closed expression.

"You haven't always lived here, have you?" she asked.

"No. I built this when I went into partnership with John on the ranch," he acknowledged.

"Have you always lived alone?" she wondered.

"I don't think my private life is any of your business," he countered without a break in his expression.

Layne sipped at her coffee, concealing the smile on her lips but letting the amusement show in her eyes. "I believe that you were the one who mentioned something earlier today about truth between friends."

"Maybe I should ask why you want to know," he challenged, almost lazily. "Are you gathering material for that piece you're going to write about ranching?"

She stiffened slightly. It had completely slipped her

mind that she had told Mattie that story to persuade her into hiring her on.

"No," she admitted frankly. "I just wanted to know more about you."

"There isn't much to know. I'm a native of the area and have lived here all my life." A grimness settled into his tight-lipped expression to accompany the challenging gleam in his eyes. Creed shifted position to rest a large hand on the mantelpiece and lean toward her. "But I have the feeling you aren't interested in my background. It's the women in my life you want to know about. Well, with this face, there haven't been very many of them. So I'm not what you would call 'experienced' with the opposite sex," he stated roughly.

It explained a few things that should have been obvious to her. There had been no practiced subtleties in their encounters, no masculine persuasion. And it bothered her to hear Creed say such things about himself. She lowered her glance to the cup in her hands, unwilling to meet his keenly assessing gaze.

"I can't believe your life has been as bereft of female companionship as you imply. You're a strong and solid man," Layne insisted.

"Maybe I should have clarified myself by explaining that the type of women I've known aren't the kind you would associate with." The dry sound of amusement was in his voice. "Be honest. I'm not the kind a girl would be anxious to introduce to her parents."

"I wouldn't have any qualms about it if I loved him," she asserted, aware of the agitated turn her breathing had taken.

"What would a beautiful woman ever see in a man who looks like me?" Creed demanded with faint self-derision, mocking her noble-sounding words.

"Looks have nothing to do with it." Her glance flared upward to lock with the penetrating study of his eyes.

"Don't they?" All in one motion, he was straightening from the mantel and hooking an arm around her waist to draw her up close to him so she had no choice but to look at the hard ridges and broad planes of his lean and unattractive features. "Could you love a man who looked like me?" Creed challenged with a sure and knowing look in his half-closed eyes.

It was an impossible question to answer, and Layne didn't even try. "I've never met such a lonely . . . and angry man before in my life," she murmured instead.

The anger she had referred to flashed in his eyes. "I don't need your pity," he growled low in his throat.

The coffee cup was taken from her hand. Layne never had a chance to see what he did with it as he bent his head to compensate for their differing heights and brought his mouth down heavily onto her lips. A second later his bear-like arms were encircling and gathering her to his lean, hard body.

This kiss held neither the cruelty of the first nor the gentleness of the second, but existed on a plateau somewhere in between. His mouth rocked across her lips with a rough hunger that was moist and all-consuming. It seared her with a rawness that hurt in the oddest way.

But that wasn't the only sensation that was rocking her. For the first time there was no heavy, bulky outer clothing to insulate her from the contact with his long, masculine body. Through his shirt, her hands could feel the bunched and flexing muscles in his shoulders and back, the source of the strength she knew so well. Her breasts were nearly flattened by the solid wall of his chest, so flatly roped and powerful, and the wide expanse of his shoulders seemed to curve around her.

A headiness reeled through Layne, heating her blood with a wild kind of excitement. His large hands arched her spine while a muscled thigh insinuated itself between her legs and applied arousing pressure to the lower part of her body. Her lips parted under the sawing force of his mouth to invite the plundering entry of his tongue to mate with hers. Layne knew that her responses were being dictated by a raw and blatant passion—not the domination of his, but her own.

The taste of him was like a wild wine, potent and intoxicating. It rivaled the rough and molding caress of his hands, which roamed her hips and spinal cord, pressing with a disturbing urgency. She, who had always been so rational and analytical in her thinking, found herself without a sane thought in her head. A whirlpool of sensuality was dragging her down, and she had no desire to be rescued.

When he dragged his mouth across her cheek to nuzzle the sensitive hollow of her ear, shivers of pleasure raised the flesh of her skin. His hand moved onto her breast and Layne was absently amazed at how perfectly its roundness fit into his large palm. She pushed against him, finding his bold intimacy more than satisfying. At the kneading pressure of his touch, she pulled in a hissing breath of sheer delight.

She was picked up with such effortless ease, then carried to the sofa. Her hands had curled themselves around his neck, her fingers gliding into the shaggy ends of his dark hair. They remained there after Creed had set her feet on the floor. He straightened to stand tall and erect, no longer bending his head to bring it down to hers.

It took a second for the aloofness in his expression to register. When he gripped her wrists to pull her hands from around his neck, Layne made no protest even though her senses continued to clamor for the intimacy of the previous embrace. She stared at him, searching for some hint of his inner thoughts. Her breathing was long and deep, slow in recovering its former rhythm.

Reaching down, Creed picked up the coat she'd draped over the sofa's armrest and held it out to her. A wry smile twisted her mouth.

"I take it this is an invitation to leave." The huskiness in her voice betrayed her attempt at a chiding challenge.

"I haven't had much sleep these last couple days. I'm tired, and I'd like to have an early night." The graveled pitch of his voice also revealed that he was not as unaffected by their passionate exchange as he wanted her to believe.

"Am I supposed to accept that as your reason?" Layne eyed him with open skepticism as she shrugged into her coat, pushing the scarf out the sleeve.

"I don't particularly care." Creed shrugged.

"Why can't you be honest?" she muttered in irritation.

"Why can't you admit the real reason you came here tonight?" he countered swiftly.

"I did!" she flashed, stung that he could suggest differently.

"Don't kid yourself," he chided with a grim slant of his mouth. "You came here tonight because you happened to like it when I kissed you this morning. You wanted to find out whether it was a fluke or if it could happen again. You weren't interested in my feelings toward you—only in finding out how it could be that you were attracted to someone like me.

She couldn't deny that it was part of her reason for seeing him. "Actually, it was a combination of both."

He breathed out a silent laugh that lacked humor. "I admit you're different from most women. They're usually too concerned about how other people would look at them if they admitted it had been a pleasant experience." Creed paused, looking at her. "Your curiosity has been satisfied so now you can leave."

His observations were a little too astute for Layne to be entirely comfortable with them. "All right, so my curiosity may have been satisfied. Where does that leave us?"

"Right where we started—I'm the boss and you're the hired hand," Creed stated.

"And what about outside of working hours?" she persisted.

He held her gaze without any hesitation. "I believe you told Mattie you were only going to work a couple of months. There's only a couple weeks to go before you'll be leaving."

"Is that the way you want it?" she demanded.

An unfriendly smile broke across his features. "I think you're finally getting the message."

"Maybe I've had trouble because you send conflicting signals," Layne said curtly and arranged her scarf over her head. "In case you've forgotten, you kissed me to start this whole thing."

"Believe me, I've regretted it since," he said dryly. "You're all too tempting, Miss MacDonald, but I'm sure you know that."

She bridled at the remark that somehow made this situation all her fault because she was an attractive female. "Go ahead and blame it on me," she snapped. "I can't help the way I was born any more than you can."

A cold draft of air hit her as she opened the door, but she didn't slow down until she was nearly to the main house. Her anger faded, leaving her with a sense of hurt and rejection. When she entered the house, her glance bounced away from Mattie's inquiring took, but no questions were asked.

"The news is just coming on," Mattie informed her. "Would you care to watch it?"

There was a reluctance to return to the privacy of her room. Layne didn't want to be alone with her thoughts. She wanted to talk to somebody; she wanted to confide in Mattie about this crazy, mixed-up situation she was caught in, but she didn't know how or where to start. So she simply sat down in one of the armchairs and looked at the television set.

But the images on the screen didn't register. With a start, Layne realized Mattie had said something to her. "I'm sorry. What did you say?"

"It doesn't matter." Mattie eyed her thoughtfully, then asked after a short pause, "Is something bothering you?"

Here was the chance she had been wanting, but still Layne hesitated, her fingers plucking at the doily on the armrest. "I went over to talk to Creed tonight."

"I figured you went somewhere," Mattie acknowledged. "For as long as you were gone, you didn't look cold when you came in, so I knew you hadn't spent all that time walking."

"How long have you known Creed?" Layne chose to back into the subject.

"He was here when I came to work for John," she replied. "I guess you could say he was the son John was never able to have. That's why John took him in and made him his partner." Mattie leaned back and gazed thoughtfully into space. "Creed was always something of a loner. I guess he had a hard time of it growing up—with kids teasing him and calling him names. When he was full size, they didn't often say anything to his face."

"I suppose he didn't date much," Layne offered.

"No. There weren't many who would go out with him. I don't imagine the pretty ones would give him the time of day. I often think it would have been easier for him if he'd gone out for sports—become a football hero or something," Mattie said with a sigh.

"Because of that, he holds it against me because I'm good looking," Layne realized, irritated that she was paying for something that was none of her doing. "So now he isn't going to let himself like me."

"Why should it matter to you whether he likes you or not? He treats you fairly."

"Because . . ." Agitated, Layne pushed to her feet and prowled restlessly to the window. "This probably sounds crazy. I know it doesn't make sense to me, but there's something about him that appeals to me. Practically every time I try to get close to him, he rejects it."

"I hope you don't think he's some overgrown stray dog that's starved for attention," Mattie chided.

"On the inside, he could be," Layne suggested cautiously.

"Attention is not the same as love. If you just feel sorry for him, then leave him alone. I can't help having some motherly feelings toward him, although heaven knows, he doesn't need me to protect him," Mattie admitted with a small shake of her head. "You probably feel an affinity for him because you felt unwanted and rejected as a child."

"So you think I just feel compassion for him." A frown knitted her forehead.

"It's a definite possibility."

Layne carefully thought through Mattie's reasoning before discarding that explanation. None of her responses had been forced; they had sprung naturally, without any prompting. Neither compassion nor pity had anything to do with the feelings she had toward Creed.

"No." She shook her head. "It's something else." She wasn't sure what she'd accomplished by talking to Mattie about this, except to learn a little more about Creed. Nothing had been solved. There was a vague disappointment that her natural mother hadn't been able to come up with the right answers for her. "It's getting late," she said. "I think I'll turn in."

"Good night, Layne. I'm sorry I wasn't more help." A wistful note crept into Mattie's usually blunt voice.

"That's okay." A shoulder lifted in a vague shrug that indicated it didn't matter. Then Layne headed for the stairwell and her bedroom on the second floor.

Hoyt stood at the half-door of the barn and gazed at the gray clouds scudding across the sky. His face wore a disgruntled look as he turned away from the door and approached the stall where Layne was saddling the roan gelding.

"Would you just look at the sky?" he grumbled. "And I thought sure spring was on its way. I could smell it in the air."

Stoney came tromping in from the barnyard, a collection of mud and manure globbed on his boots. "Yeah and it walks like spring out there too." But he lacked Hoyt's enthusiasm as he stomped his feet in an effort to rid himself of the excess weight on his boots. "I can't stand this infernal mud," he grumbled.

"Well, it won't be around long. We got another cold spell on the way. Instead of complaining about the mud, you can grumble about the ice," Hoyt declared, wrangling with the older cowboy in their usual fashion. "Nothing ever satisfies you. It's either too hot or too cold, too wet or too dry."

With the pad properly adjusted beneath the saddle, Layne bent down to grab the cinch strap and string it through the metal ring. "Did either of you catch the forecast this morning?"

"Yeah, and they called for snow, but the kid here didn't think they knew what they were talking about," Stoney returned the good-natured insult to his young friend. "Why do you think Creed's sending us out to bunch the cattle closer to home?"

He slapped the rump of the saddled horse in the adjoining stall to urge it to one side, then walked in to unfasten the lead rope from the headstall under its bridle. The roan snorted and lifted its head to gaze after the horse backing out of the stall.

"Git your horse and come on, Hoyt," Stoney chided the young cowboy for his slowness as he led his horse down the concrete walkway to the door at the end of the passageway.

"I'll be along shortly," Layne assured when she saw Hoyt look at her and hesitate.

"We'll wait for you outside," he promised, and untied his horse to lead it out.

After winding the strap through the cinch ring in a loose figure eight, Layne made the first pull to tighten the cinch. The ringing of ironclad hoofs on concrete ended as Hoyt led his horse out the far door, and a set of footsteps took the place of that sound. She recognized that long, swinging step and felt an edginess take hold of her nerves.

When they stopped at her horse's stall, she didn't glance around. Instead, she gave another tug of the cinch strap and gained another inch. She was conscious of his gaze studying her. It was an almost physical sensation. Three days had passed since she'd sought him out at his home, three days that not even the premature spring thaw had been able to melt. It was the last time she'd been alone with him until now.

He stepped into the stall and laid a gloved hand on her shoulder to nudge her out of the way. "I'll finish that for you." The impersonal tone of his voice grated at her, as unsettling in its way as the pressure of his hand on her shoulder.

Layne shrugged away from the latter. "I can manage just fine, thank you." It was a clipped answer, unaccompanied by even a glance in his direction.

She snugged the cinch up tight and reached for the stirrup hooked over the saddle horn. They both grabbed hold of it at the same instant. After a split-second's hesitation, Layne drew her hand away from the accidental contact and moved to the horse's head to unfasten the reins from the manger ring.

"What's this? You've developed a rather sudden aversion to my touch, is that it?" Creed challenged tightly.

She turned to face him squarely, a faint glare in her look. "Excuse me, but I had the distinct impression that it was you who wanted nothing to do with me."

For a long moment he held her gaze while a muscle flexed convulsively in his jaw. Abruptly he swung away. "Damn you, Layne."

His gloved hand slammed itself against a sideboard of the stall, shaking loose minute particles of dust and debris. The roan shied at the sudden, loud noise, throwing back its head and pulling against the reins Layne held. She observed the rigid tension in Creed's stance. His face was averted, but enough of it was visible for her to make out the twisted agony in its taut expression. She was too angry to feel sorry for him.

"I hope you're confused, Creed," she declared. "I hope to God you're half as confused as I am."

Maybe it was callous of her, but she wanted to hurt him. For the last three days she'd been harboring a kind of resentment. Perhaps it was natural for him to be wary of her, but she deserved a chance. She had turned the other cheek too many times to do it again.

She started to back her saddled horse out of the stall to lead it out of the barn. With a determined effort, she avoided glancing in his direction. But the minute she was level with him, his hand snaked out and caught her arm just above the elbow to pull her around so she faced him.

His teeth were bared, as if holding back all the feelings that were struggling behind his tightly controlled expression. So much was contained inside him that she was staggered by the invisible force of it.

"Layne." He ground out her name like a man possessed.

Then his hands were tightening on her arms and hauling her roughly against his jacket while his mouth swooped down to hungrily bruise her lips. It opened her up and a swell of emotions tumbled crazily through her. She was hot and on fire, her body heated by some fevered rush that weakened her legs. She swayed into him, letting him support her full weight while she tried to satisfy this giant need that claimed her.

Her fingers unconsciously retained their clasp on the reins as the shaggy-coated roan impatiently reversed the rest of the way out of the stall and walked as far as the long reins would allow. Its ears were pricked in the direction of the door where its companions had gone.

The hinges creaked loudly as the door was opened, letting a long shaft of sunlight into the shadowed barn. Hoyt stuck his head inside. "Hey, Layne! What's keepin' ya?"

The voice, the intrusion, broke the kiss, but Layne didn't immediately answer him. Her soft gaze was studying Creed's face, not noticing its homeliness but taking in its profound strength. It was lean and raw, all blunt edges and harsh contours, but underneath he was devastatingly attractive.

"Layne?" Hoyt called again.

Shielded by the high sides of the stall, she wasn't concerned about being seen, so she made no attempt to loosen herself from the circle of Creed's arms, not yet anyway. Something warm and ardent was shining in his eyes. Her horse shifted, its iron shoes scraping across the concrete.

"I'll be right there!" she finally called back.

Dragging in a deep breath, Creed withdrew his arms from around her and adjusted the scarf more snugly around her throat. "It's going to get cold out there." His voice was softly gruff as he pulled the knitted cap more fully over her ears.

Layne understood this indirect expression of concern for her well-being. It prompted a small smile. "I'll be all right," she assured him, then gathered up the reins to her horse and stepped away to lead him outside where Hoyt and Stoney were waiting for her.

Chapter 8

To facilitate the gathering of the herd, they split up to cover as much ground as possible and drift any cattle that had strayed back to the main bunch before the storm broke. In the past six weeks Layne had become familiar with the rolling land that edged the long valley where the cattle were wintered. So she rode out with confidence.

The menacing gray skies were no idle threat. By midday small flakes were drifting in the air, reminding Layne more of ice flakes than snow. The temperature dropped sharply, plummeting to the freezing level that allowed the flakes to accumulate on the ground.

Her shoulders were hunched forward inside her coat and her chin was buried in the folds of her scarf. Her legs were starting to feel numb despite the insulated underwear she had on, and she had stopped feeling her toes an hour ago. She had almost covered her section of the hills.

The red roan gelding followed the dip in the land, moving at a fast walk to indicate its own desire to finish with the job and return to the warm barn. A small ground blizzard swept the light snow in a white stream that raced hock-high at the horse's feet. It almost made Layne dizzy to watch it rush past. It made a whispering sound, almost an eerie warning of the approaching storm. But there was something reassuring in the creak of the saddle leather.

Out of the corner of her eye Layne caught a movement. She swiveled her head in that direction and glimpsed the dully rusted coat of a Hereford as it trotted quickly away from the horse and rider. She checked her horse and reined it around to pursue the cow and chase it in the right direction.

The strange ground blizzard concealed an iced-over pond until Layne's horse was nearly on top of it. It was one of those long, skinny ones, shaped to the hollow of the ground, she discovered when she halted the gelding to look for a way around it. She didn't want to waste the time to make a long detour around it, so she nudged the roan with her heels and directed it across the narrow body of frozen water.

The red roan snorted nervously and eyed the hard surface with distrust, resisting her urgings. After several prodding kicks it moved skittishly onto the ice. Halfway across it there was an ominous groaning sound beneath them. Suddenly apprehensive, Layne tried to hurry the gelding, but the groaning sound was followed by a loud pop and crack.

The gelding panicked and half reared. Layne's legs were so numb she couldn't keep her grip on the saddle, and her feet slipped out of the stirrups. As she grabbed for the saddle horn Layne saw the ice breaking up under the weight of the horse's hind legs. At the same instant the roan lunged forward and bolted for the shore. Layne had no chance to recover her balance and stay in the saddle. She was thrown sideways, falling heavily onto the already cracked ice.

It collapsed under the impact of her weight. She felt

herself land hard, then suddenly she was completely immersed in icy water. The shock of it nearly paralyzed her. Instinctively she kicked for the gray surface, the only patch of light in the murky, cold water. She came up sputtering and gasping for air. Her hat was gone, lost somewhere in the depths of the pond, and her chestnut hair was streaming down her face in clinging wet strands.

Layne had one glimpse of the roan horse galloping over a white hill, the stirrups flopping, then it disappeared. The broken edge of the ice was only a couple of yards away. She struck out for it and felt a sudden panic at the sucking drag of all her heavy, wet clothes trying to pull her under. It seemed to take all her strength just to keep her head above water. And the water was freezing cold. She wouldn't last long in it.

Sobbing with the effort, she fought for every inch of that small distance to the ice. But when she reached it, she couldn't find anything to hold on to so she could haul herself out of the water. Her hands were so wet they kept slipping off the ice. With all the weight dragging her down, Layne didn't have enough strength to lever herself out of the water. About all she could do was hold on.

"Help!" she shouted, although she didn't know of a soul who would hear her. She was frightened and growing colder by the second. "Help!"

Stretching her arms onto the ice as far as she could and clawing for a hold with her fingers, she tried again to pull herself onto the solid ice. She heard something crack. The ice wasn't strong enough to take her weight. The thaw they'd had the last few days had weakened it.

Defeat sagged through her. She rested her head on the corner of the ice and sobbed quietly, certain she was going to die. Her body felt so wooden that she couldn't even make her legs move to tread water, yet her fingers refused to give up their tiny grip on a ridge of the ice's rough surface.

"Help me." It was a pathetically weak call that she didn't expect to be heard by anyone. She was so cold, so very, very cold, that it didn't seem to matter anymore.

Her mind was drifting. Far, far away she thought she heard someone call her name, but it wasn't possible. Her hand lost its hold, and she groped instinctively to regain it. But her fingers were so numb.

The ice cracked again and Layne sobbed out loud. "No." She didn't want to die.

"Hang on, honey." That gruff, urgent voice—it sounded so near.

"I . . . can't," she answered, certain she was hallucinating. "I'm so . . . cold."

There were more ominous cracking sounds. Slowly she was losing her grip and slipping away from the edge. The heaviness of her body was pulling her down. As the numbly cold water climbed up her neck, Layne tipped her head as far back as it would go, desperately struggling for that last breath of air. Her hands and wrists were held by something, and Layne wondered if they had become frozen to the ice.

"Come on back to me, honey," the same gruff voice urged her roughly.

Mentally she kept fighting against the numbness, struggling to retain consciousness. There was a nightmarish unreality to it, as though none of it was really happening to her. Layne had the oddest sense of being pulled out of the icy water an inch at a time. It was a slow, disbelieving discovery when she realized her shoulders were out of the water and her arms were stretched flat on the ice, held by something. She made the effort of lifting her head. A large figure lay on the ice, not far from her. She stared, afraid it was another part of her nightmare and he wasn't really there.

"Creed?" she whimpered.

"Thank God you're alive," he muttered thickly.

"Help me, please." Her head sagged onto a wet arm, lacking the strength to support itself.

"Layne, listen to me," Creed urged. "This ice isn't strong enough to support both of us. I've tied a rope around your wrists. I want you to grab hold of it with your hands. Do you hear me, Layne?" he demanded.

All she could do was weakly nod her head. Her hands fumbled awkwardly for the rope, hardly able to feel anything. She made a puny attempt to grasp it, twisting it around her hands.

"I'm going to pull you out slowly," he told her. "Help me if you can."

Layne tried, but her body was so numb there was little she could do to aid him. She was a dead weight that he had to virtually drag out of the water and across the ice. Layne could feel it cracking and giving under her, nearly breaking. With each small crunch, she expected to plunge into the frigid waters again.

"You're going to make it, honey," Creed insisted and steadily pulled on the rope. There were more encouraging words, spoken with a grim determination. It was the sound of his voice she believed in more than the words he spoke.

When she was finally within reach, his hands grabbed her shoulders and hauled her the rest of the way to safety. Layne wanted to thank him, to say something, but all she could do was look at him.

His gaze bore into her while he hurriedly shrugged out of his coat and peeled off his shirt. He used it to partially rub dry her wet hair and stimulate the circulation in her face and hands. His hat was pushed onto her head, an odd thing to do, she thought at the time. Without regard for her jacket or its buttons, he began to rip it open and push it off of her. The jacket was already turning stiff.

Violent shivers began to rack her body and set her teeth to chattering. As soon as her coat was off, Creed wrapped her in his large jacket and lifted her bodily into the cradle of his arms. Layne kept thinking how cold he must be without his jacket, and only his insulated undershirt to protect him. The jacket didn't seem to be doing her much good, since it brought no sensation of warmth.

Everything was hazy to her. She was conscious, yet she wasn't. His hat sat down around her ears, its brim shutting out the sight of his face. Layne knew she was being carried somewhere because she remembered that he had picked her up, but all that registered in her mind was how terribly cold she was.

The world around her seemed gray with specks of white floating in it. There was an almost dreamlike quality about it and she wondered if she was dead. But that couldn't be, because Creed was here. She wanted so desperately to be warm again that she almost cried.

There was a loud wrenching sound, and she was jostled in his arms. An inarticulate murmur of fear came from her, certain they were back on the pond and the ice was giving way. Suddenly she could see Creed's face and the puffs of steam coming from his mouth. She was moving away from him. It seemed to confirm her terror that she was falling through the ice again, and her eyes wildly appealed to him not to let her go.

"It's okay, honey." His husky voice was riddled with the sound of his heavy breathing. "You're safe now."

A second later Layne realized she was propped on the seat of a pickup truck. It was true; she was going to be all right. Her eyes fluttered shut with relief. When she opened them to look at the man who had saved her, Creed was bending down, doing something with her legs. But her body felt so wooden that all sensation was dulled until it was almost nonexistent.

A boot thumped on the floorboards of the truck, followed by a second, plus a double pair of wet socks. She was conscious of her foot being shaken, and guessed that Creed was trying to stimulate the circulation by rubbing them, but it was difficult to feel anything. Her nerve ends were too cold to transmit any sensation of her skin being touched.

The jacket was a constraining cocoon around her. Creed straightened and swung her legs inside the truck, then shut the door. Her eyes watched him walk around to the driver's side, briskly rubbing his bare hands and hunching his wide shoulders. There was a stiff, cold look to his features when he climbed behind the wheel.

The motor kicked over with the first turn of the ignition switch. His reddened fingers reached over to the panel and switched the heater fan to its highest notch. His brown glance ran to her shivering form.

"It'll be warm in here soon," he promised and pulled her across the seat to mold her to his side.

An arm stayed tightly around her, hugging her close, while he used one hand to shift the truck into gear and hold on to the steering wheel. Her head lolled on the rounded hollow of his hard shoulder and bounced against it as the truck leaped forward, speeding as fast as the rough terrain would allow.

A thousand needle fires seemed to burn her face, the first painful knowledge that sensation was beginning to return to her. Hot air started blowing out of the floor vent, but it only made her bare feet hurt. She continued to shiver uncontrollably.

"Creed, I'm so cold." Her voice was a thready sound, helplessly appealing to him to make her warm.

"I know, baby. I know," the velvety texture of his rough voice crooned soothingly to her. "It won't be long now. Just hang on."

But the miles seemed to go on forever. Layne didn't know where they were or how far they had to go. Her body throbbed all over with the cold. Yet there was some hope because she could feel the hot air blowing from the heater vents. There was just too little of it to warm her freezing wet skin. Her body vibrated in its attempt to generate its own warmth, but the cold seemed to penetrate all the way to the bone.

"I thought I was going to die." Her voice wavered on a near sob. The terror of the incident was coming back so fresh that Layne had to talk about it to puncture the bubble of new panic inside. "I was so frightened, Creed." It took all her control to give the faint impression of rational calm.

"Don't think about it," he ordered as his arm tightened fiercely around her. "You're with me now." He turned his head, dodging the low hat brim to press his mouth to the corner of her eye in a brief, reassuring kiss.

"It happened so fast," Layne murmured in a shuddering recollection. "I spotted a stray cow on the other side of the pond. I decided to . . . take a shortcut across it instead of . . . going all the way around. I forgot . . . all about how much thawing had occurred. The ice . . . started cracking when my horse was out in the middle of it. He spooked and reared . . . I lost my balance. I—" She remembered the stunning shock of the icy water, and the words to describe it froze in her throat.

"Sssh. It's over now." Creed seemed to know exactly why she shuddered so violently. "We're almost at the house."

The seconds seemed like minutes before she heard the grinding of brake shoes and felt the truck slow to a stop. Creed dragged her bundled form sideways out of the driver's door and hefted her into his arms. The sudden blast of cold air sent more shivers racking through her body and chattering her teeth.

With long, sweeping strides, he carried her up the porch steps and propped open the storm door with his shoulder. He kicked the inner door open with his foot and swung inside with his burden.

"Mattie!" His rough voice lifted to send his urgent call through the empty rooms. "Mattie!"

He paused long enough to push the door shut with his foot, then headed for the stairs. He practically ran up the steps, with Layne joggling in his arms. All she could think about were the thick, warm quilts on her bed. But Creed carried her into the bathroom instead and stood her upright beside the tub.

His hands supported her while his gaze bore into her. "Can you stand up by yourself?"

Her legs felt so wooden that she wasn't sure. "I . . . think so," Layne said with a shivering nod.

His keen gaze lingered on her a second after he took his hands away to assure himself that she had sufficient control of her limbs to do it. But she was standing, if somewhat unsteadily. Turning, Creed bent over the tub, closed the drain stopper, and turned on the water faucets to fill the tub. After the water temperature had been adjusted, he straightened and unwrapped his jacket from around her and took off the hat.

"Start getting out of those wet clothes." There was a flick of a gaze over the length of her body before he turned to hook his jacket over the doorknob with his hat.

With benumbed fingers, Layne tried to do as she was told, but she was shaking so badly that her cold-stiffened hands couldn't seem to manage this simplest function. She sent a helpless glance at Creed.

"I can't," she murmured. "I'm so cold—"

No further explanation was necessary as he moved back to her. "I'll help you." With no hesitation, he began to unfasten the front button of her flannel shirt.

Layne was much too cold to feel any awkwardness at being undressed by him. She only wanted to get out of her wet and clinging clothes, which seemed to be freezing against her skin. There was a matter-of-fact deftness in the touch of his hands, impersonal and swift in their stripping of her blouse.

It was a struggle to pull the insulated and long-sleeved undershirt over her head. Layne helped him as much as she could, sitting down on the closed lid of the toilet seat while he tugged off her jeans and longjohns. Her bra and panties were the last to go. By then she was shivering so violently, her bare skin a mass of raised flesh, that she wasn't conscious of her nakedness.

Again Creed picked her up and she huddled against him. Her arms were crossed tightly around her stomach, trying to hold on to the little warmth she possessed. The texture of his clothes seemed abrasive against her bare skin. He started to lower her into the tub.

The instant her feet touched the hot bathwater, a moaning gasp of pain was wrenched from her throat. All that heat hurt so bad that Layne didn't think she could stand it. Her fingers curled into the wafflelike weave of Creed's insulated undershirt.

"No. Please," she protested with twisting agony, but Creed continued to lower her into the water, getting himself wet in the process.

The painful submersion didn't end until she was lying against the curved back of the tub and the water was lapping around her neck. Only then did the needle-sharp stinging finally ease and the torture of suddenly being engulfed in so much warmth finally subside. Her body throbbed with feeling that had been so long denied it. She was unquestionably alive and tingling all over. She opened her eyes to look gratefully at Creed as he stood by the tub, drying his hands on a towel.

"You be all right?" A thick eyebrow lifted in inquiry. At her affirmative nod, a near smile touched his mouth.

As he started for the door Layne remembered something she'd learned once. "There's no truth . . . in that old wives' tale about a person catching cold from getting wet." It was a way of assuring him that she wasn't in danger of contracting pneumonia from her dunking in the icy pond.

Creed paused at the door. "I wasn't worried about you catching cold," he said. "My fear was hypothermia. A severe drop in body temperature has been known to kill people." Her eyes rounded at the stark realization that even after being saved from drowning she had still been in danger. Creed pointed a blunt finger at her. "Stay in that tub for a while and soak in that heat."

As he walked into the hallway, taking his hat and jacket with him, Layne shuddered—this time in a delayed reaction to the closeness of her call instead of the cold. She sunk a little deeper into the warm bathwater until it was up to her chin and closed her eyes, absorbing the sensation of heat that surrounded her body.

How long she lay in the tub, Layne couldn't say. She was vaguely conscious of the sounds of Creed moving about the house. Once she heard voices, but mostly she was aware of the life returning to her limbs and the stiffness ebbing away.

The water temperature was just becoming tepid when she heard the approach of Creed's footsteps. He entered the bathroom with barely a glance in her direction, carrying her long terrycloth robe and her hair dryer. Turning, he removed a large bath towel from the rack on the wall, then faced the tub, shaking out the towel to its full size.

"You'd better get out of the water before your skin shrivels up like a prune," Creed advised blandly.

Layne hesitated. It was a little late for a show of modesty when he'd been the one to undress her, but she was suddenly self-conscious about her nudity even though he had seen her naked body before. Keeping her gaze lowered so he couldn't see the hint of embarrassment in her eyes, she climbed out of the tub and stepped into the oversized towel, which he immediately wrapped around her.

Decently covered, she was able to slide a look at him, but his expression was closed. Once the towel was securely wrapped around her, Layne expected him to leave. Instead Creed used the excess fold of the towel to begin briskly rubbing her shoulders dry.

"I can manage." She awkwardly attempted to assure him that she was capable of drying herself off.

"It's important to stimulate your circulation." Creed sounded so downright impersonal that it seemed prudish to argue with him.

But Layne could have told him that his mere presence was having a very stimulating effect on her system. Since he didn't seem to notice her faint agitation, she tried not to draw his attention to it. But she could feel the heat rising in her neck as his large hands rubbed the towel over her breasts and stomach.

Once Creed paused briefly to toss her another towel for her wet hair, then transferred his attention to the water trickling down her shoulder blades. She quickly realized that Creed didn't regard any part of her body as sacred territory as he roughly massaged her buttocks and inner thighs with the thick towel. In all honesty, it was more sensually exhilarating than it was embarrassing.

Her pulse was beating very rapidly when he finished and held out the robe to help her into it. Layne slipped an arm into the sleeve, then allowed the towel to slide onto the bath mat and hooked her right arm into the other sleeve. She crisscrossed the front of the robe and tied a knot in the sash belt to hold it in place.

Creed lifted the length of her damp hair out from under the collar. "You'd better dry it before you come downstairs."

"I will," she said huskily and turned to him. He stood for a minute gazing back at her, a dark and disturbing light in his eyes, the mask of indifference gone. "I don't think I've thanked you yet for saving me."

"It isn't necessary." His answer was almost curt as his jaw tightened. Despite that brief flash of grimness, he lifted a hand to brush a damp tendril of hair behind her ear. "It's a miracle you didn't get any frostbite."

"I know."

His chest lifted on a deep breath that he was slow to release. He seemed to be struggling with some inner battle. Layne wasn't sure who won when he turned on his heel and headed for the door.

"You'd better dry that wet head of yours before you get chilled again," he advised over his shoulder as he walked out of the bathroom.

It was already toweled damp-dry so it didn't take her blow-dryer long to finish the job. Her thick mane of chestnut hair glistened like silk when she descended the stairs into the living room. Creed walked in from the kitchen just as she entered the room.

Layne faltered for an instant, feeling a sensual impact at the sight of the broad, flat muscles of his naked chest. He was no longer wearing that insulated top. She vaguely remembered that he'd gotten it wet, and she could attest to the fact that there was nothing more uncomfortable than wearing wet garments.

Yet she found it unnerving, in an exciting way, to see all those sinewy, powerful muscles and that diamond-shaped patch of chest hairs. She became conscious that she was staring and turned away.

A fire blazed in the fireplace, young flames leaping high over the dry logs. She moved toward the hearth. "This looks warm and cozy," she declared. "I'm glad you started it."

Creed came into the room as Layne sank to the floor in front of the fire. "I fixed you some hot, sweet tea. It's supposed to be good for shock."

"I don't think I'm suffering from any, but it sounds good anyway." Her lips barely curved, but the look in her eyes was radiant with the inner glow of pleasure she was feeling as she accepted the cup he offered to her. He pulled a footstool closer to the fire and sat down, bending his long legs.

"Where's Mattie? I thought I heard you talking to someone earlier." Her gaze kept straying to the hard, bare muscles of his chest as she sipped at the strong, sweet tea. That indefinable male quality she had always sensed about him was more pronounced now—and more disturbing.

"She left a note saying she'd gone into town. It seems we're low on coffee. She said she was going to stop at the Powell ranch on the way back, so she probably won't be home until suppertime," Creed explained. "You probably heard me talking to Stoney. Your horse came back to the barn. They were worried something had happened to you until I told them I'd found you and brought you home."

Layne tilted her head to one side. "What were you doing out there? How did you find me?"

"I was driving the fenceline—about a quarter mile from the pond. I saw your horse . . . and noticed his legs were wet. The pond was the only place that was close by." He threaded his long, callused fingers together, absently study-ing them. "I kept hoping you'd simply been thrown."

"Then it was just sheer luck . . ." Her throat tightened on the rest of the words. "If you hadn't been there, I—"

"Don't think about it, Layne," he ordered grimly when a small shudder trembled through her shoulders. "I did find you."

"Yes." She felt shaky inside and set the cup of tea on the hearthstone. She made a determined effort to find a lighter subject. "Why did you put your hat on my head? It was about three sizes too big for me."

His glance flicked over her curled position on the floor. "A lot of a person's body heat escapes through their head. That's why in the old days, people used to wear caps to bed."

Layne turned her head to study the bright, crackling flames. Slowly she let her gaze be drawn back to him. "Isn't it crazy? Even with this fire . . . and the robe, I feel chilly."

There was a slight hesitation before Creed moved off the stool and went down on one knee to join her on the floor. When he started to gather her into his arms, it seemed the most natural thing to lay back and turn into his length so they would be lying face-to-face on their sides.

Layne pressed close to him, his arms wound firmly around her to mold them together. With the fire warming her backside, she snuggled into his bare chest to have closer contact with the body heat radiating from his hard flesh. She laid her cheek in the center of the sensually rough mat of chest hairs and inhaled his warm, male smell.

"Is that better?" The vibrations of his low voice rumbled beneath her.

Her hand stroked the hard skin stretched tautly over his ribs while Layne enjoyed the sensation of touching him.

"You must have a furnace inside you," she murmured. "Your body feels so warm."

"Does it?" His fingers spread across the hollow of her back, lightly caressing, while his other hand absently rubbed her shoulder.

"I'm glad you're such a large man," Layne mused softly, enveloped by the sensation of those wide shoulders curving around her. "There's so much more of you to keep me warm. It almost feels as if I'm crawling inside you."

There was a faint tremor in the rough fingertips that curled along the underside of her chin, silently urging her to lift her head. She raised it slowly and felt the running search of his gaze over her face. Layne sensed the tautness in his body, the stringent containment of his feelings. Then, like the slow uncoiling of a tightly wound spring, it was released as he moved toward her lips.

His mouth rolled over their soft curves, testing and tasting, while his hand cradled the back of her head in its palm. It was an instinctive movement that eased Layne around until both shoulders touched the carpeted floor. Her hands slid around his naked middle and flattened themselves along his ridged spine. Creed nibbled at her lips, taking sensuous bites of them. His fingers tangled themselves in the silken strands of her hair while he dragged his mouth over her cheek and eye, grazing along her jaw. She felt the raw shudder that claimed him when he pressed his lean cheek against hers.

"I thought I was going to lose you," he muttered thickly, close to her ear. "I was shaking so badly when I crawled onto that ice . . . I thought you were going to slip away from me before I could reach you."

She had a brief flash of insight for the hell he'd gone through. The pressure of his hands increased as she held him tightly to her and pressed her lips to his angular jaw.

There was the faintest scrape of his whiskers against her sensitive mouth when he turned to give her a more satisfactory location on which to bestow her kisses.

This time it was all raw desire, undisguised and unrestrained, as he plundered her parted lips to lick the sensitive insides of her mouth and tease her tongue, stirring her excitement. Her gliding hands reveled in the sensation of the bunched and flexing muscles beneath the hard, smooth skin of his back.

There was a spiraling pleasure stabbing sweetly through her body. When she felt his hand pushing apart the crossed front of her robe, a need to experience his intimate touch flowered deep inside her. His large, work-roughened hand slid onto her bare skin and cupped its palm over the peak of her breast.

The blood pounded through her veins and a delicious languor claimed her limbs. Shivers danced over her skin as Creed burned kisses down the sensitive cord in her neck and the hollow of her throat. She breathed in sharply at the exquisite sensation of his lips trailing up the slope of her breast and curling onto her hardening nipple.

The slipknot of her robe sash was easily dispensed with so that nothing held the robe closed. Her fingers were in the unruly thickness of his hair, its springy texture stimulating to the touch. Unconsciously she murmured his name over and over again in a fevered need. But his hands were already answering it, gliding down her stomach to her hot thighs and twisting hips.

Hungry for the taste of him, she urged him back to her lips. His devouring kiss only made the throbbing in her loins more intense, and the fine mat of hairs on his chest sensually tickled her breasts, which had been so sensitized by the manipulations of his hard tongue. She writhed against him, inviting a greater intimacy, oblivious to the scrape of the rough denim jeans against her bare legs.

When he pulled away from her to unfasten them, Layne rid herself of the encumbering sleeves of her robe. When Creed sat up to simultaneously push off the jeans and long underwear, the yellow cat appeared and strutted over to him, attempting to rub its head against his arm. Creed impatiently brushed it aside.

The cat glared at Layne and marched away in a huff, its long tail slashing the air. Her glance followed its offended departure, then swung to Creed as he lowered himself alongside her once more. His lean male flanks glistened in the firelight.

"I think Fred's jealous," she murmured and curved her hands around the strong column of his neck to bring him the rest of the way down.

"He'll have to get used to it," Creed said against her lips.

Just the touch of his mouth and the feel of his hard male body was enough to arouse her already eager flesh. She arched against him.

"I want you, Creed," Layne said, admitting all that her actions had been telling him.

"Not yet," he said thickly. "I've waited for this too long, and now I'm going to take my own sweet time about making love to you."

With his hands and his lips, he kissed and caressed nearly every inch of her until Layne was trembling with the rawness of her needs. It was abundantly clear to her that a person didn't need to be a skilled lover to know all about loving.

When she thought she could endure the agony of wanting to love him no longer, a lithe, powerful leg nudged her legs apart. She wanted to gather him in, hold all of him to her, but Creed levered the upper half of his body away from her.

"No," she whispered and pulled at him.

His resistance was only a temporary thing as he responded to her urgings and eased his weight onto her. "I'll be too heavy for you," he warned.

"No. You'll never be that," Layne murmured and rubbed her lips over his mouth.

Then he was taking her and driving into her, their lips and bodies fusing in a glorious union of souls and flesh that lifted them both. They strained together, trying to deny the physical laws that kept them two separate beings. Yet, in a swirling moment of sheer ecstasy, their essences mingled and it didn't matter.

The firelight was flickering soft and low, burning steadily but without the leaping flames with which it had so hotly begun. Her head was resting in the crook of his shoulder, their bodies still partially entwined as if reluctant to let go of that moment. Layne sighed blissfully and sensed the inquiring look Creed sent her.

"I feel all warm and soft as butter inside," she declared softly.

His hand roamed across the flatness of her stomach to the underswell of a breast. "You feel more like a woman to me," he murmured huskily.

"Oh, really?" Layne tipped her head back so she could see his face. "And what does a woman feel like?"

"All round and soft, with skin like milk." The faint smile left the edges of his mouth as his gaze darkened to search her face. "I didn't hurt you, did I?"

"No," she assured him with a small shake of her head. But his question made her remember that it was only the people a person loved who could hurt them. "Love" was a word she used cautiously, and she was hesitant to attribute it to this warm, wonderful feeling she had. She settled back on the comfortable pillow of his shoulder and shut her eyes to savor this moment of quiet closeness.

"Tired?" Creed asked and lightly stroked her hair.

"Mmm." It was an affirmative sound.

Layne felt the pressure of his mouth on her hair, then there was just the warmth of his body and the feel of his strong arms. She drifted off, not really intending to sleep, instead finding that plateau somewhere in between sleep and wakefulness. She snuggled closer to him, burrowing into his chest like a cat. She knew when he pulled the robe over her to keep her warm, and smiled at the caring gesture.

Chapter 9

A sensation of coolness stirred Layne. She pulled at the blanket on her shoulder to hug it around her neck. When she did, there was a draft on her feet. Suddenly the hardness of the bed made an impression on her, jolting Layne into remembering where she was.

But Creed was gone. She sat up and the robe slipped down. Impatiently she picked it up and pushed her arms through the sleeves as she got to her feet. When she paused to snug the robe tightly around the middle and belt it, she noticed the pumpkin-colored cat sitting in all its majesty by the kitchen door, a very smug look on his face.

"Thanks, Fred," she murmured. "I wondered if he was still here."

With a swish of its tail, the cat planted itself in the doorway as she approached, daring her to cross. But Layne wasn't intimidated by its territorial behavior and simply stepped around it.

Creed was standing near the counter when she entered the kitchen. His back was to the doorway. He sent a half-glance over his shoulder that didn't quite reach her. On the back porch the clothes dryer was tumbling.

"Fred told me you were out here," Layne said as she walked up to him and slid her hands around him to the front of his flatly muscled stomach. She pressed her cheek against his back. "I missed you when I woke up."

"Did you?" It seemed a noncommittal response. "I made some coffee. Would you like a cup?"

Slowly she withdrew her hands and pulled away from him, trying to decide whether his reception was a cool one or her expectations for a more ardent greeting had been too high.

"Sure." She swung around to the front of him where she could see his face.

His dark glance moved over her briefly, inspecting her features with an almost casual interest. "You look rested." A second cup was filled with coffee for her.

"Was I asleep long?" Layne had no idea when Creed had brought her to the house, let alone when she had fallen asleep, so there was no reason to look at the clock.

"A half hour. Forty-five minutes at the most." He turned away from her and walked onto the back porch.

"What have you got in the dryer?" She followed him.

"My undershirt," he said. "Unfortunately I left your jacket and my shirt out by the pond."

Taking a sip of her coffee, she studied him over the brim of the cup. He was so lean and brawny, roughly male and rugged. His features were too strong and too harsh to ever be pleasing to the eye, yet they were intriguing; he looked like a wild animal that possessed an indomitable spirit and fierce pride.

Her glance strayed down his muscled arms to his large hands as they tested the dryness of his shirt, then tossed it back inside the machine. Her skin still retained the tingling impression of the intimate caresses of those hands, caresses that had sometimes been rough simply because they didn't know their own strength.

Yet there had been a purity to his lovemaking that had taken it beyond a mere physical act. Layne felt the curling heat in the pit of her stomach and the swift rise of some powerful emotion that choked her throat with its sweet intensity. A misting of tears welled in her eyes as the desire surged to be held by those big, strong arms.

A tiny quiver of surprise licked through her. She was actually in love with this big brute. If she had been reluctant to admit it before, it had only been that she hadn't wanted to mistake the heat of passion for something more. She leaned her shoulders against the door frame, a little bemused by her discovery.

His knee pushed shut the door to the clothes dryer, then his glance took skipping note of her. "Don't you think you should go get dressed? Mattie will be home shortly," Creed advised her somewhat critically.

Layne straightened from the door frame as he approached, effectively putting herself in his path. The smile on her lips was warm with the inner knowledge of her feelings. Creed halted only inches from her, so she was eye level with his massive chest and its dark whorl of chest hairs. Her pulse was stirred by her nearness to the man she loved.

"Knowing Mattie"—Layne couldn't resist sliding a hand up the sinewy muscles that roped his chest—"I doubt she'll say a word if she finds me walking around in this robe in front of you."

Her hand continued its upward travel to curve along the nape of his neck while she stood on her tiptoes to kiss him, taking care to hold the coffee cup to the side of her body. Initially, his lips were unresponsive to the warm pressure of her mouth. But that didn't last as his arm hooked her waist to drag her hips into contact with his length while the driving force of his suddenly demanding mouth arched her backward over his arm.

His hand invaded the folds of her robe to take possession of her breast and roughly massage it, pinching the nipple into hardness. Her gasp of mixed pleasure and pain was consumed by his tongue, but it gentled his touch and turned it restless, gliding to her shoulder and arched throat.

When he lifted his head to gaze down at her with his eyes three-quarter lidded, Layne was conscious of the labored edge of his breathing. There was a faint grimness about his mouth even as he studied her kiss-swollen lips.

"We make a pair, don't we?" Creed muttered. "Beauty and the beast." Layne started to smile until she noticed that he wasn't amused by it. "It'd make quite a story, wouldn't it? A modern version, of course."

"I suppose it would," she conceded. "But I'd never even thought about it."

His glance raked her face. A split second later his hold on her loosened and the hand that gripped the side of her waist used its strength to swing her out of his way. She was left standing free as Creed brushed past her to enter the kitchen.

"That's what you're here for, isn't it? Doing research so you can write some stories for the paper," he stated without turning to look at her until he had finished.

A troubled darkness clouded the olive color of her eyes. Layne dropped her gaze to the coffee cup in her hand and followed him into the kitchen, not wanting to continue her lie. Yet it didn't seem fair to tell him the truth about her relationship to Mattie when Mattie didn't know. It put her in an awkward position, and there wasn't time to work out who rightfully deserved to know the truth first. Creed was expecting a response.

"Of course," Layne said, trying to sound airy.

"Your ordeal this afternoon should make good material for a story," Creed remarked as he turned to refill his coffee cup.

"I'd just as soon forget about that." Layne suppressed a shiver at the memory of those icy minutes in the water. "I prefer writing about other people's experiences."

"You've had more than enough time to accumulate all the research you'd need to write several articles." Creed studied her with a sidelong glance, a large hand resting negligently on the band of his low-riding jeans. "Why have you stayed on?"

She released an uncomfortable laugh. "You almost sound as if you want me to leave."

"I can't think of a reason for you to stay," he said evenly.

Layne stiffened at the stinging content of his words. "Not even you?" Her hurt question bordered on a demand to know exactly where she stood with him.

A cold, ruthless light flared in his narrowed eyes. "Don't try to kid me, Layne. As Stoney would say, I've been to see the elephant. Maybe it amuses you for the time being to play around with a man like me, but it won't last. I'm just an oddity to you."

"No." The denial sprang forcefully from her.

"Don't be concerned about sparing my feelings," Creed told her with a faintly contemptuous curl of his mouth. "I've wanted to make love to you. I suddenly realized there wasn't any reason why I shouldn't enjoy that beautiful body of yours, since it was so willingly being offered to me."

A confused pain flickered across her brow as Layne turned away from him to face the counter. "I can't believe you didn't feel something," she accused and abruptly set the coffee cup down.

"Oh, I felt something all right." He wandered over to her. His hands took her by the waist and turned her to face him. His dark gaze was sexually alive to her. Slowly and deliberately, his hands slid down to clasp the rounded cheeks of her bottom and insinuate her lower body to his thrusting hips, making his state of arousal blatantly obvious. "And I still feel something."

Shaking her head in mute denial, Layne looked anywhere but at him. "You don't mean what you're saying," she declared tautly and pushed at his arms.

"Don't I?" The thickness of want was in his husky voice as he bent his head and rubbed his mouth along the curve of her neck. "I could lay you down right here on the kitchen floor and take you again. If that sounds crude and heartless, you can blame it on the beast in me."

That absurd excuse merely enraged Layne. With a violent shove, she twisted away from him. It was a full second before she realized that she would never have been able to escape from those powerful arms if Creed hadn't wanted to let her go. She was hurt, angry, and confused all at the same time, but mostly angry.

"I don't know why you're acting like this, but I'm not buying any of this nonsense you're handing me!" Layne informed him in a hot rush of temper.

Creed smiled. "I'm just making sure you have plenty of subject matter for your stories—the perils of ranch life, sexual harassment on the job—"

"You're crazy." She frowned at him incredulously.

"I've thought that since the day Mattie hired you," he admitted tersely. "I don't know who or what you are—or what your game is—but I'm damned sure you aren't here to write any articles for a newspaper!"

His statement rocked her. Layne paled, unable to think of anything to say to refute him, and her senses were too disturbed by the recent contact with him to allow her mind to think clearly. His look hardened at her silence.

"I was right, wasn't I?" he muttered, almost angrily.

"Creed—" She rushed to explain but the buzzer sounded to signal that the clothes dryer had automatically shut off. Creed went striding by her to silence it and retrieve his undershirt. At almost the same instant Mattie entered through the back door, carrying a sack of groceries.

As she leaned against the door to push it shut, the suddenly speculating gleam in her faded green eyes slid first to the bare-chested Creed, then to the robed Layne. "Well, what have we here?" murmured Mattie.

Bending, Creed removed his insulated shirt from the dryer and let his glance linger for a small second on Layne. "Layne fell in one of the ponds this afternoon and I fished her out." The shirt was pulled down over his head, hands jammed through the sleeves.

The very abruptness of his answer, coupled with the grim way Creed had eyed her, prompted Mattie to guess. "And now you wish you'd thrown her back in, is that it?" she joked dryly.

"No . . ." Creed paused to send a long, considering look at Layne while he pulled the hem of his shirt down around his waist. "I have no intention of letting her off the hook."

Layne had hoped Mattie's arrival would bring an end to the conversation but it appeared that Creed was going to pursue it. She couldn't let him question her about her reasons for staying on the ranch, not in front of Mattie.

"I'd like to talk to you later tonight, Creed . . . privately," Layne said with an underlying thread of taut appeal.

His hard study of her continued while he appeared to weigh her words. "If you like," he finally conceded, then reached around the corner for his jacket and hat, hanging on a wall peg. "It's time I started the evening chores, anyway. Come over to the house after supper—and we'll have *your* talk." There was the smallest inflection of sardonic mockery in his voice.

The hat was on his head and he was pulling on his coat as he nodded to Mattie and walked out the door, slamming it with a small bang.

Mattie raised an eyebrow at his noisy exit. "It sounds like he's in a rotten mood," she observed and eyed Layne. "You look a little pale yourself. Are you sure you didn't catch a chill from that dunking?"

"No. I'm all right." Layne glanced at the door through which Creed had gone before slowly following Mattie into the kitchen.

Her thoughts were already turning to the promised meeting with Creed later that night, but it was difficult to string them together in any semblance of order when her body was flooding her mind with impressions of the heavy caress of his hands and the heady taste and smell of him.

The sack of groceries was set on the kitchen counter. "Good. There's fresh coffee made," Mattie noticed as she slipped out of her coat and unwound the scarf from around her neck to hang them both on the wall pegs by the back door. "I'm going to sit down and have a cup before I start supper," she announced. "Do you want one, Layne?"

It was a full second before the question registered. Layne reacted with a vaguely guilty start and answered quickly, "No. Thank you."

She watched Mattie pour a cup for herself and continued to stare at her when she carried it to the table and sat down. A reluctance to tell Mattie the truth tied her tongue. But it wasn't just a desire to get to know Mattie better before breaking the news that she was her natural mother which was keeping Layne silent any longer. Other reasons had come into play. The mere fact that she had waited so long made it awkward to confess now.

And she couldn't be sure how Mattie would react. There was a chance she'd ask Layne to leave, and Layne wasn't ready to go. She wouldn't have been willing under ordinary circumstances, but the way she felt toward Creed made it just that much more definite.

"Is something wrong, Layne?" Mattie said, questioning the way Layne was staring.

"No. Nothing." Layne's quickly lowered glance noticed the loosened front of her robe, created by the intimate invasion of Creed's hand. With a trace of self-consciousness, she pulled the overlapping fold more tightly across her body.

An amused sound came from Mattie, drawing Layne's glance to her again. "I may be old, but I'm not blind," she said.

"What?" Layne's voice was small and slightly wary.

"I've noticed the way Creed has been looking at you. Or . . ." Mattie paused, a faint smile accenting the age lines around her mouth ". . . maybe I should say the way he has tried so hard *not* to watch you. Any fool would know what's on his mind. It's probably on the mind of most men who look at you. Lust is a somewhat common denominator in the male species." Again that knowing smile was in place, but her gaze was keen in its inspection of Layne. "I see you're finally aware of the way he feels. In a way, I guess I've been trying to warn you."

"It wasn't really necessary." A smile fairly beamed from her face, because a warning was only needed if she had wanted to avoid Creed.

"You're both grown adults, so I'm sure you'll sort this out on your own." Mattie shrugged to indicate that it was really none of her business. Yet she added, "But things run deep with him. I mean, he isn't like Hoyt, all happy-go-lucky and carefree. Don't hurt him."

"I'd never hurt him, Mattie." Not deliberately, Layne silently qualified. But the appeal was a sobering reminder that she had to allay his suspicions surrounding her purpose for working on the ranch and explain the truth to him so he'd stop distrusting her. She fingered the collar of her robe. "I left the bathroom in a mess. I'd better go clean it up and get dressed." Layne started for the doorway. "I'll be down shortly to give you a hand with supper."

To Layne's surprise, she discovered the bathroom had been cleaned. Even her pile of wet clothes had been individually hung over a wall rack where they could drip into the tub, and her hair dryer had been returned to her room. It was obvious Creed had seen to it while she was sleeping. Undoubtedly, it was a reflexive action from his bachelor life that had trained him to a housekeeping role. Layne smiled to herself while she dressed, thinking he was a rare breed of man indeed.

There were no awkward silences at the supper table that evening, although Layne had thought there might be, considering the unfinished conversation with Creed. But she had failed to take into account that Hoyt and Stoney would expect a minute-by-minute description of her accident, both her version and Creed's, while they inserted comments along the way. Naturally they had their side of it to tell—how they found her horse running loose and intended to start a search when they came to the house and learned from Creed what had happened and that she was safe.

The subject of her near disaster dominated the entire meal. Layne suspected that Mattie was probably the only one who noticed the strong undercurrents running between herself and Creed. Layne was physically aware of him every minute, her eyes taking note of little details such as the way the lift of his hand set off a ripple of muscles beneath his shirt, the way his fingers held a knife, so she could make them part of the other intimacies she knew about him.

The few times their glances met, she saw the glitter in his desert-brown eyes, which reminded her that their conversation was yet to come. But Layne also noticed that desire that lurked in the brown depths and occasionally dragged his gaze downward to slide over her breasts as if recalling when their only covering had been his hands instead of the ruffled blouse she was wearing now.

Per routine, the men lingered over their coffee while Layne and Mattie cleared the table. With dishwater running in the sink, Layne went back to wipe the crumbs from the vinyl tablecloth. Creed pushed his chair away from the table when she walked over, and crossed to the back door to retrieve his coat and hat.

"I'll see you later." It sounded like a generalized farewell, except that his gaze was centered on her when Creed said it. But only Layne knew that the message was directed at her. No one else paid any attention.

By the time the dishes were washed, dried, and put away, it was a full twenty minutes before Layne paused in front of the door to Creed's cabin-sized house. With a mixture of apprehension and anticipation, she knocked on the inner door. His voice, muffled by the thick door, invited her inside.

His back was to the door when she entered. He was bending at the middle to lean down and crush out a cigarette in the ashtray on the low coffee table. Layne shrugged out of her coat and scarf and draped them on the hall-tree by the door.

"It's cold outside." She crossed the room as he turned and skimmed her with a glance.

"Have a seat." There was a grimness about his mouth as he took a position on one end of the long couch. His coolness gave her a few misgivings, but she avoided the large recliner as being too remote and sat on the cushion near the middle of the sofa, angling herself toward him. "Let's have it," Creed challenged without any further preliminaries. "Why are you here?"

Layne breathed out a smiling sigh. "I can explain," she assured him. "So I wish you'd quit acting like I was on trial for something."

But Creed was in no mood to be mollified by her attempt at congeniality. "Then explain," he insisted with teeth-clenched terseness. "And I don't want to hear any more of your damned lies."

"I did write for the newspaper. That much of it was true. You checked it out yourself with my editor," Layne reminded him.

His hands were tightly clasped in front of him while he leaned forward, elbows resting on his thighs. "When I went into your room to fetch your robe and hair dryer this afternoon, something bothered me." Creed spoke in a voice that was deadly quiet and flat. "I couldn't figure out what it was. Later, while you were sleeping, I went back to look again."

"You went through my things?" This invasion of her privacy left her stunned and slightly indignant.

"I admit I had no right to go through them." Creed made the concession with a smooth nod in her direction, but there wasn't even a flicker of remorse. "I was looking for something but, strangely, I didn't find it." Layne frowned when he paused, not following him. "There weren't any notes, no tapes—no information recorded anywhere for the supposed articles you were going to write.

Unless, of course, you're going to try to convince me you have a photographic memory."

"I'm not." She shook her head, eyeing him steadily. "At least now I understand why you kept on and on with all those story ideas of yours when we were in the kitchen this afternoon."

"I kept waiting for you to tell me you'd changed your mind—or admit you'd never intended to write anything," he said grimly. "But you stuck with that excuse to the bitter end. Now I want to know whether you ever intended to write anything."

"No. It was just a way of persuading Mattie to hire me." Now Layne could see that he had given her several openings to tell him the truth.

"Why was that so important? And don't feed me that old line about wanting to work on a ranch. From you, I wouldn't buy it."

"The reason is much more complicated than that. You see, I'm Mattie's daughter," she said quietly.

"You're what?" His voice rumbled with disbelief.

"I know how incredible it sounds, but it is the truth," Layne insisted firmly and met his hard and doubting look without faltering. "You already know that I was adopted when I was a baby. Off and on for the past eight years, I've been trying to locate the woman who gave birth to me. So that day I ran into you at the newspaper office, I really was tracking down my family history. Until that day the only name I had to go on was Martha Turner. Then I found the record of her marriage to John Gray, and the obituary notice told me where she lived. That's why I came here— to see her and find a way to get to know her."

All the time she had been talking, Creed had watched her with narrow-eyed skepticism. When she finished, his mouth was drawn into a thin line.

"When you come up with a story, it's a dandy," he said.

"I'd hardly make something like this up," she countered.

"I've known Mattie since she came to work for John. She's never had any children."

"I was born before she came here," Layne explained. "I don't know the whole story—only bits and pieces that I've managed to fit together from things she's told me. It's hardly surprising that she never mentioned that she had a baby and gave it away."

"You do realize I can easily find out if you're telling the truth," Creed warned. "All I have to do is ask Mattie."

"No!" The denial rushed out on a quick breath as she leaned earnestly toward him. "You can't do that. I haven't told her who I am."

His brows drew thickly together in a piercing frown. "Why? You supposedly go through all this to find her, then don't tell her who you are?"

Layne was caught up in a troubled agitation that pushed her to her feet. "I wanted to get to know her, but I couldn't know whether she would feel the same. When I showed up here that day, she thought I was applying for a job, so I let her go on thinking it. I was afraid if she knew who I was, I wouldn't be able to stay. It has to be awkward to have someone turn up out of the blue and claim to be your daughter. How do you explain that to your friends or family?"

"So she doesn't know," Creed concluded as he watched Layne moving restlessly.

"What was the point in telling her?" Layne argued. "I didn't want to hurt her or bring up any unpleasant memories of the past. It wasn't even important to learn her reasons for giving me up for adoption. I only wanted to get to know her—the way she is. I didn't come here to make her feel guilty or defensive about giving me up. And she would have if I had told her the truth."

"That telephone conversation I overheard—it was Mattie you were talking about."

"Yes." It seemed he recalled every detail, and nothing escaped his notice. She was breathing deeply and unevenly, upset by this postmortem of her decision. She wanted Creed to see her side of it, but he seemed so distant. "My parents—my adopted parents, that is—knew I'd come here looking for Mattie. When I found her and explained that I was going to stay for a while, they naturally asked what her reaction was. I had to tell them she didn't know who I was."

A silence ran between them for the span of several long seconds. Layne ceased her restless pacing to study him. Creed released a heavy sigh and pushed to his feet.

"You do believe me, then," Layne said when no more questions were forthcoming.

He raked combing fingers through the thatch of unruly dark hair and slanted a sideways look at her. "As you said, nobody would make up a story as farfetched as this."

The tension that had been building in her system was finally relieved and she could breathe easier. "You don't know how much better I feel telling you all this." She laughed faintly, smiling at him. "I've had to keep it to myself for so long that I hadn't realized what a strain it was. I guess it's always easier when you can share your problems with someone."

"You have to tell Mattie who you are," Creed stated.

"No!" Layne swiftly rejected that thought, all her nerves tightening up again. "I can't. Not yet."

"She has a right to know," he insisted tautly.

"I can't tell her now." A rawness caught her by the throat at the relentless determination in his uncompromising expression.

"If you don't tell her, Layne, I will," Creed warned.

She swallowed hard, doubting that he made idle threats. "You can't," she protested, moving a step closer to him.

"What is it? Some deep, dark secret I'm supposed to keep for you?" he challenged roughly.

"Yes," Layne retorted with an earnest sort of nod.

"Do you know what you're asking?" he demanded impatiently. "Mattie is my partner. You can't expect me to hide this from her."

"But how can I tell her the truth after all this time has gone by?" Layne argued just as forcefully. "What if she doesn't want me here after the way I've deceived her? What if she asks me to leave? You know her better than I do, Creed. How do you think she'll react when she finds out who I am?" She read the hesitancy in his expression and knew she had swayed him.

His mouth tightened in grim admission. "I don't know."

"Neither do I, Creed." Her rawly desperate glance clung to his gaze as her hands came up, unconsciously clutching at his shirt front in a silent appeal for his help. "And I don't want to leave yet."

The muscles of his chest were taut beneath her hands as Creed looked down at her, still frowning and still searching her face. Slowly his arms went around her, and his hand pressed her head to his chest in a gesture of comfort. He absently rubbed his chin over the top of her head while Layne closed her eyes and waited for him to decide whether to keep her secret or not.

His fingers twisted into her chestnut hair to pull gently and force her head back. "It's no use." A dark light smoldered in his eyes. "I don't want you to leave. And you counted on that, damn you."

His mouth came plummeting down to cover her lips in a roughly possessive kiss. It was like an explosive shock that splintered through her system and made Layne gasp at the intensely raw longing it evoked. His arm was an ever-tightening band of steel around her waist, crushing her to his length while his calloused fingers snarled the silken thickness of her chestnut hair with their restless demands for greater closeness.

Straining into his kiss, Layne opened her lips so he could invade the fragrant moistness of her mouth. She felt the blood pounding in her veins and wound her arms around his neck to hang on to him in case her heart raced away with her. Creed was consuming her and it was like dying and going to heaven.

She sensed the battle within him, the attempt to control the base instinct that drove him. Shuddering expressively, Creed wrenched away from her lips and buried his face in the side of her hair, his chest heaving in labored breaths. His arms shifted to lock around her, as if holding on to his sanity. Layne felt equally shaken and unnerved, surprised by the depths of her passion, which hadn't quelled under the ferocity of his.

"Why do you do this to me?" he murmured roughly, the husky disturbance in his low voice.

Her laugh was a breathless sound as her fingers sought the hard edges of his jaw and gaunt cheek. "It's not all one-sided, Creed. Look what you do to me."

He lifted his head to look at her passion-drugged features and the excited glitter in her half-closed eyes. "And you like it, too, don't you?" he growled in satisfaction.

His head was already coming down to take up the invitation of moistly parted lips when Layne gave him her response. "I love it."

Her fingers prized at the buttons of his shirt, not content until they could slide inside and luxuriate in the smoothness of bare skin stretched taut over lean muscles. He groaned deep down in his throat at her touch. When he scooped her into his arms, shivers of pleasure spiraled through her body.

With the toe of his boot, Creed kicked open the door to the darkened bedroom and carried her inside. Slowly he let her legs slide down until her feet touched the floor, never once letting her out of the circle of his arms.

His large hands at last cupped her face and stroked her hair. "I can promise you it will be softer than the floor," he murmured against her lips.

There were no lights in the room except the rectangular patch that fell through the open door. They undressed in broken stages, touching and kissing, unable to stay apart long enough to make it an uninterrupted process. Atop the mattress in the dark, they made tactile discoveries of each other all over again and found the same wildly sweet satisfaction in the fusion.

Layne turned her head on the pillow to gaze at the dark form lying beside her. His body was still and breathing evenly. Although it was too dark in the room to tell, she thought Creed was sleeping. She suppressed a sigh of reluctance and bent her head the few inches to kiss the hard point of his shoulder. Moving carefully, she eased herself away to swing her legs out of the bed.

"Where are you going?" Creed asked in the velvety thick voice of tired contentment.

"It's late," she said and shifted to sit on the edge of the bed. "It's time I was getting dressed and going to my own bed."

"No." A hand clamped itself around her wrist and pulled her backward away from the edge as Creed supported himself on an elbow. Layne found herself half leaning on him, crosswise. "I want you to stay here tonight."

"I can't. Mattie will be wondering what's happened to

me if I don't get back to the house pretty soon," she reasoned.

"Mattie knows exactly where you are." His hand smoothed the hair away from her neck and stroked the pulse he found beating there. "And don't kid yourself—she knows exactly what's happening too. She's been through it all before."

"I know. That's how I came to be," Layne said and kissed him quickly, slipping out of his hold while he still believed there was going to be more. "But I think I should go back just the same."

As her feet touched the floor, she felt the mattress sink, taking his full weight once more. She dressed in the dark while Creed lit a cigarette and smoked it.

Before leaving, she paused in the doorway where the light spilled into the room. "Good night." All she could see was the faint red glow of his cigarette.

His reply was slow in coming. "Good night, Layne."

It was snowing big, fat flakes when she left his house. Maybe it was shameless the way she'd given herself to him, but it seemed impossible that anything that felt so right between two people could be wrong.

Chapter 10

As the empty hayrack rattled past the opened gate, Layne jumped off to close it. The thick mud splayed under her boots when she landed, then made squishy, sucking noises with each step she took to the gate. On this mild morning she hadn't bothered to button her parka. The extra warmth wasn't needed, so she let it hang open.

Three days before, a late winter storm had held the Sand Hills snowbound for a day. Hot on its heels came the warm spring thaw to chase away the cold and leave only traces of its visit behind in the melting snowdrifts along the fence-line and the thin patches of snow cover along the north sides of buildings.

Pushing a shoulder into the gate, Layne swung it shut and braced it in position with her body until she pushed the latch into place. When it was secure, she turned away from the fence to follow after the tractor and hayrack, which was chugging to a stop by the shed. The cessation of the tractor's chugging motor made the sweep of silence seem loud. Layne slowed her steps for a minute to take it in.

The morning sun was already warming the air and infecting all who breathed it with a dose of spring fever. Layne wasn't immune to its heady stirrings, and the vague promise of something wonderful swelling inside her put a smile on her lips.

Just ahead of her, Creed had vaulted from the tractor and pulled over the hose from the elevated gasoline barrel to fill the gas tank on the tractor. His heavy winter coat had been abandoned in this mild weather in favor of a lighter-weight jeans jacket, lined with wool. Its snug fit lessened the appearance of bulk and emphasized the muscled trimness of his large build. For all that outlaw toughness about him, Layne felt a quiver of pride each time she looked at him. Love did that to a person, she supposed.

With his back to her, that wide expanse of shoulders made a broad and inviting target. Along with the burgeoning sense of spring inside her, there was a spark of mischief. It flared to life as Layne spied the small drift near her path. From experience, she knew that wet snow would pack into an excellent ball.

She glanced quickly again at Creed to make sure he still hadn't turned around, then scooped up a big handful of crusty wet snow and patted it into a round ball. There were no more than ten feet between them. At that distance she couldn't miss. Layne took aim on a point between his wide shoulders and gave it a throw.

The snowball's trajectory was a little high. Layne winced as it splatted just above his collar. Creed stiffened, then slowly turned, hunching his shoulders forward while he reached a hand behind his neck to brush the snow out from beneath his collar.

"Did you do that?" His accusing gaze gleamed narrowly at her.

"I'm sorry." But suppressed laughter gurgled in her

voice. "I must be out of practice. Actually I was aiming lower."

"You think it's funny, don't you?" Creed growled with mocking menace and took a step toward her.

When Layne saw his glance slide to the nearby snowdrift with its telltale depression made by her hands, she knew exactly the retaliation he had in mind. She started backing up, laughter still tugging at the corners of her mouth while she lifted her hands to stave off his threat.

"Creed, no," she protested with a sideways tilt of her head, the gleam still in her olive-brown eyes.

As he moved purposely toward her, Layne turned to run, but she turned too sharply. Her foot slid out from under her on the muddy ground, and she nearly fell. Before she could regain her footing and escape, Creed caught her from behind.

"Don't! No!" Breathless laughter bubbled through her words.

He had her by the waist while his hand forced its way inside the opened front of her jacket and pushed at the buttons of her blouse. All her wiggling and twisting went for naught as the buttons popped open and cold snow was rubbed across the bare skin covering her ribs.

She gasped in a shriek at the sudden iciness freezing her warm flesh. Trapped by the solid wall of his body, there was no way she could pull away from the contact. As the snow quickly melted and it was just the wetness of his hand on her rib cage, she didn't really want to avoid it.

With the slacking of her struggles, Creed loosened his hold on her so she could turn partway around. His hand remained inside her blouse while his thumb stroked the underside of her breast, deliberately evocative. A lazy, smoldering look was in his eyes when she glanced sideways at him, breathing irregularly under his familiar caress.

"Do you still think it's funny?" he murmured.

"You big brute," Layne accused, but her low voice was vibrant with other emotions, too conscious of the aroused impression his hard male outline was making on the curve of her hip.

"I wonder if I'll ever get my fill of you." The admission came thickly from some deep place inside of him as he rolled his mouth onto her lips and sensually ate at them.

The approaching sound of a pickup's motor brought a stir of impatience in him. Reluctantly Creed pulled away, turning to see Mattie driving up to the gas tanks. He disentangled himself from Layne and started toward the tractor.

"Don't mind me," Mattie said with a knowing smile as she stepped from the truck.

"I was putting gas in the tractor. It should be full now," Creed said, indirectly denying that her arrival had anything to do with bringing an end to the embrace.

Layne's smile was turned inward as she shoved her hands inside her pockets once more and used them to hold the front of her jacket shut. She had already learned in the last few days that Creed was a little self-conscious about any public display of affection. It amused her in a very tender way.

It didn't bother her that, thus far, Creed hadn't declared his feelings toward her. Love was a word that didn't come easily to a lot of men and especially Creed, she suspected. Yet he talked all around it, saying things like "never getting his fill of her." The meaning was just as clear.

"Do you need gas in that truck?" Creed glanced at Mattie as he lifted the nozzle out of the tractor's gas tank.

"Yes." Mattie took it from him and inserted it in the pickup's tank opening. "Oh, before I forget it, Creed," she said when he started to move away, "the Powells are celebrating their twenty-fifth wedding anniversary this Saturday. They're going to have a buffet supper instead of the usual cake and ice cream thing. Mary insisted that we had to come. And, Layne," Mattie added quickly to include her in the conversation, "they said to be sure to tell you that you were more than welcome too. I don't know if you remember Tom, but he stopped by a couple of weeks ago."

"Vaguely," Layne said with a nod, recalling a rancher who had come by for coffee quite a while back. She'd been busy doing something and he hadn't stayed long. She wasn't sure if that man was Tom Powell, since a couple of people from neighboring ranches had dropped by for a short visit over the last two months.

"Would you like to go?" Creed asked.

"Yes." Layne didn't hesitate. The people at the party would be his friends and neighbors, as well as Mattie's.

"You must think it's a dull bunch of people that live around here," Mattie said with a small laugh. "The weather usually keeps us from doing much socializing in the winter, but our get-togethers are fun. You'll enjoy it. And it'll give you something else to write about."

Conscious of Creed's tight-lipped expression and the hard, boring look he sent her, Layne was tense, although she was careful not to show it. "I'm looking forward to the party." He still disapproved of her perpetuation of the lie she'd told Mattie.

"I'm going to a livestock sale on Saturday," Creed announced, averting his gaze from her briefly to direct it to Mattie. "So we can start buying some calves to fatten for market. You and Layne can go to the party and I'll meet you there after the sale is over."

"That sounds good," Mattie said, nodding. "We'll probably go early to give Mary a hand with all the food." She returned the hose to its hook by the gas barrel and climbed into the truck. "See you later."

Creed watched her drive away, then started toward the machine shed to get on with the day's work. Layne fell in step with him, darting a glance at his closed expression. The line of her mouth straightened out.

"You think I should have said something, don't you?" She said what she knew he was thinking.

"Yes." It was a clipped answer.

"There isn't any easy way to back out of a lie, Creed," Layne insisted, going over old ground. "I can't very well tell her that I've changed my mind about writing that series of articles without explaining why. I just can't break the truth to her a little at a time, the way you seem to think."

"Sooner or later you're going to have to tell her," Creed stated firmly.

"I'd rather it be later." The determined set of her chin warned him that she wouldn't be swayed by his arguments. She had too much to lose.

The subject was dropped. But Layne knew it was only for the time being. The secret bothered him. In Creed's opinion, Mattie had a right to know Layne's identity.

Layne had taken Mattie at her word when she said the dress for the party was informal. The oval yoke of her cream-colored blouse was edged with ruffles, which were repeated around the stand-up collar. Her flounced skirt of brown herringbone tweed buttoned down the front, and the tops of her designer boots were just visible below the hem as she descended the stairs at a skipping run.

"I'm ready!" she called out cheerfully and picked up the suede jacket she'd left draped on a chair back in the living room.

There was a rustle of paper sacks and the sharp clip-clip of a pair of heels walking hurriedly from the kitchen. "Do you want to take this sack of dishes out to the car?" A furrow of absent concentration creased Mattie's forehead as she entered the living room and shoved the sack into Layne's arms without waiting for an answer. "I've got to get the tablecloths. I almost forgot I told Mary I'd bring them."

"Mattie." Layne stared at the woman. "You look lovely."

She didn't mean to sound so shocked, but the transformation was startling. It was the first time she'd ever seen Mattie in anything but a pair of slacks, usually an old pair of jeans. But here she was in a dress and high heels instead of jeans and work boots. The scarf and hair rollers were gone, and her youthfully freckled face was framed by soft, henna curls. The peacock-blue color of her jersey dress made her eyes appear more definitely green, although the mascara on her lashes called attention to them too.

"What? Oh, thank you." Mattie was too harried to take any more than passing notice of the compliment.

"I'm serious," Layne persisted, recovering from her momentary speechlessness. "I've never seen you dressed up before. You're a beautiful woman, Mattie."

The sincerity in her voice finally penetrated the woman's preoccupation. The tablecloths were draped over one arm as Mattie paused and looked down at herself a trifle self-consciously.

"I guess I haven't taken as much trouble about my appearance as I used to when John was alive," she admitted. A faint smile touched her mouth. "I used to turn a few heads when I was all dolled up."

"I'll bet you still do," Layne declared.

"They can turn all they like and it won't make any never-mind to me." She dismissed the notion that she had any interest in how men might look at her now. "We'd better get going so we can get these things over to Mary's before the party starts."

Spring was more than a promise in the air. Crocuses

were poking their heads out of the flower bed in front of the house while a robin hopped in the grass, looking for an afternoon snack. Layne skirted the mud puddles that had collected in the driveway, runoff from the melted snow, and walked to the car. The sack of dishes and the table-cloths were stowed in the back seat. When all was secure, they started off.

During the drive down the long lane to the highway, Mattie told her more about the couple whose anniversary they were going to celebrate. After they reached the main road, they barely traveled a quarter of a mile before Mattie slowed the car.

"What's that up ahead of us?" Mattie peered at the indistinct forms along the ditch and the grassy shoulder of the road. "Pronghorns?"

"No." They looked too dark to Layne to be antelopes. "I think it's cattle."

As they approached the animals, Layne's guess proved to be correct, and Mattie muttered a curse under her breath. "I swear those dumb animals wait until I'm all dressed up and have to be somewhere. It happens every time." She pulled the car to the side of the road and stopped it. "Come on. We'll have to go chase them in." She took no notice of Layne's startled glance as she climbed out of the car. "I knew I should have worn my boots and carried these heels."

Layne hurriedly scrambled out of the car after her. "Couldn't we just go up to the next ranch house and try to get hold of Stoney or Hoyt, so they could come out here and drive the cattle back?"

"Lord, girl, they're way the hell on the other end of the Ox-Yoke. They won't be back to the ranch house until chore time." She made it clear that no help could be expected from that quarter. "I've done this more times than I care to recall."

Sighing her misgivings, Layne set out after Mattie. Her tall-heeled boots were not designed for chasing cattle, but at least they gave her more support and balance than the spindly heels Mattie was wearing.

When the half-dozen cattle observed their circling approach, they took off at a trot. Mattie broke into a run, the jersey skirt wrapping itself around her legs as she hurried to head them off and turn them back to the break in the fence. Layne was right beside her.

As long as they had the smooth surface of the highway to run on, it wasn't so bad. Fortunately there was no traffic. But the minute they had to leave the concrete and pursue the cattle along the roadside ditch, they were in trouble. The footing was slick and the ground was uneven. The best either of them could manage was a staggering run.

The cattle were anything but cooperative. After twenty minutes of chasing, Layne and Mattie finally herded them to the section of fence where a broken post sagged the wires. Only the cattle pretended they didn't see it and stood in a wild-eyed bunch, looking at the two out-of-breath and bedraggled women with red glints in their hair.

"Oh, you dumb—" Mattie stopped as if reluctant to use the energy it would take to swear at the beasts. "Come on." She waved a limp hand at Layne. "We'll have to push them through. Watch your step. It's a bog at the bottom of this ditch."

The warning wasn't really necessary, since Layne had been forced to jump the marshlike combination of mud and grass twice to head off a cow. Her legs were shaking and the backs of her calves ached from running in the high-heeled boots, but Layne plowed through the tall ditch grass, half sliding down the slope and inching her way the last couple of feet to the bottom.

It was difficult to tell where the solid ground ended and

the mud began, but she made her guess and leaped across the ditch-bottom. The cattle nervously crowded close to the fallen fence post. All they had to do was step over the downed wires and they'd be back on home range. But they waited until Layne started up the slope, waving her arms, before they bolted in panic, nearly stampeding themselves.

A yelp came from Mattie. Layne swung tiredly around and paused to stare in amused dismay. Mattie had misjudged the width of the ditch. One foot was buried in mud up to her well-turned ankle. For an instant she stood poised in that position, then she lifted her foot. Only the shoe didn't come with it.

"Damn," she said softly and hopped to keep her balance on one foot.

With all the running and chasing, her hairdo was drooping. Her dress was disheveled and her slip was showing. Layne guessed that she didn't look much better but she started to laugh just the same.

"Oh, Mattie, you look ridiculous," she declared between breathless gasps of laughter while she pressed a hand to the ache in her side.

"Well, you don't look like a raving beauty yourself," Mattie retorted before finally seeing the funny side of the predicament. She laughed too. "Don't just stand there. You've got to help me get my shoe."

Layne wiped at the tears of laughter in her eyes. "You can't be serious."

"You're damned right I'm serious. That's my good shoe in that mud. I'm not going to walk off and leave it there," Mattie asserted.

"You mean 'hop' off," Layne corrected with more bubbles of laughter while she moved down the slope to rejoin Mattie. "I hope you don't expect me to reach down in that mud and fish it out."

"Check the trunk of the car and see if there's anything we can use to hook onto my shoe," Mattie suggested.

Layne scrambled across the ditch and returned to the car parked on the shoulder of the road. She checked out the tools in the trunk, but the tire iron seemed the most likely one suited for the job.

After several unsuccessful attempts they finally retrieved Mattie's mud-soaked shoe. Then the fence had to be jerry-rigged to keep the cattle from getting out again until more permanent repairs could be done. In all, the delay cost them an hour.

Cars and trucks were parked in the ranch yard by the score when they finally reached the Powell ranch. They had managed to straighten their clothes, brush their hair, and retouch their makeup, but there was nothing they could do about Mattie's shoe.

Creed came out of the large, modern ranch house as they started up the walk. An eyebrow shot up at the sight of Mattie walking with one shoe off and one shoe on.

"Where have you two been?" he asked. "Mary expected you almost two hours ago."

"What does it look like?" Mattie wagged her muddy shoe at him. "I had to hunt for my glass slipper." She continued past him to the door but Layne paused to explain.

"Some cattle got out on the highway so we stopped to chase them in." As she recounted the details of their zany escapade, his smile kept getting wider and wider. "So there we were prancing about in this mud like a couple of comic ballerinas, trying to hook the heel of her shoe with the tire iron."

His low chuckle evolved into deep, hearty laughter at the picture of absurdity she painted. Layne laughed with him, taking secret delight in the rich, full sound of his laughter.

It finally subsided into a broad smile. "And I thought you'd had car trouble."

"Do you know that's the first time I've seen you laugh? I mean really laugh—not one of your smug chuckles," she told him.

His expression sobered slightly, although he continued to smile with faint bemusement while he smoothed a strand of hair away from her temple with his forefinger. It was a very light caress.

"Maybe this is the first time in my life I've had something to be really happy about," Creed suggested, then met her gaze. Her heart seemed to do a skipping turn and whirl away while her throat went tight. "The party's already started." He took her arm, breaking the spell of the moment. "We'd better go inside."

"Is this one of those parties where the men go off into one room and the ladies congregate in another?" Layne asked on a lightly teasing note.

"Sometimes it happens, but usually there's an intermingling." He smiled down at her as he opened the door.

A wave of voices engulfed them when they entered the house. Every room was crowded with people, and there was a constant ebb and flow of traffic from one room to another. Creed steered her to the dining room where the buffet tables were set, crowned by a large anniversary cake. The Powells were there, the hosts as well as the guests of honor, and Creed reintroduced her to them.

"It's a shame there aren't going to be more young men here tonight to entertain you," Tom Powell declared with an admiring glance at Layne. "But it's Saturday night and most of them are out whoopin' it up. I got a feeling when they hear about you, they're gonna be sorry they missed the party."

"I think I'll enjoy the party just the way it is, Mr. Powell,"

Layne said, reserving the smile in her eyes for Creed. "Congratulations."

Creed drew her away to go through the buffet line. There was certainly no lack of food; the problem was deciding what to eat. All along the way, she was constantly being introduced to someone. Layne didn't even attempt to keep the names and faces straight. There were too many.

The house was a whirl of activity and noise, and Layne was caught up in it and swept along. Talk was as abundant as the people and the food. At some point Creed drifted away from her to speak to someone, but it was impossible to feel abandoned. There was a never-ending supply of friendly faces, male and female, eager to strike up a conversation. Several times she bumped into Mattie and went through more introductions.

It was an hour, at least, before her path crossed with Creed's. "Are you enjoying yourself?" he asked.

"I've had my leg pulled by some tale-spinner, learned all the latest gossip, and know the easy way to make bread and butter pickles," Layne said in a brief summary of the variety of conversations she'd had, and smiled. "I'm having a ball."

"I thought you were."

"How was the sale today?" She hadn't had time to ask him what the outcome had been. "Did you buy anything?"

"I bought about twenty head of young calves." His gaze made a slow sweep of the room. "You know, a lot of people are wondering why you're spending so much time with me tonight." The sweep ended with a sidelong look at her that was warm and disturbing.

"If they have eyes, they can see," she countered.

They were in the middle of a crowded room with people all around them, but she had the strongest urge to touch him and have those arms go around her. She swayed with the impulse. His broad chest lifted on a deep breath and his look darkened as if he was reading her thoughts.

"We'd better circulate," he said abruptly.

His hand applied pressure to the back of her waist to guide her into the next room. It was the family room, and the teenagers in attendance at the party had gathered there to play some records. Only a few adults had intruded on their domain. Except for the music playing, it was a fairly quiet corner of the house. Creed started to lead her away, but Layne resisted.

"Let's stay here for a while," she urged.

He hesitated, then shrugged his agreement. "If you want."

"Wanna dance?" she asked when a slow song came on the stereo.

"I can't dance," Creed said.

"Of course you can," Layne chided and grabbed at his hand.

"No. I mean it." He resisted her pull. "I haven't danced with a girl since grade school when the teacher made us choose partners. My experience is limited to that simple box step."

"I'll teach you," she coaxed persuasively.

He glanced at the young people in the room, then shook his head. "No."

"It's simple," Layne assured him, not giving up. "All you have to do is take me in your arms, stand in one spot, and shift your weight from one foot to the other."

"There's more to it than that," Creed replied with a trace of impatience.

"Couples dance like that all the time," she countered with a provocative smile. "Just try it once."

For a long second he looked at her. "All right." He seemed to give in grudgingly. "I'll give it a try."

There was an appealing awkwardness about the way he took her hand, so small that it was lost in the large grasp of his, and placed his right hand on the side of her waist. At least six inches separated them.

"You're holding me as if I were some stranger," Layne chided and positioned his right hand behind her back, then moved closer until their bodies were touching. "Isn't this better?" she murmured, peering up at him through her lashes.

His fingers spread out, fitting themselves more comfortably to the small of her back. "I don't know," he said, rocking from side to side the way she had told him to do. "Holding a woman in your arms and trying to concentrate on moving your feet is just as difficult as rubbing your stomach and patting your head at the same time. The coordination isn't always there."

"It just takes practice." She relaxed against him, swaying with his movements while she rested her head along his jaw.

"This is the way it's done, is it?" The tension was easing out of his body as he instinctively reacted to the soft pressure of hers.

"Mmmm." It was an affirmative sound. "And sometimes"—she slipped her hand out of his grip—"the girl puts both her hands around her partner's neck and he puts both arms around her."

While she linked her fingers behind his head, Creed splayed his hand over the middle of her spine. Barely any notice was taken of the music as they swayed, shifting their feet slightly, yet moving not at all.

The heat from his long, muscled body went through her clothes and warmed her flesh. The clean, male smell of him filled her nostrils with each breath she drew. Layne felt the instinctive play of his hands over her spine, pressing and caressing to fit her shape to his contours. It was all the sensation of an embrace without its accompanying intimacy. And like a strong wine, its intoxicating effect seemed to go straight to her head.

His mouth was in her hair, moistly rubbing against its silken texture. The warmth of his breath moved onto her skin, a feathery caress in itself. Her heart raced, stirring up her blood.

"Your hair smells so good," Creed muttered.

"I just washed it." There was a breathless quality to her voice.

There was a sudden tightening of his hands on her ribs as he forced a small distance between them. "Let's get out of here," he said roughly. "I've had about all of your dancing I can stand."

"Okay." The shakiness inside made Layne more than willing to agree with him.

"Let's go find Mattie and make sure she knows you're coming with me." The grip of his hand was unconsciously rough as he took her by the elbow and steered her through the crowd in search of Mattie.

Layne spied her in the living room. When Mattie saw them approaching her, she excused herself from the couple she was with and came to meet them.

"Leaving already?" she guessed with a knowing look at both of them.

"Yes," Creed said. "Layne's going to ride home with me."

"Don't wait up for me," Mattie said to Layne. "I'll probably still be here talking at midnight."

A man in a western suit came up to Mattie. Layne vaguely recalled being introduced to the tall, well-built man, close to Mattie's age.

"Looking at these two beautiful women standing here,"

he said, addressing his comment to Creed, "a man would think they were sisters."

"Blair, your flattery may have turned a lot of women's heads," Mattie declared. "But you and I both know I am old enough to be Layne's mother."

Layne stole a glance at Creed, but no expression was showing. Yet she knew Mattie's innocent remark had dampened the evening. Her deception had trapped her in such a tangled web.

"If you'll excuse us, Blair, Layne and I are leaving," Creed inserted.

At his announcement, the man turned to Mattie. "You aren't going now too?"

Layne didn't catch Mattie's answer as she moved away with Creed.

Chapter 11

When the door closed behind them, the din of all those voices was completely shut off and the stillness of the crisp night echoed around them. Layne glanced at the night's star-studded canopy and the silver sickle of a moon riding high in the sky, but it was only the silence that registered. She threw another glance at Creed, his strides shortened to match hers as they walked through the parked vehicles to his truck.

His blunted profile was etched sharply against the faint light while his Stetson hat was pulled low on his forehead, shadowing his expression. There was something condemning in his stony silence. It galled Layne that he would shut her away from him like this. It was the one trait about him that irritated her. No disagreement was ever resolved by silence.

As she climbed into the passenger side of the truck cab with the impersonal support of his hand, Layne decided he needed a taste of his own medicine. If it was silence he wanted, it was silence he was going to get.

With a forced air of calm, she settled into the seat and directed her attention to the night scenery outside the passenger window as they started for home. But her tension grew with each mile that rolled by. They weren't far from the turnoff to the ranch when it suddenly struck Layne that it was childish to maintain silence just to get even with Creed.

"This is ridiculous, Creed," she said with tightly suppressed impatience. She wanted to banish this feeling of estrangement that hurt so, but she didn't know how when their views were so opposite. "Why did we leave the party if we suddenly aren't even talking?"

His attention never strayed from the road. "I was thinking," he said finally.

"I already guessed that, so why don't you do it out loud?" she prodded.

With a turn of the steering wheel, he swung the truck onto the narrow ranch lane to the Ox-Yoke. "You told me you'd spent the last eight years looking for Mattie." Even when he glanced at her, Creed seemed distant. "You must have been very determined."

His attitude brought her teeth together. "I was." Layne tipped her head back to briefly glance at the ceiling of the truck, recalling all that that determination had cost her. Her short laugh held a note of cynical amusement. "Clyde Walters—my editor—says I'm relentless as a bulldog once I get my teeth into something. Mattie is tough and strong-minded. Maybe I take after her in that respect."

"From all you've said, you obviously had a good home, parents who loved you. Why was it so important to find her?" Creed challenged.

Despite his aloofness, Layne wondered if he was really trying to understand. "It's difficult to explain. It's something inside—a strong homing instinct—that pushes you. I just had to find her. It's a kind of compulsion. No matter how many dead ends I came across, I had to keep looking."

"Whether she wanted to be found or not," he stated in a flat voice that held no sympathy.

"I suppose you think I was wrong to look for her," Layne accused.

"I think it was wrong for you to lie about who you were when you came to the ranch that day," Creed replied.

"Maybe it was." Layne sat stiffly in her seat facing the front, irritated that they had gone full circle back to the same argument. Nothing she'd said had made any difference. "But when I met her that first time, I knew it wasn't enough just to find her. I wanted to know what she was like. After eight years of looking I wanted to spend more than a half hour with her."

The pickup came to a stop in front of the main house. "And nothing was going to stand in your way, is that it?" he suggested grimly as he shifted into park and switched off the motor.

"That's right," she flashed and slammed out of the truck to walk briskly to the house. "Why are you making such an issue over the fact that I've kept my identity a secret from her when she's kept my birth a secret for years?" It was a stiff, angry demand that Layne threw at him as Creed followed her into the house. "I'm not the only one who's guilty of keeping secrets."

Her jacket was flung off and tossed carelessly on an armchair. Without pausing, Layne continued to the kitchen, and Creed was only a step behind her. She could almost feel his gaze on her rigidly squared shoulders.

"But you have the luxury of knowing who she is," Creed pointed out and walked by her to the counter. "Coffee?" He picked up the electric percolator to make a fresh pot, sliding her a glance.

"I don't care," Layne retorted impatiently.

She was upset by all this wrangling, which served no purpose except to create an unnecessary tension between them. Her sidelong gaze flickered over him, so tall and powerfully muscled with those rough-grained features she had grown to love so well. When they had something so wonderful, it was foolish to let this drive them apart.

Needing to reestablish that contact, she reached out and rubbed her fingers over the broad back of his hand. "We've been all through this before, Creed. I don't want to quarrel with you." Layne sighed heavily.

"What do you want to do?" He shifted his stance, angling himself toward her while his fingers tunneled into the hair near her ear. His watchful gaze abandoned its interest in the action of his hand to study her upturned face. "Settle the argument the way we usually do? By putting it to bed?"

His attention shifted to her lips, and her pulse fluttered in an instinctive response to his message. While his arm slid slowly around her ribs, his dark head bent to crush her mouth under the driving force of his lips. The muscles in his arm tightened into steel bands that constricted around her until the buttons of his suit jacket made indentations in her breasts. Layne was stunned by the anger she felt in his kiss.

When he broke off the contact, twin fires of passion and desire smoldered in the eyes that studied her bewildered frown. His mouth tightened in grimness while he firmly put her away from him.

"Not this time, Layne," Creed said. "It may have worked before but that's not the way it's going to happen tonight. We're going to straighten this out once and for all."

She bridled at the arrogant assumption of his remark. "By that, I suppose you mean you're going to convince me to tell Mattie the truth."

"You'll have to, because I'm not going to be a party to your secret any longer," Creed warned.

It angered Layne that he was actually threatening to divulge the information if she didn't. "That is a private matter between Mattie and myself. It has nothing to do with you. So just stay out of it!"

"Look . . ." Creed paused, glancing away and taking a deep breath as if struggling to keep his control. Then his gaze sliced back to her. "I know you're concerned about the way Mattie's going to react to the news that you're the child she gave up for adoption all those years ago. It's bound to be a shock to her, especially when she realizes how you've deceived her. I don't expect you to face her alone. I'll come with you. If she gets it into her head that you should leave, between the two of us, we should be able to convince her otherwise."

Layne was offended by his offer. In her present mood she regarded it as an insinuation that she was incapable of successfully handling it on her own.

"This may come as a shock to you, but I don't need your help!" she flared. "I can manage on my own."

"You're going to tell her, Layne." Creed was adamant.

"But *I* will decide when that will be, not you," she retorted. "Just because I've gone to bed with you, that doesn't give you any special rights to tell me what to do."

A silence crackled in the room as Creed stiffened at her angry words. A muscle leaped in his jaw, twitching convulsively. A little shiver of alarm raced down her spine as Layne realized what she'd said. She had been attempting to assert her independence, not demean their relationship by reducing it to a purely sexual level.

"What I meant to say—" she began, trying to change the impression she'd given him.

But Creed brutally cut across her words. "I think you said it very clearly."

There was a chilling finality to the sound of the door closing behind Creed's departing figure. She had tried to explain, but he had refused to listen. And pride wouldn't let her go after him. Layne felt wretched and sick as she swung away from the sight of the door. There was an ache in her throat to go with the bitter tears stinging her eyes. She struggled not to cry.

For a long time she lay awake in her bed, staring at the ceiling. Shortly before midnight she heard Mattie return. Mattie was in bed and asleep long before Layne closed her eyes.

It was half past nine before Layne awakened the next morning, a late hour by her usual standards of predawn. Since it was Sunday, there had been no reason to set the alarm clock. Yet Layne felt neither rested nor refreshed. The ache and the dullness of spirit were still with her. She had made a mess of things. Somehow she had to find a way to set them right.

With a dressing gown over her pajamas, Layne stepped out of the bathroom and met Mattie in the hallway. "Good morning," the older woman said cheerfully, a basket full of freshly washed and folded towels in her hands. "I wondered if you were up and about yet."

"Morning." Layne managed a half-hearted smile.

"It's a gorgeous spring morning outside," Mattie declared. "I'm almost tempted to take the storm windows off and put up the screens today. Did you sleep well last night?"

"Fine." Layne nodded and moved to the side so Mattie could pass.

But Mattie paused instead, giving Layne the once-over. "You and Creed make quite a pair," she murmured.

"What do you mean?" Layne warily drew back.

"He bites my head off this morning and you aren't talking." She observed the way Layne's head dipped to avoid her gaze. "What happened? Did you two quarrel after you left the party last night?"

"Yes," Layne admitted after a small pause.

Mattie cocked her head at an encouraging angle. "Do you want to talk about it?"

The sympathetic light in those faded green eyes tempted Layne to blurt out the whole story. "I—" she began, then stopped.

Last night there had been plenty of time to think while she was lying in bed. She had decided she would seek out Creed this morning to make amends for that stupid remark she'd made last night and assure him that she would make a clean breast of everything to Mattie. But it was important for him to know her intentions before she spoke to Mattie so she could convince him of her sincerity.

"No, I don't think so, Mattie." She changed the answer she had been about to make and walked around the auburn-haired woman to her bedroom.

"I'm good at listening if you decide you want to talk later," Mattie said over her shoulder and resumed her course to the linen closet.

"Thanks." Layne paused in the doorway to her room. "I just might take you up on that." Although the subject matter would be entirely different from what Mattie expected.

In her room Layne slipped out of her robe and pajamas and hung them on the closet door. She put on a clean set of underclothes from the dresser drawer, then walked to the closet and tugged on a pair of tan corduroys. As she was rummaging through the blouses on hangers, there was a preliminary knock at her door before it was pushed ajar. Layne ducked her head out of the closet as Mattie entered.

"I washed a couple of your sweatshirts," Mattie said, indicating the garments folded neatly in her hands. "Where would you like me to put them?"

"Just lay them on the bed. I'll put them in the dresser later." Layne slipped a blue madras blouse off its hanger.

"I've already got them in my hands. Just tell me which drawer you keep them in. The bottom one?" Mattie continued into the room.

For a split second Layne didn't move, then she bolted from the closet. "No! Not . . ." Her voice trailed into silence when she saw that Mattie had already pulled the bottom drawer open.

The baby blanket was lying folded on top. It was too late; Mattie had seen it already. Like an automaton, Layne was drawn to the side of the dresser.

"What's this old thing doing in here?" Mattie appeared absently disgusted as she lifted the blanket out to make room for the sweatshirts.

Layne held her breath when Mattie took a second look at the baby blanket. She watched the woman's face closely to see if she recognized it after all this time. Her pulse quickened and her lips felt dry.

Mattie straightened. Her hand trembled as it moved over the blanket. Her skin looked pale beneath the freckles as she frowned with narrowed curiosity at Layne.

"Where did you get this?" she demanded in a low, taut voice.

Quicksilver threads of tension were shooting through her nerves while Layne tried to appear calm. "My mother gave it to me." She waited for the awareness to flash in Mattie's eyes. "It was my baby blanket."

The look in Mattie's eyes sharpened into a stabbing keenness. "Is this some kind of an ugly joke?"

"It's no joke, Mattie." A wealth of gentleness and softness

seemed to fill Layne as her lips curved in a tremulous smile, tender with understanding at Mattie's shock. "I am the baby girl you gave birth to twenty-six years ago."

Mattie's gaze flashed from the glint of rust in Layne's hair to the flecks of olive green in her eyes, then an overall sweep of her face. The skeptical doubt and disbelief remained in Mattie's expression.

"How could you possibly know about that?" she challenged stiffly.

"I've spent eight years looking for you. First I was just trying to find a woman, then one named Martha Turner." Mattie blanched when Layne used her maiden name. "Finally the trail led me to Valentine—and Mattie Gray."

Mattie looked down at the blanket, holding herself very stiff and rigid. "What do you expect me to feel? Guilt for abandoning you or a pretense of recognition, perhaps. Maybe I should be elated at being reunited with you."

"I don't really expect anything," Layne said quietly and tried to ignore that vague sense of disappointment.

"Why did you come here?" Pain glittered in Mattie's eyes as she issued the challenging protest. "What is it that you want from me?"

"Just the chance to get to know you," Layne said, earnestly trying to explain. "To find out what you were like. I've wondered about you for so long. I didn't come here to hurt you or make you feel awkward, just to . . . know you."

Mattie's look swept over her in a dazed and withdrawn rejection. "Who are you?"

"My name is Layne MacDonald. I'm your daughter." There was a childlike quality that slipped to the surface, an aching desire to please and to be accepted.

"No." Mattie shook her head numbly and stroked the baby blanket again. "They took my baby girl away a long time ago. I don't know you." Wariness and hurt were in

Mattie's accusing glance when she lifted her head. "You're a stranger."

"But I'm not," Layne insisted with a quick, anxious smile. "We have had the chance to get to know each other these last couple of months. We've worked together, talked and laughed about things."

"No," Mattie said in slow denial. "We may have done all those things but I never knew you. You slept in my house and ate at my table and played your game of pretend. How it must have amused you to ask me all those questions about my past and listen to me rattle on." The bitterness of betrayal was in her voice. "Is this the story you were going to write?"

"No." A worried frown pinched in the lines on Layne's face. She had feared that Mattie would react this way. "I never intended to write any stories for the paper. I only said that so I could persuade you to hire me."

"God, but you had me fooled." With a breathlessly bitter laugh of self-derision, Mattie turned away and lifted her chin, blinking her eyes at the ceiling.

"I was going to tell you the truth, Mattie," Layne insisted. "I never intended for you to find out this way."

"Of course you were going to tell me," she mocked.

"It's true." Layne had to make Mattie understand that. "I was going to tell you today after I talked to Creed. I—"

"Creed." Mattie whirled on her, all braced and accusing. "Does he know?"

For long seconds Layne's mouth worked with nothing coming out of it. The muscles in her throat had knotted, unwilling to release the truth and possibly alienate Mattie still more. Finally she had to say it.

"Yes."

Hurt anger raged in Mattie's expression. "Who else have you told? Stoney? Hoyt? Who else?"

"Only Creed." Layne's dark head was bent in abject regret. "Please try to understand, Mattie," she said tightly. "I never intended for you to be hurt by my coming here. For all I knew, there might have been a lot of unpleasant memories associated with my birth."

"You never cared one whit about my feelings," Mattie snapped. "You came here to satisfy your own curiosity about me. You lied, and you used me—and Creed and Hoyt—everyone."

"No," Layne protested.

"No? We took you in and accepted you for what you said you were," Mattie harshly reminded her. "We believed you."

"I'm sorry," Layne murmured helplessly.

"Now you're sorry," Mattie scoffed derisively. "Well, your cruel and selfish curiosity has been satisfied. So get out of my house and out of my life. I gave you away twenty-six years ago, and believe me, I don't regret it."

"Mattie." It was a softly anguished cry, and the baby blanket was cast at her feet in answer.

"If you aren't packed and out of this house within an hour, I'll have you thrown out," Mattie warned in a voice that was taut and shaking.

For several minutes after the door shut, Layne was frozen in place. Then she bent and picked up the blanket and held it gently against her. The back of her eyes burned with tears and she sniffed at them to keep them at bay.

With a slow awakening from her pain, she realized that she deserved some of the things Mattie had said. Some of her motives had been selfish, only she hadn't seen them that way at the time. Drawing a deep, shuddering breath, she laid the baby blanket on the bed and went to the closet to haul out her suitcase.

Her recent purchase of workclothes left her with more

garments than she had room for in her suitcase. Layne went downstairs to the kitchen for some paper grocery sacks so she could pack the extra clothing in them. There was no sign of Mattie anywhere about.

Wondering if she'd get the chance to speak to her again, Layne chewed anxiously at her bottom lip as she reached to take two of the sacks from the cubbyhole between the refrigerator and the cupboards. The back door opened and Creed walked in. He came to a stop when he saw her and seemed to draw himself up to his full height, eyeing her distantly.

"Creed." She breathed his name in a kind of relief, a smile breaking across her tense lips. "I'm so glad you're here." She was unconsciously propelled across the room by the need for his support. "Mattie knows." It crossed her mind that maybe Mattie would listen to him.

Something flickered across his tough face. "How? Did you tell her?"

"I was going to," Layne admitted, overwhelmed and agitated by that sense of frustration again because she had been denied the opportunity. "Mattie saw my baby blanket before I could tell her the truth. She thinks. . . . She was upset, Creed. She's ordered me to leave."

"What do you expect me to say?" His face could have been chiseled in stone for all the emotion it showed.

Layne drew back slightly to frown at him while she searched for some hint of regret over her imminent departure. "Maybe if you talked to her," she suggested carefully, "you could convince her to reconsider if you tried." She felt chilled by the aloofness in his dusky brown eyes.

"Mattie hired you. If she chooses to fire you, that's her business." His graveled voice was cutting in its indifference. "Did you think I wouldn't back my partner's decision?"

"I don't want to leave," Layne said and watched him with tense reserve. "And I didn't think you'd want me to go."

A long silence ran between them before Creed finally asked, "Will you need any help carrying your suitcases to the car?"

Her chin started to quiver, and Layne could feel her control breaking. "No," she said, stiff with a deep, wounding hurt, and swung away from him before he could see the glimmer of tears in her eyes. "I can manage."

Carried by pride, she left the kitchen and raced up the stairwell to her room. There wasn't time for tears as Layne hurriedly finished her packing, throwing the last of her things into the sacks. It took two trips to get everything in her car.

At the door she took one last look around the room. Her glance lingered on the baby blanket, folded in a neat square atop the bed. All through her childhood it had been one of her most precious possessions. Leaving it behind was like leaving a part of herself. But she wanted Mattie to have it. In some small way the gesture was meant to convince Mattie that she had no wish to lay claims on her. Slowly Layne shut the door and walked to the stairs.

The pumpkin-colored tomcat blocked her path to the front door. It seemed to look at her with a puzzled expression. The lump in her throat was so big, Layne thought she would choke on it. She crouched down and the cat arched its neck against the stroke of her fingers.

"This is a fine time to finally make friends with me," she said thickly.

The cat blinked indifferently and turned its head to look elsewhere. With a flick of its tail, it walked stately away from her. As she glanced after it, Layne noticed Mattie sitting in a corner of the living room, staring at the gold-framed photograph in her lap. Layne straightened with a smooth turn, observing that Mattie seemed not to have seen her.

"Mattie, I'm leaving now." She had a glimpse of the photograph before Mattie covered it. It was a picture of her late husband. There was a vacantly staring look in Mattie's pain-dulled green eyes. "You were right when you said I was selfish. And I am very sorry for that."

"Just go away," Mattie said.

Layne hesitated, then turned and walked to the door. The ranch yard seemed as deserted when she drove out of it as it had been the day she'd arrived. But the surrounding hills looked different; traces of green showing instead of the snow that had covered them on her arrival at the Ox-Yoke. New life was bursting forth and growing. A wet tear slipped over an eyelash and trickled down her cheek.

At the highway intersection she let the car motor idle. There wasn't any traffic on the isolated section of road. Her blurring eyes would have had trouble seeing it anyway. The longer she sat there, the more aware she became that it wasn't in her to give up so easily. Turning the wheel, she headed the car in the direction of Valentine.

The same wispy-haired man was on duty at the motel desk when she walked in. His flash of recognition quickly became a vaguely pleased smile as he pushed a registration slip toward her.

"Back again, I see," he observed brightly. "Be staying with us long this time?"

"I'm not sure. A couple of days maybe." Layne picked up the ballpoint pen attached to the chain to fill out the form and sniffled to clear away the tears that edged the corners of her eyes.

"Sounds like you're catchin' one of those nasty spring colds," the man said as he turned to take a room key from its slot. "Better see that you get yourself some rest. It's the best thing for it."

"Thank you." She didn't bother to disabuse him of the idea that she had a cold.

"Same room as before," he said and gave her the key.

It was all so different, Layne thought when she let herself into the room. The last time, she'd been filled with so much expectation. Now she experienced a gnawing ache over the loss of something very precious, although perhaps not completely. That was the thing she still had to find out.

The small café was teeming with morning patrons, a collection of farmers, ranchers, and stock-truck drivers. It had become a familiar scene to Layne over the last three days. There was a tumbling of voices, cigarette smoke, and coffee cups clanking. She sat alone in a corner booth, positioned to watch the door and observe who came in.

Both hands were wrapped around her coffee cup, absorbing its warmth. It was tension that made her feel cold and tied her nerves up in knots. Yet so much of it was directed to an inner awareness that she could feel the blood pumping through her veins and hear the rush of air in her lungs.

"More coffee?" The waitress stopped at her booth, a half-full pot of coffee in her hand.

"Please." Layne pulled her hands away from the cup so the waitress could fill it.

"Sure I can't get you anything to eat? A homemade roll? Toast?" the waitress inquired, darting an almost concerned look at Layne's pale and drawn features.

"Nothing. I'm sure," Layne insisted, aware of her violently churning stomach. In its present state, it wouldn't tolerate the introduction of food. The waitress shrugged and moved on.

The café door opened, and her glance sprang at the man who entered, dressed in a cowboy hat and a jeans jacket. But it fell just as quickly when Layne failed to recognize him. She stared at the coffee in her cup and tried not to give in to all the assailing doubts. The irony of her situation wasn't lost on her, but Layne refused to let it get her down.

When the door rattled open again, Creed walked in. A lump swelled in her throat as she watched his gaze sweep the interior of the café and stop on her. There was the smallest hesitation before he made his move toward the booth where she was seated.

Big and lithe, he folded his frame into the seat opposite her. His hat stayed low on his head, shadowing the hard impatience of his expression. She received no more than the briefest glance, but she felt the ripple of strong emotion come into play just at seeing him again.

"I got your message that you wanted to see me." His attention centered on the cigarette he took from his shirt pocket.

"I wasn't sure you'd come," Layne admitted with forced calm as she watched him bend his head to touch the end of the cigarette to the match flame cupped in his hand. The light glared on the outlaw-harsh angles of his face.

"Well, I'm here," Creed replied shortly and shook out the match, still not looking at her as he tossed it in the ashtray. The waitress came with a water glass, menu, and the ever-present coffeepot. "Just coffee." He shoved the menu back to her and righted the cup on the table so she could fill it.

"How's Mattie?" Layne couldn't keep her eyes off his face. It was so achingly familiar to her that it hurt not to see that special glow.

"Moody and quiet—about what you'd expect."

He thrust a look at her. "Did you bring me all the way into town just to ask me that?"

"No." She lowered her gaze and struggled to keep a grip on her composure.

"What did you want to see me about?"

"I think—" Layne hadn't expected it would be so difficult to tell him. She thought it would come out naturally; instead she was nervously tripping over it. "There's a possibility I'm pregnant." She looked at him to see if there was even a glimmer of the deep pleasure she felt.

"My God, Layne." The disgust and contempt in his expression nearly made her cry out. "I knew you were desperate to worm your way back onto the ranch so you could get in good with Mattie, but you don't really expect me to believe this phony pregnancy business?"

It was more than she could take to have Creed accuse her of lying about something like this. Blindly, Layne grabbed for her purse and shot out of the booth. She ran out of the restaurant, straight to the motel, and packed her things in a blur of bitter tears. Twenty minutes later she was driving down the highway, heading out of the Sand Hills toward Omaha.

Chapter 12

There was a crash of lightning as Layne darted out of her car and ran through the pelting rain to the roofed entrance of her parents' home. She hugged close to the door while she closed her dripping umbrella, then pounded at the door to be let in.

"I didn't know if that was you or the thunder," her mother declared as she opened the door and Layne dashed inside.

"It's pouring out there." Layne shrugged out of her dripping raincoat and left her wet shoes on the rug inside the door. When Layne spied her father sitting in his easy chair in the front room, she added, "And don't you say 'April showers bring May flowers.'"

"That's not fair." He smiled a mock protest. "You took the words right out of my mouth."

"I know," she chided him.

The umbrella and raincoat were taken from her. "I'll put these out in the kitchen for you," her mother said. "Go have a seat in the living room with your father."

"Thanks, Mom." Layne went straight into the living

room and stopped by her father's chair to drop a kiss on his forehead. "What have you been doing?" It was a general inquiry of interest.

In his middle fifties, Keith MacDonald was a slim, distinguished-looking man. His dark hair was silvering at the temples in such an attractive way that Layne had threatened to ask his barber if he bleached it.

"I just finished reading a very good article by my favorite reporter," he said and indicated the newspaper on his lap.

"Now I wonder who that could be?" Layne replied with mock innocence as she sat down on the sofa and curled her legs onto the cushions.

His expression sobered slightly. "It's good to pick up the paper again and finally see your name on some of the by-lines. While you were gone, I hardly looked at it at all. It just wasn't the same."

"I'll tell Clyde that. Maybe he'll give me a raise." Her old job had been waiting for her when she got back. It had been a relief to plunge right back into work again. That way her conversations didn't have to dwell solely on her experiences of the previous two-plus months.

"I imagine this rain has really slowed the traffic," her mother remarked as she joined them in the living room.

"It's just beginning to back up on the interstates," Layne admitted. "Luckily I missed most of it."

"Oh?" Her mother glanced at her in surprise. "But when I called the newspaper, they told me you'd left over two hours ago."

"I did, but I had an appointment along the way," she explained. "How long before dinner's ready?"

"Another half hour. I thought we'd eat late."

"Good. I was hoping we'd have a chance to talk without sitting down at the table right away," Layne replied, since there was much she needed to tell them.

"How about a drink before dinner?" her father suggested, rising out of his chair.

"A gin and tonic will be fine for me, dear," Colleen MacDonald replied as he walked to the small home-bar in the corner.

"Just some tonic water for me," Layne said. "With lemon if you have it handy."

"Tonic water?" Ice clinked in the glasses as he fixed drinks for the three of them. "When did you turn into a teetotaler? Not that you ever did drink much."

"Just recently," she admitted, and waited until he was on the way back to them before she continued. "I have some good news for you. At least," Layne added to qualify her statement, "I hope you'll ultimately regard it as good news."

"What's that?" Her father passed them their glasses.

"You'd better sit down, Dad," she suggested gently. After a skeptical glance, he returned to his chair. "You see, you're going to be grandparents."

"What?!" said her father, fairly exploding.

"You aren't serious, Layne." Her mother simply stared.

"How can that be?" her father demanded irately.

"It's very simple, Dad. I'm going to have a baby." There was an air of serenity about her. All the soul-searching hours had already been spent. The confirmation had been made—just this afternoon by her family doctor. "I know I probably shouldn't sound so proud of it," Layne conceded. "But I've had a lot of time to think. And I want this baby. I'm going to love it, and I'm not going to be ashamed to bring it into this world."

"Layne," her mother murmured, moved to tears by the calm declaration.

"Who's the father? That's what I want to know," her father demanded, always the more volatile.

"Creed Dawson," Layne replied evenly.

"The man you told me about? The one who was a part-ner on the ranch?" her mother asked and received an answering nod.

"Just exactly what all went on at that ranch? What kind of woman is this Mattie Turner that she'd let a thing like this happen?" The drink was slammed on the round table by his chair as her father pushed out of it, ready to blame anyone but his "little girl." "I knew I should have gone and taken you away from there the minute your mother told me you were going to stay there for a while. I knew it was a mistake!"

"Calm down, Keith," Colleen MacDonald admonished. "You may not have high blood pressure, but at this rate you're going to get it." She turned again to Layne. "Does he know about the baby?"

"It was before I found out for sure. I don't think he quite believed me," Layne admitted and tried to shrug away that painful memory. "It doesn't matter anyway."

"Didn't quite believe you, eh?" her father repeated angrily. "I'd like to get my hands on him."

"Oh, Daddy, I don't think so." Layne tried to suppress the smile that tugged at the corners of her mouth as she looked at her father's slim build. "Creed would make two of you."

"You'll have to tell him, Layne," her mother inserted.

She glanced briefly at her hands. "Yes, I'll . . . write him a letter." Only because she believed he had the right to be informed, not because she thought it would change any-thing.

"I'll have my attorney write him a letter," her father stated.

"No, you won't," Layne countered and swung her feet to the floor to walk over to him. "Come on, Dad." She put an arm around him and hugged him in a cajoling fashion. "I'm not upset or angry. Don't you be."

The anger faded reluctantly from his expression as he looked at her with grudging acceptance of her attitude. "Did you love him?"

"Yes." She still did; nothing had changed that. "And I'm going to love his baby just as much. Try to be happy, Dad," Layne urged gently, a smile slanting her mouth. "We're going to have a baby."

He shook his head in mild dismay, but there was already a faint smile showing on his face when he hugged her. "You always could wrap me around your finger," he declared. "You're going to move out of that apartment and come back home to live."

"I'm going to do no such thing," Layne said firmly even as she smiled at him.

"When's the baby due?" her mother asked. "You can't be very far along."

"About a month." She still experienced that tingling sense of awe whenever she thought about the life growing inside her. It was scary and exciting all at the same time.

"You found out so soon?" her mother said with some surprise. "But how did you know?"

"I guess I suspected because I had this vague nausea in the mornings, but mostly it was this feeling of something happening inside me." Layne searched for a way to explain it, finally feeling free to talk about the wonder of the experience. As she looked at her mother to expound on the theme, she saw the flicker of pain and knew instant regret. "Mom, I'm sorry."

"Don't be," Colleen MacDonald hastened to assure her. "I never had the privilege of knowing what it was like to have a baby grow inside me, but you're going to experience that miracle. And I'm happy for you."

"Now let's don't all start crying," Keith MacDonald said at the sight of the tears building in the eyes of both his women.

"We won't," Layne promised with a sniffling laugh.

"There's so much to do before the baby comes," her mother declared. "I don't know where to start."

"Here she goes," her father muttered, but with fond indulgence.

"Keith, there's all those boxes of Layne's baby things that we stored in the attic," she recalled. "Clothes and toys and crib sheets—and I don't know what all."

"You still have all that?" Layne was amazed.

"And more," her father assured her. "Your mother saved everything."

"Well, not quite everything," her mother protested, not too vigorously.

"In case you've forgotten, I'm the one who carried all those boxes up to the attic," he reminded her.

"Let's get them down," Layne urged.

"There's bound to be a lot of it that you can use once we start going through the boxes," her mother said.

"Not tonight," her father said with an adamant tilt of his head. "Have you forgotten dinner, Colleen?"

At the prompting question, Colleen MacDonald started backing toward the hall. "We'll get them down this weekend, then," she said, agreeing to the postponement.

Her father's arm remained around her shoulders as Layne watched her mother leave to check on dinner. A silence drifted into the room. She turned her head slightly to look at this man who had cherished her and protected her from the time she'd entered his life. The shadow of pain and regret darkened the love that was in his eyes when he looked at her.

"A grandfather, huh?" His smile was tight, and a little on the crooked side.

"This isn't the way you thought it would happen, is it?" Layne murmured softly with a twinge of pain. "You wanted to be able to go around to all your friends, pass out cigars, and brag about the baby your little girl was going to have." The caressing stroke of his hand on her hair lightly pressed her head to his shoulder. "That's the way I wanted it to happen, too, Dad. I loved him so much. And I was so sure that big ugly brute was just as crazy about me. You aren't the only one who wanted the rice and the wedding cake to come before the baby powder and formula. So did I, Daddy."

Tears slid down her cheeks to be absorbed by his shirt. He said nothing and just held her more closely to him. Daddies don't cry, so he hid his red-rimmed eyes in her hair.

In the early afternoon on Saturday, Layne carried the last armload of books out of the small den and dumped them on the couch in the main room of her apartment. When she had rented the apartment several years ago, the agent had referred to the small room off the living room as a second bedroom, even though it was barely large enough to accommodate a single bed and dresser. Layne had converted it into a cozy den with a desk and shelves where she could do her writing.

Now, of course, it was the perfect size for a nursery. Layne returned to the room and looked around. A bronze band was tied around her forehead, the color emphasizing the russet highlights in her hair. Her hands were perched on the hips of her snug-fitting jeans, which showed a flat stomach. The sleeves of her tawny gold sweatshirt were pushed up around her elbows while the loose bulk of the material concealed the fullness of her breasts and the slender curve of her waist.

The desk, with its side extension for a typewriter, was all that was left in the room, except for the bookshelf stands.

When her parents arrived, her father could give her a hand moving the desk into the living room, but Layne thought the shelves might be useful to hold the baby's things.

Maybe it was premature to turn the room into a nursery when she still had nearly eight months to go before the baby was born, but it somehow made things more definite. She smiled with an exhilarated kind of satisfaction at this first step she was taking to prepare for the baby's birth.

The doorbell to her apartment rang and Layne went to answer it at a loping jog, anticipating the arrival of all the things that would start to fill the nursery. When she opened the door, her mother peered around the cardboard boxes stacked high in her arms. Layne grabbed the top one before she moved out of the way to let her parents in.

"Good grief, what did you do? Bring everything?" She laughed when she saw the way her father was loaded down.

"I thought you might enjoy looking through some of your baby keepsakes even if you can't use them," her mother explained.

"We might as well just pile them all here on the floor so we can start sorting through them," Layne instructed, picking an empty space in the middle of the room.

"I'll go get the baby bed out of the car and be right back," her father said, and he headed for the door as soon as he had set down his load of boxes.

Not wasting any time, Layne sat cross-legged on the floor among the boxes and started opening them. "It's like Christmas!" She laughed to her mother as she began to drag out the baby items.

Together they sorted through the articles, setting aside the ones she could use and repacking the others. Her father's return with the baby crib was a minor interruption that lasted no longer than it took for Layne to send him to the junk drawer in the kitchen for the tools to reassemble it.

"Look at this." Layne held up a tiny undershirt. "I can't believe I was ever small enough to wear this." The doorbell rang and she scrambled to her feet to answer it, casting a puzzled glance at her mother. "Did Dad go out to the car again?" she asked on her way to the door.

Her mother frowned. "I thought he was in the nursery."

The instant Layne opened the door, shock rooted her to the floor. A pair of hesitant green eyes looked back at her as Mattie stood solemnly in the outer corridor.

"Mattie." She finally recovered her voice. "What are you doing here?" The question contained her dazed feeling of disbelief.

"I came mainly to apologize," Mattie stated with her usual bluntness while a rueful smile slanted her mouth. "After I spoke to your mother on the phone the other night—"

Layne whirled about to stare at the slim blonde woman who was already gravitating toward the doorway. "You spoke to her?!" Incredulity and question ringed her voice.

"Yes," Colleen admitted, a trifle guiltily. "After you told me how upset Mattie had been over the way you had deceived her, I realized I was partly to blame for that. I'd made such an issue about protecting her from any rude shock out of her past that I felt I had influenced you into concealing the truth from her. So I called her to explain that. And partly"—a faintly embarrassed smile crept into her expression—"to make sure she didn't think I had raised you to be thoughtless and self-centered."

"Oh, Mom." Affection choked Layne's voice as she smiled at this woman who had loved her and stood by her through everything. "You're really something, do you know that?"

"Yes, she is," Mattie agreed with a matter-of-fact ease. "When I got that phone call from her, I had already realized why I had been so hurt and angry over the way you had deceived me. It was the guilt and shame that I felt. I have to be honest, Layne, and tell you that I didn't feel guilty for giving you to a couple who would love you and provide a good home. It was the way I had deceived John all those years, never trusting his love for me enough to tell him about you. So all those hateful accusations I was saying to you were really the way I felt toward myself. So there I was when your mother called, feeling rotten for the way I'd treated you and certain you wouldn't want to ever hear from me again after the way I practically threw you out of my home."

"That isn't the way I felt at all, Mattie," Layne declared earnestly.

"Your mother managed to convince me of that." Mattie smiled at her counterpart. "That's why I'm here . . . to say I'm sorry . . . and to give you this." She handed Layne the package she was holding. "It's your baby blanket," she explained. "I thought you might want to have it for your baby."

Too overwhelmed by emotion to speak, Layne tightly clutched the soft package to her body. She supposed her mother had told Mattie of her pregnancy when she phoned. Before Layne had a chance to confirm that, her father came out of the new nursery.

"The crib's up," he announced, then noticed the third woman standing in the open doorway and smiled pleasantly. "Sorry, I didn't realize you had company."

"Come here, Dad." Layne extended a hand to draw him into their circle. "I want you to meet Mattie Gray."

No more identification than that was needed as his attitude immediately turned stiff and cool, prompted by a touching jealousy that the appearance of her natural mother might, in some way, deprive him of Layne's love and devotion. It was an unreasoning fear that Layne understood very well.

"How do you do, Mrs. Gray." He shook her hand formally.

With her usual astuteness, Mattie eyed him directly. "You should be very proud of your daughter, Mr. MacDonald." There was a hint of a smile around her mouth. "And don't look so skeptical. If you knew me better, you'd know that I never say anything just to be tactful. Whenever I look at Layne, I have to consciously remind myself that she is the baby girl I had. She will probably always be a person I've grown to like first, and a daughter to me second."

There was an almost visible relaxation of his defenses. Layne was relieved to see there was a chance that they could all get along and she wasn't going to be caught in the middle of some tug-of-war.

"What are we all doing standing in the door?" she questioned with a discovering laugh. "Come on in and sit down." Her turn led Mattie into the apartment. She stopped near the center of the living room to pick up a box and clear a path to the chairs. "It's a mess in here, I'm afraid. We've been sorting through my old baby clothes."

When Layne looked back to make sure she was being followed by the others, her glance went straight past the others to the man who suddenly filled the door frame. Dressed in a western-cut blazer of dark brown corduroy and wheat-tan denims, Creed stood motionless, staring at her from under the brim of his brown Stetson.

"Where did you come from?" The question was driven from her, and a second later her gaze was running to Mattie as the source of his presence.

"I guess I didn't tell you Creed came with me," Mattie said, watching Layne closely. "I came on up to your apartment to make sure you were home while he parked the car."

Suddenly he was moving past her stunned and staring parents straight to Layne. Her heart rocketed into her throat at the sight of him.

"You shouldn't be carrying that box in your condition," he said gruffly and took it out of her hands when she thought he was going to take her into his arms.

It stung to know that his first thought on seeing her was for the child inside her. "Less than three weeks ago, I was throwing around sixty-pound hay bales and it never bothered you," she said, mocking his sudden concern.

With iron-jawed grimness, Creed ignored her observation. "Where do you want me to put this?" He stood expectantly in front of her, holding the box in his arms.

"In here." Stiffly she circled around him and walked to the new nursery, leading him inside. "You can set it in the corner behind the door," she directed.

Pausing in the middle of the small room, Layne waited while he swung the door partway shut with his elbow and set the box on the floor in the corner. When he straightened, she looked away so he wouldn't see the hunger in her eyes. The silence grew heavy but Layne was damned if she was going to be the one to break it.

Creed wandered over to the newly erected crib and accidentally knocked his hat on the hanging lamp suspended from the ceiling. He removed his hat and combed his hair with a rake of his hand to ease its flatness while Layne covertly watched him.

"I guess you've decided to keep the baby." His hands turned his hat in slow rotations.

"Of course, I am." It hurt her to think he believed she wouldn't want it.

"You might have decided to have an abortion—or give it away," he replied with a hint of a challenge.

"How could you even think such a thing?" she demanded.

"I don't know." He kept turning his hat. "You were so obsessed with Mattie, I thought, maybe, you'd do the same as she had done."

"The situation and the circumstances are different," Layne said, at last understanding where he'd gotten the idea. "I want this baby. I love it and I'm going to keep it."

There was another long pause while she felt his gaze wandering over her. "It doesn't look like you've gained much weight."

"Only a couple of pounds." Her hand moved instinctively across the flat of her stomach. "It'll be a while before I start showing."

The room was small and Creed was so big and tall that he just made it seem that much smaller. Every nerve in her body was conscious of him. She ached to feel his arms about her and taste the rawness of his kisses.

"I guess you've already made a lot of plans." He bent his head to study the sweatband inside the crown of his hat.

His face was so damned expressionless, and she wished he'd quit messing around with that hat. It was impossible to see what he was thinking, but Layne supposed he was wondering if she expected any help from him, financial or otherwise. She wanted none that was not willingly offered, so she tried to make sure he understood that she could manage on her own.

"I've got a good job and I'll be able to work right up until the baby is born. Afterward my mother is going to take care of the baby so I can go back to work. Later I'll find a good day-care center."

"Layne." There was something poignantly haunting about the way he looked at her, holding her gaze. "No woman has ever had my child before. I want us to get married so this baby can have my name."

He suddenly seemed so raw and exposed, all that tough-looking exterior melting to show a sensitive man who wanted a baby. She remembered Mattie telling her about the way some women had recoiled from his brutally cut features. But inside he was like any other man, wanting children, a home and a family. Layne didn't care that he wanted to marry her just for the sake of their child.

"All right." She kept her acceptance simple and direct.

Creed took a step toward her, which didn't leave much distance between them in the small confines of the room. "I believe a child should be raised by both parents."

"So do I," Layne replied with growing softness.

"I don't know how long it takes to get blood tests. We'll have a justice of the peace or a minister marry us as soon as we can get a marriage license." With just his fingers, he lifted her left hand. "Would you like a diamond ring or just a plain wedding band?"

"It doesn't matter." It was difficult for her to talk about such things without any emotion. She didn't understand how he could do it.

"I suppose it doesn't," he agreed flatly, and let her hand slide off his fingers. "You do understand that when I talked about marriage and raising our baby, I meant that we would live together in the same house."

"Yes, I know." Her voice kept getting huskier.

"I'll be a good husband to you, Layne." A muscle twitched along his jaw. "I know you love this baby. In time I hope there will be some left over for me."

"Left over," she said on a breath, and suddenly realized what he was too proud to put into words. "You have it all backward, Creed. It's because I love you so much that I have enough left over for our child."

A look of pain flashed across his face. "Don't pretend anymore with me, Layne." He was withdrawing behind that hard, stony shell where he hid his feelings.

"I'm not pretending, Creed. I never have pretended about the way I feel toward you. I know you're not handsome, but your looks have never mattered to me." She pried gently at the crack she'd found in his armor and discovered a deep well of tenderness within herself that she hadn't known she possessed. "It was the proud, gentle man I found inside whose rare smiles were to be treasured and whose caresses gave pleasure without expecting any in return."

The longing in his eyes was dark and intense as Creed weighed her words, bearing the scars of too many burns to readily trust the flame again. She took his hand and pressed it to her stomach, flattening her own hand over his.

"I'm going to have your baby, Creed," she said. "Doesn't that prove how much I love you?"

A low groan rumbled from his chest as she was swept into his arms. He kissed her eyes, her cheeks, her lips, and bit at her ears and her neck while tremors shuddered through him. It was an intensely deep and passionate outpouring of love as his arms strained to hold her more tightly and his hands moved over her body with raw and restless urgings. There was a spilling over inside her of a love so wild and sweet it tore at her heart.

Never letting her go, Creed made a small turn and sank onto the edge of the desk, as if his legs could no longer hold him. Yet his lips continued to devour her while his arms made a crushing attempt to merge their bodies into one and his thighs spread to fit her body between them. The pounding of her heart became all mixed up with the wild thudding of his pulse.

Then he dragged himself back while his trembling hands moved over her as if feeling for broken bones. "My God, what am I doing to you?"

"I won't break," Layne promised him and arched her

hips more intimately against the hard, aroused need of his loins, conscious of the tingling ache it created within herself. "If you ever hurt me, I'll tell you. Just don't stop loving me."

"That's impossible," he muttered thickly.

"How could you ever believe I was only pretending?" she murmured with a wondering shake of her head.

"Don't you know how incredibly beautiful, intelligent, and alive you are?" Creed countered. "The first time I saw you, I was staggered. But I also saw the way you looked at me—the way all women have looked at me, even the plain fat ones—recoiling a little, fascinated a little."

"It's true. I can't deny that." Layne only wished she could as she traced his face with loving fingers. "But it was before I knew you."

"It was such a torment to have you around." His hands tightened their grip on her briefly. "When you started paying me attention, I thought you were flirting with me just for kicks, and I nearly hated you. But it was hard to hate you. Then you started making me believe you really cared."

"I did care—always. How could you doubt that I loved you when I was practically shameless about it?" She breathed a bewildered laugh.

His hands began to move caressingly over her arched back, touching her with a wondering quality. "When I pried that secret about Mattie from you, I started thinking the lovemaking was just a bribe to keep me silent. It was one helluva bribe. Most of the time I was so drunk with loving you, I didn't care. I tried to make myself believe that I would enjoy you for as long as I could have you, but it didn't work."

"You thought I was using you," Layne realized with a bitter pang.

"That's precisely what I thought." Creed nodded grimly.

"And that stupid, thoughtless remark I made to you in anger that going to bed with you didn't give you any right to tell me what to do—it convinced you, didn't it?" There was hurt in her eyes as she looked at him. "All I wanted was to make it clear that no man was going to dictate to me and blackmail me with the love I gave."

"I can't imagine any man dictating to you." A smile lifted the corners of his mouth.

"And you wouldn't talk to Mattie for me when she ordered me to leave, because you thought I was still trying to use you." The pieces were falling into place with remarkable clarity. "Even when I told you I was possibly pregnant."

"I thought once you were back in Mattie's good graces, a couple weeks later you'd make the happy discovery that you weren't pregnant after all. But God, Layne, when you first said it—" When Creed looked at her with that wondrous, seeking light in his eyes, she felt the same dazed awe he knew. "I wanted desperately for it to be true. That you would have *my* baby."

"I was going to write you a letter after the tests were confirmed but I guess Mattie told you."

"If you hadn't agreed to marry me, I think I would have carried you off."

"I'd suggest that you do it anyway, but I have a feeling my father would have something to say about that," Layne murmured, nuzzling his chin.

"That reminds me, I'm going to have to talk to him . . ." Creed paused as her lips made a tantalizing brush over his mouth. ". . . later."

Not sure what to read next?

Visit Pocket Books online at
www.simonsays.com

Reading suggestions for
you and your reading group
New release news
Author appearances
Online chats with your favorite writers
Special offers
Order books online
And much, much more!